The door opened on well-oiled hinges

It led out onto a bare stone ledge. Kane didn't hesitate about following it, because there was nowhere else to go. In seconds he was on the ledges above the front of the gaudy.

Bodies stretched across the ground on pools of blood-black sand. Burned wags and burning wags left smoky smudges against the pale blue sky. Kane glanced at the wag they'd arrived in. By some miracle, it was still in one piece. But there were at least thirty Tong warriors on the ground. He had no idea how many were burning up their back trail.

Other titles in this series:

JAMES AXLER

OUTLANDERS®

SARGASSO PLUNDER

A GOLD EAGLE BOOK FROM

WORLDWIDE®

TORONTO • NEW YORK • LONDON
AMSTERDAM • PARIS • SYDNEY • HAMBURG
STOCKHOLM • ATHENS • TOKYO • MILAN
MADRID • WARSAW • BUDAPEST • AUCKLAND

First edition August 2001
ISBN 0-373-63831-0

SARGASSO PLUNDER

Special thanks to Mel Odom for his contribution
to this work and to Mark Ellis for his contribution to the
Outlanders concept, developed for Gold Eagle Books.

SARGASSO PLUNDER

The Road to Outlands—
From Secret Government Files to the Future

Almost two hundred years after the global holocaust, Kane, a former Magistrate of Cobaltville, often thought the world had been lucky to survive at all after a nuclear device detonated in the Russian embassy in Washington, D.C. The aftermath—forever known as skydark—reshaped continents and turned civilization into ashes.

Nearly depopulated, America became the Deathlands—poisoned by radiation, home to chaos and mutated life forms. Feudal rule reappeared in the form of baronies, while remote outposts clung to a brutish existence.

What eventually helped shape this wasteland were the redoubts, the secret preholocaust military installations with stores of weapons, and the home of gateways, the locational matter-transfer facilities. Some of the redoubts hid clues that had once fed wild theories of government cover-ups and alien visitations.

Rearmed from redoubt stockpiles, the barons consolidated their power and reclaimed technology for the villes. Their power, supported by some invisible authority, extended beyond their fortified walls to what was now called the Outlands. It was here that the rootstock of humanity survived, living with hellzones and chemical storms, hounded by Magistrates.

In the villes, rigid laws were enforced—to atone for the sins of the past and prepare the way for a better future. That was the barons' public credo and their right-to-rule.

Kane, along with friend and fellow Magistrate Grant, had upheld that claim until a fateful Outlands expedition. A displaced piece of technology...a question to a keeper of the archives...a vague clue about alien masters—and their world shifted radically. Suddenly, Brigid Baptiste, the archivist, faced summary execution, and

Grant a quick termination. For Kane there was forgiveness if he pledged his unquestioning allegiance to Baron Cobalt and his unknown masters and abandoned his friends.

But that allegiance would make him support a mysterious and alien power and deny loyalty and friends. Then what else was there?

Kane had been brought up solely to serve the ville. Brigid's only link with her family was her mother's red-gold hair, green eyes and supple form. Grant's clues to his lineage were his ebony skin and powerful physique. But Domi, she of the white hair, was an Outlander pressed into sexual servitude in Cobaltville. She at least knew her roots and was a reminder to the exiles that the outcasts belonged in the human family.

Parents, friends, community—the very rootedness of humanity was denied. With no continuity, there was no forward momentum to the future. And that was the crux—when Kane began to wonder if there *was* a future.

For Kane, it wouldn't do. So the only way was out— way, way out.

After their escape, they found shelter at the forgotten Cerberus redoubt headed by Lakesh, a scientist, Cobaltville's head archivist, and secret opponent of the barons.

With their past turned into a lie, their future threatened, only one thing was left to give meaning to the outcasts. The hunger for freedom, the will to resist the hostile influences. And perhaps, by opposing, end them.

Chapter 1

"Reminds you of the old days, doesn't it?" Kane remarked. "Busting down doors, busting heads. Hoping we didn't get busted up ourselves."

Kane studied the gaudy house built into the side of the red stone wall in front of them. It was more of a fort, actually. Whoever had first designed the building had buried three-quarters of it inside the cliff, and it was at least two stories high, judging from the front it presented. The construction crew had even taken time to cover the facade with tightly fit cut stone blocks.

Bullet scars pocked the stone, most of them old but a few of them recent. The right corner showed cracks, indicating a grenade or some other type of explosive had been used against it at one time. Two iron-bar-covered windows occupied the wall on either side of the metal entrance door.

Kane knew the windows were intended more as gun ports than for letting light into the building. A crooked sign stood on the arched roof on stilted wooden legs, proof against the heavy snows that sometimes came in the vestiges of the nuclear winter. Tyson's Y'all Cum Bakk Saloone stood out in dust-covered purple letters two feet tall.

More than two dozen wags sat in front of the gaudy house, clustered in groups. Hard-eyed men and a few women burned dark by the desert sun and dressed in leather and patched clothing sat in some of the vehicles. They kept their blasters at the ready, guarding the vehicles while their partners were inside.

"In the old days," Kane told Grant, "we didn't think there was a chance we'd get busted up."

Grant nodded, surveying the gaudy house. A thin smile twisted his lips. "Coming in without Mag armor like this, I feel naked."

"You are naked," Kane replied. "Don't forget that and mebbe we'll get out of here alive today."

"Cheerful soul, aren't you?"

Kane ignored the comment. The crowd around Tyson's was definitely rough trade. He recognized the men and women as natives of the outer Cobaltville and Utah mining territories. But there were other men there, as well.

Chinese Tong, their vehicles identified by bright scarlet chops, had moved into the area lately, vying for the iron ore coming out of the hardscrabble mines. Kane knew the Tong were from the Western Isles by the chops, the scarlet Chinese characters marked on their vehicles, and he knew whom they belonged to because he recognized the symbols.

"Wei Qiang's boys have made themselves at home," Grant said.

"Not easily." Kane watched the various camps of men and saw the wariness each group had for the other. Some of the men belonged to the independent mine caravans that ferried the iron ore from the Utah territories to Cobaltville. Others were traders who'd scavenged supplies and tools the mines bought or traded for. A few of them were coldhearts, men and women who preyed on the weak living off the harsh land.

All of them gave the Tong members a wide berth. Wei Qiang, the warlord of Autarkic in the Western Islands, hand-picked his men, and all of them were hardened killers. Their chosen weapon for close-in fighting was a single-bladed hand ax. They'd invaded the Western Isles some time in the past and had set up an empire there.

Kane pushed up from the wag he and Grant had driven from the Cerberus redoubt in the Bitterroot Range. More than two hundred years ago, before the world had died in a nuclear inferno, the wag had started life as a mil-spec jeep. Since then, it had been pieced back together at least a half-dozen times by people with various degrees of skills and limited access to parts.

Metal patches welded over the body showed signs of rust, ripped open in places by dents and dings. Kane and Grant had captured it from a band of Roamers who'd been traveling through the Bitterroot Range near the redoubt a few weeks back. The encounter had resulted in some of the new bullet holes decorating the wag's body. But the vehicle provided good cover for their present op. They'd left the Sandcat all-terrain vehicle back at the redoubt for the same reason they opted not to wear their black Magistrate armor; the Sandcat and the armor would invite precisely the kinds of questions that they wanted to avoid.

"Let's do it," Kane growled, knowing his stomach was knotting up in ways it hadn't when he'd been a Cobaltville Magistrate. But he knew it was the waiting that took its toll on him. Once the action started, he chilled out. As a Magistrate, he'd worn the black armor of Baron Cobalt's enforcers and had been feared. Here in the Outlands, that black armor would have been a target for jackals who felt capable of taking down a lone wolf. Dying was a way of life in the Outlands. A survivor often paid for his or her life with the blood of others.

Grant stepped out of the wag holding the M-14 he'd chosen from Cerberus's extensive armory. The rifle was serviceable and fired a 7.62 mm round heavy enough to knock a man down, and it looked scuffed enough that no coldheart would kill him just to take it from him—if he could. As former Cobaltville Mags, both he and Grant were accustomed to Copperhead close-assault weapons and Sin Eater handblasters, but they would also have drawn unwanted attention.

Grant stood over six feet tall, massive and broad-chested. His coffee-brown skin gleamed with a sheen of perspiration from the heat covering the desert lands. Gray stained his short, curly black hair. A gunfighter's mustache curved around his lips and ran down to his chin. Smiles didn't come easily to him; usually, as now, he wore a dour expression.

He was dressed in faded denim jeans and a red vest that had once been a corduroy shirt. A scarred ammo belt looped his waist, carrying extra clips for the M-14, as well as extra rounds for the .44 Colt Magnum blaster riding in a cross-draw holster in front of his flat belly.

Kane slipped a Mossberg pump shotgun from between the seats and pulled the nylon strap over his shoulder. He let the riot gun hang down beside his leg, ready for instant access. He carried a .45 automatic blaster on his right hip in a cut-down holster, extra clips riding on the belt. He pulled twin bandoliers of shotgun ammo across his shoulders, an advertisement to everyone that they were well armed and equipped. The handle of a long-bladed military fighting knife barely showed above his boot top.

Without another word, he led the way toward the gaudy. He stood an inch over six feet, a lean wolf of a man who carried most of his weight in his arms and shoulders. His dark hair was matted from the hard days of road travel and clung to his nape. He wore a green denim shirt with the sleeves hacked off and denim pants in the same shape as Grant's.

His point man's senses swept the surroundings, picking up the attention from the hard men around him. None of them made eye contact, but he knew they were looking all the same. He and Grant were strangers in their midst, and the stripped-down wag they'd arrived in didn't give much indication of what they were about.

The land around the gaudy was broken and fell away in miniature cliffs that provided a clear view of the surrounding countryside for miles. Tyson's saloon didn't have many surprise visitors. Sparse vegetation, no trees, dug into the sand and rock and found just enough water to survive. A well-worn trail packed the dry earth in front of the building. The blue sky lay open and huge all around the area, smudged by orange-

and-green chem clouds carrying deadly acid rain far to the south.

A fat man in soiled overalls sat on a three-legged stool outside the gaudy's front door. A machete hung at his side, and his thick hands held a cut-down double-barreled shotgun. The fat man's face was round, childlike, but the dark eyes carried malevolent glints. He raised the shotgun slightly, stopping Kane and Grant in their tracks just out of arm's reach.

Kane ignored the shotgun. The man had already let them too close to stop them, but he wasn't the real threat. He was only cannon fodder for the men on the other side of the door.

"Ain't seen you around before," the fat man challenged.

"We've been around," Kane replied.

The fat man shook his head. "Not here."

Kane narrowed his flinty blue-gray eyes. "The gaudy open for business or not?"

"Depends." The fat man's gaze flicked between Grant and Kane.

"On what?" Kane growled irritably.

"On what business you got."

"None of yours," Kane replied.

The fat man's features remained placid, not taking offense. "I'm making it mine."

Kane grinned at the man coldly. "Even with all that ass filling those pants, you ain't got enough ass on you to lean on me."

"Son of a bitch," the fat man said without emotion. He shifted on the three-legged stool and the wooden joints creaked in protest. The shotgun started to come up.

"Up until now," Grant warned in a soft voice filled with menace, shifting a little to let the fat man know he had a clear field of fire, "you've only been guilty of being a social retard. Don't go adding stupidity to it. And you can take an ace on the line for that."

The fat man drew the shotgun back.

"I'm a man who's got scrip to spend," Kane said. "That's all I know any gaudy owner's ever been interested in."

"There's an entrance charge," the fat man said.

Kane paid the price for Grant and himself. "There a back way out of this place?" Kane asked. The idea of walking into a place with only one exit didn't appeal to him.

"You get this door," the fat man said, poking the bills through a slot in the wall. When they disappeared, the fat man rapped his knuckles on the door. A moment later, the sound of locks being thrown ratcheted loudly and the door opened.

Kane stepped through the open door, his point man's senses flaring. As a Magistrate, he'd been through plenty of dangerous doors with Grant covering his six. He'd never gotten accustomed to the feeling of unease at stepping into potential trouble. But that had probably been what helped him stay alive. He kept his right hand near the Mossberg's pistol grip.

Cool air bumped up against Kane, letting him know there were tunnels dug into the back end of the gaudy. Judging from the coolness of the air, he was willing to bet the tunnels led down to caves.

The massive earthshaker bombs that had destroyed the western coast of the United States and put most of California beneath the sea had also reshaped a number of areas above, as well as below, the surface. As a Cobaltville Magistrate, he'd had firsthand knowledge of the cave systems in the area. Slaggers had often used the cave systems for hiding, as well as for storage areas.

Tables of all shapes and sizes filled the center of the gaudy's huge main room. Kane's boots scuffed against the stone floor as he continued inside. Whoever had built the place had taken time to put down a permanent floor rather than a wooden one. Still, the floor wasn't completely level and rolled underfoot in places.

A long mirror occupied the wall behind the bar. Bottles of whiskey and other liquors from scavengers' booty sat side by side with homegrown popskull and beer. The labels on the former easily identified them to those who could read, while the labels on the latter carried words and pictographs.

"My, my," Grant said softly. "Bet you get service with a smile here."

Kane followed his friend's line of sight. Two women worked the bar, looking enough alike to be sisters. They wore yellow silk blouses with belled sleeves, the buttons open enough to show a lot of cleavage, and shimmering dark red pants that clung to every curve. Both girls had short-cropped brunette hair that curved in at their cheeks.

Kane knew the hairstyle also served to keep an overly aggressive gaudy patron from grabbing them by the hair easily. The girls poured drinks quickly, taking scrip automatically, and chatted readily. It was easy to understand why so many mining caravan drivers and guards, traders and coldhearts made it a point to stop in at Tyson's.

Since the place was packed, finding a seat that covered the bar, as well as the door, proved difficult. The best seats in the house had already gone to the first arrivals.

Kane chose a small round table that listed unsteadily underneath a mutie alligator head a full yard long that was mounted on the wall opposite a small stage. The table was uncomfortably close to the large fireplace where a cow and a pig turned on a spit over the banked coals. The heat from the fireplace baked into him, but it was still cooler than the noonday sun outside.

The orange glow from the coals washed out into the room until it was overcome by the yellow glow of the bear-fat lanterns hanging around the room. The black smoke from the lanterns eddied against the stone ceiling in drifting pools and filled the gaudy with an undeniable stench.

"They should do something about that damn stink," Grant groused. "This place is more than habitable, but that sure takes the edge off."

Kane silently agreed. He took a pair of cigars from his

pocket and passed one to Grant. "Self-defense," he said. They lit the cigars from the small bear-oil lamp on the table.

Grant blew out the oil lamp's flame to avoid the stench, as well as drop the light level around them so they'd be even harder to see in the gloom filling the enclosed room.

Aware of the men around him and knowing how volatile their natures were, Kane didn't let his gaze rest on any of them too long. The gaudy's patrons sat segregated into groups, blasters in plain sight. Kane's point man senses picked up other watchers, as well. He took a deep drag on his cigar and scanned the ceiling again. The smoke was obnoxious but it worked against the gaudy in other ways, too. Smoke had a tendency to seek out higher ground.

He watched the smoke swirl around the stone ceiling, then move into holes in the walls at either end of the bar. He barely made out the rectangular shapes nearly hidden in the shadows. If the smoke hadn't fanned out and revealed the top half of the rectangles, he'd never have seen the men inside. He puffed on his cigar, releasing a plume of smoke that joined the clouds already drifting overhead. He caught Grant's eye and cut his own toward the rectangles.

Grant shifted slightly and let his gaze slide over the walls. He nodded. "No sign of our guy," he said.

"No," Kane agreed. "I'll get us some drinks."

"Let me know if they look as good up close."

Kane nodded and rose from his seat. With the cooling wind filling the room, the sweat covering his body was starting to turn to ice against his skin on the side not facing the fireplace.

He pulled up his shirttail and mopped his face, then scrubbed the grit and sweat from the back of his neck. More than anything right now he wanted a bath and a bed to sleep in. Those had been things he'd taken for granted as a Mag except when he'd been on an extended stay outside the ville. He leaned on the bar, feeling hostile stares scraping against his back.

"I said I wanted something stronger than the watered-down

piss you been pouring in my glass.'' The speaker was a man three down to Kane's left.

Lean and leathery, a few radiation sores scabbed over on his face and neck, the man looked like a desert rat, one of the independent scavengers who worked the Utah territories. Kane knew the reputation of such men. They turned from scavenger to coldheart in an eye blink.

One of the bartenders moved toward him. A brilliant smile formed on her full lips. "I'm sorry," she said pleasantly. "I didn't exactly hear what you said."

Kane picked up the razor-edged threat in the woman's voice, surprised that the rat didn't. He turned slightly, making sure he was out of the line of fire. He had no doubt that the rectangles in the walls held gunners responsible for covering the sec inside the gaudy.

"I said this shit you been pouring in my glass for the last hour is just a bunch of piss," the rat roared drunkenly. He looked like a bundle of sticks gathered inside his dusty clothing.

The woman leaned closer to the man, her cleavage threatening to spill from her blouse. The smile never left her crimson mouth. "You stupe bastard, you can't even keep your excretions straight."

The desert rat blinked at her once, and Kane knew everything was about to go to hell in a handbasket. Without warning, the rat came up with a long-bladed knife, slashing for the bartender's throat.

Gliding athletically on the balls of her feet, her eyes widening only a little with the sudden adrenaline flow, the woman dodged out of the way of the knife. Her right hand came up and a small blaster shot from the belled sleeve, filling her hand. Her finger tightened on the trigger.

The hollow boom of blasterfire filled the gaudy's main room.

Chapter 2

Brigid Baptiste halted the horse high on the hill overlooking the trail below. Moving slowly, knowing the trees around her wouldn't protect her from a keen-eyed observer who noticed a motion out of place in the surroundings, she stepped down from the saddle. The stink of sweaty leather and horse filled the still, humid air around her. It had stopped raining less than an hour ago, and she was soaked.

The dark gray shirt and black denim jeans she wore blended in with the brush and trees, and she knew she was only one shadow among others. A couple years back, while she was still an archivist working on the baron's projects in Cobaltville, she wouldn't have been able to move with such grace in the wild. She'd learned a lot because her life had depended on it more than once. She knew she'd probably never be able to move with Grant's or Kane's skill, but she was good enough for this.

Silently, she wished that Kane were there, even though she knew that probably wasn't a good thing to wish for. Kane would have handled the present situation a lot differently than she was willing to. He didn't like to exercise the patience she knew he had unless he was forced to.

And violence had a way of turning up around Kane, as if he were some kind of magnet for it.

She opened the straps on the saddlebag and took out a pair of binoculars. Wrapping the bridle reins around a nearby tree limb, she tethered the horse and moved a little farther down the hill, staying well within the sheltering cover provided by the dense brush and low-hanging branches. Then she hunkered

down to spy on Donald Bry, the man she'd followed from the
Cerberus redoubt for the past two days.

Just under six feet tall, Brigid was slender and full breasted.
Her red-gold hair normally hung well below her shoulders, but
she had it up now in a French braid to provide less of a target
for branches and brush. Her green eyes looked like dark em-
eralds in the shadows left over from the rain. A mini-Uzi was
slung at her shoulder. She fitted the compact binoculars to her
eyes and gazed down the trail.

She didn't focus the binoculars on the two men talking. The
man she didn't know wasn't a danger as long as he was talking
to Bry. Instead, she swept the terrain around the narrow clearing they'd met in. A sniper hiding in the brush would end
everything she'd been working to do for the past two days.

She scanned the brush with the patience and skill she'd
developed while working in the Cobaltville archives.
Breathing slowly and shallowly, she moved methodically from
sector to sector.

The man talking to Bry had arrived in a wag nearly completely hidden in the brush. To the left of the wag, over a
hundred yards back, a stripped-down motorcycle lay on the
ground under a tall spruce tree. Only a faint gleam from the
rusted metal frame caught Brigid's eye.

She tracked up the tree with the binoculars and found a
gunman sitting among the branches. He'd gotten bored with
watching over the other man, and careless. His rifle lay across
his knees, and he gave only cursory attention to the terrain.
She spotted two more men who completed a rough triangular
fall-back path for the man talking to Bry.

Drawing a calm breath and forcing the anger she felt away
from her mind, Brigid focused on the two men talking down
in the clearing. She didn't know why Bry had betrayed them
or how. But that was only for now. She would learn.

Donald Bry was a small man with round shoulders and blunt
features papery white from living indoors far too long. His
thick shock of copper-colored hair lay plastered to his head

from the rain. He wore a gray-white trench coat over his clothing that was dark with mud smears. A bolt-action .30-30 rifle occupied a sheath hanging down the front of his horse's saddle, canted butt forward so it could be easily pulled.

Brigid didn't know for sure if Bry knew how to use the weapon. Even after two days of following the man, she couldn't believe he was out in the wilderness across the Bitterroot Range. And she hadn't been able to think of a single reason why.

The man Bry talked to was overweight and paced constantly. He wore a raincoat and flat-brimmed hat. He didn't look happy at all.

Bry didn't, either. Brigid thought the man even looked more than a little afraid. She didn't blame him. If Bry was betraying them, and if Kane found out, Brigid was certain Kane would kill him.

Raindrops gathered on the leaves above her, falling across her shoulders and back. A couple splashed down her collar and ran down her spine. Goose bumps covered her back for an instant before the humid heat surrounding her melted them away.

Bry and the man talked for a few minutes, with the man growing increasingly angry while Bry appeared more agitated. Brigid wished she were close enough to hear the conversation.

At the end of the conversation, Bry dug in his saddlebags and handed a thick package to the other man. Brigid rolled the adjustment knob on the binoculars, focusing on the package. It wasn't much bigger than Bry's blunt, short-fingered hand, square in shape and between three and four inches thick.

A package that size from most men wouldn't have worried Brigid much. But Donald Bry was the computer specialist at Cerberus redoubt, second only in his knowledge in that field to Lakesh. Someone like Bry could deliver a hell of a lot of information in a package that size. And information was one plentiful resource that distinguished the Cerberus redoubt.

She watched Bry as the two men continued to talk. The

other man appeared to be mollified somewhat, but he threw a finger in Bry's face, obviously chastising him.

Whatever Bry had been supposed to do, Brigid reasoned, hadn't been accomplished to the other man's satisfaction. She felt her thighs starting to burn with the strain of sitting hunkered down, coupled with all the hours of being in the saddle. Bry hadn't traveled quickly from the redoubt, but he had traveled steadily.

Brigid was reluctant to shift, though, knowing the three men watching over the transaction might catch her movement, however slight.

Her initial thought was that Bry was betraying the Cerberus redoubt and Lakesh in some manner. There was no other way to explain this clandestine meeting.

In a way she couldn't blame the man. Like herself, Grant, Kane, DeFore and others among the present redoubt personnel, Lakesh had engineered events that had put them in danger in their home villes, leaving them no option but to flee the death squads that had been hunting them. In the end they'd each had to accept the help Lakesh had offered, never suspecting for a time that he had virtually impressed them into his service.

Even though the life they had now was in most ways better than what they'd had in the villes, they were fugitives hunted across most of the Outlands.

Brigid's mind, ever curious and ever watchful, trained to take a few facts and build theories that remained to be weighed and judged by the addition of more facts and suppositions, concentrated on Bry and the transaction she'd just witnessed.

Of all the personnel Lakesh had recruited to the Cerberus redoubt, Bry most times seemed the happiest. The little man had access to more, bigger and better computers than he'd ever had before. Not a day passed that Bry wasn't digging into the computer files Lakesh gave him access to.

So did the package contain something Lakesh hadn't wanted Bry to have? Or any of them?

The questions rested uneasily in Brigid's mind. With her

background as an archivist, she was used to being persevering when it came to waiting for answers. The problem was that in Cobaltville lives hadn't hung immediately on those answers. Now they did.

The other man turned away from Bry and walked back along the trail toward the hidden wag. Bry stood there with the horse's reins in his hands, looking lost and alone. Brigid thought maybe he'd been expecting to go with them. Instead, it looked as though the little man was being abandoned.

Brigid stretched out carefully, no longer able to ignore the pain in her thighs. She continued watching the man in the hat through the binoculars. Fat raindrops beat against her sodden clothing intermittently, making faint pops. At first the sound drowned out the other noise, but as it drew closer, the slithering attracted Brigid's attention.

She turned her head cautiously, primitive instincts slowing her movements even as her heart raced to flood her system with adrenaline. She lowered the binoculars, turning them down quickly so no light reflected to the three men watching over the meeting. When she saw the snake lying in the grass less than a yard away, her breath locked in her throat.

Masked as it was in the grass and the brush, Brigid didn't know if the snake was twenty feet long, but it was every bit of fifteen feet in length. The reptile lay in loose, powerful coils, heaped around behind her and to her left, blocking her way back to the horse. If it had come from farther uphill, as she guessed, it had bypassed the horse and chosen her for the weaker kill.

Brigid froze, staring back into the hypnotic black eyes. The forked tongue flicked out, scenting the air. The snake's head was wedge-shaped, like one of the trenching tools they carried in camping backpacks, and more than a foot across. The coloring of the scales was splotchy, mostly greens with a dash of purples and reds thrown in. A thick black circle collared its neck.

The wedge-shaped head wavered, holding almost steady a

foot above the ground. The tongue flicked out again as the creature stared at Brigid.

She wasn't sure if the snake's progenitors were native to the Bitterroot Range, but she was certain its genetic makeup had been altered somewhere down the line. Snakes didn't grow that big in the area.

Cold fear lanced through Brigid's stomach as the snake oozed through the brush and came closer. She tried to swallow, but her mouth had gone dry. Movement, she decided, as long as it wasn't sudden was a good thing. Cautiously, she gathered her feet under her.

The weight of the mini-Uzi on her shoulder was in no way comforting. Even if she managed to free it before the snake struck, the shrill sounds of blasterfire would attract the attention of the men below. She felt certain they wouldn't simply let her go.

And perhaps they wouldn't let Bry go, either. She wasn't sure what she owed the computer specialist in light of the present events, but she was determined not to endanger him if she could help it.

The snake's mouth opened soundlessly, releasing fangs that popped into place. The fangs were easily twice as long as Brigid's fingers. Saliva strands ran from the fangs to the pink-and-white mouth. The head rose higher, coming a full three feet off the ground and gliding closer to Brigid.

She continued moving slowly because she had no choice. Her feet weren't under her yet, and she knew she couldn't throw herself far enough away to escape the snake. Her heart beat frantically, hammering inside her chest. In another moment she had one foot solidly under her, the other one coming.

The snake didn't give her time to finish. Bent over as she was, using her hands against the ground to keep her balance, she was almost eye to eye with the creature and less than two feet away.

The snake struck with a smooth flex of scaled muscle, launching itself like an arrow from a bow. The wedge-shaped head opened so far it looked like the creature was trying to turn inside out. The fanged mouth jutted out, streaking for Brigid's face.

KANE WATCHED the desert rat rock back, pulled hard to the right when the derringer bullet struck him. Blood immediately drenched the rat's right shoulder. The old man swore fiercely as he regained his balance. His hand still clasped the knife, but the blade was wet with his own blood.

"Go ahead and fuck up again," the woman told him. The small blaster centered on the man's face. Her eyes were wide with excitement. "I've got another barrel left."

The desert rat froze. "Fuckin' bitch! Don't you ever—"

The bartender shot him between the eyes. The man's head popped backward. Blood spurted from the small crater above the bridge of his nose as the corpse dropped.

The men at the bar around the dead man stepped back as two sec men leaned out of the wall areas with assault rifles.

"I won't stand for any name-calling." Calmly, the bartender broke open the two-shot derringer, popped the empty brass casings into the air and thumbed fresh shells into the small weapon before the casings pinged against the stone floor. The smile never left her face.

Her weapon reloaded, the bartender vaulted lithely over the bar and landed astraddle the dead man. She knelt and quickly went through the corpse's pockets. The scrip she found quickly disappeared into her cleavage. The gaudy crowd erupted into cheers and laughter as she robbed the dead man.

The fat man who'd sat on the stool outside the front door strode into the room with his shotgun at the ready, a rolling mountain of flesh. Several of the gaudy patrons moved surreptitiously, turning so they had the big man covered in case anything further broke out.

"Stand down, Hickey," the woman warned, shoving her derringer out at the big man. "You done missed all the excitement."

Hickey hesitated, shifting uneasily on his feet. "I gotta drag the fucker outside, Carrie. Means I get a cut."

"You get bupkiss," the woman said. She aimed the tiny blaster at Hickey's crotch. "Might not chill your ass with either one of these bullets, but I'll make sure you have a harder time finding your johnson than you do now if you take one more step." Her free hand never stopped patting down the corpse. She turned up another wad of stained notes inside the dead man's shoe. That disappeared, as well.

Hickey cursed, totally unhappy with the situation. But he didn't take another step. A handful of gaudy patrons laughed at the fat man and made derisive comments.

Carrie stood and kicked the dead man. "Take this shitbag away, Hickey." She backed into the bar near Kane and hopped up onto the surface. Lifting her legs, she pivoted on her butt, still keeping the derringer on the fat man.

His ears red with embarrassment and still muttering curses, Hickey leaned down and fisted the dead man's shirt, then dragged the corpse from the room, leaving a trail of blood. He slammed the door behind him.

Carrie pushed the tiny blaster with its telescoping spring into the holster inside her belled sleeve as she walked toward Kane. "Something I can get for you, handsome?"

"Two beers," Kane replied, dropping scrip on the bartop.

"Draw or bottle?"

"Bottles," Kane told her. "I've seen you draw." He also didn't trust the local water supply. The scattered mines created toxic waste from the digging going on inside them, and none of it was getting taken care of. He'd heard stories of babies being born worse off than any of the muties he'd ever heard about from the old days.

"Local or import?" Carrie turned back to the shelves behind the bar.

"Import," Kane growled. "And I'll know the difference if you just refilled the bottle."

Carrie picked up two long-necked bottles in one hand and

turned to Kane with a grin. "A man like you, mebbe you would know. But you might want to watch your tone, see to it mebbe I don't take offense. I'm a harsh woman when I think I've been slandered."

Kane grinned at her, a thin rictus devoid of humor. "I've seen you draw," he told her quietly, "but you haven't seen me."

The smile stayed on the woman's face, but her eyebrows lifted. "Planning on staying long?"

"No."

Coolly, she shrugged and said, "Too bad. Could be fun."

Kane saluted her with both bottles in one hand, leaving his other hand free to go for either the shotgun or the pistol. He turned and headed back to the table, knowing Grant sat there covering him.

He really didn't expect any trouble from the woman despite her temper, but gaudies in the Outlands were capable of producing all kinds of violence. A boy no older than eight or nine walked into the room from a door beside the stage with a bucket in one hand. The boy studied the blood patterns for a moment, as if they had something to tell him, then took out a small plastic shovel and started spreading sand over the crimson stains.

Grant accepted his beer and twisted off the cap. "You know, you always take me to the nicest places."

Kane resumed his seat, scanning the gaudy's interior. "Just be glad I keep taking you home, too."

"I got a candidate in mind for this little meeting."

Kane raised an eyebrow as he uncapped his own beer.

"Man in the corner," Grant said. "The one with the scar around his head that makes you think mebbe he's had a lobotomy."

Taking a drink from the beer, Kane glanced in the far corner of the room by the door. The beer tasted bitter, but it was cool. Cold would have been better.

The man was tall and scrawny, almost lost in the stained

white shirt he wore, looking like some disease had wasted away the better part of him. A fringe of shoulder-length graying brown hair surrounded his bald head. He wore a beard hacked off to only a handful of inches and mostly squared off.

The scar Grant referred to ran from where the man's left ear had been, up across his temple, then diagonally across his forehead until it reached the hairline on the opposite side. The scar was old, almost disappearing into the seams of the man's face. A dozen other scars kept the big one company. Despite his thinness, the man's feet and hands were huge. A scope-equipped lever-action .30-06 rifle leaned against the wall beside him within easy reach.

"Looks like whatever he ran into got the better part of him," Kane commented.

"He's still got a heartbeat," Grant replied.

Kane silently agreed and took another drag on his cigar. Those scars guaranteed most people would leave the old man alone. But they also meant if anyone braced him it would be a pack rather than an individual—or someone who would shoot him from behind and be done with it. "What makes you so sure he's who we're here to meet?"

"The way he keeps eyeballing us tells me he's real interested in us." Grant rounded the gray ash from his cigar into the bear-oil lamp. "He came in while you were at the bar and rousted a couple guys from that table."

"They went?" Kane sipped more beer and felt closed in again.

"Like they were trained."

Kane glanced speculatively at the old man again. "He's not here alone."

"That's what I was thinking. The two guys he moved are at four o'clock from you."

Kane pulled on the cigar, then breathed out a plume of smoke. He squinted through the haze and spotted the two men against the wall on the opposite side of the room.

Both were young and big, showing signs of rough-and-tumble lives in the scars that covered their faces and arms. They'd worked together for a time, Kane knew, because they never looked at each other while they talked, their eyes constantly on the move around the gaudy.

"Mebbe we should go knock on his door," Grant said. "I hate waiting around."

Kane nodded and rolled his shoulders to loosen up some of the tension he felt. "So do I. But it's been their show so far. Let's leave it there for a little while longer."

"Mebbe he doesn't know it's us," Grant said.

"That would be kind of hard to figure," Kane said. "We're the only black-and-white team in here."

"Mebbe he hasn't noticed."

"You get as old as that and tore up that much along the way, you notice."

The bartender who'd killed the desert rat walked over to their table. She leaned down with her hands on the tabletop, giving Kane a direct sight line down her blouse. "We're serving lunch if you're interested."

"What?" Kane asked. The smoke was so thick in the room it masked the scent of food. As he looked around, though, he noticed a number of the tables had big platters of food.

"Barbecue," Carrie answered. "Ribs, brisket and potatoes any way you like them. Homemade bread and honey."

Kane and Grant both ordered the ribs, baked potatoes and a loaf of bread. He also asked for two more bottles of beer. The cost was expensive but he'd known it would be. The surrounding terrain was too inhospitable to raise livestock, and he doubted anything would grow nearby except the sparse brush and cactus.

The meal arrived in just a few minutes. The thick, smoky spice of the barbecue sauce dolloped generously across the ribs overcame even the smell of burning bear fat. The potatoes were as big as Grant's fists, split open and filled with yellow butter, chives and bacon bits.

Kane and Grant dug in with gusto. Lunches during the overland trips had consisted of ring-pulls and self-heats, as varied as they could be but still tasting as if they'd all come from the same tin container. Wild rabbits had contributed to the limited menu on a couple suppers, but the meat had been gamy and tough. The meat on the ribs, however, practically fell off the bone.

They ate without talking, as accustomed to the casual conversations they'd had over the years as they were to the comfortable silences that came between them. Kane surprised himself with his appetite. He nursed his beer, not wanting to chance falling under its influence. The harsh heat trapped outside the gaudy's front door had left them on the dehydrated side, and their bodies soaked up anything wet way too fast.

"Company's coming." Grant spoke in a low rumble that didn't go much past the perimeters around the table.

Kane slathered honey on a chunk of homemade bread. "It's about damn time." He stuffed the bread into his mouth. The honey was sweet and pure, providing an almost instant sugar rush. With food this good, it was no surprise Tyson's Y'all Cum Bakk Saloone had regular business.

The scrawny man stood just out of arm's reach, his rifle held close in one hard-knuckled hand. "Name's Remar," he stated in a husky voice. "I think we got some bidness to attend."

Kane gazed at the man for a short time without saying a word. Remar didn't flinch from the scrutiny, didn't appear interested at all. "Mebbe. Pull up a chair and we'll talk."

Remar hooked a nearby chair with his foot and yanked it across. He dropped into the seat with a sigh, laying the rifle across his knees. He eyed the plates of ribs on the table with a look of total larceny.

"Have you eaten?" Grant asked.

"This morning," Remar told him. "Ain't got around to it since."

Grant pushed over his plate of ribs. Kane slid over the remaining half loaf of bread and the ceramic honey pot. It was good that the meat was so tender because it didn't look like Remar had a tooth left in his head.

The scrawny man ate as if he'd stopped one step short of

starvation. Kane and Grant watched in silence, amazed at the amount of food the man put away—especially since he ate one-handed. He kept the other hand on his rifle below the table. Kane didn't doubt the rifle's safety was off or that the man's finger was curled around the trigger.

Remar glanced up at them, evidently somewhat uneasy about their quiet attention. "Fuck, you gonna talk or stare at me? Ain't you ever seen a man eat before?"

"Not like that," Grant said.

The old man's eyes knotted up, and his face flushed deep red with anger. For a moment Kane thought they were about to lose their only lead, and have to kill the old man at that.

Then a big grin like that of a shy youngster spread across Remar's lips. "I was the youngest of thirteen kids. Getting to the dinner table was a tussle. Getting something to eat was like going to war."

Kane sipped his beer and watched the old man work at the meat and bread.

Remar spooned honey out onto a piece of bread he'd torn from the loaf, then wadded it into a ball and shoved it into his mouth. He chewed a few times, then swallowed. His Adam's apple strained with the load but managed it. He belched softly, covering it with his forearm.

"My pa kept a farm in the Ohio River valley," the scrawny old man said. "Pigs and cows, them were things we sold off to the baron's men for taxes or swapped with traders for seed and equipment. Pa kept a lot of range-fed chickens, and them we could eat. Till I was ten years old, though, I thought all a person cooked up of a chicken was legs and the neckbone. Then I got some size on me and made me a knife. Only had to cut a couple of my brothers to let them know I wasn't just eating legs and neckbones no more."

Kane laughed at the man's honesty despite the tension that had brought him and Grant down from the Cerberus redoubt. He was well acquainted with men like Remar. They were deadly and dangerous, but a man knew where he stood with them.

"I guess you ain't here to talk about menus, though," Remar said.

"No," Kane agreed.

Remar stuck another piece of sauce-drenched meat into his mouth. His hooded eyes turned speculative. "You brought the scrip?"

"I wouldn't be here otherwise," Kane said.

Remar nodded. "Wanted to ask. Some people sell me a little short, think mebbe they can shine me on with big words or a fancy way of saying things. But I understand all right, and I can tell when most folks are lying to me."

"Me too." Kane returned the old man's gaze full measure.

"Knew you could." Remar tore off another piece of bread and used it to sop up barbecue sauce from the empty meat platter. "So you understand I ain't in here alone?"

"Two men inside." Kane nodded in their direction. "They're a little green. I keep finding them looking at me."

Remar shrugged. "They'll learn or they'll die."

"Most do," Grant added.

"You ain't been green in a long time," Remar said.

"Not since I started putting on my own drawers," Grant told him.

Remar gave a short, barking laugh. "I got six more men outside. Just so's you know the score if something breaks loose in here."

"That's good to know," Kane said. "When a funeral's done right, six men carry a corpse to the grave."

A grin split Remar's thin lips, pulling at the maimed side of his head where his ear had been. The purple knot that occupied the ear space had hairs sticking out of it that quivered. "You got no backup in you, do you?"

"Never learned how," Kane replied.

"You got another cigar?" Remar pointed to the butts sticking up from the bear oil lamp.

Kane took three more cigars from his pocket, and they used Grant's lighter to fire up all the way around. Remar rolled the cigar in his toothless mouth with obvious relish. "Good smokes,'' the old man said. "Ain't hand-rolled. At least not in this century. You got access to a redoubt nobody's found yet?''

"No,'' Kane answered. "I traded for them. Same as I'm trading with you now.''

Remar's lips pursed again as he blew out a smoke ring. His voice lowered when he spoke again. "What kind of tech are you looking for?''

"What have you got?''

Remar shrugged. "All kinds. Comp progs. Meds. Books. Surgical equipment. You name it, we can get it.''

"That's a big promise,'' Grant stated.

Remar nodded. "And I mean ever word of it.''

"Sounds like you're the one who found a virgin redoubt,'' Kane commented, but he and Lakesh knew it was probably worse than that. On their last brush with the Utah territories, they'd been tracking down the source of predark tech that had been pouring into Cobaltville. That had led into the Western Isles and their first brush with Wei Qiang, the Tong warlord. Recently, the baronial alliance had fractured, and Cobaltville had been attacked by Barons Samarium and Mande. Baron Cobalt would seize any advantage he could in his quest for supremacy over the other barons, and his interest in predark tech was renewed after his Mags repulsed the forces of Samarium and Mande. The situation was unstable, and no one knew where the barons might strike next—or with what weapons.

Lakesh still had a few sources in the archives, people he kept track of that didn't know they were being spied on. But it had been Grant and Kane who'd trolled through the Outlands until they'd found out about Remar. They hadn't gotten their contact's name, but they'd gotten a message to him to set up the meet today.

"Hell, son,'' Remar said, "Tyler Falzone done found better than a redoubt. He uncovered the Lost Valley of Wiy Tukay.''

Chapter 3

Brigid threw herself back and sideways, lunging to avoid the striking snake. The creature streaked by her, missing by inches. She kept moving, knowing the snake was already preparing to strike again from the sound of the scales gliding through the underbrush.

Desperately, Brigid rolled, coming over on her butt then trying to get to her feet. Branches and brush tore at her, ripping scratches on her face and exposed arms, pulling at her clothing. Despite her control, she gave a choked cry of fear and frustration as the snake struck.

Falling back, trying to get more distance between them, Brigid lifted the binoculars, hoping to fend off her attacker. The snake's fangs hammered into the binoculars. Venom slid hot and wet across Brigid's fingers, sending a stinging burn into the scratches the thorns and branches had left. The dull thud echoed among the trees.

The snake appeared dazed for a moment. Brigid took advantage of the brief respite and pushed herself to her feet. Her stomach quivered and tried to turn flips. Her knees quaked and barely got under her in time to keep her upright.

Abruptly, two branches dropped from overhead. In the adrenaline-driven moment, everything seemed to take place in slow motion. She noted the blaze-white ends of the finger-thick branches and the way the leaves shimmered as they fell to the ground. Both of the branches fell from a fairly straight path.

Brigid instinctively looked up, thinking something had to have been in the trees overhead. Her imagination summoned up more snakes draped over the thick limbs, waiting to reach down and seize her.

Then the sound of the explosion rolled over her, a sharp crack that she instantly identified as a rifle report. Realizing she was in as much danger from the men she'd spotted earlier as she was from the snake, she ducked low and threw herself into the brush away from the snake.

More bullets raked the tree line. Her horse pulled at the tethered reins, rearing frantically as all hell seemed to break loose.

Brigid rolled into cover behind a tree and pushed up into a squatting position. Silently, she cursed herself for being so far from help and for trailing Bry by herself. It was a stupid thing to do, maybe lethally so. And if she survived the encounter and Kane heard about it, she knew he'd tell her that.

She slid the mini-Uzi from her shoulder and cradled it in both hands. Exchanging blasterfire with men equipped with rifles wasn't a good plan, either. The subgun was deadly inside a certain radius, but the range was too far and the 9 mm subsonic rounds would bounce off even pencil-thick branches.

Leaning around the tree, Brigid gazed down the hill toward the path. The man Bry had met had already disappeared into the forest, but Bry was still on the trail trying to control his skittish mount. Brigid let out a sigh of relief, knowing the men he'd met hadn't faulted him for them getting spied on. At least not yet.

She held the mini-Uzi in both hands and fired a full clip at Bry, intentionally missing the man. The bullets slapped into the loose black earth, flinging grassy clods in all directions only a few feet from the computer specialist.

Bry's horse gave another series of convulsive heaves and succeeded in unseating its rider. Bry fell heavily to the ground and curled up in a fetal position, his arms wrapping around his head. When the bullets stopped striking the ground nearby, he pushed himself to his hands and knees and crawled toward the nearest shelter. His horse vanished in a heartbeat, kicking up its heels.

Satisfied she'd helped convince the gunmen that Bry wasn't responsible for the present problem, Brigid whirled back around the tree. Her breath tore rapidly through her throat in burning gasps. She hit the mini-Uzi's magazine release and dropped the spent clip.

Automatically, the reflexes drilled into her by Grant and Kane, she scooped up the empty magazine and shoved it into her pants pocket. Empty casings were more plentiful than spare clips. She tugged another clip free of her belt and slid it into the weapon.

Bullets continued ripping through the nearby trees, but they were coming more slowly now. At least one of the gunmen had picked up on her position, though. The vibrations of the big rounds striking the trunk carried through the tree she leaned against and echoed against her back.

Remembering the snake, she scanned the underbrush again. She saw nothing and didn't know what was worse: seeing the snake in front of her or not knowing where it was. Brush shivered on her right, uncomfortably close to her feet. She yanked her legs back, expecting the snake to jump at her from the brush. With the sounds of the blasterfire echoing around her, she knew she wouldn't be able to hear the snake's approach.

Feeling vulnerable, Brigid glanced uphill, thinking everything would be better once she got the hell out of the area. Kane and Grant weren't expected back from their road trip for another few days, but the possibility that they'd returned early existed.

She picked up a long dead branch and used it to beat the brush ahead. She kept the mini-Uzi tight in her fist, her finger resting outside the trigger guard as Kane had taught her. The snake's twenty-foot length made it incredibly dangerous, but it would also be hard to miss.

The bullets came more slowly now, but they also came

closer. Grass and brush jumped and flew as the rounds cored through them, and bark splintered beside her head, peppering her cheek with splinters. Tears stung her eye and blurred her vision as she ducked out of reflex.

She kept heading uphill, hoping her horse didn't tear itself free before she reached it. Another round cut through at her side, tearing a thumb-sized hole through her shirt and narrowly missing flesh. Two days' ride out from Cerberus was no place to be with any kind of wound, she realized.

Her lungs burning with the need for oxygen, Brigid kept moving, taking cover wherever she could. Less than fifteen feet from her rearing horse, she slung the mini-Uzi and pulled the fighting knife from her belt. There wasn't time to untie the bridle reins, and she intended to slash them.

She took a final deep breath as bullets cut through the branches overhead, then she pushed up and sprinted for the horse. All she needed was a little time to put some distance between herself and her pursuers. They wouldn't chase her far through unknown territory, not if they'd gone to such lengths to keep their meeting with Bry secret.

Her legs crashed through the waist-high brush, and she vaulted over a fallen tree that had become a home for a tribe of large black ants. Her hand crushed some of the hard bodies as she went over and she felt the unpleasant jolt of stingers plunging into her palm. She almost fell on the other side of the tree when she landed, and her feet sank into the soft loam. She stumbled and caught herself, then aimed for the bucking horse again.

"Easy, easy," she said when she reached the animal.

The horse's eyes rolled white and it trembled even as it reared. It whickered plaintively and tried to back away from her. Bullets crashed into the trees overhead, knocking down raindrops, leaves and branches.

She grabbed the reins in her empty hand, ignoring the burning pain left from the ant stingers. A quick slash of the knife in her other hand and the leather parted. The horse shied away from her, trembling and bucking, stumbling through the thick underbrush.

Brigid resisted the impulse to cry out in frustration at the horse. It was as frightened as she was and had its own plans for escape. She sheathed the knife at her hip, unable to even duck the bullets that slammed into the hillside. Lunging forward, she grabbed a fistful of the horse's wiry mane and pulled herself closer.

When she managed to grab the pommel with her other hand, she held on to the horse and saddle and pulled herself up off the ground and against the animal. She held on desperately, trying to anticipate the frightened beast's movements. She shoved her left foot forward and finally succeeded in sliding it into the stirrup. Pushing off from her foot, she hauled herself into the saddle, hanging on as the horse reared again, going nearly straight up. The horse's head went back so fast and so far that she couldn't avoid it.

Hard bone and muscle collided with Brigid's face with enough force to nearly knock her unconscious. Dazed, she hung on to the saddle pommel with both hands, losing the reins. The metallic taste of blood trickled through her mouth, letting her know her lips had split from the impact. She blinked her tearing eyes open and searched for the reins. Spotting them, she leaned forward across the horse's neck to reach them. Her fingers grazed the rough leather, narrowly missing the thin bands.

Warm and sticky bright crimson blood sprayed over the side of Brigid's face.

At first she thought the blood came from her, gushing from an injury the horse had done to her face. Then she realized it was coming from the horse. She captured the reins and drew them back even as she became cognizant of the fact it was already too late.

A bullet had cored through the horse's head, entering the other side and ripping out a crater that covered the animal's eye and half its long face, barely missing Brigid as it passed through. Horror swept over her as she surveyed the terrible wound, the ruined red flesh and the broken white of shattered bone. She felt the bullet's impact then, carried through the horse's body and echoing against the inside of her thighs.

For a moment, Brigid sat on top of the frozen horse, then it fell like a marionette with the strings cut, tumbling to the ground like a flesh-and-blood avalanche. She tried to kick free of the saddle, but her foot was tangled in the stirrup. She fought free, knowing the deadweight of the horse would break her leg or at the very least trap her.

When her foot came free, she fell off balance, striking the ground hard on her side. Her breath left her lungs in a painful rush, and black comets whirled in her vision. Her foot was jammed under the dead animal. Placing her other foot on the horse's back, she pushed hard and wiggled her trapped foot. Rocks and roots tore at her leg, tearing through the thick denim in places. Blood from her nose leaked down her chin and rattled in the back of her throat.

Another bullet struck the horse's exposed stomach. The sudden eruption of intestines squirming out of the bullet hole let Brigid know how the side of the horse's head had been blown away. One of the three gunmen was using explosive bullets. The ropy twists of guts spewed into the grass and brush, freeing a rush of stink and blood.

Free of the horse, Brigid turned over and stayed low in the brush. Bullets dug craters in the ground around her and left jagged white scars on the nearby trees. Her body shaking with adrenaline and fatigue, she half ran and half crawled straight into the snake.

Brigid had one terrified instant of recognition before the snake struck. She tried to throw herself back, but there was no time. The snake sank its fangs into her chest and clamped down.

Screaming in fear and anger, Brigid gripped the snake behind its wedge-shaped head and tried to pull it from her even as she fell to the ground. The burning poison raced through her body, followed almost immediately by numbness.

She pushed against the coils of scaled muscle between her hands and knew she couldn't force the snake away. Then blackness closed in all around her.

Chapter 4

"The Lost Valley of Wiy Tukay?" Kane repeated. He rolled his cigar, tasting the tobacco and the residual tang of the barbecue sauce. He tried to remember if he'd ever heard of the place during his days as a Mag or during the intervening time he'd spent at the Cerberus redoubt. "I've never heard of it."

Remar puffed contentedly on his own cigar, leaning back in his chair expansively. "Not surprised. It was lost for a bastard long time."

Grant swapped looks with Kane, his dark eyes revealing hooded doubt. "But this Tyler Falzone found it."

Remar nodded.

"Sounds like a line of bullshit to me," Grant stated.

Remar shook his head, not taking offense. He leaned forward and placed his free elbow on the table, giving himself enough room to maneuver the .30-06, and lowered his voice. "It's not bullshit. It'd be kind of stupe to think me or anybody else is pulling all that tech out of our asses, now, wouldn't it?"

Kane silently agreed. A few months back they'd first come across a trader named Chapman who'd been trading tech to Baron Cobalt. While investigating Chapman and his sources, Kane, Grant, Domi and Brigid had ended up in the Western Isles. Ambika, the warrior queen who'd ruled the Isles of the Lioness, had tried to kill them before they could discover anything more about the tech recovery Chapman was connected with. A Mag commander named Kearney from Cobaltville had told them about the operation in what had been Seattle, but the information they'd been able to discover since that time had been sparse.

They did know that Baron Cobalt was very interested in the recovered tech and had been dealing steadily with the traders that dealt in it. The recent attack on Cobaltville had only underlined the importance of any advantage that salvaged predark tech could provide, and Cobalt had increased his activity in the Northwest Territories. The baron's interest in the tech had spurred Lakesh's interest. Kane had agreed on the necessity of investigating the situation. The Cerberus exiles couldn't stay hidden forever, and when the time came to fight back Kane wanted every advantage he could get. The split in the baronial alliance might even work in their favor.

"What is the Lost Valley of Wiy Tukay?" Kane asked.

Remar blew out another lungful of smoke. "Ain't no fucking paradise, I'll tell you that. It's the ass end of the world, is what it is."

Kane resisted the impulse to hurry the man's story. It wouldn't have made a difference to someone like Remar.

"Ever hear of a place called Seattle?" Remar asked.

"Yeah," Grant replied. "It's up in the Northwest Territories. Back during the nukecaust it was one of the hardest hit places."

"For a long time after the nukecaust," Remar confirmed, "the whole Northwest Territories were thought to be completely destroyed. And what wasn't destroyed was covered over with rad burn."

Radiation sickness was still a problem in a number of places. Kane had seen what happened to the people who mistakenly chose to live around such areas. "It takes hundreds of years to get rid of the nukecaust fallout."

Remar nodded. "Don't get me wrong, there's still places up in the Northwest Territories that'll guarantee fucked-up kids or barrenness, or just flat chill your ass. But Falzone found a way through that."

"So Falzone went looking for this Lost Valley?" Grant asked.

Grinning, Remar shook his head. "Fuck no. Falzone was just like most folks with an adventuresome spirit. He wasn't up there looking for no gaudy tale."

"He was running," Kane said, understanding.

"Yep," Remar replied. "Falzone got crossways with a trader he'd been working with. This trader had a big-time op going, one of the first to get into the more livable areas in the Northwest Territories. Falzone got to thinking mebbe there was enough room for a couple traders to operate out of the area."

"The trader Falzone was working with didn't see it that way," Grant said.

Remar gave a short bark of laughter. "Pretty much. But what really put the turd on the birthday cake was Falzone taking off with the old man's woman when he up and left. Carson put a lot of stock by that woman. She was a looker, by God."

"You were there?" Kane asked.

"Yeah. I ran sec for Carson."

"But you went with Falzone?"

Remar rounded off his cigar and nodded. "Carson was an old man." He glanced at Kane and Grant. "Older than me. And Carson had a scared man's belly. He was playing it safe, had been for a while. Falzone's got some curiosity about him. Like the bear that went over the mountain to see what he could see."

"Lot of bears get chilled doing that," Grant pointed out.

"Mebbe," Remar agreed. "But I've always been a curious-bear type, too."

"That's why you got that fucked-up ear," Grant said.

A thin smile spread across Remar's lips. He reached up to touch the scarred purple knob on the side of his head. "Fucker that gave me this ear never got to see another sunset."

Kane drained the rest of his beer and placed the bottle on the table. "So Falzone was on the run."

"Yeah," Remar said. "Carson chased us for a couple months, drove his wags into areas nobody had been into in years probably. And kept driving us right before him."

"Carson must have thought a lot of the woman," Grant commented.

"She was a beautiful one. Had dark hair and Spanish eyes, the kind that see right through a man and don't give nothing away themselves, the kind that just makes a man put a tent up right there." Remar shook his head. "She'd just been a kid when Carson found her, dancing in some gaudy to get by. But Carson, he convinced himself he loved her, and he tried to convince her, too. But she wasn't having any. So Carson rolled an armored wag into the middle of that gaudy and took her. She tried to kill him three times that I know of, and Carson wouldn't have took that from any man, woman or beast even once."

The front door opened and Kane tracked the newcomers automatically. There were six of them, all Chinese Tong hatchetmen. The group stayed together and moved slowly through the room. Kane's point man senses flared, and he cut his gaze across to Grant, who gave a slight nod, indicating he'd marked their arrival, as well.

"All those years," Remar continued, "I never thought I'd see that woman care about anything in her whole life. Five years Carson kept her, took her to bed and raped her every night. But something happened between her and Falzone."

"She saw a way out," Kane said. It was an old story, one of the first he'd learned about women. When a woman didn't have scrip, she could always trade out sex. A strong man traded out his blaster arm and his willingness to kill. In hard territory like the Outlands, sex and strength were still commodities in demand.

Remar shook his head. "Hell no. Falzone wasn't no cherry. Man had his fill of women. Every ville we rolled into, Falzone could walk up and have his pick of the litter. Problem was him and Carson's woman fell in love."

Kane watched the Tong hatchetmen sit at a table near the bar. The line of men talking to the two bartenders partially blocked his view. A crawling sensation tickled the back of his neck even though the Tong members didn't seem to even look in his direction.

"And I'm talking about true love," Remar said, shaking his head. "Never saw anything like it before in my life. Don't think I'll ever see it again." He glanced at Kane. "You only see the six of them?"

Kane glanced at the old man, his respect for the man's ability to survive rising. Remar had marked the Tong hatchetmen, as well. "Yeah. Friends of yours?"

"Nope," Remar replied. "Competitors. There's a Chinese baron out in the Western Isles."

"Wei Qiang," Grant said.

Remar nodded. "You've heard of him."

"Everybody out in the Utah territories has heard of him," Grant said. "Qiang's men and Baron Cobalt's keep running gun battles going over the mines."

"That's right." Remar looked reluctant about finishing his beer but did so anyway. "Qiang's short of steel out in the Western Islands, the way I hear it, and Baron Cobalt ain't so keen on sharing what's getting dragged out of the mines around here. Wei Qiang's interested in the tech Falzone's recovering, too. The Tong has got some camps in the Northwest Territories, always staying on the prod for the traders we send down this way. They've taken down a few shipments, and we've chilled a few dozen of them in return."

"They know you?" Kane asked.

"I guess they do now. Unless you boys have done something to piss off the Tong."

"No," Kane replied.

"Good to know. I hate when things get complicated."

"Getting out of here might be complicated," Grant stated sourly.

"Hell, son," Remar said with a laconic grin, "you and me both know there ain't but one way we're getting out of here alive."

"Shit," Kane said, starting to lean forward toward the old man.

Remar stood in one fluid motion and lifted his rifle. The Tong hatchetmen still weren't completely caught by surprise. They scattered from the table, going low to put the other gaudy patrons between themselves and Remar, their quick response reminding Kane of a seasoned Mag unit. The old man stood his ground and brought the .30-06 to his shoulder. When he touched the trigger, a massive boom filled the gaudy's main room and a Tong hatchetman went back and down, his chest a bloody ruin.

Kane snarled an oath as he dived from the chair an instant before a hail of bullets smacked into the wall where he'd been sitting. Grant was in motion, as well, moving in the other direction so they could lessen their chances of both being hit and try for some kind of cross fire.

In a heartbeat the gaudy turned into a war zone.

Chapter 5

"DeFore, I need you now."

The irritation she'd felt the first time Lakesh had called her over the intercom drained from DeFore when she heard his second call. In all her years at the Cerberus redoubt, she'd never heard that note of near hysteria in the old man's voice.

"Collins," DeFore said softly to the man who lay on the bed in the operating room she ran. She wore her ash-blond hair pulled back from her face, contrasting starkly with the deep bronze of her skin. She was stocky and buxom, but she looked good in the one-piece white jumpsuit most of the redoubt personnel wore.

Collins struggled to focus on her, blinking his eyelids a few times before he was finally able to keep them open. The painkiller she'd given the man packed a punch. "What?" he asked in a dry voice. He was a middle-aged man with a thick shock of brown hair and freckles scattered across the bridge of his nose.

"I'm going to have to leave you for a moment, but I'll be back." DeFore took an inflatable cast from the nearby stainless-steel shelf. The infirmary was top-of-the-line, better stocked than anything she'd ever worked with before, and even though she'd been there for years, she still marveled at the redoubt's extensive inventory.

"Sure," Collins said drunkenly. "I'm just going to stay here."

"That's a good idea." DeFore slid the cast over the man's lower right leg. The fibula had been snapped in two in a particularly nasty greenstick fracture as a result of a fall while climbing with a hunting team from the redoubt. Despite the fact that Cerberus was fully stocked with self-heats and ring-pulls and tons of food, the small community that lived within the vanadium walls preferred fresh meat, as well as the pre-served supplies.

"You're going to be back?" Collins asked, touching her arm with a lax hand.

"I'm going to be back," DeFore assured the man. When the hunting team had returned with him, Collins had been a basketcase. It wasn't often a man got to see one of his own bones sticking out of his body.

"I'm going to stay here," Collins said again.

"I think that's a good idea." DeFore hooked an air hose to the inflatable cast. She peered through the plastic at the dozens of bright blue sutures she'd threaded through the torn flesh of Collins's leg. She didn't like being hurried through one of her operations, and she damn sure intended to let Lakesh know that.

Everything seemed in order. Blood still stained the wound, but the surgical salve she'd put over it would keep bacteria at bay. The wound would clean up better the next time. With any luck, Collins wouldn't even walk with a limp when she was finished. DeFore did excellent work; she didn't settle for any other kind.

She pulled the straps across the man, belting him into the bed. In his present state of shock and with the meds in him, she was certain Collins wouldn't be able to get up from the table.

"DeFore," Lakesh called again, "I really must insist on your presence here."

Finished with the straps, DeFore stripped the bloodstained surgical gloves from her hands, stepped on the pedal of the biohazard garbage can and dropped the gloves inside. Angrily, she pressed the intercom button. "What?"

She breathed out, trying to get control of her emotions. Lakesh had that effect on most people, she'd noticed. Although they had their differences and decidedly conflicting points of view at times, she thought that Kane handled the old man better than anyone at Cerberus. Kane wasn't hesitant about airing his frustration with Lakesh.

"It's Brigid." Disbelief and pain echoed in Lakesh's voice. "I'm afraid we've lost her."

KANE DROPPED to one knee as he leveled the Mossberg shotgun. He aimed at one of the Tong hatchetmen and squeezed the trigger, riding out the savage recoil.

The tight pattern of double-aught buckshot caught the Tong member in the side of the chest and lifted him from the floor. The man sailed back a good three feet and landed on the floor, his lungs ripped to bloody tatters. Incredibly, he managed to get to his feet again and raise the blaster in his fist.

Racking the shotgun's pump, Kane fired at the man again, aiming across the barrel of the man's blaster and putting the pellets into his face. No matter how much opium the hatchetman had in his system, Kane knew the guy wasn't getting up again.

The bartenders had ducked behind the bar before the first shot was fired. Bullets ripped splinters from the wooden walls and tables, thudding into the heavy bar and shattering the bottles and the long mirror behind them. A round caught the chair Kane had been sitting in and sent it spinning onto its side.

The gaudy patrons resorted to savage instinct, firing at everyone but the groups they'd come in with. In seconds the body count had climbed into double digits. Corpses lay across chairs, tables and the floor, and wounded squirmed toward the nearest hiding place.

Remar worked the lever on the rifle calmly, shoving another round into the breech, then fired again, putting a bullet through the head of the hatchetman he'd already gut shot.

Kane glanced to the right and spotted a dead man facedown into a stacked plate of ribs. Blood and rib sauce clung to the corpse's agonized features. Knowing they couldn't hold their present position without serious risk, Kane rose in a half crouch and ran for the table. He hit the dead man and the chair with his shoulder, overturning them both. Then he kicked out a boot and knocked over the heavy table.

"Grant!" Kane bellowed as he took a moment to reload the shotgun's spent shells from the bandoliers.

Grant fired his M-14 at point-blank range into a man who'd been sitting behind him. The man had been leveling a hand-blaster at Grant until the rifle round knocked him back. There was no way to tell if the man was a true coldheart or a simple mine train sec man. But he hadn't been checking Grant's pedigree, either.

"Remar!" Kane yelled. He pushed himself up on one knee and threw the shotgun's muzzle over the tabletop. One of the hatchetmen screamed in his language as he fired an AK-47 from the hip. The unmistakable sound of the Russian blaster filled the room. A line of 7.62 mm rounds buzzed across the room, cutting down two other men as he tried for Remar.

Kane wrapped his finger around the shotgun trigger and squeezed. The pellet burst shattered the Tong hatchetman's chest and knocked him across the table behind him.

Grant slid into place beside Kane. With both men behind it, the table space was crowded. "They came for Remar."

Kane nodded, studying the back wall behind the bar speculatively.

"Both of Remar's buddies are down," Grant added.

"They put six men inside," Kane said grimly. "Want to bet how many they've got outside?"

Grant scowled. He glanced over the tabletop. The wood vibrated from the rounds repeatedly striking it. "We got the front door, but there's already a crowd there. And if you're right, there's an execution squad outside."

Sudden machine-gun fire ripped through the gaudy's two front windows. Shattered glass scattered across the room. The heavy slugs even knocked some of the iron sec bars out of place, striking sparks that cascaded in wide arcs.

Remar dropped to his knees behind Kane and Grant. A wolf-ish grin twisted the old man's battered face. Blood seeped down one arm in steady streams.

"Mebbe we got more than the front door," Kane said. He swept the room with his gaze. No one was making a move toward their position except the Tong warriors. Everybody else was trying to hole up.

"What?" Grant asked.

"The bartenders aren't around anymore," Kane said. "Remember the breeze we felt earlier?"

Clarity eased some of the tension in Grant's face. "Escape route."

"Got to be," Kane said.

Remar loaded his weapon with fresh shells.

"You hit bad?" Kane asked the old man.

"Through and through," Remar answered. "I've been hit worse and lived to tell about it."

"We're going to try for the bar."

Remar gave him a tight nod. "Don't slow up unless you want to get bred."

Without another word, Kane shoved himself to his feet, both hands holding the shotgun. He wished he wore the bulletproof black polycarbonate Mag armor. Fear thrummed inside him, but that wasn't what made him wish for the suit. He was a fighting man, a warrior who took every edge he could in survival.

The Mossberg held seven rounds, and he fired steadily as he ran for the bar. Everyone on the other end of the room sweeper went to ground, including the Tong hatchetmen. Kane didn't know if he hit any of them or not. He didn't try to go around the bar; he threw himself on top of it, sliding toward the edge.

Before he dropped over the side, a Tong warrior stood at the other end of the bar, an Ingram submachine gun clenched in his hands. The Chinese man's face was a mask of rage, marked by blood from a scalp wound, as he screamed and fired.

The bullets cut the air over Kane as he extended his arms and fired the Mossberg. Without the chance to properly brace the weapon, the shotgun slammed back into Kane's cheekbone hard enough to blur his vision. But the tight pattern of buckshot was on target. As Kane went over the side of the bar, he watched the Tong gunman pinwheel back.

Kane landed on broken glass and shattered mirror fragments that cut into his clothing and flesh. The alcohol puddle that spread across the stone floor soaked into his clothing and burned the dozens of cuts he received.

Groaning, he rolled onto his stomach, getting cut more in the process, and pulled the shotgun to his shoulder in the prone position. His point man's senses had already cued him into the shifting shadow patterns at the end of the bar. When the Tong hatchetman stepped into view, he spotted Kane and immediately threw himself back.

Kane dropped the shotgun sights from the man's body to the leg the man had pushed off on, still visible beyond the edge of the bar. He heard Grant crash to the floor behind him and start cursing at once even as he fired.

The shotgun pellets struck the Tong hatchetman's leg and knocked it into the air and back. The man's scream rose above all the other noise in the gaudy. If he wasn't dead or dying, Kane felt certain the man was crippled.

Pushing himself into a hunkered position, aware of the bits of glass stuck in his hands and arms that caught the light and glittered, Kane glanced back behind the bar. A small opening no more than two feet across was revealed behind a section of the back wall that hadn't been properly replaced.

Remar came around the end of the bar opposite where the Tong had showed up. Blood streaked his face. "That lead out?"

"It better," Kane replied grimly.

The old man scuttled forward, staying below the line of

bullets that knocked more mirror fragments and bottles from the wall above.

Kane dropped the shotgun's muzzle on the man.

Remar stopped, his face hardening. "I usually don't let a man draw down on me and live."

"I usually don't draw down on a man and not chill him," Kane replied evenly.

Remar laughed.

"One of us goes first," Kane said. With Remar between them, he figured there'd be less chance of losing the man. It also provided that their backs didn't become tempting targets.

"Get it the hell done, then," Remar ordered. "Otherwise we're all going to have a seat on the last train west."

Kane glanced at Grant.

Grant shook his head. "That's a small hole. If I get stuck, we're all fucked. You go first."

Kane didn't argue because it was true. He slithered through the hole, angling his broad shoulders to get through. He knew Grant would have an even harder time of it, but he felt certain the big man would make it.

The hole opened up on a landing on the other side. It was too dark to properly see inside the corridor, but his exploring hand found the wall on the other side, the wall to his left and the stairs that headed down to his right.

He crawled through and tried to stand. He cursed when his head hit the short ceiling. Bullet holes across the wall facing the bar let in stray fingers of yellow-and-orange guttering lamplight from the gaudy and let Kane know someone was using high-caliber slugs. Dust flurried in the beams of light.

Remar came through next, oozing through the hole as if being reborn. "Son of a bitch, it's dark."

"Unless you've got a lantern in your hip pocket, it's going to stay that way," Kane replied. He shifted so the shotgun was almost pointing at the man.

Remar noticed the weapon but didn't say anything about it. He tested the stairs with a foot.

"Wait," Kane ordered.

"Those people out there are going to find this, too," Remar grumbled. "Especially now that we showed them the way. You don't think they're going out that front door if they've got a choice, do you?"

Kane knew the old man was telling it true, but he wasn't leaving without Grant.

It took some work but Grant forced his way through the bolt-hole. "The going gets any smaller along the way, and we're going to have real problems," the big man grumbled.

"I'll let you know," Kane said. "Let me borrow your lighter."

Grant passed it over, then stepped in behind Remar, stooped by the short ceiling.

Kane took a moment to feed more shells into the shotgun before he slung it. He slipped the .45 free of the hip holster because it would be easier to use in the narrow confines of the stairwell. Holding the lighter above his head, he flicked the wheel. The flint caught the wick on fire, sending shadows whirling and spinning in a sudden maelstrom around Kane.

Only partially revealed, the stairwell curled in on itself and plunged down into rock. The cool air coming from below set the lighter's flame wavering. Kane took the draft as a good sign. If the other end of the stairwell was blocked, the draft wouldn't exist.

Bullets hammered a staccato tune against the gaudy wall. One of the rounds penetrated and chipped rock from the wall beside Grant, who ducked out of reflex. The big man still had his cigar clenched between his teeth and he puffed on it till the coal was a bright orange in the darkness.

"We going?" Remar asked sarcastically. "Or mebbe I should have brought me a bedroll?"

"We're going," Kane said. But he wished they'd had more information about Tyson's saloon. The stairwell could lead from the frying pan to the fire. He watched Grant, knowing what the big man was doing.

Satisfied that the cigar stump was burning as hot as it was going to, Grant flipped it back through the escape door. The orange coal splatted into the pool of liquor and alcohol behind the bar, rolled and smoked for a moment until Kane thought it was simply going to go out.

Then the alcohol caught, spreading quickly in a liquid pop that was audible in the hidden stairwell even over the sound of blasterfire. Blue flames whirled up from the alcohol to block the escape door. Smoke spilled into the hidden passageway slowly, since it was coming against the breeze crowding out into the main room, but Kane felt it already burning his nasal passages and the back of his throat.

"Goddamn son of a bitch!" a woman yelled from the other side of the wall. "Vann, I'm on fire, goddammit!"

"Then put yourself out, bitch," a man roared back. "We all got our problems!"

Kane knew the alcohol fire would consume itself quickly, and if it didn't catch fire to the bar in that time, it would go out. Made primarily out of stone, the gaudy could take the damage being meted out and be back in business in less than a week provided the owner had the wherewithal to replace the lost supplies.

The lighter grew hot in his hand with the continued use. He turned his attention to the narrow spiral staircase and started down, following the .45's lead.

Chapter 6

"What the hell is going on?" DeFore demanded as she charged into Cerberus redoubt's central control complex. She was slightly out of breath from running through the halls to reach the room.

The complex was the nerve center of the redoubt, housing more predark computer equipment than DeFore had ever seen in her life. Filling one wall was the huge Mercator map, with blips of light that showed all the functioning mat-trans gateways around the entire planet. Thin lines of illumination connected the blinking lights.

"It's dearest Brigid," Lakesh stated worriedly. He sat at one of the many computer stations, staring into the screen above laced fingertips.

DeFore shoved her anger aside for the moment. She wasn't exactly close to any of the other personnel at Cerberus, except maybe Grant, but she knew she had a vested interest. They were all exiles and there was safety in numbers.

She crossed the room to stand by Lakesh, dwarfing the small man. "What's wrong?" she asked, looking at the screen to scan Brigid's transponder readings.

"I don't know," Lakesh said in a small voice. "As you can see yourself from the transponder reports, dear Brigid has undergone some kind of trauma."

Short and slender, Mohandas Lakesh Singh had recently undergone a startling physical transformation. On his return from their most recent mat-trans jump to China, Lakesh no longer appeared the frail old man DeFore remembered. His glasses were gone, as was the hearing aid, the liver spots on his hands had vanished and his hair was iron colored rather than ash-gray. He attributed the reversal of the aging process to a realignment of his cellular structure and recalibration of his body's enzymes and alkyglycerol level, but Lakesh could be maddeningly vague and disingenuous.

Even after years, DeFore wasn't sure how she felt about Lakesh. The old man had set her up in her own ville and turned her into an outcast so he could recruit her. But during the time she'd been at Cerberus, she'd operated on him and looked after him. And despite all her professionalism, she couldn't help feeling close to him. But that was only at times. During the other times she sometimes thought she'd be better off if she never saw him again.

Part of her enchantment with him, though, was a result of his history. Lakesh had been born before skydark. He'd seen the world before it had died, had memories of times well before skydark. Back then Lakesh had been a willing recruit of the Totality Concept, the organization responsible for building all the hidden redoubts.

After the world had ended in nuclear fire, Lakesh had volunteered to be placed in cryogenic suspension. He'd slept in the Anthill, the master center of the redoubts located in Mount Rushmore, for more than a century, and was awakened more than fifty years ago to take his place in the plans of the nine barons.

However, everything he'd seen and lived through, everything he remembered from the past, had served to alter Lakesh's alliances. Instead of remaining a supporter of the baronial oligarchy, he'd become its most dangerous adversary. Over the years he'd covertly put his plans into action. His chief strength lay in the fact that he'd known the Cerberus redoubt was still active when all nine barons believed it was destroyed.

"Where is Brigid?" DeFore demanded. Lakesh had a habit of sending Grant, Kane, Brigid and Domi out on missions and not telling everyone else at the redoubt where they'd gone. "Can we get to her quickly?"

Lakesh shook his head. "Brigid is over twenty miles southwest of us."

DeFore looked at the transponder readings again, willing herself not to lose control. Even by Sandcat, the armored wag Cerberus personnel used for overland travel, and running at full speed, the broken territory would take more than an hour to cross. "How the hell am I supposed to help her if I can't get to her?"

"I don't know," Lakesh replied. "I only knew that I couldn't help her."

As DeFore watched the monitor, the transponder readings continued to slowly drop. She reached for the keyboard and opened another window on the screen, bringing up a graph that measured the drop in Brigid's life signs against the time frame it had occurred in.

The transponder was a subcutaneous biolink that every Cerberus member had to submit to. Once injected into a person's body, the nonharmful radioactive chemical bonded with the person's glucose and middle epidermis, providing a signal that could be tracked through a Comsat satellite Lakesh had access to. The transponder transmitted location, as well as heart rate, respiration, blood count and brain-wave patterns.

According to the report DeFore pulled up, Brigid Baptiste had started dying only moments ago.

"What's the matter?" Lakesh asked.

"She's in shock," DeFore said.

"Has she been shot?"

"Was she in a place where there was a chance of that?" DeFore countered.

Lakesh remained silent, but his blue eyes reflected worry.

DeFore knew the old man genuinely cared about Brigid. He'd worked with her in the Cobaltville archives, training her and secretly arranging her advancement, pushing her toward the day he could betray her and turn her into an exile with no choice but to call Cerberus home. But while Lakesh cared about people in his own way, DeFore believed that no one there was anything but a means to an end, an avenue Lakesh had to pursue to assuage his own guilt for his part in the Totality Concept.

"Is Kane with her?" DeFore asked.

"No," Lakesh responded. "Kane is elsewhere."

"Is anyone?"

"Darlingest Domi is there." The old man spoke quietly, his eyes once more on the monitor. "Perhaps."

"Perhaps? What the hell do you mean, perhaps?"

"I mean, my dear DeFore, that Domi is in the general vicinity of dear Brigid's present position, but I do not know if she is aware of how critical Brigid's situation is."

"Is there a way to get a message to Domi?" DeFore asked. She glanced around the nerve center, noting an absence that she should have noticed before. Donald Bry wasn't at one of the workstations, and the tech was always there except when he was sleeping. "Where's Bry?"

Lakesh hesitated. "In his room. He isn't feeling well."

"What's wrong with him?"

"I don't know."

DeFore looked at the monitor again. The transponder life signs were slipping more slowly now, but they were still going down. "For someone who loves knowing more than anyone else does, there's a lot you don't seem to know."

Lakesh said nothing.

"If Bry isn't feeling good, why the hell hasn't he let me know? I'm supposed to be the doctor."

"Perhaps," Lakesh suggested, "he hasn't felt it was anything to concern you with."

"Anything that would keep Bry away from these computers would be a matter of life or death to anyone else." DeFore forced herself to concentrate on the immediate problem facing her. "Brigid hasn't been shot."

Lakesh let out a tense breath. "That's good news."

"She's been poisoned," DeFore went on, hammering Lakesh with the diagnosis. "From what I'm seeing here, Brigid's going into anaphylactic shock. If she's not treated in the next few minutes, she could die. Can I take a Sandcat and go to her?"

Showing the great discipline he was capable of, Lakesh stood up straight and laced his fingers behind his back. Still, he didn't face her. DeFore didn't think he dared at the moment. "Would you have time to reach her?"

"I don't know."

"Then the outcome doesn't justify the risk." Lakesh delivered his words without inflection. One of his major concerns was keeping the redoubt hidden from the barons, something that was getting increasingly difficult.

"She's dying," DeFore implored.

"I heard you. Perhaps she will recover, and perhaps Domi is more aware than I have been led to think."

"And if frogs could fly," DeFore exploded, "then they wouldn't bump their asses on the ground when they hopped." But she knew from the set of the old man's jaw that he wouldn't change his mind. "What was she doing out there, Lakesh?"

Slowly, Lakesh said, "I don't know."

Frustrated, unable to tell if the man was lying or not, DeFore returned her attention to the monitor. Brigid's life signs continued to fade. "You know if Brigid dies," she said softly, "Kane is going to have your ass for it."

"Yes."

As HE DESCENDED the spiral staircase with the overheated lighter chasing back the complete darkness, Kane tried to remember how many steps he'd come down but quickly lost count. He was too busy trying to keep track of the noises that echoed in the tight confines, separating those that came from the gaudy house above from the ones that came from below.

Remar breathed heavily behind him, wheezing and rasping

in pain as he tried to catch his breath. Twice, the man let his rifle buttstock collide with the wall, and Kane knew the solid thumps probably carried to the bottom of the stairwell.

Kane remained leaning toward the inside curve of the steps, following them down and around, partially to keep himself from getting dizzy or disoriented and partially so he could quickly dodge back.

The two bartenders had left the gaudy in a hurry. They had somewhere to go.

As they descended, Kane noted that the breeze coming up from the narrow tunnel continued to grow colder. They were deep underground now, and for there to be that much of a chill in the air he was certain that the passageway led to a cave or caves.

A half-dozen steps later, Kane reached the bottom. The lighter's flame was nearly spent, so weak that he didn't recognize that the step ahead of him was the floor. He stumbled and nearly fell.

He leaned against the wall, knowing the lighter made him vulnerable. The breeze blew more strongly against his face, coming cool enough now to raise goose bumps on his arms and the back of his neck. The sweat in his shirt turned to ice.

Kane's mind raced as he released the lighter's flame button. The guttering yellow-gold illumination died away in the space of a drawn breath. He used his peripheral vision, knowing it would be a few minutes before he could see clearly in the dimness.

Only it wasn't as dark as Kane had expected. Pale gold lantern light limned the carved stone doorway just beyond arm's reach. Lifting the .45 beside his jaw, he stepped forward.

Behind him, Remar made a surprised "Urk."

"Wait," Grant ordered in a harsh whisper that barely reached Kane's ears.

Kane halted again at the carved doorway. The gurgle of running water provided an undercurrent to all the noise still coming from the gaudy. He swept the cavern with his gaze, spotting the small stream of sluggish dark water in the center of the uneven stone floor. Oil lanterns hanging on the walls reflected against the stream surface. Dark smoke pooled against the ceiling briefly, then swept through the roof cracks.

Pallets containing supplies sat in heaps around the cavern. There wasn't enough light to read the ingredients at a distance, but Kane felt certain they were food supplies. White PVC pipe stabbed into the stream from the cavern roof.

Moving cautiously, Kane stepped into the cavern. The alcohol fire Grant had started had probably petered out by now, and whatever survivors were left would be coming down the stairs after them.

Lantern light splintered against a sharp edge as it cut the air toward Kane. He was already in motion, his point man's senses warning him before he realized what the threat was. His free hand came up, blocking the attack, then swept under the arm, trapping it. He stopped short of breaking the limb when he heard the feminine squeal of pain.

Despite the gender, if the woman had kept struggling against him, Kane would have killed her. Instead, he threw her back against the wall, jarring the breath from her.

Carrie the bartender smiled coldly at him. "Sorry. I thought you were someone else."

Kane nodded, close enough to her to smell the alcohol on her breath. "If you'd have chilled me, would you have cared?"

Her eyes met his honestly. "No."

"Me neither." Kane was definitely aware of the resilient woman's flesh pressing against his body. Her nipples were firm against his chest and he had his thigh between her legs, keeping her shoved back against the wall. She pulled her thighs together, reminding him she was there.

"You're a hard man," she said.

Grinning wolfishly, Kane said, "Not even close." He pressed the .45's muzzle into the hollow of her throat, then used his free hand to search for other weapons she might be carrying. He reached into her sleeve and plucked the derringer from the holdout holster strapped to her wrist. "Where's your friend?"

"Mebbe close by," Carrie taunted.

Kane's search yielded nothing more than the pocket blaster. He kept his voice low enough it wouldn't travel far over the sound of the gurgling stream. "You might want to tell her to come over here," he said. "One of you two could end up chilled."

Carrie hesitated only a moment. "Beth. Come on out before you get us chilled."

Footsteps sounded to Kane's right. He clamped a hand around the woman's neck and yanked her from the wall, pulling her in front of him as he turned to face the other woman.

Beth stepped from the darkness, a cut-down double-barreled shotgun in her hands. Blood smeared her face, still dribbling from a bullet that had torn through her cheek. "Mebbe I don't give a shit about getting chilled," she said, her words slurred by her injury. "Caught a bullet up there that's going to change the way I look and live, and that's an ace on the line."

"Get your friend here chilled, too," Kane promised. "We haven't got a lot of time here. People from upstairs are going to be downstairs pretty quick."

"Not friends," Carrie said, and Kane figured she was reminding the injured woman more than she was telling him. "Sisters. C'mon, Beth, your face ain't so bad. We can fix it. If we can't, we'll find someone who can."

Silvery tears sparkled on the woman's cheeks, running to her chin on one side and mixing in the blood on the other. "Don't want to live ugly, Carrie. Ugly women only get paid for flat-backing, and me and you always agreed that wouldn't be for us. Not after the way we were raised."

"I know," Carrie said. "I know, baby, and that's not going to happen to us. We got a good thing here. That ain't going to go away."

"Kane," Grant called in a whisper.

Kane nodded, knowing his friend had already stepped into the shadows. With the lanterns on around them, Grant was nowhere near invisible, but his movements remained slightly masked, just one shadow moving among others.

Carrie stiffened in Kane's grip, and for a moment he thought she was going to warn her sister. "Big mistake," he whispered in her ear.

"It's going to be okay, baby," Carrie coaxed. "Just put the blaster down and we'll all walk out of here. You want to do that, don't you?"

Beth shook her head and Kane's stomach tightened, knowing the woman was over the line either from pain or shock. "No," Beth replied. "Don't give a shit at all."

The woman raised the shotgun, and Kane knew she was going to fire. He just didn't know if Grant was going to reach her in time.

Chapter 7

Born a feral child of the Outlands, Domi blended into the grassy slope overlooking Brigid Baptiste's position without being seen by the woman's pursuers. She'd watched as Brigid had been discovered, then tried to break for freedom.

If it had been her, Domi knew, she wouldn't have tried for the horse. Getting on the horse had only made a bigger target for the snipers.

Two days ago Domi had noticed Brigid leaving the Cerberus redoubt. The young outlander had followed the woman out of boredom. Curiosity had never been a big issue with Domi. Too often curiosity killed not only the cat but everything around it.

She lay on her stomach in the grass, feeling the noonday heat bake into her back, warming muscle that had been tempted into turning lethargic until the first blaster shots sounded. When she saw the horse rear and drop like a rock, she was sure Brigid hadn't been hit.

The snake diving at Brigid's chest was a surprise. Domi thought the woman had driven it away after the first attack. She watched it now, coiling around Brigid, hanging on where it had bitten the woman.

The gunmen closed the distance. Donald Bry sat astride his horse at the edge of the forest, looking up apprehensively but making no move to help Brigid.

Domi didn't really blame the little man. She figured Brigid was already dead. Plus, it didn't look as if Bry had been out in the wilderness on business that Lakesh would approve of, and his newfound friends definitely wouldn't have appreciated his interest in what they perceived as a threat or an enemy.

Lying still in the grass, Domi knew she couldn't be seen. Albino by birth, her skin was normally pale as creamed milk. Since being in the wild, she'd taken care to cover her exposed skin with a mixture of berry and grass juices that kept most insects away. She'd scrubbed in dirt to give her skin more color, reverting to savage.

Her bone-white hair was wilder than normal because she'd braided broken twigs with green leaves to disguise most of the color. She was every inch of five feet tall and weighed a hundred pounds that her slight, curvy figure belied. Her eyes were grim ruby drops of blood.

She'd left her own horse nearly a half mile back. After discovering where Brigid was spying on Bry, Domi had taken the horse back so it wouldn't whicker and give her presence away. She knew more about hiding and spying than Brigid did.

The snake continued crawling around Brigid, constricting her.

Cursing, Domi pulled the M-14 rifle from the ground beside her and brought it to her shoulder. It was a duplicate to the one Grant had chosen to take with him. The blaster had a matte black finish, and she kept it below the line of underbrush.

She tracked the three men as they continued leapfrogging up the hill, taking turns providing cover fire for one another. Still lying prone, the young albino sighted on the lead man through the open sights, then kept both eyes open as she moved up to the sniper scope. Experience told her that she had to aim under her target to properly hit it when aiming downhill.

Breathing in, Domi put the crosshairs over the center of the lead gunman's chest. She breathed out half a breath as Grant had taught her, held it, then squeezed the trigger.

The heavy rifle stock slammed back into her shoulder. The joint twinged in protest. Months back, a bullet had destroyed the bone. DeFore had replaced the shoulder joint with an artificial ball and socket. After long weeks of painful therapy, Domi had returned to full strength. However, impacts against the joint still caused occasional pain.

The bullet caught the gunman high, ripping through his throat just below his chin and lifting him from his feet. Domi saw the bright scarlet blossom on his neck just before he dropped into the brush. By that time she was already focusing on the second gunman. She squeezed the trigger, knowing at that distance the sound of the first shot would reach the gunmen only a heartbeat ahead of her second shot.

She'd deliberately aimed even lower, adjusting from the first shot and knowing the man would automatically go to ground. She watched the man through the scope, spotting the telltale shudder that told her the bullet had struck him.

A handful of rounds from the third gunner raked the trees. None of them were close. The gunner didn't have her position. She stayed with the second man, spotting him crawling through the brush. Her next round slammed through the man's back and nailed him to the ground. If he wasn't dead, the man wasn't going to survive the perforated lung.

The third man broke from cover and ran for the hidden wag, where the man Bry had met sat behind the wheel.

As the man climbed into the wag and it took off, Domi glanced at Bry. The computer specialist hesitated, overcontrolling the horse and causing it to turn circles beneath him. Then whatever war he fought within himself was decided, and he kicked the horse in the flanks, charging through the forest away from Brigid.

Maybe Bry hadn't known who'd been spying on him, Domi told herself, but the man had to have been able to guess that it was someone from Cerberus. She fed new cartridges into the M-14's magazine, then slipped it back into the weapon.

Once the sound of the wag had disappeared, only silence reigned in the forest.

Rising as gracefully as a leopard, the young albino jogged

down the hill, dropping in controlled slides down the steep areas. The mutie snake heard her coming and coiled protectively around Brigid's limp body. The wedge-shaped head rose high from the ground, and the massive jaws opened.

Domi locked eyes with the snake, a chill threading down her spine. She approached the creature at a normal gait, dropping the M-14 as she closed.

Brigid was unconscious or dead, her skin tone already turning blue.

Ignoring the Detonics .45 holstered at her hip, Domi reached down and drew the knife from the sheath tied to her right calf. The blade was long and wickedly serrated, a memento she'd kept when she'd been Guana Teague's sex slave for six months in the Cobaltville Pits. She'd sold herself into slavery in an effort to get a piece of the good life available to ville dwellers. In the end she'd cut Teague's throat with the blade.

Domi kept walking toward the snake, both hands in front of her and spread out to the sides. She focused totally on the snake's movements. There was no choice about heading into the snake's attack. If she tried to hold back, to keep herself prepared to dodge to one side or the other, her reflexes wouldn't be as fluid as she needed them to be.

When Domi was less than four feet from the snake and its prey, the snake struck.

The young albino slapped out with her free hand, catching the wedge-shaped head behind the gaping jaws on the inside of the strike and pushing her attacker aside. She thrust the knife, sinking it deeply into the thickly muscled neck. As the snake tried to twist, Domi yanked the knife. The serrated edge sliced the throat open, releasing a rush of blood.

Domi blocked the head again, then watched as death claimed the huge creature. Paroxysms shivered through the snake as the head thumped against the ground. The rest of the body coiled and uncoiled.

Moving quickly, Domi grabbed Brigid and pulled her free. Unable to carry the woman, the young albino dragged her

several feet away from the flopping snake coils. She laid the
woman down and placed her fingers against the side of her
neck.

The pulse was thready and weak. Thrusting her arm out,
Domi found that Brigid's breath barely moved the hairs on
her arm.

Domi cursed again, cursing Brigid, Bry and her own bad
luck at coming. She examined the woman, searching for the
bite marks she knew had to be there. She sliced through Brigid's shirt buttons and pulled the garment open.

The fang marks stood out in livid purple against the pale
flesh of Brigid's breast. Blood streaks ran from the bite marks
and across her flat stomach.

Taking a deep breath, Domi pushed back one of Brigid's
eyelids. The eye was rolled back in her head, only the bloodshot white showing.

"DOMI'S WITH BRIGID," DeFore announced. She knew Lakesh could read the information himself, could see the two
transponder signals almost on top of each other now, but it
felt better just to be saying it.

Lakesh nodded. "Then we can hope for the best."

"Hope for the best?" DeFore echoed his words in disbelief.
She turned on him. "Lakesh, we need to get a team out there."

"By the time you could get there, it will already be too
late," Lakesh said. "You've already said that."

"If she survives, she's still going to need medical attention."

"Which she'll get as soon as she arrives here."

"You mean if."

Lakesh's voice hardened. "I mean when. That's what I said,
my dear DeFore."

"Why did you call me up here?" DeFore demanded. "You
knew there was nothing I could do from here."

"I didn't know." Lakesh turned his attention back to the
computer workstation, flicking quickly through the sec menu.

The program accessed the motion detectors around the Cerberus redoubt, the sec cams, as well as the heat sensors.

"You goddamn well did know," DeFore accused. "You just didn't want to be up here by yourself in case Brigid bought it on your shift because of something you did."

"That will be enough." Lakesh's voice was sharp. "I'll not speak again on this matter."

Frustrated, knowing she was well past her own lines of control, DeFore turned and walked toward the door. "If you need me again," she snarled, "I'll be in the infirmary, helping the people that I'm allowed to help."

"Sarcasm doesn't become you," Lakesh chided.

"Perhaps not, but it makes me feel better."

"We must be patient," Lakesh said. "We must trust darlingest Domi to care for Brigid until we are able."

"We're talking about anaphylactic shock," DeFore called from the door. "That's more than Brigid just having an upset stomach or PMS. She's been hurt bad. And trusting Domi to handle a medical emergency is really low on the list of things I want to do."

Lakesh crossed his arms over his chest and regarded the computer screens.

Without another word, DeFore stomped out of the room. She'd called it right about Lakesh's reluctance to stay there alone if Brigid died, and she knew it. But there was more involved than just Brigid. DeFore knew that, too. Lakesh was too focused, too cold for nothing to be going on.

She headed down the dimmed hall, deciding that Collins could wait a few minutes more. There was a stop she intended to make on the way back to the infirmary.

KANE SHOVED Carrie over and down. The double-barreled shotgun discharged over their heads. Pellets ricocheted from the walls, striking sparks, and thunder cannoned through the cave. He landed on top of the woman and swung the .45 toward her sister. By rights the shotgun would be empty, but if Beth tried to reload, he intended to drop her.

Grant charged from the darkness as Beth broke open the weapon, sending the empty casings spinning. She took two fresh rounds from an ammo pouch on her hip. Before she could seat them, Grant stepped beside her and backhanded the woman hard enough to knock her from her feet.

Carrie screeched and clawed at Kane's face. "Don't hurt her, goddammit! Don't you dare!"

Kane caught the woman's flailing hand, pinning her with his body. "She's not dead. Just unconscious." He pushed himself to his feet and yanked her up, as well. "How do we get out of here?" He raked the wavering shadows with his gaze, finding Remar easily.

"Company's coming," Remar said, nodding at the stairs.

Fear filled Carrie's face. She glanced at her unconscious sister, no longer the tough woman who'd killed the man who'd insulted her just a short time ago. "I'm not leaving my sister."

"You're not leaving her," Grant growled. "We're not leaving her." He reached down and easily picked up the small woman, draping her over one broad shoulder. "Now show us where the damn door is."

Carrie ran, leading them past a gasoline generator that Kane assumed was used to pump water into the gaudy proper. The stream in the middle of the floor stayed underground, disappearing under the wall Carrie led them to.

"Where's the rest of the gaudy staff?" Kane asked. He'd never looked into the kitchen adjoining the main room, but he'd assumed the small boy who'd carried the bucket of sand to clean up the desert rat's blood hadn't been alone.

"There's another tunnel that feeds off the kitchen," Carrie answered. "The gaudy was designed so we wouldn't be trapped with only one way out. A small system of tunnels runs through the cliff the gaudy is built into." She stopped near the lantern on the wall and took a torch from an oil-stained box. She lifted the lantern's hurricane glass and lit the torch.

"You could take the lantern," Kane said.

As the gold flames spread along the torch, Carrie shot him a look of reproach. "Lanterns break, and they're expensive. After this blows over, we'll be back." She shoved the torch forward and followed it to a line of carved steps leading opposite the gaudy.

"Who owns this place?" Kane already had his suspicions. He reached into the box of torches and took one out for himself, lighting it quickly from the lantern. The light spread over the uneven cavern roof above, leaving dimples of shadows that pockmarked the surface.

"Me and Beth." Carrie walked up the steps. "Old man Tyson died three years back. His health had been failing for a long time. This place sells liquor and food, and passable entertainment from time to time, not personality. Old man Tyson's long suit was never personality. If it wasn't for the scrip the traders and miners brought in, he would have just as soon been shut of them."

Kane followed the woman up the narrow stairs. The edges of the steps were so worn they were rounded. Coupled with the small surface available, walking on them was tricky. Judging from the layout of the cavern and the presence of the tunnels Carrie had mentioned, he guessed that the place had once been a mine that had petered out long ago, perhaps even before skydark.

"Me and Beth found Tyson dead in bed in one of the upstairs rooms," Carrie went on. "We didn't mention it to nobody. Just buried his ass down in the cave and went on with business as usual. We've done okay for ourselves."

"Until today," Remar said from behind Kane.

Kane glanced at the man, then past him, seeing Grant walking with the unconscious woman riding on his shoulder. The big man carried the extra weight as if it were nothing.

"Tyson's been chased off before," Carrie stated. "Ain't the first time folks have brought their problems to our doors.

We've gone away for a few days, then come back and set up shop again.''

''Nobody tried to take over?'' Kane asked, intrigued.

Carrie stopped for a moment at a landing. She held the torch up high, scaring off a small cluster of brown bats that fluttered more deeply into the cave. ''Damn things. I can't stand them. Fucking flying rats if you ask me.'' Once the bats had gone, she stepped into a passageway cut through the rock. ''Nobody's tried to take over. Running a gaudy ain't as easy or as exciting as pulling sec work on mine trains or being part of a gang that's hijacking mine trains. Tyson hadn't been so old, he probably wouldn't gone into the business himself. But it's just fine for me and my sister.''

Voices drifted up from the cavern. Halting at the entrance to the new tunnel, Kane looked back and down, spotting a handful of men and women stepping into the main cavern. One of them held a small lamp that had been taken from one of the gaudy tables. The man raised the lamp to spread the light better, flooding the lower half of the room.

''Why don't you stand up here like a goddamn beacon a little longer?'' Carrie whispered angrily in Kane's ear. ''I think there's some poor son of a bitch in the back who hasn't seen us yet.''

The back of his neck burning because he knew he deserved some of the rebuke, Kane herded the woman into the tunnel. ''I like to know who's on my backtrail.''

''You know them?''

''No.''

Carrie moved forward through the tunnel, walking confidently. ''Those Chinese men opened up on you back in the gaudy.''

''Yeah.'' Kane was glad the passageway roof was tall enough for Grant to carry Beth without having to stoop.

''Why?'' Carrie asked.

''Don't know.''

Carrie snorted in disgust. "People you don't know always trying to chill you?"

Kane grinned at her. "At least I got your name before you tried to take my head off."

Chapter 8

Searing pain flooded through Brigid's breast. She struggled to open her eyes, but it felt as if someone had stitched them shut. Sunlight burned down on her face, turning the inside of her eyelids bright red. She tried to take a deep breath, then thought the snake still constricted her chest because her lungs hardly filled at all.

She was no longer aware of the cool scales of the snake wrapped around her. She guessed that the poison in her system had already numbed her body to an extent. An arctic chill filled her body, but her head pounded with heat.

A moan escaped her lips when a new, searing fire filled her breast. She tried to raise her arms and push the snake away, certain that it still had its fangs locked into her flesh. Her arms didn't move. Fueled by panic, she tried to open her eyes again. She knew the excess adrenaline squirting through her system was bad for her because it carried the snake's poison along faster.

More than anything, she wished Kane were there. If she had to die, she didn't want to be alone. After being raised in Cobaltville and her training as an archivist, she'd learned to relish her periods of solitude, but she'd never been truly alone. People had filled the ville around her, a constant backdrop to her own life.

Lying here in the forest, she knew dying alone had to be the worst end anyone ever met. Birds called out in panicked voices around her, reminding her that the birds and the bugs would be the first to strip the flesh from her bones.

She tried to move again and moaned with the effort. She

thought perhaps one of her hands had closed in response. She wanted to cry, but she couldn't do that, either. Then she imagined what Kane would have thought of her lying there like that. He was a fighter, a warrior honed by the harsh life he'd led as a Mag. He wouldn't have given up.

And he wouldn't have allowed her to give up, either. His voice echoed in her head. *Anam-chara.* It was the name they had for each other, learned during the mat-trans jump to Ireland. The term meant "soul friend." Morrigan, the blind telepath, had told Kane that their souls were inextricably bound.

Kane chose not to believe it. At least, that's what he'd told her. But he never forgot the term, and the chemistry between them was undeniable. It was also unacceptable.

Were those bonds woven tightly enough, Brigid wondered, that Kane would somehow know the exact moment she died?

The searing pain stabbed into her breast again, bringing agony that splintered her thoughts.

She focused on the anger and fear that filled her. The poison had turned her body cold, but the other emotions burned hot. She used them to muster her failing strength and keep the blackness away.

Slowly, she forced her eyes open. The green of the forest blurred into view, and she shifted her head, glancing down. Her vision remained blurry, but she saw the white wolf suckling at her breast. Crimson stained the creature's maw. It gazed back at her with bright red eyes and barked something she almost understood.

Then the blackness pulled Brigid away again.

"THERE'S THE DOOR."

Kane looked ahead to the end of the tunnel. He'd have seen it even if Carrie hadn't pointed it out. Light framed the opening and let in some of the oppressive heat waiting outside.

It also let in some of the noise of what sounded like a full-scale battle. Blasterfire echoed in the tunnel, punctuated by occasional explosions.

"They're going at it hard and heavy," Grant commented.

"Yeah." Kane squatted in the passage, using the shotgun as a brace. In the tight confines of the passageway, the double-aught buckshot would be devastating to anyone who made the mistake of following them. Sweat caused his shirt to stick to his back. During the final hundred yards or so of their climb, the temperature had risen dramatically. His hair was matted at the back of his neck.

Remar squatted on the other side of the passageway. "Got any more of them cigars?"

Kane rummaged in his pocket and found more bent cigars. He passed them out to Grant and Remar, keeping one for himself. He glanced up at Carrie.

She shook her head, looking anxious. "What about my sister?"

"She's still sleeping," Grant answered as he accepted a light from the torch Kane held. The big man squatted with a tired sigh, carefully placing the unconscious woman on the stone floor of the passageway.

Carrie approached cautiously and placed a hand on her sister's bloody throat.

Kane watched, taking Carrie's torch and holding his own and hers up so she'd get the best light. The wound on Beth's face ran from the bottom of her ear almost to the point of her jaw. With all the blood covering it, it was difficult to see how bad the damage truly was.

"Has anyone got any water?" Carrie asked. She tore at the bottom of her shirt, trying to rip a piece free.

Gently, Grant took the woman's hand in his, dwarfing hers. "Leave it alone for now," he told her softly. "That wound needs to clot good first or you're going to just rip it open and cause more blood loss."

Carrie nodded, then ran her fingers through her sister's hair slowly and tenderly.

Kane directed his attention back to Remar. "Do those Chinese men know about the Lost Valley of Wiy Tukay?"

"Mebbe."

"How much do they know?"

Remar looked uncomfortable. A pained look crossed his face. "Listen, you let enough scrip hit the table that Falzone thought mebbe it was an idea I come talk to you, but that don't mean he figured mebbe I should tell you everything."

Kane chewed the butt of his cigar, waiting while blasterfire rang outside the door. He never broke eye contact.

"Shit." Remar spit a glob of phlegm onto the stone floor and smeared his boot over it. "What was in the package you sent Falzone?" Remar asked.

Kane remained silent. Truth to tell, he didn't know exactly what was in the package. Bry and Lakesh had put it together. The tech Falzone sold was old. Some of it Lakesh had commented should never see the light of day again, and he'd been more than a little concerned about it.

Much of the recovered tech, Lakesh had said, Falzone didn't understand. What Bry and Lakesh had offered were manual printouts that explained and clarified some of the tech they knew the man was selling. When a man was selling something, learning about it and what it was truly worth to others was priceless. That was only part of what Lakesh had put on the table.

Another explosion blasted in the distance.

Remar flicked ash from his cigar. "The Tong have learned about the tech."

"How?"

Shrugging, Remar said, "If you've been around these people, you know how they are. They move into a territory and set up a strong-arm operation, as well as put people in place who gather information. Qiang's probably got himself quite an empire over in the Western Isles."

Kane knew that was true. Wei Qiang's Tong had made tremendous inroads in the Utah territories despite Baron Cobalt's army. "Why haven't they gone to Seattle to discover this Lost Valley of Wiy Tukay themselves?"

"Qiang has put his hatchetmen up there." Remar smiled grimly. "They usually don't live too long. Lucky for us right now, the old bastard isn't too willing to overextend himself. But he isn't the only problem."

"Who else is interested?" Kane was surprised Remar was being so free with his information.

"A group called the Heimdall Foundation that's interested in getting their hands on as many of those progs as they can. They paid good—until they ran out of scrip. Now they're more interested in collecting more on their own or hijacking our runners. They're just big enough to be more than a slight annoyance."

Kane filed the name away, thinking maybe Lakesh or Brigid had mentioned it before.

"And then there's the Futurists," Remar said. "They're the most trouble. They're a religious group, dedicated to their god, Wiy Tukay."

"What's he the god of?"

"She," Remar corrected. "She's the goddess of destruction. The Futurists believe it was Wiy Tukay who brought about the nukecaust."

Kane wasn't surprised about the religious belief. After the world had ended, cults had sprung up all throughout the Deathlands, each with its own reasons for why the nukecaust had happened and who had caused it. The death of a world inspired zealots everywhere. New cults still sprang up occasionally, sometimes as whole new mythologies and sometimes as variations of others that had come into existence.

"What do the Futurists want?" Kane asked.

"To get Falzone out of the area," Remar said. "They believe everything he's doing is going to stir up Wiy Tukay again and destroy the rest of the planet." He released a lungful of smoke. "Then there are Baron Cobalt's Mag teams who've been out poking around."

"You paint a rosy picture," Kane commented, swapping a quick look with Grant.

"You done me a good turn getting us out of the gaudy," Remar said. "Figured I'd return the favor."

"Or," Kane replied, "if you thought mebbe I was a curious man, you've just tried to set the hook."

Remar grinned. "Falzone told me you wouldn't be an ordinary guy."

Kane didn't say anything. Falzone would know that anyone who could put together the package Bry and Lakesh had assembled wouldn't be ordinary. The hook had been set both ways. If he decided to follow up on the information.

As voices echoed in the passageway behind them, growing stronger, Kane rose and dropped the cigar butt. He stomped it underfoot so it wouldn't allow potential gunners to aim at him. He lifted the shotgun, then lifted his voice. "Stand back!" he warned.

As the lead man carrying the lamp hesitated, dropping lower, the other shadows moved around him.

Kane heard the order in Chinese, understanding the intent even though he didn't understand the words. Blasterfire raked the walls. He lifted the shotgun and fired three rounds as quickly as he could pump the shells into the chamber.

The first or second pattern spread caught the lamp and shattered it. Flaming ropes of oil splashed back over a man wearing Tong black. Fire wreathed him as he screamed in agony. One of the men next to the human torch pushed a handblaster into his face and squeezed the trigger. The dead man fell back on top of his companions, who roughly kept pushing his body back and down.

"Damn!" Kane swore. He glanced at Grant, who was already shouldering the unconscious woman. "Remar! Cover our backs!"

The old man raised the .30-06 and banged out two shots that screamed from the passageway sides. The shadows around the flaming corpse went to ground.

Kane took point, his senses coming alive as he charged up the incline to the opening at the other end. He replaced the spent cartridges in the shotgun, then stepped out onto a bare stone ledge. Kane didn't hesitate about following it because there was nowhere else to go. In seconds he was in the ledges above the front of the gaudy.

Bodies stretched across the ground on pools of blood-black sand. Burning wags left smoky smudges against the pale blue sky. Kane scanned the wreckage, noting the pocket-sized battles still spread out across the broken terrain in front of the gaudy. The Tong hatchetmen had the high ground with an armored wag housing two heavy machine guns. They hammered .50-caliber bullets into anyone who hadn't already run away.

Kane glanced at the wag they'd arrived in. By some miracle, it was still in one piece. But there were at least thirty Tong warriors on the ground. He had no idea how many were burning up their backtrail.

Just as Grant and the others joined him on the ledge, seeing for themselves how limited their choices were, Kane heard a familiar drumming fill the air. He glanced up in time to see the first Deathbird streak across the sky. There was no doubt what the target objective was.

"Fireblast!" Kane swore. Deathbirds were refurbished Apache attack helicopters, and they guaranteed death from above.

The Tong warriors never spotted the Deathbird until the nose-mounted 20 mm cannon spit destruction in a line headed straight for the armored wag. Explosive rounds burst thunder against the thick ceramic-armaglass shell of the Tong wag. The men standing closest to the wag were blown away.

"Shit!" Grant exclaimed as they hunkered down.

Kane nodded, glancing back at the wag. "There's only one way out of here."

Grant resettled the unconscious woman across his shoulder. "Down this damn incline while dodging bullets and hoping the Mags working the Deathbird don't decide to use us as moving target practice."

Kane grinned at his friend. "You left out the part about not getting chilled while we're doing it."

"That was the understood-without-saying part," Grant bit out sourly. "Looks like we're working on another one-percenter here."

Chapter 9

"Bry." DeFore pressed the button beside Donald Bry's door. She heard the chimes echo faintly inside. It was hard to wait patiently after the confrontation she'd had with Lakesh.

No one came to the door.

DeFore pressed the buzzer again, holding it longer this time. The ring of the chimes carried through the door and out into the empty hallway. The Cerberus redoubt was a multilevel complex of living quarters, labs and armory. Built back in the 1990s, the redoubt had been intended to house more than a hundred people. Less than twenty people lived there now, leaving cavernous hallways and dozens of rooms that were never used. It was easy to get lost in the redoubt, and solitude was often in oversupply.

Bry couldn't hide, though. DeFore knew where he lived. Usually if the computer specialist wasn't in the nerve center, he was either in his room at the workstation there or in the commissary.

For the first time, DeFore wished she'd gotten to know the man better. Of all the personnel at the redoubt, Bry seemed the most content with his present lot in life. He also seemed to be the closest to Lakesh.

Except for Domi, DeFore amended. Lakesh obviously cherished the little outlander, not put off at all by her ways or her appearance. Or Domi's habit of running around the redoubt nearly naked. The old irritation when she thought about Domi rose in DeFore.

Almost immediately, DeFore started feeling guilty. Right now Domi might be the only person standing between Brigid and death. Instead of resenting the girl, she should be hoping the best for her.

Giving up on the doorbell, thinking maybe Bry was truly sick enough to be in bed and unable to hear the chimes, DeFore rapped her knuckles against the metal door. "Bry," she called again.

Although she waited much longer than she believed it would have taken Bry to reach the door, there was still no answer. DeFore glared at the unanswered door. If Donald Bry was in his room, he wasn't seeing anyone. And if he wasn't in his room, where the hell was he?

DOMI LOWERED HER MOUTH to Brigid's bare breast, centering her lips around one of the fang marks left by the snake. She sucked hard, noticing the way Brigid's nipple hardened. She chose to view that as a positive response. If the woman had been too close to death, there would have been no response at all.

The dry, bitter taste of the venom trickled into Domi's mouth. When she'd sucked as hard and long as she dared, afraid she was accidentally swallowing some of it, the young albino drew her head back and spit the mouthful of saliva and poison into the hole she'd dug in the ground.

Already light-headed from her exertions and maybe from the poison, as well, Domi wiped her lips with a handful of grass and blew the air from her lungs so she wouldn't hyperventilate. She kept her ears cocked for any sounds and paid attention to her peripheral vision. Her senses were preternatural, making her another wild thing in the forest.

Birds had returned to the area. They fluttered and chirped through the trees, flitting from branch to branch and watching her cautiously. Some of the more bloodthirsty species had already descended on the corpses of the horse and snake.

Domi knew larger predators would be along soon; she and Brigid had to be gone by then, because some of the mountain cats in the Bitterroot Range were deadly and fearless.

The young albino examined Brigid's wounds. She'd used her knife to cut an X over each puncture, inciting a fresh blood flow that would hopefully help drain the poison from Brigid's body. The woman's flesh was already cool to the touch from the sluggish blood flow. Passing out when she did had probably helped save her from some of the poison's effects.

Domi bent back to the task, sucking on the other puncture this time. Little of the bitter taste of poison remained, which she hoped was a good sign.

"D-Domi?" Brigid's voice was weak and hoarse.

"Yeah." Domi rocked back on her haunches. She stuck her finger down her throat and made herself throw up into the hole she'd dug. The thin, brackish bile clung to her lips until she brushed it away. If any of the poison had found its way to her stomach, she hoped the retching would bring it all back up. The danger that she might have absorbed some of the venom through a small cut in her mouth or on the inside of her cheek still existed.

"I thought you—you were a wolf." Brigid's green eyes were frightened and round, but the pupils were pinpricks.

Despite the situation, Domi thought Brigid's words were hilarious and laughed loudly. The raucous noise frightened away some of the nearby birds. The young albino spit, trying to clear some of the bitter chalk taste from her mouth. "How you feel?"

"My head hurts and I'm freezing." Weakly, revealing the modest nature she had, Brigid tried to cover her bare breasts. She glanced around fearfully. "Where's the snake?"

"Chilled it," Domi answered, pointing at the snake's body. The movement scared away a half-dozen black crows that had descended on the creature and started tearing at the flesh with their sharp beaks. "Want fangs for souvenir?" Domi grinned.

"No." Brigid closed her eyes. "I've got a med kit in the saddlebag on the horse. The supplies contain a snakebite kit that has antivenin for most of the poisonous snakes in the area."

"I sucked out most of the poison," Domi said, feeling angry that Brigid didn't choose to recognize or trust in her efforts. But she went to the dead horse. She raided the saddlebags until she found the med kit, then took the half-full canteen for good measure.

Brigid struggled to sit up but didn't have the strength. That she had any at all amazed Domi. Brigid took the snakebite kit from the young albino and prepped the needle with shaking hands. She tried to give herself the injection but couldn't.

Domi took the syringe from the woman. The young albino hadn't had the opportunity to give many shots, but DeFore had demonstrated the basic techniques. Plus Domi herself had had a number of cortisone shots while DeFore reconstructed her shoulder.

When the snakebite injection had been given, Brigid said, "Thank you," and passed back out.

"Fuck," Domi said with real feeling, realizing Brigid was going to be deadweight while she tried to get the woman out of the area. Good deeds never went unpunished.

KANE WATCHED the Deathbird wheel for another pass over the Tong war wag. Black-clad Chinese warriors lay broken and scattered across the ground from the first assault.

The wag's machine gunners tracked the deadly craft, their big .50-cals hammering out a death song. The big rounds drummed against the Deathbird's armored hide.

"Stupe bastards," Grant growled above the rumbling rotor wash. "Ought to know you can't crack a Deathbird open that easy. They should be aiming at the rotor, hoping they get lucky as hell and break one of the rotors if the damn fool's going to fly in that close to them."

Kane silently agreed, but his mind was on figuring a way out of their own situation.

"Don't mean to rush you," Remar yelled over the sound of the Deathbird's thrumming engine and the battle, "but we're about to get joined."

"Grant," Kane called, "you're going to try to carry that woman?"

"If I can." Grant's face remained stoic.

In the daylight now, Kane saw where blood striped the big man from dozens of superficial lacerations from their trip through the glass behind the bar. He guessed he didn't look much different himself. "If it gets to where you can't carry her and save your own ass," Kane stated, "drop her."

Grant nodded.

"You can't do that," Carrie protested.

"Yes, I can," Kane replied, turning his harsh gaze on the woman. "Cut your cost between two dead people versus one. You can stay behind if you want to."

Carrie looked hesitant, but her eyes dropped away from Kane's, letting him know she was aware he meant it.

"Ready?" Kane asked.

"As I'm going to be," Grant agreed. He shifted the unconscious woman around, cradling her in his arms across his massive chest.

"We'll wait for the Deathbird to make another pass," Kane said, eyeing the aircraft. "The rotor wash is throwing up a lot of dust. Mebbe it'll buy us a little time to get to the wag."

"When you jump," Grant said, "that'll be me on your ass."

"We ain't exactly got a lot of time here," Remar grumbled.

"You want to lead," Kane said, watching the Deathbird swoop closer for another pass, "that's fine by me."

Remar muttered darkly and pulled the .30-06 to his shoulder. He fired a couple shots, and the resulting scream of pain told Kane the old man wasn't just firing warning shots.

A cloud of yellow dust as thick as fog rose up behind the Deathbird. The Tong war wag hammered .50-cal rounds against the aircraft's armor, seemingly to no avail. Another cloud of dust gathered momentum to the east, streaking for the gaudy.

Even without binoculars, Kane knew it would be ground

support for the Deathbird from the Cobaltville Magistrate Division. Deathbirds softened up a hardsite so the hard-contact Mags could move in.

Kane watched as the dust cloud spiraled up, following the Deathbird. The dust didn't fall quickly, but hung in the hot dry air. "Move." He slid over the side of the gaudy, aiming for a steep incline where rainwater had washed over the side of the cliffs for thousands of years, creating a small gully in the rock. The gully was too steep to climb, but it did slow the descent.

The rough rock ripped Kane's shirt and pants and abraded his skin as he slid. A heartbeat later, his boots jarred against the ground with almost enough force to buckle his knees. Holding the shotgun in one hand, he turned as Carrie slid down the rock.

She landed hard and would have smashed her face against the rock if Kane hadn't caught her around the waist with his free hand. Before she even got her balance completely, he shoved her away to clear the way for Grant and Beth.

Grant slid with a lot of momentum due to the young woman's extra weight. Knowing there was no way the big man could handle the landing on his own, Kane stood ready. Grant's feet hit the ground, driving sand and rock over Kane's boots from the impact. The big man let out a low groan when his knee joints popped from the effort. He went down into a squatting position in an attempt to absorb the landing but couldn't maintain his balance. He fell forward, unable to keep his feet under him.

Kane grabbed Grant's shirt and jerked his partner up and forward, pulling them both into a shambling half run until Grant found his balance.

The .30-06 banged at the top of the cliff. Return fire bounced from the rocks around Remar as he assumed a prone position at the top of the cliff.

Kane glanced up at the man as Grant started for the wag at

a dead run while the dust cloud partially masked their movements. "You coming?" he shouted up at Remar.

With a quick movement, the old man rolled from the cliff's edge and skittered down the gully, hitting the ground hard. Even as Kane reached to help the man, Remar shoved himself upright, flashing a lopsided grin. "Am I coming? Hell, son, I ain't even breathing hard yet."

Kane turned and sprinted toward the wag, quickly catching up to Grant. Carrie struggled to keep up with the big man even though he was carrying a lot of extra weight.

The thick dust cloud swirled over Kane, sticking to his skin and clothing, drawn and held by the perspiration filming his skin and soaking his clothes. He hacked and coughed as the dust coated the inside of his mouth. Automatically, he closed his mouth and breathed through his nose the way he'd been trained to as a Magistrate. He slitted his eyes, feeling his lashes and eyelids crust up.

The thunder of the Deathbird drummed overhead. Even without looking, the change in the rotor roar told Kane the attack craft was already coming back.

He drove his feet hard, reaching the wag only a few steps ahead of Grant. He flung himself behind the steering wheel and felt the wag's rear drop as Grant climbed aboard with the woman. Kane keyed the ignition and heard the engine catch smoothly. Before they'd taken the road trip after confiscating the vehicle, they'd replaced the engine from the Cerberus redoubt stores.

Grant left the woman in the rear and dropped heavily into the passenger seat. He unlimbered the .30-30. Dust covered his dark features and beard.

Carrie pulled herself up into the wag and lay protectively across her sister. Bullets chopped into the earth around the wag, then cored through the metal above the left tire.

"Fireblast!" Kane snarled. If one of the rounds blew through the tire, they were dead. He let out the clutch as Remar grabbed the wag's side.

"Son of a bitch!" Remar gasped, redoubling his efforts to keep stride with the wag. He faltered and slipped, stretching out full length for a moment while he kept his hand locked on to the wag. He pushed against the ground, trying to get his feet under him again. He cursed steadily.

"Shut up and run!" Kane ordered.

A line of bullets stitched across the wag's engine housing. Metallic whumps split the air as dents appeared on the housing's surface. He pulled hard to the left, trying to avoid the machine-gun fire spilling from the Tong war wag.

Taking advantage of the favorable turn, Remar leaped and hauled himself aboard the wag's rear deck, landing heavily on the two women. Carrie screeched at him and shoved him off her sister and herself.

Grant pointed out the rolling wag to Kane's left. A V-shaped nosepiece was attached to the front bumper, and a support bar hooked through the rear deck. Caravans used reinforced wags to break through hijacker blockades.

Kane shifted gears, popped the clutch and dropped his foot heavily on the accelerator. The engine growled in protest but responded with a surge of power that churned all four wheels. The blockade runner missed the wag by inches as a torrent of blasterfire cut the air above Kane's head.

The Deathbird dropped from the sky again, the scorpion-shaped shadow flitting across the broken terrain. Kane tracked the aircraft and changed directions, heading straight for it.

"What the hell are you doing?"

Kane ignored Carrie's screamed demand. He kept the wag hurtling under the Deathbird's path. Dust driven by the rotor wash whipped around the cracked windscreen and covered him again.

The 20 mm cannon opened up suddenly, ripping craters in Kane's path as broad as ax handles. Rock and sand blew back over the wag and rained on Kane and the others as crashing thunder blew away all other sound.

Grant threw a hand on top of the windscreen and set the

M-14's muzzle across it. He shouldered the weapon and aimed quickly, then fired steadily.

Kane listened to the sharp cracks, knowing Grant would either aim for the vulnerable tail rotor or the pilot. The Plexiglas bubble was bullet resistant, but the impacts still created webbed cracks that reminded the pilot he was being shot at.

When the last cannon round hammered the ground less than ten feet in front of the wag, Kane pulled hard to the right, positioning Grant for a shot at the pilot while avoiding the cannonfire. The right front tire rumbled over the earthen clods and rock dug up by the cannon round. The rotor wash beat down on them for just a moment, then passed. He glanced in the rearview mirror and spotted the first line of the Mag Sandcats arriving at the gaudy.

The Sandcats quickly deployed in a loose half circle around the eastern side of the gaudy. The familiar forms of the black-clad armored shock troops spilled from the vehicles.

"They've got a royal hard-on for somebody," Grant roared over the wag's straining engine.

Kane upshifted a final time and kept the accelerator on the floor. He roared under the Deathbird's shadow, heading west. "Yeah." He glanced in the rearview mirror and watched Remar looking back at the arriving Mags. "I'll give you three guesses who they're looking for and the first two don't count. And we're going to find out why."

Chapter 10

"You're not very friendly all of a sudden."

Kane returned Remar's gaze fully. To the old man's credit, he didn't blink or look away. "I tend to get that way when I buy a man a meal and it turns out he's got a full squad of Cobaltville Mags washing up on his backtrail."

Remar shook his head. "Not my fault."

Kane shook his head in disgust. "You're right." He turned and walked back up the trail to the rickety cabin leaning against a sandblasted cliffside thirty miles from the gaudy. Not all of that thirty miles had been as straight as a crow flew.

Carrie had told them of the place after they'd gotten clear of the gaudy. The old man who lived there did medical work. Once, according to the tale Carrie had been told, Doc Crawford had worked in the Cobaltville labs. She didn't seem to know what had brought the old man from the ville.

Constructed of scrap wood and rusted tin, held together with baling wire and nails, burned by the unforgiving sun and leeched of color, the shack almost faded into the rock behind and on one side of it. The building tilted precariously, the angled roof piled with sand and rock to prevent the tin from flapping in the wind. The two walls not facing the rock each held one window covered with wax paper. It was easier to replace paper than glass.

Flowering cactus bearing fist-sized yellow blossoms stood in a small garden to one side of the shack's only door. A stone path, carefully laid out in the dust and rock, led to a weathered privy. A child's carved wooden soldiers occupied positions on a pile of sand farther up on the incline behind the privy where Grant sat as lookout.

Kane walked through the shack's front door and into the main room. The house was bigger on the inside than it looked from outside.

Carrie knelt beside the hammock Doc Crawford used as an operating table. She held her sister's hand and made cooing noises while Crawford stitched up the big gash.

"This isn't going to heal too badly," Crawford stated quietly, peering through the magnifying glasses he wore. He was a lean rake of a man with cottony white hair that fell well past his shoulders. A thin beard clung to his chin, and a ragged mustache shadowed his upper lip. His scrub-whites had gone gray with age, and were held together with patches a half-dozen different colors.

Kane guessed the man was in his sixties or seventies, but his hands were smooth as glass as they glided around each other to tie the knots in the stitches he'd put in Beth's face. He glanced at Kane as he worked, never any hesitation at all.

Beth pulled at her sister's hand.

"She wants to know how bad is the scar going to be," Carrie said.

"It's going to be a hell of a lot better than being dead," Crawford said. He shrugged, starting a fresh piece of nylon stitching through the needle's eye. "It was a nice cut, both sides good and straight. The thing that worries me most is the muscle that got cut. If I put everything back together right, her smile will even be okay and there won't be any draw to her lip."

Beth made a mewling sound. Carrie held on to her hand with both of hers.

"I'm really sorry I don't have any anesthesia," Crawford said. His hands wove their designs on the wounded woman's face. "This would be a lot easier on both of us if I did, but it's damn hard to get hold of out here."

The main room had a door in the back wall that Kane

guessed led to the kitchen area. He'd spotted the chimney flue on an earlier recce of the area before he'd followed Carrie's directions to the shack. A ladder beside the room's fireplace led up to a loft covered by a faded quilt with knights on horseback.

There were other people in the area who knew a little about medicine and how to care for wounds, but Carrie had insisted on Crawford. The man took care of the more seriously injured that came through the gaudy, as well as abortions that the girls who worked there needed upon occasion.

Crawford tied off one more stitch, then ran his bloody hands into the pan of sterilized water beside the hammock. "I do have something that'll help you sleep."

"That would be good," Carrie said, tears bright in her eyes.

"I'll fetch it." Crawford rose from the floor and walked to the back room.

Automatically, Kane moved from where he'd been standing. When Crawford came back, Kane wouldn't be standing in the same spot. He crossed the room to the two women, his hand almost resting on the .45's butt.

Beth's face looked a lot better than it had. The stitches had closed the wound neatly, pulling the flaps together in a straight line. Blood streaked her face, but Carrie was gently cleaning that away, as well. Beth's whole jaw was swelled, and her eyes were fever-bright.

"He did good, sweetie," Carrie whispered softly. "Doc Crawford did real good. You're going to be pretty as you ever were. Men are still going to look at you the way they always did."

Tears leaked from Beth's eyes, helping wash away the crusts of blood on her face.

Movement in the loft drew Kane's attention. He glanced up and watched a corner of the quilt drop back into place. Someone had been watching.

Crawford reentered the room carrying a long-necked glass bottle and four glasses. "I've got some of that homemade mash you girls have been paying me with. In the shape you're in, Beth, what with the excitement and all, I don't think you'll have to drink much before you're sleeping like a baby.''

Kane watched the quilt more directly, knowing Crawford would notice.

The old man sat the glasses on the floor, then yanked the cork from the bottle. He poured a couple fingers of the amber liquid into two of the glasses and handed them to the women. Carrie helped Beth drink hers, cradling her sister's head in her arm.

"Can I buy you a drink, mister?" Crawford asked.

"Sure," Kane said easily. "But why don't we invite your friend up in the loft to join us?"

"Do you just like a big crowd?" the old man asked. He splashed whiskey into his own glass, then quickly gulped it down. A look of sour pain filled his face for a moment, and he wheezed.

"I like to know who all the players are," Kane stated.

"He doesn't want a drink."

Kane cut his eyes to the old man. "Why don't we ask him?"

"I don't have to."

Kane put steel into his voice. "I'd like to hear you ask."

Crawford hesitated for a moment, then poured more whiskey into his glass. "Kenny."

"Yeah, Pa?" The voice was deep and mature, but held a youthful uncertainty.

"Come on down."

There was silence for a short time, then the sound of bed slats shifting. "Are you sure, Pa?"

"Yes, Kenny."

"'Cause you always tell me to stay up here out of the way when you got folks inside the house." The tone grew more petulant.

"I know I do," Crawford said. "And I mean it. We're just going to do this now, this one time."

"'Cause it's a surprise?"

"Yeah, Kenny, because it's a surprise." Crawford poured himself another drink, then freshened Beth's.

The wooden slats shifted again, creaking as if from a great weight. Then a thickly muscled leg poked out from the quilt and searched for the ladder until the toes curled around one of the rungs.

Kane watched in silence as a giant of a man climbed down the ladder.

Kenny stood nearly seven feet tall, deep and broad through the chest. His arms were so muscled they wouldn't hang straight. A shock of blond hair hung into his aquamarine eyes and framed a moon face that showed anxiety and fear. Except for his expression, he looked every bit of thirty years old. His expression belonged on a boy of eight or nine. His homespun clothing showed care, though, in just the simple fact that they fit him.

"It's okay, Kenny," Doc Crawford said softly. "This man isn't going to hurt us." He swirled his drink in his glass as he watched Kane. "This is my son, Kenny."

The young giant stepped forward and offered his hand.

Kane tentatively took the man's hand, feeling the incredible strength in the fingers and grip.

"I'm Kenny," the man said. "Who are you?"

"Kane." Taking his hand back, Kane looked up into the aquamarine eyes.

"Nice to meetcha." Kenny grinned happily, then folded his hands behind his back. He took a step away. "I don't want to step on your toes. When I step on your toes, they hurt awful bad."

Kane smiled back at the huge man. "I bet it would."

Kenny nodded and brushed the hair from his eyes.

"I thought I recognized you," Crawford said. "I knew your father."

Kane shifted his hard gaze to the old man. "That's history, and I'd prefer we left it that way."

Crawford nodded and tossed back the rest of his drink. "Okay, Kenny, have a seat and stay back out of the way."

Kenny nodded, then went and sat with his back to the wall. "Can I go outside?"

"No, it's getting dark."

Kenny eyed the light falling against the wax-paper-covered window. "It's not dark yet, Pa."

"It will be."

"I can play for a little while."

"Not now, Kenny. Please try to be a big boy."

Kenny pursed his lips and nodded slowly, clearly unhappy with the decision.

"Get your book and read," Crawford advised in a soft voice.

Kenny pushed himself up and retreated to the loft briefly. When he came back down he carried a large book titled *King Arthur and His Knights of the Round Table*. The child-man sat down again and opened the book. He gazed at the colorful pictures on each page in rapture.

"You see why I left Cobaltville," Crawford told Kane.

Kane nodded. Children born with defects that kept them from being useful citizens of the ville were put to death at birth. Someone as large and as strong as Kenny would have been put down in the Tartarus Pits until he died or was killed by others in the forced-labor populace.

"I couldn't let him grow up there." Crawford poured himself another drink. "Maybe growing up here isn't any better, but he gets to play here."

Kane nodded. "It must've been hard getting him out of there."

"It was even harder keeping him a secret." Crawford watched his son with a mixture of sadness and joy. "For the first ten years of his life, we kept Kenny in a closet. Raised him there and taught him he wasn't supposed to be seen by anyone else."

"Where's his mother?" Kane asked.

"I don't know," Crawford said. "I knew as big as Kenny was getting and him getting anxious to explore everything that we couldn't keep him hidden much longer than we already had. I made the decision to get him out of Cobaltville and head west, take our chances out here. She didn't want to take any chances. She stayed behind."

The hardship Crawford had to have endured touched Kane. But the closeness between the two was something to be envied.

"She's sleeping," Carrie announced.

Crawford knelt to examine Beth. He peeled back an eyelid and checked the pulse at the side of her neck. He turned the woman's head so the stitched wound was easy to get to. "Get a rag from that pile," he said, pointing at a group of carefully wrapped towels on a shelf on the wall. "Hold it under the side of her face."

Carrie did as she was told.

Crawford uncorked the whiskey bottle again, then spilled some of the contents over the long cut. Beth whimpered and tossed her head in discomfort, but she didn't wake. "It's the best disinfectant I've got now."

Carrie mopped at her sister's face and wound, cleaning up the extra liquid.

"I've got some antibiotics in a med kit," Kane said. "I'll get them for you."

Crawford raised a speculative eyebrow at him. "You're well provisioned."

Kane shook his head. "Don't even go there. I cut my ties with that place and Baron Cobalt a damn long time ago. But when we cross paths, I don't hesitate to take what I need."

"No," Crawford agreed, "I suppose you wouldn't."

"I've got some liquid bandage, too," Kane told the man. He headed out the door. They'd hidden the wag near the cliff and the shack, piling on dead brush to break up the vehicle's lines and camouflage it so no one could see it easily from the air or ground.

Remar fell into step beside Kane. "That's a good man in there."

"Yeah." Kane nodded.

"That's been a hard row to hoe, him taking care of that son of his."

Kane didn't say anything as he made his way to the wag. He dropped to the ground and squirmed under the vehicle until he reached the false plate that held the med kit. Meds out in the Utah territories were valuable enough to kill over.

Remar stood beside the wag, waiting. "You were right about that Mag group looking for me."

Kane listened but concentrated on freeing the plate. The bolts were grime encrusted, but they came loose after some serious twisting. He dropped the metal case inside onto his chest. It was as big as a briefcase and had been hard to hide. But DeFore had insisted and Kane had agreed. Even if they never used the med kit, the contents could be used for trade to get other things they might have needed along the trip.

"Falzone has been doing some regular trade with the barons," Remar said, "but you probably knew that. He's been giving them progs and hardware he's turned up in the Lost Valley of Wiy Tukay in exchange for blasters and heavy armament. It's gotten bad up there, what with the Tong and the others trying to take access to the valley away from him. If we lose the blasters and equipment we've been trading for, we might as well roll up our tents and move on. That isn't a generous or hospitable land up there."

Kane crawled back out from beneath the wag, spitting road grit that had fallen into his face. "Did the baron decide it wasn't too inhospitable or too ungenerous? Is that why he wants you?"

Remar shook his head. "Oh, hell no. It's much worse than that."

Chapter 11

"Do you speak English, you fucking slant-eyed bastard?" Mallet knelt down in front of the Tong captive, close enough to breathe in the sour stench of sweat clinging to him.

The Tong warrior said nothing. The two black-armored Magistrates holding his arms jacked up behind his back while forcing him into a kneeling position pulled on his arms harder. Pain lanced raw, dark lights into the man's hazel eyes.

"I said, do you speak English?" Mallet roared again.

The captive bit his lips to keep from screaming. Blood leaked from the corner of his mouth.

With a practiced roll of his shoulders that allowed no warning, Mallet smashed the back of his armored glove against the prisoner's face.

The Tong warrior's head turned sideways from the impact. Flesh split open over the man's cheekbone like the rind on a fresh melon. Blood wept down his face, clinging in drops to his jawline. Shaking with pain and fury, the man turned his hard gaze back to the Mag leader.

Mallet glanced at the Mag on the right. "What did this man have on him, Stewart?"

"Nothing like what we're looking for, sir." Stewart was young, the first in a new line of Mags coming into their own in Cobaltville. The battle against Kane, Grant and the other outlanders, as well as the Tong and mine train hijackers, had taken their toll on Cobaltville's resources, which had already been depleted by the battles with invading forces of Mags from other baronies. Where the Magistrate Division had once been able to hold its ranks with generation after generation of warriors, they were now in the position of securing new blood.

In Mallet's opinion, allowing in the new breed was thinning the blood of the old-line warriors. "I'm talking about opium, Stewart. These stupe bastards chew that shit all the time. Keeps 'em brave and makes 'em hard to chill."

Stewart looked embarrassed and uncertain. "I don't know, sir."

"Fucker looks like he's flying high now." Mallet rocked back on his heels. At thirty-plus years, he had a good fifteen years in with the Mag Division at Cobaltville. He stood just over six feet tall, a lean, rangy man with dark features and dark eyes. A knife scar seared his right temple and left a line of white hairs in its wake.

He left on his helmet because a Mag brought more fear to his enemies with all the gear in place, and because he knew some of the men they'd ran from the gaudy had fled into the hills. He'd put patrols out earlier, but with the approaching night, he'd pulled them back into the perimeter and posted guard. Motion detectors and sec men with night-vision capability watched over their campsite in front of Tyson's saloon.

Mallet grabbed a handful of the Tong warrior's hair and pulled it back painfully. "Tell me about a man named Remar."

The prisoner yelped in pain, squeezing his eyes tightly shut. "Fuck you!"

Mallet grinned evilly. "Now we're communicating." He deliberately looked over the battle zone. A couple wags still burned, something Mallet hadn't been happy about because those vehicles could have been salvaged either whole or for parts.

When he'd first come up through the Mags, Mallet had been assigned to recover wags and supplies from outlanders who'd discovered them on their own or had stolen them from the ville. He hadn't lost that scavenger's eye.

The dead, all except for the three Mags who had been lost

while taking the gaudy, lay across the ground where they'd hit. Remar's two accomplices had been located and positively identified. Remar had been one of the few who had gotten away. So far a few of the trails were being ferreted out, but Mallet didn't fool himself. Finding anyone in the sun-blasted Utah territories was damn near impossible unless their location was known.

"Tell me about Remar," Mallet commanded.

"Why should I?"

"Because I'll chill you if you don't."

"You'll chill me even if I do," the Tong warrior said.

Mallet shrugged and nodded. "Yeah, but if you talk to me, I'll chill you quick. Otherwise, I'll open your guts up and stake you out here for the local wildlife to feed on." Baron Cobalt had sent him into the field, and he didn't intend to fail no matter what it took to get it done.

"I will not dishonor my mission," the Tong warrior replied. "Nor will I dishonor Wei Qiang."

"Qiang doesn't give two shits about you," Mallet stared harshly.

"It doesn't matter."

"Brave talk." Mallet stood. "Iverson."

"Yes, sir." An older Mag in bulky armor looked up from the self-heat he held in his hand.

"Do you still have that hatchet you collected from one of these stupe bastards?"

"Yes, sir." Iverson was a noted collector among the Mags, generally of weapons that he took in battle. He reached down beside him and held up the single-bitted hatchet.

Mallet held his hand out, and Iverson tossed the weapon to him. The Mag leader caught the ax by the haft. He swung it experimentally, getting the heft of it. "All right, we're going to do this the hard way." He dropped back into a squatting position and locked eyes with the prisoner. A smile he could never quite erase at times like these twisted his lips. This was another facet of the Mag business that he truly enjoyed. "Give me his right hand."

The two Magistrates behind the prisoner pushed the man forward. The Tong warrior fought against them, but his slight size against the bigger men and the armor they wore left him no match. They lay on him and stretched him out, extending his right arm.

"What do you know about Remar?" Mallet demanded again.

The man's body quivered in fear. He shook his head from side to side. "No."

"Has Remar been trading with Wei Qiang?" Mallet drew the keen ax blade across the back of the man's wrist. Blood welled up in the slight cuts left by the razor edge.

"No."

Mallet reached down and ripped the shirt off the man's back. He tore it into strips, making a production of the effort. Taking two of the strips, he wound them around each other. Then he wrapped them around the man's wrist. "Someone's been trading with Qiang."

"Yes."

"Who?"

The Tong warrior struggled again, tightening his hand into a fist. "I don't know."

Mallet took a finger-thick stick from the ground nearby. He hooked it into the cloth and twisted, drawing the slack from the cloth and cutting off circulation to the man's hand. "Who told you to come after Remar?"

"General Leung."

"How were you supposed to know him?" Mallet glared into the man's frightened eyes, looking at the road maps the red veins made in the white.

"Pix," the man cried. "We were given pix to know Remar."

"What were you supposed to do with him?"

The Tong warrior's nerve broke then and he wept openly, his voice keening across the campsite.

"Answer me, damn you!" Mallet caught the man's imprisoned wrist. He raised the hatchet in warning. Light from the nearby campfires glinted on the blade.

The man spoke rapidly in his native tongue, fear dripping into every syllable.

"What were you supposed to do with Remar?" Mallet asked.

"Capture him!" the man screamed. "We were supposed to take him captive and take him back to Qiang! Lord Qiang wants to know the location of the Lost Valley!"

"Remar knows where the Lost Valley is?" Mallet demanded.

"Yes."

"How do you know?"

"We found one of Falzone's men," the Tong warrior said. He flexed his fist, trying desperately to reclaim it. "We made him talk."

"Who's Falzone?"

"The man who discovered the Lost Valley and took it from the followers of Wiy Tukay."

"Who are they?"

"Religious zealots. They believe that Wiy Tukay ended the world through the computers because men were reaching too high, aspiring to become gods themselves."

"Stupe bastards."

"It is their belief."

"Tell me about Remar."

The Tong warrior swallowed hard. "He is one of Falzone's handpicked men."

Mallet felt the sweat covering the prisoner's wrist, slick enough to make hanging on really hard. "Where did Remar go?"

"I don't know."

"What does Qiang want with Falzone? Is he wanting to cut a deal for the tech?"

"No. Lord Qiang wants to locate Falzone and the Lost Valley, then he wants to take it away."

"Was Remar here to meet you?"

"No."

"Then who?"

The Tong warrior shook his head. "We never learned. Remar knew we were after him. He and the men he met chilled my men inside, then they fled out the back. They escaped in a wag just as you arrived."

Rage filled Mallet. He'd been minutes only behind Remar, had probably even seen him out on the battlefield. Now the man was gone. "Did Remar tell you he'd sabotaged the latest comp progs he'd sent to Cobaltville?"

"No."

The last batch of comp progs had contained a virus of some sort that had never been seen before. Power in twenty percent of Cobaltville had been shut down for nearly an hour before the techs repaired the damage. At least, they hoped they'd repaired the damage.

Mallet knew there was a lot of concern that the comp prog had left something behind, something that would interfere with the Cobaltville comp systems at some other time. That was why Baron Cobalt had instituted a scorched-earth policy against the tech traders. No more trading would be done until they could assure the comp systems wouldn't be violated.

"Did Qiang know about it?" Mallet demanded.

"I don't know Lord Qiang's mind," the man replied.

Mallet knew he'd exhausted the man's knowledge, but he pressed on anyway. Now that he'd done his job, he could turn his attention to his passions. "Where is Remar?"

The Tong warrior shook his head, knowing the question signaled an end to whatever mercy he might accept.

"That's too fucking bad," Mallet stated. "I think you're lying to me, and lying's just cost you a hand." He raised the hatchet and brought it down, listening to the satisfying crunch of the blade biting through flesh and bone.

The man's agonized scream echoed over the Mag campsite, riding the winds high up into the hill country.

THE SCREAM SURFACED in Brigid's mind like a bubble oozing up through a quicksand mire. She struggled through the layers of sleep, only to feel the heat of the fever gripping her and causing disorientation.

Her heart hammered in her chest as she gazed up at the encroaching darkness filling the sky. She lay still, remembering how important Grant and Kane had always said waking was.

She didn't feel any eyes on her, but she didn't have their training or the animal instincts that Domi possessed. Remembering the young albino triggered a feeling of ill ease. Brigid knew the girl should have been at her side.

Cautiously, aware of the bile rising in her throat, Brigid sat up. For a moment she thought her head was going to continue floating up from her shoulders. A sleeping blanket lay beneath her, zipped open and containing a thermal blanket that was damp with the sweat from her fever.

A horse whickered nervously thirty or forty yards away. Brigid couldn't see the animal through the thick copse of trees around her, but it made sense that Domi would have staked it a short distance away from them. The horse served as an early-warning system and wouldn't give away their exact position.

The gathering gloom and the fever plaguing Brigid contributed to her lack of clear vision. She found the mini-Uzi under the sleeping blanket within easy reach. Gathering it up, she automatically checked to make sure it was fully loaded before placing it in her lap.

A canteen sat next to the sleeping bag, as well. Brigid took off the cap and drank slowly, trying to ease the pain in her parched throat and not wanting to incite the nausea twisting slowly in her stomach to full riot.

She wished she knew where Domi was. Being born with an eidetic memory, if she'd seen the young albino leave she'd have remembered it. She didn't. All she could remember was a scattered handful of images after Domi had sucked the snake's venom from her body.

Experimentally, Brigid opened her blouse. Bloody patches across the front had dried stiff. Domi had left her bra off and the two punctures on her breast uncovered. Both of the small wounds were ringed with bruises, and brackish pus flowed from them. Thankfully, she didn't see any red lines of infection.

Out in the darkness, the angry cry of a big cat filled the night.

Brigid's thoughts immediately turned to Domi. She pushed herself up, then studied her surroundings. Dense forest separated her from the horse to the west. North was still upland, while the stream to the east flowed south. Tall grasses filled the banks on either side of the water that caught the light like a glass sheet.

The stream meant game trails. Domi liked to hunt and didn't care much for self-heats.

However, suspicion lurked in the back of Brigid's mind. Domi had offered no explanation why she was there, or if she had, Brigid hadn't been conscious for it. The young albino had either followed Brigid or Bry.

Brigid wasn't sure which of the two possibilities displeased her more. Domi's presence was certainly no accident.

She took a fresh grip on the mini-Uzi and pulled her blouse more tightly around herself. The wind carried a cutting chill, but she knew most of that was from the fever. She headed south, swaying slightly from weakness and nausea.

If Bry and Domi were together in whatever they were doing, Brigid wasn't sure she wanted to be at the campsite when they returned. But if Domi was in trouble, she couldn't ignore that, either.

The mountain lion cried out again.

Brigid kept walking, hoping she wasn't just getting lost.

KANE CARRIED a plate heaped with food to Grant's position. Doc Crawford and his son had surprising culinary tastes. The shack's larder was impressively stocked; a boon for a man in his profession, Crawford had stated.

"How's the girl?" Grant asked as he accepted the plate.

"Asleep."

"Is she going to be okay?"

Kane sat on the rock and looked out over the terrain before them. Nothing moved out in the full dark that had descended when the sun plunged below the western rim. The temperature had dropped at least thirty degrees, a remnant of the nuclear winter that had stalked the Earth after the nukecaust. "He's got good hands, a good touch. I haven't seen many who worked neater."

"Mebbe her face has a chance."

Kane nodded and shifted, trying in vain to find a comfortable position. The cuts from the glass back at the gaudy had been treated. None of them had been serious, but several of them would be painful for a couple days until they healed over better. "Have you seen anything out there?"

"No." Grant turned most of his attention to the plate. "Roast? Is this real?"

"Yeah," Kane said. "I didn't ask what kind of animal it came from."

"Don't get me started on that end of things." Grant used his fork to prowl through the other items on the plate.

Kane had marveled himself. Crawford had proved to be a generous host in spite of the unexpected company. Besides the roast, he'd added new potatoes, baby carrots and peas. Despite the heat of the desert, the physician and his son maintained a garden in a greenhouse farther up the cliff. He'd tapped into the underground stream and used a pump to draw water for the crops. Taking care of the garden was one of Kenny's duties.

"I found out why the Mags are so interested in Remar," Kane said.

The old man had remained in the shack below to play cards with Crawford, who was also proving generous with his whiskey supply. Carrie slept on the floor beside her sister.

"Yeah?" Grant forked a new potato and popped the whole thing into his mouth. He chewed slowly, savoring the meat juices that had soaked up into the vegetable.

"The last shipment Remar took into Cobaltville was tampered with," Kane explained, cutting down the story he'd gotten from Remar.

"I thought Remar wasn't going to talk about this."

Kane shook his head. "The problem was getting him to shut up once he started."

Grant grinned. "He came across like he was all innocent and you coaxed the answer out of him?"

Kane nodded.

"He's pretty good with that poor-innocent-me act."

"I've seen better," Kane replied.

"Not much." Grant plucked up one of the two thick chunks of homemade bread and used it to sop up meat juices. "So what happened with the last shipment?"

Kane resisted the impulse to pull a cigar from his shirt pocket even though nothing except the nocturnal desert crowd moved around them. "Evidently, the baron's techs tried to run it through their systems and ended up shutting down part of Cobaltville for nearly an hour."

"How?"

"Remar doesn't have a clue. He's not even sure that the progs he gave them would do something like that."

"Was it intentional?"

Kane hesitated. "I don't think so. Falzone needs the blasters, equipment and supplies Baron Cobalt had been trading with him."

"Just to play devil's advocate here, Falzone could get those from Qiang."

"According to Remar, Qiang trades out everything but weapons."

"Qiang doesn't want to equip an army he's planning on facing," Grant said.

"That's the way I have it figured."

"If Falzone didn't cross Baron Cobalt, who did?"

"That's a good question," Kane answered. "I've been thinking on it myself."

"What about the other groups Remar's been talking about?" Grant asked. "The Wiy Tukay followers?"

"They don't mix with the tech side of things too well the way Remar tells it," Kane answered. He stared out into the darkness overlying the broken land around Doc Crawford's shack and let his mind run through all the permutations of the problem he'd already come up with. "They've got a few systems operational, but they prefer to leave everything buried."

"Getting Baron Cobalt pissed at Falzone would go a long way toward keeping things buried."

"The Wiy Tukay group is more interested in chilling Falzone's inner circle, the people who actually know where the Lost Valley is. Once they're dead, everything goes back to normal."

"Except the Tong and Cobaltville Mags will still be searching for the mother lode of lost tech." Grant's teeth tore into the roast, peeling the meat easily from the bone.

"Yeah, but that's better than having your god disinterred bit by bit every day. Remar said the Wiy Tukay people don't have the sophistication to tamper with the comp progs he delivered at Cobaltville."

"What about the Heimdall Foundation?"

Kane shook his head. "We don't have enough information on them. I recall hearing about them somewhere, but I can't put anything definite with it."

"Brigid will know."

Kane silently agreed. Unbidden, he thought about Brigid Baptiste. The last time he'd seen her was days ago. They'd parted amicably, both of them on the same side for a change because both of them had been interested in getting to the truth of the matter regarding the location of the lost tech that had suddenly started reappearing across the Outlands.

They hadn't talked much before Kane and Grant had loaded the wag and started for the Utah territories. But driving down the mountains from the Cerberus redoubt, Kane had caught sight of Brigid standing on the ledge above. She'd waved, then disappeared in the distance.

"Anam-chara," Kane whispered as he felt the familiar ache fill him whenever he thought of Brigid. The jumps into the parallel worlds had revealed a lot to him, and he was certain she felt the same way. On those three alternate worlds, their doppelgängers had engaged in lovemaking, a move neither of them seemed inclined to commit to in this world.

Yet, if the shared memory they'd experienced while in Russia confronting the Tushe Gun was correct, they had been together before. A sick knot twisted through Kane's stomach. The memory hadn't had a good ending, and there'd been no guarantee how together they'd been. Even Morrigan had told them they'd been together and separated a number of times in past lives.

So what was it going to be in this life? he asked himself. Did they already know the answer, or did they fear the answer, not wanting to draw any closer than they had to in order to fulfill whatever grand scheme they were supposed to be inextricably linked to in this life?

All the supposing made Kane's head hurt. It was also possible that he and Brigid just found each other to be too much of a pain in the ass. That put a damper on love and sex, whichever it was they felt for each other.

"Coming back?" Grant asked in his deep voice.

Kane glanced up. "I didn't go anywhere."

"Right. I've noticed what effect Brigid's name has on you this last couple days."

Kane frowned. "I'm not looking forward to getting back to

Cerberus and having an argument with her over whether we should pursue this."

"You think she'll argue?" Grant seemed unconvinced.

"Mebbe."

"This lost tech could be important. And if Baron Cobalt's so interested in it, I'd like a peek at his hole card, too."

"That's exactly how I feel," Kane said, "which is why I think Brigid is going to argue about it."

Grant shrugged and gave a half smile. "The two of you don't always argue."

"We will."

"You ever wonder," Grant asked, "what it would have been like if you two had met in another time and another place?"

Images of their encounter in past lives and alternate worlds came to Kane's mind, filling him with the chill of a night far colder than the one they sat in at present. His heart pounded as visions of violence, mayhem and brutal death overwhelmed him.

Kane sucked in a sudden draft of air as the power of the vision lifted from him. His heart still beat frantically.

Grant shifted beside him. "Are you okay?"

Kane wiped at his face and found it was covered with sweat. "Yeah. I'm fine."

"You don't look fine."

"Mebbe I just need a good night's sleep," Kane said sharply. "That's something we haven't had in over a week now."

"Hey, easy," Grant said, holding up his hands. "I didn't mean to strike a nerve there."

"You didn't," Kane growled. The vision remained vivid in his mind, and he knew he wouldn't sleep well that night because Brigid's face would haunt him. He wished he knew that she was all right so the uneasy feeling he'd had since the escape from Tyson's saloon would leave him. Then he told himself that nothing would happen to her at the redoubt. She was just fine.

Grant stood, road dust clinging to his clothing. "Where to next—back to the redoubt?" he asked.

"I figure so." Kane made himself as comfortable as he could on the bare rock. The cold seeped into him, biting at his bones. "We'll fill in Lakesh and Brigid, then set up to go out west, see if we can find Falzone and this Lost Valley of Wiy Tukay."

"There's something else you've got to consider," Grant said.

Kane looked up at his friend.

"If somebody tampered with those comp progs Remar delivered to Cobaltville and it wasn't a freak happening," Grant said, "it can only mean one thing."

"Somebody's got a person inside Falzone's inner circle." Kane nodded. "I've already thought about that."

"If we step up into that, we're going to have to watch our backs."

"I know."

Grant stood and started down the hill. "I'll bring you back a blanket to knock off the wind before I turn in, and see if the doc has a pot of coffee somewhere in the house."

Kane watched his friend go and wished he could think of something else besides Brigid Baptiste.

Chapter 12

Because of the fever delirium filling Brigid, the shadows seemed to take on lives of their own, pulsing slowly at times while twisting madly at other times. She held the mini-Uzi in both shaking hands. The blaster was almost too heavy to carry.

A footfall sounded behind her.

For a moment Brigid thought it was her mind playing tricks on her, but she spun. The movement caused the wounds left by the snake to throb painfully, echoing the angry resonance already playing in her head that came with the fever.

Only shadows confronted her. She watched them carefully, struggling to remain standing. Was it Bry, back to finish the job the snake had started? Or was it the men he'd met with?

"Walking in the dark is pretty bastard stupe for a woman supposed to be smart." Domi stepped out of the shadows, letting the moonlight catch her milk-white skin.

"I thought you were in trouble," Brigid said. She didn't lower the mini-Uzi. Paranoia rattled around in her mind, whispering that Bry and Domi were coconspirators in whatever deadly game the computer specialist was playing. Her finger lingered on the trigger.

"Do you know where you are?"

"No," Brigid admitted. "I was following the stream because I figured you had."

"For a little while," Domi agreed. "Then I went into forest. Big predators stay by water at night. Feed on smaller animals drawn to the water."

"I knew that."

Domi smiled the cruel little witch-grin she seemed to save

for other females. "You know you're not the biggest predator out there? Mebbe got more snakes. Big cats learn to like man-flesh."

"I heard a mountain lion."

Domi's white teeth gleamed in the darkness. "Won't hear it no more. Not that one."

"Why did you leave?" Brigid couldn't help thinking maybe the albino girl had met with Bry or his cohorts.

Domi held up a cord with three rabbit corpses. "Dinner. You need more than self-heats to get strength back quick."

Feeling guilty, Brigid slid her finger from the mini-Uzi's trigger. "I thought you needed help."

Domi snorted. "First rule survival—never help. Second rule survival—only help others if able help self first." Without another word, she led the way back toward the camp.

Swaying, her head pounding, Brigid stood her ground for a moment. Stubbornness flared through her, making her resistant to following the girl's lead. Then she took stock of the situation. Pride at this point was something Kane would lose himself to. Her mission remained clear. She had to let Lakesh know Donald Bry was meeting with others outside the redoubt.

And she wanted to ask Bry to his face how he'd been able to sit there and watch as his new friends tried to kill her.

Brigid turned and followed Domi, who moved soundlessly and looked like a pale white ghost drifting through the trees and underbrush.

KANE LISTENED to the scuff of leather across solid rock as he watched the shadow creep up the cliff side overhanging Doc Crawford's shack. He eased the combat knife from his boot, the movement masked by the wool blanket Grant had brought him a short time ago. He held a cup of hot chicory coffee in his hand, intending to throw it in the face of the potential assassin. His point man senses were on full alert, searching for any other shadows that didn't belong in the darkness.

The scent of fresh lemons tickled Kane's nose, throwing him off stride mentally for a moment.

"Are you awake?"

Kane stared into Carrie's eyes through the darkness. Moon glow highlighted the planes of her face and reflected slightly from the shiny fabric of her blouse. "I'm on guard duty," he replied, irritated. He didn't want anyone else around at the moment. Grant had started enough troubling thoughts.

"Mind some company?" Carrie stood in front of him, shifting her weight to throw her hip out.

"It might not be safe out here." Kane watched the woman, taking in the sleek lines and the full breasts straining at the blouse. The garment had suffered damage during their escape, and he saw patches of flesh through it.

"It's not going to be any safer in there." Unbidden, Carrie sat beside Kane. She wrapped her arms around herself and shivered. She smiled at him uncertainly. "It's cold."

Kane hesitated for only a moment, then flung the blanket open. Carrie sat beside him and huddled close for warmth. Kane felt the chill that had dug down deep into her body, but he felt the soft woman flesh, as well. Her hip nestled against his, firm but giving. Her touch sparked the lonely resonance inside him that had been keeping him company.

"I've got coffee," he offered.

"I'd like that."

Since there was only one cup, Kane freshened the dregs in the cup from the thermos Grant had brought. He passed it over.

Carrie took the cup in both hands and sipped slowly. She looked out over the landscape. "The Mags were after your friend, weren't they?"

"He's not a friend," Kane replied. "We just met today."

"But they were after him?"

"Mebbe."

"You're up here keeping watch."

"I'd do that anyway." Kane felt Carrie shift beside him, trying to get closer. The lemon scent was stronger now that it was trapped inside the blanket wrapped around them. He felt the heat of her pressed against him. The contact stirred an arousal in his loins. Images of Brigid in those other worlds appeared in his mind.

"You're a careful man."

"I try to be." Memory of the woman blasting the desert rat in the gaudy chilled some of Kane's ardor. He looked at her wrist, wondering if she still carried the hideout pistol, but the blanket wrapped around at the bottom of her palm so he couldn't see. An uncomfortable itch started between his shoulder blades. "How's your sister?"

Carrie sipped her coffee again and nodded. "Resting. Doc says he thinks her face is going to be okay."

"That's good." Kane felt a little relieved. The closeness between the two sisters also made them dangerous.

"I know. She's a pretty woman. She doesn't deserve something like that." Carrie turned to Kane. "I wanted to thank you for helping to get her out of there. I don't think we'd have made it on our own."

"Mebbe you would have."

"I wanted to thank you."

Kane nodded.

"And I didn't want to be alone tonight," Carrie said. "I thought mebbe you'd like some company."

Kane tried to think of what to say, but his throat felt suddenly dry. The lemon scent was overpowering. Carrie put the cup aside and reached for him, wrapping strong arms around his neck as she threw a leg over his waist.

She looked down at him from her position, her eyes gleaming with passion. "I don't like worrying about things. I've always found getting laid kind of takes the edge off, you know?"

Kane's senses whirled, and her touch seemed electric. Her weight across his groin felt entirely too comfortable, too right.

Carrie drew her blouse off, revealing generous breasts capped with nipples already hard from the cold. And maybe from something more. She placed her hands against his chest and moved, grinding against him. "Been a long time?"

"Yeah," Kane responded. "It has."

"Good." Carrie reached down for his pants and started unbuckling them. "Get naked."

"YOU SAW BRY?" Brigid asked.

Domi took one of the spitted rabbits from the fire, gazed at it in open speculation, then bit into it with strong white teeth. The meat separated from the bones like tissue tearing. "Yeah."

Brigid hesitated, not expecting the young albino to answer positively so quickly. She gazed into the flames of the small cook fire, fighting through the nausea that still gripped her. After they'd returned to the campsite, she'd intended to help Domi prepare their meal and see to her wounds. Instead, she'd curled up and gone to sleep again, waking only moments ago. She'd kept the mini-Uzi gripped in her hand the whole time. "Did he see you?"

"Don't think so." Domi wiped a forearm over the meat grease that had dripped on her chin. "Saw you."

That thought proved unsettling to Brigid. Although she didn't know Bry that well, she would have guessed he'd try to help her in the situation she'd been in. "What did he do?"

The shadows hung close to the campsite, creating a small bubble of illumination around them. The horse whickered again off in the distance but didn't sound perturbed. The breeze that blew across them was filled with a hodgepodge of scents, sweet and sour, thick and cloying and just the thinnest trace of fragile fragrances. But the smell from the meat searing over the fire was the strongest.

Brigid's stomach quietly revolted against the grease smell, but her saliva glands kicked up in anticipation. She decided to wait a moment. Even sitting up brought a wave of dizziness.

"Bry did nothing," Domi stated.

Brigid let out a long, slow breath.

Domi looked at her and raised her eyebrows. "Surprise you?"

"No. That's what I thought I saw."

"Bry didn't risk his neck to help you. Get him chilled, not much use."

"Not much use for what?" Suspicion flared anew in Brigid as she wondered how much Domi really knew about Bry and the meeting.

"Himself. If he tried to help, his friends would chill him, too." Domi took another bite and chewed contentedly. "Supper's getting cold. I worked hard for it."

"I know. Thank you." Brigid took one of the two remaining rabbits from the fire. Grease dripped from the seared meat, and she held it above the grass. She used her fingernails to pluck the meat free, then dropped it into her mouth. Her stomach almost rebelled at the strong taste as the grease clung to the inside of her mouth.

"Bry had a blaster," Domi said. "Didn't shoot at you." She shrugged. "That's good."

Silently, Brigid had to admit that was true. She finished chewing the meat and swallowed it, choking back the retching reflex. "What was Bry doing there?"

"Talking to men. That's what I saw."

"Do you know who they were?"

"No." Domi turned the rabbit in her grease-covered hands. Bone showed through in places. "Never seen them before."

"Why did you help me?" Brigid asked.

"Because I could." Domi shrugged. "Thought snake chilled you for sure, though."

"Me, too," Brigid admitted. Her breast and chest areas were still tender to the touch, but no infection appeared to be spreading. She fixed the young albino with her gaze. "What were you doing out there?"

"Following you."

"From Cerberus?" Brigid couldn't believe it. Surely she would have noticed someone following her. But then, she told herself, Bry hadn't seen her. Unless he'd deliberately led her into the trap. That possibility didn't sit well with Brigid at all.

"Yeah."

"Why?"

"Grant was gone from redoubt," Domi answered. "Lakesh was being all secret. I got bored."

"So you followed me?"

Domi nodded. "Looked like fun. If I got bored, I could go back to the redoubt."

"Did anyone know you went?"

"Got transponder, same as you. Anyone could look at comp for transponder signals to know where we are."

The realization hit Brigid that Lakesh was probably monitoring Kane's and Grant's signals while they were away on their mission. Her transponder signal—as well as Domi's and Bry's—would have been available for Lakesh to see. If Bry had been away on redoubt business Lakesh would have tracked him, but Lakesh could have done that anyway. And if Lakesh hadn't wanted her anywhere around Bry, she was certain he would have intervened.

The thoughts troubled her, especially since she didn't know Lakesh's agenda.

"Meat okay?" Domi asked.

Startled, Brigid looked up suddenly, which started a fresh bout of nausea rolling through her stomach. She nodded, then cut that short as well when the headache slammed against her temples. "Yes. It's fine. Thank you."

"Then why you not eat?"

"I don't feel well."

Domi snorted and shook her head. "'Course not. Snakebit like that, you feel bad for a while. Only way to feel better is to eat. It's why I went after fresh meat instead of self-heats you packed."

"I know, and I appreciate it." Brigid felt she owed Domi an explanation. Domi probably didn't care, and her feelings didn't get hurt easily by anyone other than Grant. "I've just got a lot on my mind."

"What?"

Brigid paused. That was the downside to talking to Domi and treating her like a friend. If something hit Domi's mind, it came out almost immediately. "I'd like to know what Bry was doing out here."

"Meeting people."

"Yes, but I'd like to know why."

"Then ask."

Brigid pinched off another bite and popped it into her mouth to buy herself some time. "It's not that easy."

"Yeah, it is. We get back to Cerberus, I'll show you."

"He could lie."

"Why?"

"Bry didn't exactly leave word and tell people where he was going."

"Did you?" Domi's ruby gaze flickered highlights from the cook fire.

"No." Guilt swirled around in the nausea Brigid was experiencing.

"Why?"

"I wanted to see where Bry was going."

"Could have told Lakesh."

Brigid shivered from a chill that thrilled through her. Her head hurt from thinking so much. None of this was easy, and it didn't promise to get any easier. "No."

"Why?"

"I didn't feel like it."

"'Cause you think Bry was sent out here by Lakesh."

Brigid nodded.

Domi grinned and shook her head. "Pretty stupe. If you're out here, Lakesh knows." She broke the leg bones and sucked out the marrow.

"Then why didn't Lakesh send someone after us?" Brigid let some of her irritation and anger sound in her words. "He would have been able to tell I needed medical attention from the vitals being transmitted back on the transponders."

"Lakesh knows I'm here." Domi shrugged and tossed the rabbit skeleton away. "You don't need anyone else. And we're far from the redoubt. Mebbe people out there now hunting us."

The possibility ignited more uneasiness inside Brigid. She glanced down to make sure the mini-Uzi was still at her side. The distance from the Cerberus redoubt was a definite factor. She looked back at Domi, who sat cross-legged and contentedly stripped meat from the rabbit carcass.

"Look," Brigid said, fighting her awkward tone, "I appreciate everything you've done for me today. You saved my life, and I won't forget that."

"Oh?" Domi arched her pale eyebrows. "We keeping count now?"

"No," Brigid said. "But I wanted you to know."

Domi nodded. "Okay."

Brigid finished as much of the rabbit as she could, then offered the remaining portion to Domi, who eagerly accepted. Still fighting the nausea and headache, Brigid lay back on the bedroll the young albino woman had made for her. The fever seemed to have abated somewhat. The air no longer felt freezing and only carried a cool comfort with it. She pulled the lightweight blanket over herself and gazed at the stars.

She tried to think of how she was going to handle Bry back at the redoubt, but she knew that was going to depend on the reception that awaited her. The fact that Lakesh hadn't sent out a search party for her when he'd seen her vitals on the transponder program bothered her. She'd always considered herself important to Lakesh. After the way he had recruited Beth-Li Rouch and attempted to set up his own genetic farm by pairing her off with Kane had been the first indication that he cared more for his own agenda than for the feelings of others.

Despite her long training in staying focused and reasoning

things out, Brigid found her thoughts wandering to Kane.
She'd made her peace, as much as she was able, with whatever
demon haunted their relationship. She wished she could have
defined the thing that existed between them, but she couldn't.
The possibility of past lives they'd shared threw any conjec-
tures she might make even further into a cocked hat.

Without warning, a memory of Ambika mounted on Kane
back in the Western Isles invaded Brigid's mind. She tried to
force the image away, but it wouldn't go. Ambika had been
beautiful, as tall as Kane with bronze skin and bluish-silver
hair. She'd held a knife at Kane's throat as she'd taken him
deep inside her, hammering her body against his.

Brigid had been trapped in a cage beside the bed, a prisoner
and captive audience. She and Kane had never talked about
that day, or about what he'd felt or thought. Maybe she didn't
even want to know, she told herself. And she damn sure didn't
want to try to explain how she'd felt. With Beth-Li's arrival
at Cerberus and the woman's interest in Kane, Brigid had
stepped aside, willing to let whatever happened between Beth-
Li and Kane happen. Brigid hadn't needed, or wanted, another
enemy at the time. However, nothing had happened between
Kane and Beth-Li.

And now Beth-Li was gone.

A longing filled her, but she couldn't put a name to it. Over
the pop and crackle of the cook fire, she heard Domi still
eating. "Domi," she called out, unwilling to meet the young
albino woman's eyes.

"Yeah. Want meat back?" Domi sounded reluctant to be
so generous.

"No."

"Okay."

"If Grant did allow his defenses down and let you inside,
where do you think it would go from there?" Instantly, Brigid
felt awkward for having asked the question. If it hadn't been
for the fever, she knew she would have been more disciplined.

"Don't know," Domi replied. "Don't think about it. That

too far away. Mebbe one of us get chilled before it go any further than fucking. Still, fucking would be fun.''

"How do you feel about him?''

"Want to fuck him. Want to be with him. Don't think any further than that. That's your problem, Brigid, you want to know too much. Life kind of just happens, and you want to control it. Not meant to be that way.''

Brigid snuggled in the blanket, finding more comfort than she'd imagined would be possible. The meat finally rested easily in her stomach. But her thoughts turned to Kane, wondering how he was doing with his current mission—and who he was with.

Chapter 13

Carrie covered Kane's mouth with her own, breathing sweet alcohol fumes into his lungs. Her hot, naked breasts pressed against him. His hands held her bare shoulders, feeling the chill of her skin. Her hands fumbled with the front of his pants, reaching for the erection beyond.

Out in the distance, a mournful coyote howl echoed, rolling across the uneven hills and through the cliffs.

Even as his senses reeled on the edge of giving himself totally over to the woman's obvious experience, Kane remembered that coyotes mated for life. He couldn't recall who'd told him that, or what the circumstances had been.

His desire melted away almost instantly. His hips stopped straining toward Carrie.

"Hey," she grumbled as she felt him through the material, "what's going on here?"

"Nothing," Kane growled irritably. "That's exactly what's going on." Using his strength, he pushed the woman back and sat up. "Get your clothes on before you freeze."

Carrie looked at him uncertainly. "Is it something I did?"

"No." Kane straightened his pants, buckled them and kept his eyes averted from the woman.

"Got some kind of injury you haven't told me about?" Carrie sounded aggravated.

"No." Kane didn't meet her eyes.

"Then what the hell happened here?"

"Just stopped a mistake, that's all." Kane picked up her blouse from the ground and tossed it to her. She tried to ignore the garment and stare him down, but it was too cold.

By the time she had the blouse back on, Carrie's teeth were chattering. "You going to kick me back down on the cliff, or can I at least warm up before I go?"

Kane hesitated just a moment, feeling foolish and angry with himself. Even though the erection had died away, a part of him still wanted the woman. Hell, a part of him still wanted any woman. He pulled the blanket from his shoulders and tossed it to her.

She accepted the blanket and wrapped it around herself. "You're going to freeze."

"No, I'm not," Kane stated calmly.

Carrie sat only a few feet from him. "You always this picky about your women?"

"I'm not being picky."

"Then what do you want to call it? A few minutes ago you seemed pretty interested in what was going on."

"If I felt like talking about it," Kane told her, "I would. Since I'm not, that probably means something."

"Don't be a shit."

Kane started to make a scathing reply, then stopped short at the last minute. She deserved to get some shots in. It hadn't been her fault, and he hadn't tried to explain. "Okay."

At first he thought she was going to try to carry on the argument. Instead, her voice softened. "You got any coffee left in that thermos?"

Kane picked up the thermos and poured a fresh cup of coffee. He handed her the cup, watching the steam curl up over the lip and get whipped away by the slight wind. The chill cut into him like a knife. He sat with his knees drawn up, his elbows resting on them, and tried not to think of the cold.

Carrie sipped the coffee, never once taking her eyes from him. "Is it me?"

"No," Kane said tightly. Silently, he cursed himself for being so weak as to ever allow the situation to get started. Then he cursed Brigid for a while, even though it wasn't her fault, either.

"I can count on one hand the number of times I've been turned down," Carrie said. "And don't go thinking I'm all that easy."

"Never crossed my mind," Kane said. The taste of her lips still lingered in his mouth.

"Well, if you ain't looking for a virgin and it ain't me, it can only be one other thing," Carrie stated. "There's another woman."

Kane started to object, then didn't. "Yeah."

"Your wife?"

"No."

"Ah, it's even worse, then. You're in love with someone who doesn't love you back."

When Kane glared at Carrie, the woman only grinned at him. "You talk too much," he said.

Carrie pulled the blanket more tightly around her, bringing it up to the bottom of her chin. "Since neither one of us can sleep at the moment, why don't you tell me about her?"

Kane ignored the woman. He tried to lose himself in the terrain, tried to imagine where Mags might try to hide in the dark, but that wasn't exactly relaxing, either.

"Do you still see her?" Carrie asked.

The silence weighed heavily between them until Kane broke it. "Yeah," he said. "I still see her."

"A lot?"

"Sometimes."

"What color is her hair?"

"Red-gold," Kane said softly, imagining the way Brigid's hair caught the light in the sun.

"Does she know how you feel?" Carrie asked.

"No," Kane said hoarsely. "I don't even know how I feel. Two years ago, I lived in a ville. I had a job that offered security and a future. Hell, there was even a pension plan if I lived long enough."

"A lot of outlanders would chill their mothers for a chance

at something like that. Was she somebody's wife? Somebody powerful enough to chase you off?''

Kane shook his head. "It wasn't like that. We left together." He found himself wishing he could talk about everything he'd been through, then cursed him for being weak. All his life he'd been trained to take care of his own problems.

"Then why aren't you together now?''

"We never were together," Kane replied. Then memory of the past lives tumbled through his head. "Mebbe. I don't know. It gets confusing.''

"Have you ever been in love before?''

Kane laughed bitterly and looked at her. "I don't know if I'm in love now. And if I am, all I can say is it's pretty fucking miserable.''

"Sometimes that's the way it is,'' Carrie told him. "My mother used to tell me a story at bedtime when I was a little girl. Beth and I used to beg her to tell it, and most nights she would. It's a story from before the nukecaust.'' She held out the coffee cup.

Kane took the cup and drank. The hot liquid ran down inside him, beating back some of the chill.

"See,'' Carrie began, "there was this gaudy slut who kind of got forced into the business because she needed the jack. But inside she was a good girl and looked forward to meeting a man, settling down and having kids. Only she figured nobody's have her 'cause she was a gaudy slut.''

"Sounds depressing,'' Kane commented. "I'd prefer *Little Red Riding Hood*, even the version where the granny gets eaten.''

"This story gets better,'' Carrie promised. "One night while this gaudy slut was working, this guy with a lot of jack came by in a new wag. But he couldn't drive the wag, so she offered to help him out.''

"She could drive the wag but he couldn't?'' Kane shook his head in disbelief. "The guy must have been pretty stupe.''

"Before skydark things were different. Anyway, she helps

him drive his wag to where he's going. He knows she's a gaudy slut, right? But he offers her jack anyway to help him out for the next week.''

Kane yawned. The story was so far-fetched he had a hard time focusing on it. But it helped him keep his mind off Brigid and the guilt he felt for his involvement with Carrie. Guilt wasn't a normal feeling for him. As a Mag that emotion had been all but trained out of him. The only thing to feel guilty about was failing a mission.

"To make a long story short," Carrie continued, "the man falls in love with the gaudy slut because he's a lonely man, and she makes him start living his life for the first time. He takes her away, and they go live in his castle.''

"I guess it's a good story if you're a kid," Kane said.

"Especially since a move up from your present place in life is becoming a gaudy slut. Beth and I still take turns telling each other that story." Carrie fell silent for a short time. "It might be a while before we tell it to each other again.''

Kane refilled the coffee cup, already regretting the decision to give away the blanket. He drank down the scalding contents, hoping to nurse the inner warmth for a little while.

"I guess what I was trying to say was that love, at least true love, doesn't always give you time to think about it. You don't get to pick and choose so much. Sometimes you have to just take it the way it is. You might want to keep that in mind." Carrie stood and pulled off the blanket. She draped it over Kane's shoulders. "I'm warm enough to go find my way to the bed Doc promised me. You take care of yourself." She turned and walked down the cliff, arms wrapped around her.

Kane watched her go without saying another word. He pulled the blanket tight around him. Even though the chill gradually left him, the loneliness gnawed at his guts.

BRIGID WOKE with the rising dawn. The nausea had left her during the night, and she'd actually gotten half a good night's sleep. When she moved, her body protested. Aches and pains assailed her.

Jaundiced orange clouds lined the eastern horizon above the tree line. Dew glinted on the grass, scattering tiny rainbows in all directions. Cries of morning birds greeting another day split the air. If it hadn't been for her swollen breast and the soreness that filled her chest, she might have thought the events of the previous day had been a bad dream.

The aroma of cooking meat mixed in with the other morning fragrances. She sat up slowly, feeling her senses spin slightly. When she paused and closed her eyes for a moment, the sensation faded into a dull beat at her temples.

With the approach of morning, Domi had let the cook fire burn down. Little more than a handful of orange coals littered the patch of ground covered by gray ash. Small branches carved into short stakes held two cuts of meat above the heat. The outer surface of the meat had burned black in places, promising the meat had been cooked all the way through.

Brigid surmised that Domi had left breakfast. But the young albino woman had also left. The blankets she'd used to sleep on the previous night lay rumpled and empty.

Suspicion instantly flared through Brigid again. She eased herself to her feet, fisting the mini-Uzi automatically. She dropped the magazine out for an instant to check the load. Satisfied, she popped the magazine back into place.

She wasn't moving at her best, but Brigid felt confident about handling herself. She crossed to the other side of the campsite and peered through the limbs. The horse remained ground-hobbled next to the trees where it had spent the night. The horse's presence made her feel somewhat more hopeful.

Domi had evidently gone off on her own. Brigid was certain no one could have taken the young albino woman without a fight, not without waking her. It also stood to reason that if any of Bry's new associates had come calling that they would have taken her instead of the younger woman. It was also possible, Brigid had to admit, that Domi had gone to meet with Bry's associates herself.

"What you doing out of bed?"

Brigid turned quickly, too quickly for her head and stomach not to react. Her temples throbbed and her stomach sloshed warily. She brought up the mini-Uzi, turning sideways as Kane had taught her to present a smaller target.

Domi stood at the other side of the campsite, her Combat Master pistol in one hand and a small blue nylon net bag in the other. The net bag was filled with berries and tubers.

"Where have you been?" Brigid demanded.

The young albino made a face. "Took bath in stream. Gather more breakfast. Mebbe you should gather your own since get up so bitchy." Angrily, she stalked over to the cook fire and hunkered down. "Hoped mebbe you'd get enough sleep to feel better."

"Did you see anyone out there?" Brigid asked, lowering her blaster.

"No."

Brigid let out a tense breath. "I thought you'd been captured."

An amused smile eclipsed the scowl on Domi's face. "Mebbe you sleep through it, but no one never take me that quiet. I ain't no stupe out my first time."

For a moment Brigid thought maybe the tension between them had passed, then she realized the declaration could have been pulling double duty as an insult. "How cold is the water?"

"Plenty chill this high up in the mountains." Domi rummaged in the nylon net bag, taking out a handful of blackberries. "Get clean. Mebbe good for fever."

"The fever's almost gone." Brigid hung the mini-Uzi from its shoulder rig and walked over to the saddlebags Domi had stripped from her horse. She dug inside and came up with a change of fresher clothing. Riding through the forested mountains didn't allow for a large wardrobe. "I'm going to take a quick bath, then I'll be back for breakfast."

Domi put a hand across her forehead and made a production of gazing around the nearby trees. "Be fine. If crows don't get breakfast first."

"My appetite will be better after I've had a bath," Brigid explained. "I'll be more appreciative."

"Hope so."

Brigid ignored the gibe. "Do you have any soap?"

Domi shook her head. "Use sand and grass. It cleans good."

Turning back to the saddlebag, Brigid took out a small cake of soap she'd packed back at the redoubt. She added a small hand towel. Saddlebags didn't have much space, but she'd known how to pack in an organized fashion.

"Better be careful," Domi advised. "Saw a couple snakes in water."

An immediate chill of lingering fear ran through Brigid. She guessed that Domi was only saying that out of spite, but with the way wildlife had mutated as a result of the nukecaust, it was possible. "I will."

A few feet from camp, Brigid found a small game trail and followed it down to the stream. The water ran clear enough to show the shallow bottom, nestled comfortably between two meandering banks. Cattails lined the banks in a half-dozen spots, providing homes for birds and frogs. As she neared the edge of the stream, a red bird erupted from the nearby stand of cattails and took wing with angry cries.

The movement startled Brigid into an automatic dive for the ground. She landed hard and off balance, the wind partially knocked from her. She took a couple shuddering breaths to get her heart rate under control again, then got up.

She unlaced the calf-high boots and eased her feet out. Judging from the odor coming from them, sleeping in them the previous night hadn't been the best idea she'd ever had. Her feet immediately felt better when she peeled off the socks.

Resting a moment to let the nausea pass from all the bending, she gazed around the countryside. She tried to tell herself that she was protected, that no one was out there because Domi would have known.

However, she realized, that didn't mean that Domi would have told her.

She hated the insecurity that she suddenly found running rampant in her. Paranoia wasn't an attitude she wanted to adopt. But being around Lakesh and Kane had taught her facets of paranoia that she'd never known existed. Both of them rebelled against being led around by others, but neither of them had a problem manipulating other people for their own causes.

Even the duties she'd done as an archivist had taught her that lifestyle. Back in Cobaltville she'd progressed enough in her chosen profession that she'd been entrusted—and ordered—to rewrite history in accordance with the line handed down by the baronies. In Cobaltville, though, she'd felt she'd at least been privy to what was truth and what wasn't. Yet even that had been stripped from her by Lakesh's machinations.

Her thoughts grew more troubled. Bry's presence at the site was undeniable, but she didn't think that would be the case when she returned to the Cerberus redoubt. Donald Bry was an intelligent man; she just hadn't known he'd be versed in subterfuge, as well.

Deliberately, she stood. Her instincts told her she was alone, safe from unfriendly eyes at the moment. She chose to trust herself. She stripped out of her pants and panties and dropped them into the grass, then followed them with her blouse. A bra had been out of the question.

Naked, she stepped into the water, finding it as cold as Domi had promised. Chill bumps raced across her exposed flesh. She carried the mini-Uzi with her and held the soap in her other hand. Once in the water, she paused, noting the birds flitting around in the cattails. If someone crept up on her, the birds would probably be her first sign or warning.

Her attention was diverted to the water, too. She didn't think snakes would be in the stream, but she couldn't keep her eyes from it, either. She washed thoroughly, using only one hand and swapping soap and machine pistol as she needed to. She plunged her head under the water to wet it, then to wash the soap from it. Being clean had always made her feel better, giving her a sense of being in control of her situation. It worked now.

Finished with her bath, she walked back to the bank where she'd left her clothes and the hand towel. She dried as best as she could with the towel while holding on to the mini-Uzi. Still somewhat damp, she found a rock that had already started to warm with the morning sun and sat cross-legged.

The wound on her breast was still swollen and more discolored than it had been the day before. No red lines of infection had appeared, and that made her feel better. The slight breeze wrapped around her and finished the drying process in a matter of minutes.

While she sat there, she focused on her anger and frustration until it pushed the fear from her mind. No matter what game Bry was trying to pull, she wasn't going to allow it. The Cerberus redoubt was the only home she had, and she wasn't going to let it be destroyed.

She dressed quickly, wadded the old clothes into a ball and walked back to the campsite.

"You look better," Domi stated when she returned. She wrinkled her nose as she sat by the campfire tending to the two stakes. "Smell better, too."

"It's the socks." Brigid folded the old clothes into the saddlebags and went to join the young albino.

"You walking slow. Sore?"

"Yes."

"Going to have to take it easy getting back to Cerberus."

Brigid looked into the ruby eyes, wondering if Domi had

only said that out of respect of her wounds and general condition, or if there was an ulterior purpose. Like allowing Bry more time to return to the redoubt. She didn't like the way her thoughts were suddenly twisting and turning through her head so that she had to question everything that crossed her mind.

"We'll go as fast as we can," she told Domi. "The only thing that will slow us down will be riding double, not me."

Domi shrugged.

"I want to get back to Cerberus as quickly as we can."

An anticipatory grin filled Domi's pale features. "Going to toast Bry's chestnuts?"

Brigid knew Domi had been listening to Grant and Kane talk too much. "Yes. For starters." She took one of the steaks from the sharpened sticks. The meat was warm to the touch, but not too hot to hold. She bit into it, savoring the juices. The meat was tougher than she'd thought it would be. She chewed with effort and swallowed. "What is this?"

"Mountain lion," Domi answered simply. "Stupe bastard thought it would eat me last night. Instead, me and you eat it. Red meat is red meat."

Brigid didn't ask any more. She hoped Domi was only teasing her in an effort to get under her skin. But she didn't turn away from the meat. Her body needed to be strong, when she arrived back at Cerberus.

She fully intended to get to the bottom of the mystery of Donald Bry.

Chapter 14

"Is this where the Lost Valley of Wiy Tukay is?" Kane scanned the map Remar had unfurled across Doc Crawford's table in the center of the breakfast dishes.

Remar weighted down one corner of the map with a salt shaker and another corner with a heavy pocketknife that looked as if all it had ever known was abuse. Flakes of rust clung to the scars in the exposed tops of the blades, and Kane felt certain they were blood remnants.

Grant covered the other corners of the map with a knife and fork he'd wiped clean.

"No," Remar answered, sitting back in his chair across from Kane.

Crawford and Carrie were feeding breakfast, thin oatmeal gruel, to Beth. Kenny was outside.

Kane sat in his chair and tried not to look at Carrie. Neither of them had spoken of the previous night, but Grant had been more attentive than usual, though he didn't speak whatever was on his mind. Sleeping outside had left Kane stiff and irritable.

"This is where I'd like to meet up with you," Remar went on.

"Why?" Grant asked.

Remar glanced around the table at both men. "To give you Falzone's answer."

"His answer about what?" Kane asked.

Remar gave them a lopsided smile and pulled at his nub of an ear. "About whether he'll consider bringing you into the Lost Valley of Wiy Tukay. All this pussyfooting around you're doing here, don't you think I've got an idea of what you really want?"

"Going there wasn't it," Kane told the old man.

Grinning like a possum, Remar leaned back in his chair and laced his fingers over his crotch. "Sure, it was. Do you take me for some kind of stupe?"

"If you're thinking like that," Kane said, "mebbe we should start."

"Look," Remar said, "I knew I had the Cobaltville Mags on my ass. Do you think I would have made the meet at Tyson's saloon if I hadn't thought meeting up with the two of you wasn't important?"

"Leading an assault force of Mags to us isn't exactly impressive, either," Grant stated flatly.

"Mebbe not," Remar agreed. "'Course, they came on a little more pissed than I would have thought. But it did manage to wipe out a few of Wei Qiang's people, too."

"And two of your own," Kane said softly.

Remar nodded. "Yep. I'm going to miss those boys. They knew how to listen when a man was talking, and they weren't bad in a firefight."

"We didn't come here to sign on," Grant said.

Kane sat back and took cigars from his pocket. He passed them around, and they lit up. He puffed contentedly, his mind whirling. Lakesh's main objective had been to make some kind of contact with the tech traders and open up a dialogue with them. Then again, Kane didn't entirely trust Remar.

"I know you ain't going to sign on," Remar said. "I figure you two probably have your own group you work with. Falzone couldn't believe the work that had been done on those progs you sent me back with last time. Nobody he's got can do that sort of thing."

"Neither can we," Kane said.

Remar nodded. "I figured that, but you know who can." He paused, rounding his cigar on his empty plate. Ash fell into the remnants of the biscuits and gravy. "That's going to be one of my selling points to Falzone."

"Mebbe we aren't interested," Grant said. "After all, yesterday we found out as far as the Cobaltville Mags are concerned, it's open season on your ass. Anybody hanging around you is going to be a target, too."

Remar's expression tightened. "All I was thinking is that mebbe we could help each other out. Baron Cobalt figures he's been set up, and I can't prove it wasn't our fault. Falzone and me, we're going to have to come up with something to fix that. The baronies buy most of the stuff that we turn up, and pretty often they're using it against each other where they can. The situation's already pretty dicey."

The recent baronial war was one of the reasons Lakesh was so interested in the tech trade, Kane knew. And it was one of the reasons he'd agreed to take a hand in things.

"If we lose the baronies—" Remar said.

"You lose the blasters," Kane finished.

Remar twisted his nub of an ear. "That's the ace on the line. We can still do trading with the baronies farther east, but it's a lot harder getting back with those shipments with all the Roamers and coldhearts between here and there. And the other baronies ain't exactly keen on us trading with the others, but they put up with it. A little. It don't stop them from taking down an occasional caravan we put out."

"What do we get out of it?" Kane pressed.

"That's why I want to talk to Falzone," Remar explained. "I've seen you and your partner work. You're pure hell on wheels, and you've been together for a while. It shows. Plus, you've got access to the guy who fixed those progs. Getting him to us is going to burn your bridges with these other people, and I know that. I just put myself in your shoes, wondered what I'd take to buy into an operation while I'm stepping away from a pretty good deal." He met both their gazes levelly. "Me, I wouldn't settle for anything less than all the way in."

"I'm listening," Kane said.

Remar pointed back at the map. "You boys show up here, and I'll meet you, give you Falzone's answer."

Grant hardened his voice. "That's out to the Western Isles. I don't intend to travel all the way out there for a rejection."

"I don't think you will. When I tell Falzone about Baron Cobalt's progs, he's going to know we have no choice."

"You could find another comp engineer," Kane stated.

"Sure, but mebbe not somebody as good as your guy. Plus, I get to pick up the two of you. Until this thing gets cleared up with Baron Cobalt, I'd rather have somebody as seasoned as the two of you walking sec for me."

Kane puffed on his cigar and looked at the old man through the smoke. "We'll think about it."

BRIGID PULLED BACK on the reins and stopped the horse. The animal nickered quietly as it halted, swishing its tail at the flies that had chased them for the past half mile.

Stiff and sore, Brigid swung down out of the saddle. The impact against the ground almost folded her legs double under her. Despite the fact that the temperature was generous, especially in the deep shadows of the forest she'd been traveling, she was bathed in perspiration.

Birds cried out in protest overhead. The leaves rustled in the slight breeze, creating a wave of quiet noise.

She took the canteen from the saddle pommel and uncapped it, then drank deeply. The water was cool and soothing as it went down. The ride was making her more frustrated. Even though they'd gotten an understandably late start that morning, she'd hoped to make better time than they were.

"What's wrong?" Domi eased out of the underbrush only a few feet from Brigid. "Why stop?"

Standing only a few feet away from where the young albino had put in her appearance, Brigid had never heard Domi approach. She glanced at the younger woman and felt even more frustrated. Domi rode double with her only occasionally, wanting to rest the horse. Also, she was able to keep up foot with the pace Brigid set on the horse through the brush and because of her health.

"I'm resting the horse." Brigid capped the canteen and hung it from the saddle pommel. The way a new wave of perspiration suddenly chilled her and further soaked her blouse made her think everything she drank was pouring right through her.

Domi walked up to the horse and held some potato-like tubers she'd found in the area. The horse showed little interest until the young albino thrust the tubers under its muzzle. Once she had the animal's interest, she removed the bridle so the horse could eat and held on to the harness. "Horse looks okay. Not even sweating heavy."

"I'm resting me, too," Brigid explained.

Domi nodded and continued feeding the horse. "Like this, take us an extra day to get back to the redoubt."

"I know," Brigid acknowledged. She chafed at the loss of time, wanting to find out what was waiting for them at the Cerberus redoubt.

Chapter 15

"Actually, friend Kane, I think the prospect of you and Grant journeying out to the Western Isles is a good idea."

Kane stared into Lakesh's gaze, but the former Cobaltville administrator never flinched. They sat in the operations center inside the Cerberus redoubt. Kane swapped looks with Grant, but the big man only shrugged.

After taking a drink of the coffee in front of him, Kane asked, "Why?"

A wry smile twisted Lakesh's lips. "I promise, your reaction in this regard is most vexing. If I had disagreed with you, I'd have expected an argument. Yet, now that I agree with you, I find that I have to explain my decision—a decision, I remind you, that apparently was not mine to make in the first place."

Kane didn't buy Lakesh's statement. Over the years that he'd known him, Lakesh always played an angle. "If this was something you hadn't agreed with, you'd have argued."

Bright lights twinkled in the youthful eyes. "Exactly." Lakesh folded his thin fingers together.

"I'm liking this less and less," Kane said.

"Yet it was your idea. Perhaps you're becoming less enchanted with your own solution." Lakesh waggled a finger at the huge Mercator map on the wall. "It is a long trip into uncertain conditions."

"Not quite as far as Russia or some of the other joy spots you've sent us into," Grant observed.

Lakesh sighed, as if suddenly tired of the whole argument. "The lead you turned up in regard to the comp progs and other tech Falzone and men like him have been trading to Baron Cobalt concerns me. There are things that would be better off buried.''

"Then why have Bry fix up the bundle of comp progs for us to trade with Falzone?'' Kane asked.

Shaking his head, Lakesh said, "Surely you don't need me to explain the intricacies involved in buying into someone's trust. Your background as a Magistrate for Baron Cobalt covered that.'' He settled back into a chair. "Besides which, the progs Bry prepared for them were nothing more than a few executable files involving word processing and graphic abilities. With a few selected histories and predark geopolitical thinking thrown in for good measure.''

Kane believed that. Although Remar had seemed genuinely happy with the condition of the progs they'd delivered, Lakesh would never part with anything that would have been harmful to the redoubt or given an outside force an edge.

"When were you thinking of leaving?'' Lakesh asked.

"The sooner the better.'' Kane emptied his coffee cup, barely noticing that the contents had grown cold. "Remar is expecting us within a few days.''

"There is a gateway that has survived near there.''

Kane knew that. "Grant and I will go overland. If we show up looking fresh without the signs of a harsh trip on us, Remar's going to get suspicious.''

"Looking fresh after a mat-trans jump,'' Grant stated, "usually isn't the way those things work.''

Memories of past jumps filled Kane's mind. A headache that lasted for hours, combined with gut-churning nausea and nightmares, was the general order of the day. Things usually got worse from there.

"I'm not sure traveling overland is the wisest choice,'' Lakesh replied.

"Mebbe not, but it's the way we're going.'' Kane was surprised at the relief he felt at Lakesh's reluctance about the mission. "We'll make the necessary draws from stores later today and head out first thing in the morning."

Lakesh nodded, but he didn't look happy about the decision. Or maybe, Kane amended, he deliberately tried not to look happy about it.

"As you wish," Lakesh answered. "You have my thoughts on the matter."

Kane knew he didn't have all his thoughts on the matter. Lakesh generally always held something back. "We'll want a few more comp progs to take with us."

Lakesh looked surprised. "Why?"

"To sweeten the pot," Kane answered. "Buy a little more of that trust Falzone's willing to give us."

Lakesh nodded. "I'll attend to it."

"Why not Bry?" Grant asked softly. "I noticed he wasn't at his perch. That's not like him."

"Bry is ill," Lakesh stated.

"Never known him to be ill," Grant continued.

"Ask him about it," Lakesh said. "Although I must warn you that Bry takes his privacy about personal matters most seriously."

Kane let the comment pass and focused his attention on the coming mission. Now that Lakesh had agreed to it so readily, he no longer looked to it quite as favorably. "What about the problems Remar said Baron Cobalt's people were having with the progs Falzone had traded him?"

"You know as well as I do, friend Kane, that anything taken from the predark days isn't the most trustworthy. Time and the near destruction of this planet have taken a major toll on most things. And from what you say, Falzone and his people are taking some of the tech and progs from underwater."

"Cobalt and his people would know that," Grant said. "They'd be guarding against something like that. The way Remar tells it, Cobalt believes he was set up."

"Comp progs have never been entirely trustworthy. Besides the incompatibility some of them had with the machines designed to operate them, there were a legion of people in the predark days who lived for the opportunity to infect progs with viruses created for the sole purpose of disabling the very systems the progs were constructed to run. In the last few months of 1999, there were those who believed the world would come to chaos on January 1, 2000, because the software engineers forgot to factor in the years after 1999. Mass hysteria nearly flooded the globe. End-of-the-world parties were held. Survival rations were hoarded and stocked by several people. Terrorist groups—coldhearts, for lack of a better term—struck at the nations of the world to escalate the fear.''

"You think Cobalt was infected with a bug left over from the prenukecaust days?" Kane asked.

"Do you have another solution?" Lakesh asked.

"The progs could have been deliberately tampered with."

"You said Falzone was desirous of getting blasters from the barony," Lakesh replied. "Would deliberate sabotage of the progs he was trading to Baron Cobalt be conducive to that arrangement?"

"No." Kane felt himself growing a little irritated with the conversation. It troubled him even further that Lakesh's arguments were sound, probably even ones he'd have himself.

"Mebbe Falzone's got someone else in his group who isn't all that happy about the relationship Falzone has with Baron Cobalt," Grant said. "Remar did mention there are other groups interested in what's been found so far in the Lost Valley of Wiy Tukay. Mebbe if they get Falzone discredited, they could set up a deal of their own."

"Grant does have a point," Lakesh stated.

"Yeah." In a sour mood, Kane pushed himself up from the conference table. Despite the fact that he was calling the shots, he still didn't feel in control of the situation. Part of it, though, he realized, stemmed from the thoughts he'd been having about Carrie and Brigid.

He and Grant had been back at the redoubt for a handful of hours. Neither Domi nor Brigid appeared to be about, but he'd refrained from asking about them. There were days that passed in the redoubt when he didn't see Brigid Baptiste once. However, the same couldn't be said about Domi and Grant. The albino girl hung around Grant whenever he was there.

"Perhaps we should adjourn this meeting," Lakesh suggested. "I think we're all a little fatigued." He stood up from his chair. "If you need to talk to me further, I'll be here."

Kane surveyed the little man with a Mag's suspicion but found nothing to hang it on. Lakesh's comments had been totally understandable; the only thing Kane distrusted was the reasoning behind them.

Before the three of them could clear the conference room, a young man in a white jumpsuit stepped into the room. "Excuse me, sir," he said to Lakesh.

"Yes?"

"We've got a problem, sir. Brigid Baptiste and Domi are arriving on horseback. They're about twenty minutes out." He slapped the trans-comm at his hip. "The scout I talked to said Brigid wasn't looking any too good."

The announcement sent a cold chill ghosting through Kane. *Anam-chara.* "What's wrong?"

"Walking Dove didn't say, sir. Only that there was an obvious problem."

Walking Dove was one of the Amerindians who lived in the foothills beneath Cerberus redoubt. Kane had established an informal alliance with the tribe, part of which included scouting for intruders.

Kane was on the move at once. "Where has Brigid been?" he demanded in a hard voice.

"Nowhere that I sent her," Lakesh responded.

"You could have followed her transponder."

"She remained within the area, but I don't know what she was doing. As you well know, no matter how much I try to orchestrate events here in this redoubt, you, Brigid, Domi and Grant continue to harbor actions based solely on your own judgments."

"So whatever's wrong is her fault." Kane checked the action of his Sin Eater on his right forearm. The big-bore automatic handblaster was one of the badges of office a Magistrate carried.

Stripped down to a skeletal frame, the Sin Eater was barely fourteen inches long. Holstered on his right forearm, it was attached with actuators that flipped it into his waiting hand when he tensed his wrist tendons. The clip held twenty rounds of 9 mm ammo. There was no trigger guard, no wasted inch of design; it was one of the most wickedly efficient blasters ever made.

"I didn't say that," Lakesh protested.

"You didn't have to." Kane took the lead through the door with Grant at his heels. Lakesh trailed after them.

"WHERE HAVE YOU BEEN?" DeFore challenged.

"Sick," Bry answered.

DeFore glared through the narrow gap between Donald Bry's door and the frame. In truth, the little man did look more pallid than normal, but DeFore's skepticism ran high. Over the past couple days, she'd continued stopping by Bry's room only to get no answer. This day she'd been somewhat surprised when he'd opened the door.

"Why didn't you come see me?" she asked.

Bry blinked at her like an owl. The gap in the door was barely wide enough to reveal one bloodshot eye. "Why?"

"You were sick."

Bry nodded, as if carefully considering her words. "It was the flu. Nothing special."

"The flu?"

"Yeah." Bry shrugged. "Maybe I should have come to see you, but I figured I could tough it out on my own. I've been through worse before."

"You should have visited me." DeFore made her voice stern. "An outbreak of any kind within these walls can be dangerous. A communicable disease can run through the personnel in this redoubt in days.''

"Has anyone else been sick?" Bry asked calmly.

"No. Not with anything that's been as incapacitating as you've evidently had these last few days."

Bry nodded. "Is there anything else? I'm still feeling kind of weak."

"Let me in." DeFore pushed on the door.

Bry held the door steady, blocking it with one foot. "Why?"

"So I can take a look at you."

"I'm okay."

"Damn it, Bry, when I have a problem with one of the med comps in the triage, I don't just slap it and hope it gets all better. I call you."

"I'm better," Bry insisted.

"That's your opinion. You could relapse."

"I don't think so."

DeFore fixed him with her harsh gaze. "Open this door."

Bry hesitated for a moment, then reluctantly stepped back from the door and allowed it to open. He moved back into the center of the room.

DeFore felt uneasy as she stepped into the room. As far as she knew, she was the only person in the redoubt who'd ever entered the little man's private quarters. She carried her bag in one hand as she followed him.

Cerberus redoubt was honeycombed with rooms, from labs to the massive armory to the infirmary, as well as the operations center that Lakesh had claimed as his own. But there were also many private quarters.

Bry's rooms were small compared to DeFore's. Shelves held hundreds of books, although they weren't neatly put away, but a sense of organization reigned. More shelves held comp hardware, some of it looking functional and other pieces in various states of repair or cannibalization. Spools of wire leaked tendrils.

The main room contained a broad chair that held a couple pillows and a thick blanket. However, the chair in front of the comp station against the wall to the left showed signs of obvious wear. The comp screen flashed as numbers and letters cascaded across it.

Schematics covered the walls, inscribed with tiny lettering that DeFore recognized from memos written to her concerning her own comps that belonged to Bry. Additional papers taped next to the schematics offered more-involved views of the various projects or expansions.

The room behind the main room held a bed and closet space. It wasn't nearly as neat. Clothing draped the bed, some of it clean and some of it obviously piled awaiting washing. A dank musty smell pervaded the room, mixed with the scent of heated electronics. DeFore got the feeling the bed was never slept in.

"Didn't anyone ever teach you to clean up after yourself?" DeFore asked.

Bry appeared defensive, though it was unclear whether it was about the room or something else. "I don't spend a lot of time here."

"You sleep."

Bry shrugged. "Occasionally."

DeFore pointed to the big chair. "Sit."

Reluctantly, Bry sat. "I'm fine. Why won't you believe me?"

"You haven't been outside of this room in days," DeFore said. "That's not like you."

"I've never been sick like this before."

"All the more reason to check you out now." DeFore unlimbered a stethoscope and placed the circular disk against Bry's thin chest. She listened for a moment. The little tech's heart beat strongly, the pulse only a little elevated. "When was the last time you were out of the redoubt?"

Bry shrugged. "Weeks. I don't care much for outside."

DeFore listened as the man's heart sped a little. Lying, she knew, could cause heart-rate acceleration. "What did you do?" She moved the disk on his chest.

"I don't remember," Bry replied irritably. "Probably Lakesh wanted me to repair one of the outside sec alarms."

DeFore noticed the accelerated heart rate again. Bry had learned to lie with a straight face some time ago, but it was obviously a stressful experience for him. "Haven't you heard me beating on the door the past few days?"

"Yeah."

"Why didn't you answer it?"

"If I'd wanted to see you, I knew where to find you." His tone was belligerent.

"Yeah, I guess you did." DeFore took out a blood-pressure cuff and a thermometer. "Roll up your sleeve."

Bry glanced away from her petulantly, then reluctantly rolled up his sleeve. "You don't need to do this. You could simply check my transponder readings."

"I haven't had access to them lately. I figured you knew that." DeFore slipped the thermometer into Bry's mouth, then fastened the blood-pressure cuff. Minutes later, both readings came out normal and nearly so. Elevated blood pressure was another sign of stress.

"Well...?" Bry demanded.

"You're fine." DeFore tucked her instruments back in her bag.

Bry smiled a little, positively gleeful for him. "I told you."

DeFore moved toward the door. "I'd like to give you something."

"What? You just said everything was normal."

"Some advice," DeFore said. "I'd stay out of Kane's and Grant's sight for a little while. Brigid and Domi are returning to the redoubt, and Brigid isn't doing very well."

"She's all right?"

"She's alive," DeFore answered.

Bry couldn't quite cover the look of relief that washed over him.

"And mistakes like that are going to get noticed. Grant and Kane have been up against a lot tougher guys than you."

"I don't know what you're talking about," Bry said.

"I'm talking about the scratches on your cheek and forehead. I'd say they're from branches. And then there's that unaccustomed sunburn. Maybe you haven't noticed because you haven't been exactly cozy with a mirror lately, but they're there."

Bry touched his face. His fingers left momentary white spots on his pink flesh.

"You'd better hope Brigid Baptiste is all right," DeFore said, "because if Kane ever figures out you left her out there on her own in the shape she was in, he's going to take a pound of flesh from your ass." She closed the door behind her, enjoying the apprehensive look on Bry's face.

Chapter 16

Kane stood outside the Cerberus redoubt and scanned the mountainside below with a compact pair of Bausch & Lomb microbinoculars. The figures in the distance were only a moving blob to the naked eye, but through the lenses he spotted Brigid Baptiste barely hanging on to the saddle pommel of the horse Domi led through the sparse brush covering the foothills of the Darks. When he saw how weak Brigid was, his chest felt too tight.

"Where the hell has she been?" Kane demanded.

"Friend Kane," Lakesh said worriedly, "you would have to ask her to find out the answer to that question."

Kane bit back a scathing retort. He knew Lakesh's own feelings toward Brigid ran strong. After all, the former administrator had helped shape her entire destiny and had hand-picked her for the Cerberus redoubt.

Hooves rang on stone behind Kane.

Grant led two horses up from the small corral they kept for short overland travel, guessing that Brigid had gotten her own mount from there, as well. The horses were supplied by the Amerindians who lived in the foothills below the redoubt. Kane took one of the horses from Grant without a word, slipped his foot into the stirrup, grabbed the pommel and pulled himself into the saddle.

The horse shifted under him, reminding him how much he hated the rolling motion that was so graceful for the animal yet went against everything he'd been trained for. He guided the animal down the steep, narrow trail. The saddle scabbard held an M-16 with an M-203 gren launcher. From what he'd been able to see, Domi and Brigid weren't being pursued.

At the bottom of the foothills, Kane kicked the horse gently in the sides, guiding it into a gentle gallop. Once he was down in the tree line, he lost sight of Brigid and Domi for a few minutes. The tree line didn't last. On the other side of it he spotted Brigid and Domi immediately. He swept the terrain around them out of habit.

"Hey, Grant," Domi called out when they reached her, offering him a bright smile.

"What happened?" Kane demanded.

Brigid glanced up from her slumped position in the saddle. Her complexion was pasty and dark circles ringed her eyes. Fatigue hammered the horse's muscles.

"Snakebit," Domi answered. "Got most of the poison out. Told her to rest, but she wanted get back here. Pushed too hard, without letting her body heal some first."

Without thinking about it, Kane rode over to Brigid's horse, yanked the reins to still the animal, then took the woman into his arms. He could feel the fever in her body against his chest.

"I'm not happy about it, either, Kane." Brigid's voice was whisper thin. Her emerald eyes shone bright with fever and anger.

Kane realized his own aggravation at his wayward thoughts had shown on his face and Brigid had assumed it was directed at her. "Take it easy, Baptiste. I'm going to get you to DeFore."

"I could have gotten there on my own," she insisted weakly.

"Yeah." Kane grinned tightly. "I know you could have." He took up the reins to his horse again in his left hand, cradling Brigid's upper body against his arm. He kept his right arm around her, holding her close, and the action seemed to bring back memories of similar incidents. "Easy, Baptiste, you're going to get there."

She didn't hear him, though. When he glanced down, he

saw that she'd curled in tight against him and either passed out or fallen asleep. He urged the horse to go a little faster.

A THIN COLD WIND FILLED the western mountain pass.

Mallet sat in the passenger seat of the Sandcat at the bottom of the narrow trail leading up through the pass. He'd been that far west of Cobaltville before, but he could count the number of times on one hand with fingers left over.

"Sir?" the Mag behind the wheel asked.

"Wait," Mallet said. He released the door lock and stepped out. Sand and rock crunched underfoot. The sky above was swirled purple and yellow with chem clouds that held the promise of blistering acid rain. On this side of the mountains it rained often.

Four men dressed in worn clothing and animal skins rode horses out of the rocks ahead. They carried rifles across their pommels. All of them had wrinkled, seamed features below their fur caps. Two of them wore necklaces of human teeth, some already turning black with rot.

Six skeletons, some of them missing limbs, hung from stakes driven deep into the ground near the entrance of the pass. Two other stakes held corpses that were only days dead. Small gray birds flitted around them, stripping the flesh from the face near the hollowed-out eyes. Insects trooped along the flaccid flesh under the ragged pieces of clothing that had been left to them.

Two other Mags, dressed as Mallet was in the long Kevlar-weave coats that covered them from neck to calves, stepped out of the Sandcat, as well. They fell into step behind Mallet, flanking him on either side.

Mallet strode purposefully forward, keeping his hands empty and in sight.

"That's far enough," the lead rider said. He shifted the Sharps .50-caliber buffalo rifle on the saddle pommel to cover the Magistrate. "Name's Goldberg, and this here's my pass. I know you're wearing a bulletproof jacket, but I've seen this old fifty penetrate that armor sometimes. And when it don't, just stopping a round from this big-mouthed bastard leaves a man all busted up inside.''

Mallet stood his ground twenty feet from the men, looking up at them across the steep incline. They didn't step down from the horses. The Mag commander glanced up at the high mountains surrounding the pass. They were too steep to allow the Sandcats up, and even a man on foot would have a hard time of it. Farther up there was little protection in case the acid rain clouds opened up. The pass was wide enough to allow only one Sandcat to drive through at a time.

"If you recognize the jacket and the wag," Mallet said evenly, "then you know what I am."

Goldberg leaned out over his horse, never taking his eyes from Mallet, and spit a long stream of tobacco juice. "Mags don't cut much ice up here in the high country. Don't much give a fuck who or what you say you are. This here's my pass, and anybody ever going to travel it is gonna pay the toll. Gimme the scrip or go back."

"Never met a man who owned part of a mountain range." Mallet showed him a thin grin.

The click of the Sharps's hammer drawing back sounded loud even over the purr of the Sandcat's engine. "Not the whole range," Goldberg growled. "Just this one little pass. You don't want to pay the toll, you can go over or around."

"I'm looking for a man," Mallet said, and pointed to his ear. "He's real noticeable. Scarred up and only got one ear. Name's Remar."

"Information costs extra."

In spite of the situation, Mallet laughed. Black spots of rage spun in his vision, and he felt the killing urge sweep over him. "Mebbe you ain't met many Mags, old man. You're looking at one Sandcat, but I got five more stopped only a short distance away. I put a call through on the trans-comm, and you got nine kinds of hell breathing down your neck."

Goldberg spit another stream of tobacco and smiled in anticipation. "Six Sandcats, huh? Well, me and the boys, we ain't never had a payday like this before."

"The twin machine guns on the Cat here could take out you and your buddies," Mallet said.

"Before or after I put a round into your chest?" Goldberg asked. He shook his head. "Even then, you ain't gonna stop the grens set up along the mountain ridge that will fill this pass with rock if you try anything."

Mallet glanced along the ridges on either side of the pass. Nothing moved, but he was sure Goldberg wasn't bluffing. "Sir," Teach said over the trans-comm plug in Mallet's ear, "we're in position on both sides of the pass. Confirm three coldhearts on either side of the pass. We have them all in our sights."

During the trek out from Utah, the Magistrate group had heard about Goldberg and the pass. Mallet had sent his men on foot an hour before they'd rolled into the area.

"Remar," Mallet reminded.

"Let me see the color of your scrip."

Mallet tagged the trans-comm button in his left hand. "Take 'em down," he ordered in a low whisper that carried over the throat mike.

Almost immediately, blasterfire echoed along the ridgeline. The three coldhearts with Goldberg glanced up. Only Goldberg retained the presence of mind to lift the heavy Sharps to his shoulder.

Mallet was already in motion, tensing his wrist to flip the Sin Eater into his waiting hand as he dived to one side. The .50-cal bullet ripped through the space where he'd been standing, and he heard Cramer grunt in pain behind him.

"I want Goldberg alive," Mallet growled as he threw the Sin Eater straight out. "Kill these other coldheart bastards." He stroked the trigger and sent a 3-round burst crashing through the head of the horse Goldberg rode. The animal died instantly, its legs splaying out while the coldheart leader struggled to feed another round into the single-shot rifle.

Goldberg slithered free of the saddle and moved for cover provided by a large boulder on one side of the pass. Before he reached it, a bullet-riddled corpse dropped from the ridge above and smashed against the ground only inches away.

One of the other riders got off a spray of blasterfire that peppered Mallet's long coat. The bulletproof weave easily stopped the rounds. The Mag commander strode forward as he was trained, relying on the fear of the Magistrate Division. Every slagger and outlander knew that Mags were relentless. The rider pitched from his horse in the next breath, 9 mm bullets punching his face into crimson ruin.

Goldberg thumbed a cartridge into the rifle's receiver. His eyes looked as hard as gun sights as he stared at Mallet.

The blasterfire on the ridges above lasted only a moment longer. "Sir," Teach called calmly over the trans-comm, "confirm all the targets are down. No one escaped. We're removing the grens now."

"Good." Mallet raised the Sin Eater again and sprayed Goldberg's legs.

The old man proved tougher than Mallet would have thought because he pulled the heavy buffalo rifle to his shoulder defiantly, screaming out in murderous rage.

Disregarding the instinctive impulse that fired through him and tried to take him to ground, Mallet aimed at Goldberg's exposed left shoulder and squeezed off a single round. The thunderclap of the Sharps's detonation cracked and filled the pass with echoes.

Goldberg went backward immediately, but Mallet wasn't sure if it was from the buffalo rifle's recoil or the 9 mm round hitting him. The old man reached for the blaster again, screaming curses at his legs as they gave out beneath him.

Mallet stepped on the rifle, pinning the weapon to the ground. Goldberg ripped a skinning knife from his sleeve with his good hand, pushing up and slicing at Mallet's face.

The Mag commander dodged back, but not in time to completely evade the vicious blade. The razor-edged tip scored his right jawbone from the lobe of his ear almost to the point of his chin. The icy shock of the wound burned along his jaw.

"Damn," Mallet swore as he felt warm blood running down his neck. He drove a boot into Goldberg's face, pulping the old man's nose and knocking out his two front teeth.

Goldberg's head hit the ground, then he came back up with the knife, spitting blood and broken teeth that splashed across the Mag commander's chest.

Mallet caught the knife on the Sin Eater, then grabbed Goldberg's wrist in his empty hand and twisted. The old man's arm broke like kindling. Even as he screamed in pain, hatred still burning in his eyes, Mallet kicked him in the face again. Goldberg hit the ground, then lifted his head and spit blood again, drops coloring the Mag commander's face.

"Old man's like a broke-backed snake," Iverson said as he stepped up beside his superior. "Gonna have to chill him to put him down."

"Mebbe," Mallet grunted. "But stepping on his head will slow him down some." He planted a boot on Goldberg's throat and held the man on the ground, then shoved the Sin Eater's wicked muzzle against the old man's cheek under his left eye. "Tell me about Remar."

"You go to hell!" Goldberg shouted. "Chill me and fucking be done with it."

Mallet grinned. "It's not going to be that easy." He thrust the Sin Eater's barrel into Goldberg's mouth, sliding it easily across the blood-slickened lips and through the gap where the missing teeth had been.

The old man screamed at the searing pain from the heated barrel blistering the inside of his mouth. He gagged on the blood, finally having to swallow it. Bright red bubbles burst around the Sin Eater's barrel.

"We lost Remar's trail yesterday," Mallet said. "Looking at the map, knowing he was head out west, this was the closest pass we guessed he'd head for."

"Never seen him," Goldberg choked out around the blaster in his mouth.

"I don't believe you." Mallet twisted the Sin Eater inside the old man's mouth, placing the muzzle against his cheek and pressing hard.

Goldberg's eyes widened when he realized what the Mag commander intended.

"That's right, you old fucker," Mallet said. "You ain't ever met nobody like me. Me and other people's pain, we've spent a lot of time together." He touched the trigger and blasted a round through the old man's cheek. He held the heated muzzle against the wound to maximize the pain and minimize the blood loss by cauterizing it. He settled back and listened to Goldberg's screams.

KANE STARED at the angry red infection staining the twin puncture wounds between Brigid Baptiste's breasts. He stood behind DeFore as the woman prepped the operating tray.

"Big snake," DeFore commented. "If Domi hadn't sucked the venom out right after the strike, Brigid would have probably been dead right there." She used a scalpel to open the Xs that had already been cut into Brigid's flesh. Thick greenish pus spurted from the wounds.

"Is she going to be all right?" Kane asked in a hoarse voice.

"Yes." DeFore wiped away the infection, then used a swab to clean the wounds. She kept up her efforts until fresh blood flowed more freely than the pus. "Another few days of pushing herself like that without the proper treatment, those wounds would have turned nasty."

Kane stared at Brigid's pale features. Since he'd taken her into his arms, she'd never regained consciousness. Seeing her like that, so helpless, wasn't easy.

"As it is," DeFore said, "with the proper treatment, a good line of antibiotics and a few days' bed rest, she'll be up and around.'' She prepared a syringe, tapping a fingernail against the side to make sure all the air bubbles were gone.

Kane stood there with his arms folded across his chest. "What was she doing out there?"

DeFore plunged the needle into Brigid's arm, then depressed the plunger. "I don't know. Did you ask Lakesh?"

"He says he didn't know."

DeFore applied thick yellow antiseptic to Brigid's wounds. "Do you believe him?"

"No."

"Me neither." DeFore unfastened Brigid's belt. "Give me a hand undressing her."

Kane hesitated.

"Don't play shy. You've seen naked women before. Help me get her comfortable so I don't dump her off the table and hurt her worse than she is."

Reluctantly, Kane helped. They stripped Brigid's clothing and underwear from her and laid her in the center of the bed. Kane couldn't help looking at the long-limbed beauty and feeling more than a little uncomfortable. When DeFore pulled a clean white sheet and blanket over her, Brigid shifted restlessly, her features waxen from the low-grade fever that filled her.

"Did you notice Bry's absence?" DeFore asked.

"Lakesh said he's been sick."

"That," DeFore said, "might be worth asking about, too."

Chapter 17

In the stillness of the infirmary, Kane came awake when Brigid's hand twitched in his. He stood up from the chair where he'd been sitting and looked down at her.

"Kane?" Brigid's emerald-green eyes searched his face, then roved the darkened room.

"Yeah. Relax, Baptiste, you're going to be fine."

"I knew that. Generally, waking up is a good sign." Brigid lifted the sheet and peered down at her chest, careful not to expose her nudity to Kane. The chill air in the room had formed small, hard peaks at the tops of her breasts. "Did DeFore look at me?"

Kane nodded.

Brigid let the sheet drop, trapping it under her armpits. She pulled her hand from his, having to make two attempts because Kane forgot he was holding it and instinctively tightened his grip.

"How long have you been here?" she asked.

"Since I brought you here."

"Oh." Brigid was quiet, and Kane knew she was thinking about all the implications of the announcement.

"It wasn't anything I hadn't seen before, Baptiste," Kane growled, then changed the subject.

"Mebbe we could talk about how you came to be snake-bit."

Brigid shifted her gaze to him. "Why?"

Kane shrugged and ticked off points on his fingers. "You're too careful to get accidentally bitten by a snake. Traveling away from the redoubt isn't something you're normally prone to do. And there's still a horse missing from the corral.''

"It's dead," Brigid stated flatly. "A coldheart band shot it out from under me."

"What the hell were you doing out there, Baptiste?" Kane couldn't believe she'd left the redoubt on her own.

"No more than you would have done," Brigid replied.

Kane breathed evenly through his nose and swore to himself that he wasn't going to lose his temper. "Going out into the mountains and getting bitten by a snake is not something I would have done."

Brigid's eyes narrowed. "Things didn't exactly work out the way I'd planned them, Kane."

"Seeing you coming in here half-dead, I kind of figured that."

She arched her brows, studying his face. "How did things go down in Utah territory? Judging from the scrapes and cuts I can see even in this dim light, I don't think things went exactly according to plan, either."

"We made contact with the man we were looking for."

"I didn't fail at what I was doing." In spite of the hoarseness in her voice, Brigid's words rang strongly in the quiet room.

"I didn't say you did, Baptiste. What I meant was that you and Domi didn't have to go alone. There are people here who could have gone with you."

"Domi didn't go with me."

Kane shook his head and crossed arms over his chest. "Going out there by yourself is damn stupe."

"There wasn't any other way."

"There's always another way," Kane argued. "Even a seasoned Mag doesn't walk into a situation without backup."

"You weren't here, Kane. The decision I made was valid."

"And getting chilled would have given you even more validation?"

"That's not what I said. Even on my own, that coldheart band spotted me."

"You should have waited till Grant and I got back," Kane said, trying to understand what had possessed Brigid enough to try something like that on her own. "We're better at this than you ever will be."

Brigid pushed herself up from the bed, her back ramrod straight. She stood on the floor, the bed between them, trying to wrap the sheet around her and maintain her dignity. The dignity worked, but the sheet cascaded around her briefly, revealing a quick glimpse of her rounded buttocks. Brigid quickly hauled up the sheet and turned to face him.

"Don't lecture me, Kane," she told him sternly. "I can remember a few times when I put everything on the line to save you and Grant after one of your plans went awry."

Kane raised his hands in surrender, wondering again what it was about Brigid Baptiste that sometimes kept him on the edge of anger. It would help, he felt, if she would just listen to him. "That's not how I meant it, Baptiste."

"Yes, it is."

"Okay, mebbe I meant it, but I didn't mean for it to come out so bald-faced like that."

"An insult doesn't feel better just because it sounds better."

"I didn't mean it as an insult," Kane said. "It was an observation. I mean, if something needs to be researched, would you want me and Grant trying to find it?"

"No."

"That's all I'm getting at."

Brigid lifted her chin stubbornly. "I'm better than what you may want to believe, Kane. These last few years have been an education for me. If it hadn't been for a little bad luck, they'd never have known I was there."

"A little more bad luck, Baptiste," Kane said soberly, "and mebbe you wouldn't be here at all."

"It didn't happen, so deal with it."

"What were you doing out there?"

Brigid's brow knitted in puzzlement. "Lakesh hasn't said anything?"

"Only that he didn't know where you were. Or why you were there." Kane studied Brigid's face, knowing from her inattention to him that her mind was busy thinking about what he'd told her. "Did he know?"

"Lakesh could have tracked my transponder."

"I thought of that."

"But it's possible he didn't."

Kane shook his head. "Did you tell him you were going?"

"No. I didn't expect to be gone more than a day."

With effort, Kane curbed himself from pointing out Brigid's further lack of planning. "But once you were, and Lakesh would have noticed you missing after a few hours, he'd have checked on you."

"And what would he have done then?" Brigid demanded. "Sent someone after me and had them haul me back to the redoubt?"

"He didn't," Kane pointed out. "But you can bet he knew where you were and that you were in trouble. So why didn't he send help?"

Brigid's tone was more neutral, more evidence that she was thinking the situation through, as well. "Domi was there. If he knew about me, he knew about her."

"Why was she there?"

"She claimed she got bored."

Kane nodded. Where the albino was concerned, he could believe that. "Mebbe. And mebbe Lakesh sent her."

"Why?"

Kane locked eyes with Brigid. "I guess that depends on why you were out there."

Brigid dodged the question. "What happened in Utah?"

Surrendering for the moment, Kane gave her a quick rundown on everything that had happened with Remar, leaving out the details about Carrie and her sister.

"You're planning on going out to the Western Isles?" Brigid asked when he'd finished.

"Yes."

"When?"

"Tonight."

Brigid's face hardened. "You just got back."

"The trail's only going to get cold if we wait, Baptiste. Baron Cobalt's Mags and the Tong are already barking at Remar's heels. If he didn't escape them, he may lead them straight to Falzone and the Lost Valley of Wiy Tukay."

"I'm in no shape for that kind of trip."

"You weren't going."

"Why?"

"This isn't something you should get overinvested in. Me and Grant are going to be bouncing between Falzone, the Tong and the Mag pursuit group. On top of that, Remar says Falzone's got his own problems with other people."

"I see," Brigid said coldly.

"It's going to be a hard trip, Baptiste, not something you want any part of."

"I'm tougher than you think, Kane."

Kane nodded. "I already knew that. You don't have anything to prove to me."

"That's not how it feels."

"Mebbe not, but that's coming from you—not me."

Brigid turned and searched the nearby cabinets. The sheet she'd wound around herself came open a little, revealing the glorious expanse of one long leg. The dim light set fire to her red-gold hair.

"What are you doing?" Kane asked.

"Looking for my clothes."

"DeFore threw them out. There wasn't any way of saving them. There's a bag there that has your personal effects."

Brigid took the bag from one of the pegs inside the clothing cabinet, pulled the sheet more tightly around herself and walked unsteadily toward the door.

"Where are you going?" Kane demanded.

Brigid opened the door. "To my room. I can lie here or there, and if I get to choose—which I do—I'm going to do it there."

"I thought you were going to tell me what you were doing away from the redoubt."

Brigid eyed him levelly. "Don't worry about it. It's nothing I can't handle." She paused. "It's not something you'd want to overinvest in." She stepped into the silent hallway and left Kane alone in the room.

"WHERE'S BRY?" Kane demanded a few minutes later.

Lakesh turned from the comp monitor he'd been working at. "He's in his room. He's been sick for days."

"Sick with what?" Kane stayed relentless. He was still angry with the way the conversation had gone with Brigid, and with the fact that he felt like the last one to know what was going on at the redoubt.

"A viral infection, friend Kane," Lakesh replied. "It's nothing you should concern yourself with. Another day or two and he should return to his post in full health."

"That's convenient."

Lakesh blinked innocently. "I beg your pardon."

"That he's not here now," Kane said, "as we're getting ready to leave."

"You could go by and see him for yourself," Lakesh suggested.

"I tried," Kane replied. "I beat on his damn door but I got no answer."

"Perhaps he's asleep."

"Mebbe he's not even in there," Kane suggested.

"Well," Lakesh said, "there is a quick remedy for that concern." He tapped the keyboard and pointed at the Mercator map on the wall. "Donald Bry's transponder location."

Kane watched the map, seeing the blip that showed up suddenly on the topography. He instantly identified the area as the Darks. In the next moment, a screen opened below the Mercator projection, tightening the transponder scan. Cerberus redoubt showed on the screen, continuing to enlarge and shift as the transponder was tracked down through the various rooms and levels of the complex. When the search finished, the blip beat constantly, flashing in the personnel quarters.

"Donald Bry is in his room, friend Kane," Lakesh said. "According to the readout, his heart rate is accelerated and he seems to be somewhat stressed."

"There's no fever?"

"None that I see. But that could come and go."

"You have the master key to every room in this redoubt," Kane said. "Let me have it."

"I can't do that," Lakesh said. "I won't. Each person in this redoubt has the right to privacy."

"Since when?" Grant asked as he strode into the room, Domi drifting along at his side.

"Privacy is a creature necessity I willingly honor as long as it doesn't conflict with the most important needs of this complex," Lakesh answered. "I would expect you to honor and agree with that view." A bright smile filled his face as he held out his hands. "Darlingest Domi, how nice to see you again."

The albino girl raced across the room and took Lakesh's hands. Both of them looked elfin.

Neither of them, Kane had to admit, looked guilty.

"Was there anything further you had to say on the matter of Donald Bry's absence, friend Kane?" Lakesh looked up at Kane, still holding delicately to one of Domi's hands.

Kane briefly considered forcing the issue. "No. I'm done here."

"Good. Then we can move on to other business." Lakesh reached for an old, weathered leather satchel sitting by the monitor worktable. "I have the comp progs you can take to Falzone and his group of scavengers."

Kane took the satchel and hung it over one shoulder. "This stuff all works?"

"Yes, friend Kane. I guarantee that Falzone will be interested in this sampling of the progs Bry and I have unearthed from the Cerberus archives. After listening to your tale of how his people are searching underwater for the items they're retrieving, I think he'll definitely be interested in this particular batch."

"We'll find out soon enough," Kane growled.

"When are you leaving?" Lakesh asked.

"Tonight. Like I said, there are a lot of miles between here and the Western Isles."

"As I pointed out, friend Kane, there exists the possibility of using the gateway to jump there and save yourselves considerable wear and tear on that journey."

"And if Falzone or Remar have a secondary group coming after us?" Kane pointed out. "That country up there gets tight. A number of the mountain ranges are impassable, and we just show up there with someone coming along our backtrail, we might as well flush whatever trust we've earned so far."

"Perhaps you are right," Lakesh admitted.

"That's an ace on the line. Easy isn't always." Kane turned on his heel and strode toward the door. Grant fell in behind him.

"Friend Kane," Lakesh called, "please make sure the transcomm in the wag is in good working order before you leave. Communications may prove impossible along the way at different points, but I'd like to maintain it where and when we're able."

"Right," Kane growled.

Chapter 18

"Things didn't go well with Brigid?"

Hair wet from the quick shower he'd taken, Kane swung into the jeep's passenger seat. For their long overland journey, the jeep would be more comfortable—and less noticeable—than a Sandcat. Like Grant, he'd put on fresh clothing, including a shirt with long, loose sleeves that concealed the Sin Eater strapped to his right forearm. "She's hardheaded."

"True." Grant smiled as he keyed the ignition. The sound of the powerful engine filled the underground garage. "But that's one of the things we both admire about her."

"She's also up to something."

"About Bry?"

"Mebbe." Kane turned and flipped open the cargo hatch containing self-heats, ring-pulls and extra ammo for their weapons. The cargo box had a false bottom where they stored their black polycarbonate Mag armor. Kane had decided to pack it in case events in the Western Isles turned out to be a cast-iron, one-percenter bitch. There were plenty of people in the Outlands who hated the Mags and the barons they stood for, but they also feared them. And the armor had stood between him and a lot of damage for years. "DeFore warned me about him, too."

"What did she say?" Grant steered through the long corridor.

"DeFore suggested that Bry might not have been as sick as we've been told."

"And?"

"And nothing," Kane said irritably. "I don't think she knows anything more. Did you talk to Domi?"

"Yeah."

"What did she have to say?"

"Little Miss Innocence," Grant replied. "Just happened to be there in time to save Brigid's ass when she got bitten by the snake."

"Do you believe that?"

Grant lifted his massive shoulders and dropped them. "Mebbe. Domi said she got bored, noticed Brigid leaving and took off after her, not letting Brigid know she was there. Like it was a game. I can see that."

Kane studied the massive vanadium door waiting at the end of the corridor. "Me too. But if she was there, she probably saw what Brigid saw. And neither of them is telling us the whole story."

Grant spoke into his trans-comm. A hidden comm aboard the jeep boosted the signal, guaranteeing that they'd be able to stay in touch with Cerberus most of the trip. "Open the damn door, Lakesh."

A moment later, the lights went out as the huge vanadium door hummed and slid into the housing beside the doorway. The wag sped through the opening. As the vanadium door slid closed like an accordion behind them, Grant slipped on a pair of NVGs. Kane did the same, letting the lenses strip the night from the surrounding terrain, turning it into a blend of greens and blacks.

Grant pulled onto the main access road leading down from the redoubt.

Sensing someone's eyes on him, Kane turned in the seat. With the NVGs on, he could just make out the feminine figure standing on one of the higher mountain peaks where the chain-like fencing ran. She watched until the steep grade took her from Kane's sight.

"THERE'S NO OTHER WAY but that pass. Unless you want to add a day or two travel time across some really rough country."

Standing beside the wag, Kane trained his binoculars over the mountain pass. They were long, hard days from Cerberus. Other than two skirmishes with scavenging Roamers and a confrontation in a roadhouse that had turned both bloody and deadly, the trip out west had been relatively quiet.

"They've got a group of coldhearts working a toll." Kane surveyed the high walls towering over the narrow pass. Even with the wag's four-wheel drive, going over the mountains was out of the question. He focused on the standing crosses, spotting the bodies hanging from them. Three of them looked fresh.

"We've got the scrip," Grant said.

"If that's all they're after." Kane put the binoculars away. "Let's roll."

Grant put the wag in gear and drove up the steep incline toward the pass and the waiting coldhearts. He took a mini-Uzi from under the seat and laid it just under his thigh for easy access.

Kane took up a Mossberg pump riot shotgun with a pistol grip from the floorboard. A short bandolier was mounted below the shotgun's action, and Kane had extra shells in the jacket he'd put on against the morning's chill.

As the wag drew closer, the coldhearts moved into position. Only one man stood in the center of the pass, but Kane counted nearly a dozen blasters trained on their wag.

Grant kept his foot steady on the accelerator. "Got a hinky feeling about this."

"Yeah," Kane agreed, cradling the Mossberg in both hands.

The coldheart in the pass waved them to a halt. Grant stopped short fifteen feet away, one hand on the wheel and the other on the 9 mm blaster beside his leg.

"No need to be shy, gents." The coldheart was short and scrawny, dressed in remnants of a mil-spec uniform. Gray duct tape was wrapped raggedly around his hard-used boots. He carried a bolt-action .30-06 canted on his hip. Radiation burns had left scarred ruins on the right side of his face, turning his eye milky white with blindness. "We're open for bidness."

Kane dropped the shotgun muzzle over the man's chest and said easily, "So are we."

Some of the confident smile left the coldheart's face. "I wouldn't want to open the ball on this patch of trouble, I was you."

"The last son of a bitch I'd want to be in this situation," Kane said, "is you." He moved the shotgun meaningfully.

The coldheart paled. "Just doing bidness here, that's all. Can't let you go through for free. We spent some blood getting set up here and deserve something for keeping this pass free."

"How much is the toll?"

The coldheart raised his voice. "Morgan? How much for a wag and two riders?"

"Shit," Grant breathed quietly, "if they don't have a set price, they're either real damn new at this or they haven't been charging the people who have been going through this pass."

"Yeah." Kane waited, the shotgun's muzzle never wavering.

"You running jolt or pop-skull?" one of the men taking cover called down.

"No," Kane replied.

"You ain't no trader, and you don't look like no settler passing through. What bidness you got out this way, then?"

"None of yours," Kane said.

The coldheart standing in the pass tried to take a step back.

Kane looked at the man down the shotgun barrel. "Don't move."

The man froze.

"The toll's fifty for the wag, twenty-five apiece for riders," Morgan called out. "Brings the total to a hundred."

"You're too high," Kane replied without hesitation.

"It's my pass," Morgan replied. "I reckon I know what

it's worth to pass through. If you don't have the scrip, we can work out a trade for one of those blasters you're carrying."

"It's worth fifty to me not to have to go around."

Morgan was quiet for a short time. "I'll take the fifty."

"Send your man over for it," Kane instructed.

"Kelly," Morgan ordered, "go on over there. We got your back."

Obvious reluctance filled the man as he walked over to the wag. Kane used one hand to take the scrip from his shirt pocket, flipping out the fifty in greasy notes they'd traded for at a roadhouse yesterday. He tossed it onto the ground at Kelly's feet.

The coldheart licked his lips nervously, then bent to clutch the notes in a dirty, scarred fist.

"Step aside," Kane ordered.

Kelly trotted backward, almost tripping himself in his haste. "I got it, Morgan."

"Let 'em go," Morgan yelled.

Kane watched the men shifting on the mountainsides, picking up more of them along the towering ridges. His point man's senses flared to life, picking up more movement than he thought was necessary.

Grant let out the clutch and the wag's four-wheel drive spun all the tires until they found traction. He kept the mini-Uzi under his thigh.

Kane watched the ridges, realizing how vulnerable they were to an avalanche of rock that could be spilled down onto them. Figures flitted on both sides, visible for only a moment, then dropping into new positions with cover.

"Damn!" Grant growled as a diesel engine's roar filled the pass.

Looking forward, Kane watched as an eighteen-wheeler pulled into the pass, blocking the way. The huge wag had pieces missing that revealed the large engine and the tops of the tall tires. Smoke billowed from the rusted stacks that vibrated and shivered. The windshields had been broken out long ago, but someone had replaced them with steel plating that showed bullet scars.

Grant jammed on the brakes, holding the wag straight. Gears ground as Grant tried to force the transmission into reverse. The tires stuttered against the stones lining the pass, burning off rubber.

Kane aimed the shotgun at the small rectangular aperture left in the steel plating over the wag's windshield and squeezed the trigger. The double-aught buckshot slammed against the rusted steel, striking sparks and leaving dents but not penetrating. The face on the other side ducked out of the way, unharmed.

The mighty wag kept coming and gunners stepped out onto armored platforms on either side of the cab. They fired their blasters but the vibrations shivering through the big wag, as well as the rugged trail, left them unable to shoot accurately.

Kane shot at the coldhearts on the wag to keep them honest and concerned about their own necks.

Swinging his arm over the back of his seat, Grant peered behind them and pressed the accelerator to the floor.

Kane turned back, hunkering down as Grant did, and barely caught sight of the chains dragging a group of flat metal trays across the ground. Sunlight glinted from the sharp points mounted on them.

"Spikes!" Kane roared. He tried to target the men pulling the chains, but they'd taken cover on either side of the pass.

"I see them," Grant yelled. He stepped down hard on the brakes again, barely controlling the wag as it skittered across the loose rock covering the floor of the pass.

The spiked platforms covered the end of the pass as the diesel came slowly forward.

"I don't want to risk four flat tires," Grant stated.

"Neither do I," Kane said. "Even if we managed to get away from here, I don't want to be left without transportation."

Bullets ricocheted from the wag and shattered rocks around them.

"Around the wag, then?" Grant asked.

"It's the only chance we have." Kane drew a bead on a coldheart along the ridgeline above. The twenty-five-yard distance with the shotgun fully choked kept the buckshot tight.

The coldheart's head disappeared in a sudden burst of crimson even as the buckshot that hit his shoulder spun him. The dead man tumbled on the ridge and fell down, starting a small avalanche of rock and dust. The corpse plummeted to the jeep's hood, getting hit by at least two more rounds.

Grant shoved the gearshift into first again and popped the clutch, launching them forward. Kane left the dead man across the wag's hood as extra protection from the coldheart blasters.

Grant closed the distance on the diesel truck. The grade to the left looked slightly less steep, and scraggly brush that might provide a small amount of traction peppered the side. If one of the tires didn't get cut out from under them, he thought they might have a chance.

Grant pulled hard left at the last minute, neatly avoiding locking bumpers with the massive diesel. Even with four-wheel drive, the jeep dug frantically for traction, barely able to pull them up the incline out of the diesel's path.

The ride was bumpy, violently rocking Kane and Grant back and forth. They lost the coldheart's corpse almost immediately. The body dropped to the ground and disappeared under one of the churning tires, losing a couple feet of the precious height the wag had fought for. The wag's rear bumper grazed the diesel's side with a squeal of tortured metal.

The coldheart riding shotgun on the specially built platform at the diesel's side tried to bring his blaster to bear. Kane twisted and turned, shoving the Mossberg toward the man, squeezed the trigger and blew a hole through the man's chest.

Dust clouds spumed up, filling the air as the wag continued to struggle to hold the grade. Kane slitted his eyes against the stirred-up grit, reducing his vision to shadows and guesswork. He fed more shells into the shotgun.

Grant kept a death grip on the steering wheel, his foot pressing on the accelerator. Dust masked his features, highlighting his black skin with amber powder.

The wag slipped suddenly, the rear end dropping under the front wheels until the vehicle was almost pointed straight up at the ridge. Grant cut the wheels to the right and kept the engine revved. Stubbornly, the wag clung to the ridge side, creeping past the diesel instead of driving. But they were still moving in the right direction.

Morgan yelled out behind them, his voice strong and hoarse, but his words lost in the rumble of the engines. The coldheart leader broke cover and ran toward the diesel, waving the driver back.

Raising the shotgun, Kane fired at Morgan, knowing that he didn't have a chance in hell of hitting the man. The buckshot slammed into the earth and stone nearly six feet away and short of the man. Still, it was close enough that the coldheart leader dived for cover again.

The diesel driver stopped with a loud hiss of air brakes, the huge wag trembling. Gears ground. It started to reverse, finding purchase. Suddenly, the jeep's front wheels lost traction, letting it drop back against the diesel. Caught against the bigger machine, the jeep was carried along as it rolled backward.

A coldheart stepped from the back of the diesel. She fired a .30-30 rifle at almost point-blank range, sending a round through Kane's seat and narrowly missing him. He felt the vibration of the seat getting slammed as the coldheart levered another round into the chamber.

Unable to bring the shotgun around, Kane tensed his wrist and the Sin Eater slid into his waiting palm. He tasted dust on his tongue as he watched the coldheart's mouth round in surprise. A Mag's weapon was the last thing she'd expected, and hadn't expected him to be able to target her at all.

Kane touched the trigger twice, coring one round through

the woman's throat. Blood pumped from her neck as she staggered back, then dropped behind the big wag's wheels. Her body spun out in front of the wag, ripped to pieces. Kane twisted his wrist and reholstered the Sin Eater.

The jeep found traction again and leaped forward, propelled by the diesel's greater weight and momentum. Grant shifted into second and floored the accelerator again. The diesel's huge tires rubbed the jeep's passenger side only inches from Kane. The jeep stuttered and jumped, batted away for a moment, then lost traction and hammered against the diesel again.

Holding on to the dash in front of him, the wag now almost perpendicular, Kane spotted four coldhearts erupting over the top of the ridge in pursuit. He couldn't return fire without falling back into the huge eighteen-wheeler. One of the coldhearts slipped, tumbling the length of the ridge to disappear under the big truck's wheels.

Then the jeep shot past the diesel, skidding down the ridge threateningly. For a moment Kane thought they were going to flip, then the wag dropped back to all four wheels and raced across the uneven terrain.

"Damn!" Grant swore.

Kane glanced ahead and spotted the three wags already in position. One of the men knelt by the wags with a long tube over his shoulder. Grant lifted his arm, getting ready to pop the Sin Eater free.

"Wait," Kane said, recognizing the one-eared man standing beside the man with the tube. "They're not after us."

The tube belched flame and smoke. A shriek filled the air, followed almost immediately by an ear-splitting detonation that ripped into the diesel rig. The big wag kicked over nose forward, driven by the explosion from behind that gutted the cab. Flames clung to the quivering hulk.

The coldhearts came to a sudden stop, but Remar waved his teams into action. The three wags leaped forward, equipped with .50-caliber machine guns mounted behind armor plating. The first wave of bullets hammered three coldhearts to the ground. The wags roared in pursuit of the others, cutting them down efficiently.

Remar strode over to Grant and Kane. The old man fished in a shirt pocket and took out a hand-rolled cigarette. He lit the twist of paper at the end with a disposable lighter and sucked the cigarette into a full burn.

"I hadn't figured on you boys making such good time," Remar said, "or we'd have been here sooner."

"You knew about the coldhearts?" Kane asked. The blasterfire bursts had died away to single shots.

Remar nodded. "We run convoys through here, trading goods we find for goods we need. Morgan and his gang of slaggers waylaid the last convoy through here. Luckily, two of the sec team got away and managed to get to us." The old man breathed out a wreath of smoke that curled around his head. "I told Falzone we needed to keep this pass clear, and he agreed. So here we are."

"Just in time, too," Kane said.

Remar shrugged. "Mebbe. Looked to me like the two of you had cleared the worst of it. Once you were loose, it would have been Morgan's mistake to try tracking you."

"I take it Morgan's not the man who normally watches over the pass," Grant said.

A grin split Remar's face. "Now that there's a funny story."

Chapter 19

"This is Goldberg."

Kane looked up at the old man's corpse, hanging on the cross at the mouth of the pass. The wound in his cheek showed black tattooing from gunpowder and the raw, angry meat of a burn. The scrawny frame was a map of abuse, from burns to deep cuts to an amputated foot. Ribs showed through on the left side, and a broken cheekbone gleamed through shredded flesh.

"Goldberg ran this pass for years." Remar touched a small cut under the dead man's chin. "It wasn't the amputation that chilled him. They took care to put a tourniquet on that and cauterize it. And you could say mebbe it was the aggregation of all the other wounds that did it."

"Aggregation?" Grant echoed with a raised eyebrow. "Mebbe you've had a little more schooling than you let on."

Remar grinned and shrugged. "Mebbe part of what you saw back in the gaudy was a little put-on." He puffed on his cigarette and spit out loose tobacco. "The worst thing you can ever do for a curious man is to teach him to read. A man gets into all kinds of trouble after that."

Kane gazed at the other bodies. "You're saying that little cut along Goldberg's throat is what chilled him?"

"Yeah. No doubt about it." The coal at the end of Remar's cigarette glowed orange. "They tortured him to get their questions answered, then they bled him out, took their time watching him die."

"Who is 'they'?" Grant asked.

Remar walked over to one of the other bodies hanging from

the cross. The corpse was tall and broad, the blond hair short in a military cut. Bootless from one of the scavengers that had passed through since death, the only clothes remaining on the dead man were a shirt and pants too bloody for anyone to want. Sparse stubble dotted his chin. Ants tracked across light blue eyes that had partially dehydrated and sat loose in their sockets.

"What do you make of this?" Remar asked.

Kane surveyed the body. Deep cuts decorated it, as well, but very little blood had seeped from them. "All the wounds were made after he was dead."

"Yeah. So why make them?"

"Opening him up like that would let in the scavengers and insects more quickly," Grant suggested. "A few more days hanging out exposed like this, even his own family wouldn't recognize him."

Kane's mind worked at the mystery, irritated that Remar could have seen through the subterfuge so quickly while he was still missing important parts. He drew his knife from his boot and lifted the man's shirt.

A single bullet hole centered over the heart held a cluster of green bottle flies. White maggots already squirmed in the bloated flesh around the wound.

Remar waved the flies away, but there was nothing to be done about the maggots. "The shot to the heart chilled him, but why?"

Kane surveyed the dark bruising around the wound. It hadn't turned purple and green as it would have if the flesh had gotten the chance to start healing. But he recognized the patterns. "He was hit with a big-bore blaster."

"Goldberg carried an old Sharps .50-cal buffalo rifle," Remar said.

"This guy was wearing a bulletproof vest," Kane said, "but the vest didn't hold up against the blunt trauma. The impact busted up his chest." He opened the dead man's nostrils and found dried blood caked inside. "Looks like broken bone punctured his lungs, or at least tore them up."

"Good," Remar said approvingly.

"He'd have needed medical attention or plenty of time to heal up," Kane said.

"Yeah," Remar said, "but the people he was with didn't want to wait. So they chilled him. Leaves the question of who."

"You're not going to know who he was unless you find some kind of identification," Kane said. "But you'll know what he was." He used his knife and slit the man's right shirtsleeve. Indentations left by the device that had been strapped to the dead man's wrist still showed in the waxy flesh. "Bulletproof armor and a Sin Eater only add up to a Magistrate."

"I knew you were a smart one, as well as good with weps," Remar said. "I told Falzone that."

"They'd have been better off burning the body," Grant commented.

"It's what I would have done," Remar said.

"The Mags have pursued you from Utah territory?" Kane asked.

"It looks like it," Remar answered.

"If they'd have been close to you, you'd have run across them coming back here."

"Yeah. Goldberg had a working relationship with us," Remar said, "but he didn't know where Falzone's operation is. Once you're past this pass, there's still a lot of land to cover if you don't know where you're heading."

"But the Mags are out there somewhere," Kane said. "Still searching."

Remar nodded and spit his cigarette stub to the ground, then crushed it underfoot. "I guess Baron Cobalt's more pissed off about things than I'd thought."

Kane turned and surveyed the pass. Remar's people worked quickly; they hauled the coldheart corpses to the burning wreckage of the eighteen-wheeler and threw them on. The sweet scent of burning flesh filled the air, noticeable even in the scorched-rubber smell from the flaming tires.

"What are you going to do about the pass?" Kane asked.

"There's a man named Grady to the south of here," Remar said. "He's been interested in taking over the pass if it ever came open. I'll send a couple riders over to his place, let him know the pass is his if he can hold on to it. It's better to pay a toll for every shipment we put through here and not have to fight our way through a bunch of coldhearts every time."

"Why not post a team out here?" Grant asked.

"Manpower is limited," Remar answered. "Word is starting to spread concerning the salvage we're doing. Cobaltville's interest is only going to make things more intense. The only ace on the line we have right now is that most people don't know where the Lost Valley of Wiy Tukay is. All our people do. If we stationed a team in the pass, they'd be vulnerable, more of a target for other scavengers. If the team out here got taken and questioned, it'd be like giving someone a key to the front door."

Kane studied the burning bodies on the flaming eighteen-wheeler, watching some of them squirm as weak screams rent the air. Not all of the coldhearts had been dead.

"But you're going to take us there," Kane told Remar. "We're going to know where the Lost Valley is."

"I'm going to take you there," Remar agreed, "but you're not going to know."

THE TALL BUCK STOOD in the shadows of broad oak trees nearly two hundred yards from the wag convoy as they continued to head north, northwest. The incline was hard going, covered over with dense grasses that rose only minutes after they'd passed. The pace was simple enough that Remar had no problem dropping over the side of Kane and Grant's wag and staying on his feet.

Kane glanced at Grant.

"Don't like the idea of getting split up," Grant stated in a low rumble, "but I like the idea of Remar wandering around out of our sight even less. That man's got some really despicable turns about him."

"Yeah, I know." Kane stepped from the passenger seat and landed easily on the ground. Their wag was second in line, with two more of Remar's wags after them. There was no disguising the fact they were there to keep close watch over Grant and Kane.

The wag riders glanced at Kane but made no move to pursue him.

After the last wag had passed, Kane followed Remar. The old man stayed low in the grass, easing toward the buck among the trees. Emulating Remar's caution, Kane stayed low and moved slowly. The buck had excellent eyesight and hearing, but the convoy's passage drew most of its attention and clattered noisily past.

Forty yards farther on, the buck twisted its muzzle. The tall antlers raked the leaves of the branches overhead. A foreleg quivered as it glanced at the two men.

Remar turned to stone for a few heartbeats, the wind blowing the fringe of hair around his head. Kane froze, as well, knowing the old man's attention was as fully on the buck as the animal's was on the two men.

"It's been a while since I had venison," Remar whispered. He eased himself to ground and slipped a .303 bolt-action hunting rifle from his shoulder. The safety snapped off with a click. The old man took careful sight through the scope mounted on the rifle.

Kane held his position less than three feet from Remar. His mind was still filled with questions, but he hadn't gotten many answers over the past few miles they'd traveled from the pass. Remar had proved plenty willing to talk, but the man didn't talk about things he didn't want to discuss.

There had been no clarification as to how Kane and Grant were going to be taken to the Lost Valley of Wiy Tukay without knowing where it was.

The buck locked into position, staring straight at them.

Kane heard Remar let out half his breath and hold it. The rifle thundered and the recoil shoved Remar's shoulder back.

The buck staggered for a moment, shook its head, then gathered its legs and sprinted. Birds exploded from the tops of the trees and took flight.

"Bastard bad luck!" Remar exclaimed, pulling the bolt back. "I hit the son of a bitch, but I didn't get a chilling shot. Damn thing will probably run a mile before it gives up and dies, and I still ain't going to have anything to show for it."

Kane dropped his shotgun to the ground. "Let me see the rifle."

Remar handed it over. "She's a good blaster, Kane, but you're talking about a running target."

Kane took the heavy weight of the rifle into his arms, slipped the sling around his left forearm and pulled it to his shoulder. He kept both eyes open, the right focusing through the scope while he used his left to keep the buck in sight. Trying to find the fleeing animal through the powerful scope only would have proved impossible.

The buck sprinted for the heights above the trees, bounding in great strides.

"Waste of a good bullet," Remar commented.

Kane ignored the statement, used his left eye to zero the scope in over the running deer, then found his target. He moved the crosshairs up, leading the animal a little, then squeezed the trigger. He rode out the recoil and counted down the second it took for his round to reach the buck.

The animal had hit the straight stretch leading up the ridge, and there wasn't time for another shot. Without warning, the buck twisted in midbound, the hindquarters suddenly going limp. The beast crashed to the ground.

Remar wore a grin that went ear to ear. "Damn if that wasn't some of the finest shooting I've ever seen." He pushed up from the ground and took the rifle when Kane offered it.

"Mebbe it was a little luck," Kane replied.

"Have it any way you want it," Remar said. "Me, I'm gonna have that buck in steaks thick as your eyeball and seared only enough to scare some of the pink off the meat." He reloaded the rifle, then shouldered it again.

Kane followed the old man up the incline, surprised at how well Remar moved.

The buck was still alive when they reached it, glassy-eyed and bleeding through its nostrils with every shuddering breath. Remar drew a straight razor from behind his neck and slit the buck's throat. Then he gutted the animal and started field dressing it.

Kane sat back on his heels a few feet away, the shotgun resting across his knees. From his position he could survey the ground around easily. "We need to talk about traveling north."

"Relax." Remar reached into the dead animal and scooped its guts out with his hands. "I got it all worked out."

"I don't," Kane replied.

"You should be patient."

Kane eyed him levelly. "That's not going to happen."

THE SMELL of cooking venison flooded the campsite Remar chose in the hollows of surrounding foothills. The fire hissed and spit as grease dropped into it from the meat placed on a section of chicken wire. Black smoked roiled upward, caught in a gentle breeze that threaded it into the wind and blew it westward. Guards occupied posts well away from the campsite, and the rest of the men hunkered down, talking and joking.

Remar sat with Grant and Kane apart from the other men. The old man reached out and smoothed the loose sand that powdered the rocky surface that clung to the foothills. "We're here." He stabbed his knife into the sand, creating a dimple. "The Valley of Wiy Tukay is three days from here. That's hard driving and assuming we don't get jumped along the way and lose time being pinned down by hostiles or suffer a wag breakdown.''

"What's between here and there?" Kane asked.

"You ever been out this far west?"

"Western Isles," Kane replied.

"This far northwest?"

"No."

Remar dragged the knife point through the sand in a wavy angle. "By late tomorrow, we should hook up with a station Falzone set up along the Salmon River. More or less a hidden fort and resupply station. Men there, they don't do any trading, but they trap and hunt, and occasionally venture out to a few villes managing to live off the land around here. Mighty hard living, too, but if people's got a big enough need, there's enough for them to make do."

Kane nodded, listening to the whisper of the men around them mix with the sizzle of the steaks.

"At the Salmon River, we'll take a boat all the way to the Spokane River, which takes us into the heart of what used to be Washington State before the nukecaust."

"I don't like the idea of leaving our wag," Kane said.

"You won't have to." Remar grinned. "The river may make things easier, mebbe a little faster, but I damn sure ain't going nowhere I can't wrap a little armor around me and keep some wheels on the ground. The boat Falzone rebuilt is more like a flatbed barge. It'll haul your wag, and the one I'm taking back with me. The other two stay at the fort. I borrowed 'em to make this meet with you. They stay there as support to the caravans we send back and forth to the baronies."

"The river big enough to handle that kind of load?" Grant asked.

Remar grinned, flashing pink gums. He scratched at the nub of his ear. "Hell, son, you ain't seen the rivers this place has got up here now. It's big enough and deep enough. Back before the nukecaust, this place was just plumb sorry with rivers and lakes." He got up and wiped his hands on his pants.

"You'll get to see it all in a couple days. Right now, that steak's calling out to me."

"It's calling out to me, too," Grant said.

Kane nodded.

"Do you feel any better about the trip we're about to make?" Grant asked.

"No. The river trip isn't something I'd do if we had a choice, but I will." Kane uncoiled, getting to his feet as Grant did. "One thing that would make me feel better is knowing who betrayed Falcone." That question had been preying on his mind a lot, and he didn't like where his thoughts were taking him.

Chapter 20

"Bry." Brigid watched the short man's rounded shoulders hunch up instinctively. She'd waited patiently until she'd caught him out of his room. It was almost midnight, and the lights of the redoubt had dimmed to simulate the outer darkness.

Bry turned without saying anything. He shoved his hand deep into his lab coat.

Brigid stood with her arms folded across her breasts. Over the past few days she'd recovered nearly all of her strength. There were only moments of weakness. Even the infection around the bite marks had dimmed to an angry red. "What were you doing out there?" she asked.

"I wasn't out anywhere," Bry insisted. "I've been in my room. Sick."

Brigid ignored the response. "Who were the men you met?"

"I don't know what you're talking about." The food tray Bry held in his hands shook. The fork clinked delicately against the metal surface.

"You were there," Brigid said. "I want to know why."

"You must be mistaken," Bry protested. "Maybe you just saw someone who looked like me. They say you were hurt pretty badly. Maybe that confused your memory."

Brigid closed on the shorter man, causing him to draw back into the wall behind him. "I'm not mistaken. You're just lying, and I mean to find out why."

"It wasn't me." Bry sounded petulant.

For a moment Brigid felt bad about pushing the man. Bry

hadn't exactly come across as a true friend since they'd been at the redoubt, but he'd worked hard in his capacity to make sure they returned safely from the places they'd journeyed.

Neither Bry nor Lakesh talked of where the little man was from. Brigid knew it couldn't have been good. Nothing around the baronies was. And with Bry's skills, she felt certain that he'd spend that time under a baron's thumb.

Brigid steeled herself, imagined in her mind that she could grab Bry and shake him until the truth fell out. The surge of adrenaline rushed through her weakened system and made her feel nauseous. She knew she couldn't do it.

And she knew from Bry's eyes that he knew she couldn't do it, either.

However, Kane would have had no problem at all. In that moment Brigid wished they were a little more alike, wished that the differences between herself and Kane were a little smaller.

Angrily, she turned on her heel. She even swallowed the threat of telling Bry she was going to keep her eye on him because that would have been redundant. As she walked away from Bry, the only sound in the hallway was the click of her shoes against the concrete floor.

THE RIVER BARGE WAS nearly eighty feet long and twenty-five feet across, yet the Salmon River still managed to make it look small. The barge had been put together from salvaged parts that looked mismatched. No real care had been given to make it look pretty or even confidently serviceable. Rubber tires roped to the sides provided a cushion of sorts as it wallowed between the sides of the wooden platform where it was berthed.

"I don't know which looks worse," Grant commented. "That boat or the damn dock."

The dock extended from the hillside of the valley that had been carved by the swollen Salmon River during flood times, pitched precariously over the elbow where the river made a sudden turn. From the way the current ran swiftly eastward, Kane figured the water was deep. Whitecaps showed over a gaping set of fanged rocks less than a hundred yards distant.

"Hell," Kane said, "you haven't mentioned anything about the trip downriver yet."

"I was thinking mebbe we could talk our way out of that. Whitewater isn't exactly the place I'd want to take a boat flat as that. Looks like a damn stick floating on the water."

Kane silently agreed. Ropes on both sides of the barge held it between the dock, which twisted and jerked uncertainly as the boat pulled on it. The way the boat bounced, he guessed that it had little draw.

"According to Remar, overland travel would take another five or six days," Kane stated. "And that's through hostile territory and places still hot with rad pits. At least the barge is armored up."

Two 20 mm cannons, one fore and one aft, were mounted on the deck. Four .50-cal machine guns stood at attention on port and starboard sides. Each gunnery position had abbreviated shielding that protected the men stationed at them from enemy fire.

Grant glanced at the churning water. "Somehow, I don't find that as reassuring as you seem to."

Ahead of them, Remar waved one of the wags onto the barge. The wag moved slowly, inching across the planks that spanned the distance between the dock and the barge.

Kane watched the planks give slightly, and held his breath, waiting for the wood to give way and drop the wag onto the pitching barge. He was certain the river current would swiftly carry away the vehicle, as well as the man driving it.

In another moment the wag rolled onto the barge's deck and kept going forward. Men spread out around it, uncoiling chains, and quickly lashed the wag to cleats mounted on the deck.

Remar stood on the dock and waved to Kane. "Let's go."

Grant hopped out of the wag as Kane put it in gear.

"Where are you going?" Kane asked.

"Getting ready," Grant replied. "In case I have to chase along the riverbank to save your ass." His face was totally somber, but his eyes flashed with hidden mirth.

Kane pressed the accelerator and started the laborious climb up the planks. He felt them giving under him, and hoped that his wag wasn't just heavy enough to shatter the boards and send him plunging down into the river. His gut churned anxiously, and he felt sweat gather between his shoulder blades, turning cold as the wind hit it.

The wag shifted from side to side, following the barge's movements. But in another couple minutes, he pulled the wag to a stop only a few feet behind the first one. He switched off the engine as the crew threw chains over the wag and secured it, as well.

Climbing out of the wag, Kane stood with difficulty as the barge surged like a live thing fighting the anchoring ropes that bound it to the dock. He cursed.

"You get used to it after a while," a young man told him as he pulled a chain tight around a cleat. "And once we get moving, it ain't so bad."

Kane doubted that but didn't say so. He took a cigar from his pocket and lit.

The fort stood on top of the hillside towering over the river. The structure was built low and squat so that it had blended in with the surrounding forest. But as they'd gotten closer, Kane had noticed that the field of fire in front of it was meticulously laid out.

From the way the floor had sounded hollow inside the building during the brief visit there, he guessed there was at least a hidden story beneath and probably escape tunnels, as well. Falzone was a man who planned his strategies carefully.

Remar and Grant joined him. Remar ordered his crew into action, bellowing commands over the roar of the passing river. Diesel engines chugged to life reluctantly, sending a new series of shudders through the craft. A moment later the fort crew cast off the lines and the deck crew reeled them in.

In the stern Remar manned the huge tiller, pushing them out into the center of the river. A ball cap pulled down low on his head shadowed the grin he flashed at Kane and Grant as they joined him.

"Do you like river rafting?" Remar asked.

"No," Grant answered for both of them. "Especially not on something this big."

"Trust me," Remar said, "you'd like a smaller raft even less. We tried smaller ones for a while. Lost about a half-dozen cargoes before Falcone said fuck it and built this monster."

"How did he know to build something like this?" Kane asked.

"Falcone's got a sharp mind," Remar said, pulling hard on the tiller to shove them more deeply into the swift current. The barge shuddered for a moment, fighting the pull of the current, then suddenly gave up.

Kane felt the change immediately. The barge squirted forward, the ride now smoother but definitely faster. He wasn't sure if it was an improvement because it moved fast enough now to guarantee a hell of a pileup if it hit something.

"I've seen him take a lot of equipment even most trained scavengers would have given up on and make it work. Ol' *Bessie* here became important to him." Remar nodded at the savage tree-and-boulder-studded country passing them on both sides. "A man traveling overland, he don't stand near the chance of getting to the Lost Valley as we do, and we can do it in about a third of the time."

"What about the Cobaltville Mags?" Grant asked. "You know from those bodies back at the pass that they haven't given up. And if they've come this far, they won't. Even if it takes them three times as long."

Remar scratched at his nub of an ear. "I know. But it'll give us some room to work with."

"To do what?" Kane asked.

"The only thing we can do," Remar answered. "Get the hell out of the valley or try to chill them all so they can't let others know where we are."

"Getting out would be your best bet," Kane offered. "We're talking about a full Mag contingent here. You saw what they're capable of back at the gaudy."

Remar nodded. "I know. I've seen them in action before. That's what convinced me I needed to talk to you boys, see if you were interested in signing on with me. With Falcone." He pulled on the tiller, making another adjustment as the river slapped at the steel hull. The dual diesel engines throbbed under the deck, sounding like muted thunder. "When it comes to chilling or being chilled, the two of you know how to handle yourselves. Figured mebbe we could use that."

"We'll see," Kane said. "But taking on a group of Mags isn't something I'd choose to do."

"Not," Remar agreed, "unless you had the right reason."

EVEN AS SHE ENTERED the door to the redoubt's central control complex, Brigid knew something was wrong. And she did something she would never have believed she'd have done only a few short years ago, she reached for the weapon that habitually rode her right hip while she was out in the field.

Only it wasn't there. While the team was within the redoubt, Lakesh forbade the wearing of weapons. They were too well insulated from the outer world, too secure to have to worry about someone getting close to them without some kind of forewarning.

Quietly, feeling the oppressive silence that filled the room, Brigid went forward, breathing shallowly.

Lakesh was sprawled in the floor, blood seeping from a cut on the back of his head, matting his hair.

Brigid froze, feeling the security that usually existed within the redoubt suddenly stripped away from her. She maintained her position, listening the way Grant and Kane had trained

her. It was always better to walk into a situation prepared—
or to simply walk away from it altogether.

Knowing that she would walk away from Lakesh for the
time it took to get a weapon surprised her. Despite the way
Lakesh had sometimes treated her since she'd arrived at the
Cerberus redoubt, she still cared deeply for him. He had been
her mentor for years, had pushed her into learning more—
until the day she'd learned too much.

Certain the room was empty, she crossed to Lakesh, pressing her fingers against the side of his neck as she knelt. His
pulse was slightly thready but seemed strong. Brigid reached
up to the comp console and keyed the intercom.

"Yes," DeFore answered.

"There's been an accident," Brigid said. "Lakesh is hurt
and unconscious."

"I'm on my way."

Gently, Brigid touched Lakesh's scalp, examining the laceration there. It was not quite two inches long, but it looked
even worse now that the swelling had set in. From the tacky
feel of the blood, the fact that it had only started to congeal,
she knew whatever had happened hadn't been that long ago.

"Darling Brigid?" Lakesh's eyes fluttered. He twisted his
head, trying to see her.

"Easy," Brigid advised. "Just lie still. DeFore is coming.
I don't want you moving until she checks you out."

"Lying on this floor is discomfiting at best, and near to
agony physically. Really, I think I would be much better if
you would help me up."

"No."

Stubbornly, Lakesh tried to push himself up, but his arms
shivered under the strain and didn't accept the burden he was
putting on them. Gasping, his complexion much paler than
normal, he slumped back to the floor. "I had forgotten how
much one's head hurt upon occasions such as this."

"What happened?" Brigid asked.

"I was hit on the head," Lakesh answered.

More nervous now, Brigid glanced around the control center. But the only thing that looked suspicious about it was the fact that Donald Bry was not at his post. "Someone is in the complex."

"Actually, darling Brigid, someone is very much out of the redoubt, I fear." Lakesh reached shaking fingers to the back of his head.

Brigid trapped his hand and kept it from the wound. "Don't touch it. You'll only cause more potential infection."

Lakesh sighed. "I am quite capable of taking care of myself."

"Get argumentative," Brigid promised, "and we're going to find out. Who hit you?"

Lakesh hesitated, as if he couldn't believe he was going to say what he said next. "Donald Bry."

"Why?"

"I don't know." Lakesh shifted again as if trying to get comfortable. He grimaced, letting her know he hadn't been successful.

"I'll get a sec team in here," Brigid told him. "We'll find him."

"He's not here," Lakesh said. "I walked in on him this afternoon and found him accessing the mat-trans. I asked him what he thought he was doing. Before I knew it, he was on me."

Despite Lakesh's words, Brigid had a hard time figuring out why Bry would even want to use the mat-trans unit. Uneasily, she glanced at the gateway unit. The brown armaglass walls were opaque, offering no clue about what had happened. "Why would he be using the mat-trans unit?" she asked.

"For the same reasons anyone else would," Lakesh answered somewhat testily. "To get to somewhere else."

"Where did he go?"

"Really, darling Brigid," Lakesh said, "I don't think Bry would have knocked me out just so he could tell me where he was going."

DeFore arrived and quickly started examining Lakesh.

Brigid held his hand in hers, feeling it shake. "Bry gave no warning?"

"If he had," Lakesh said dryly, "I think I would have called a security team."

DeFore poked and prodded, and Brigid noticed the woman was professional but none too gentle. "In all the time that Bry's been here," DeFore said, "he's never done anything that wasn't sanctioned by you."

"I've nearly had my head bashed in," Lakesh protested weakly, "and yet you insist on finding me suspect?"

"It's amazing how easy that is." DeFore glanced at Brigid. "He's going to be okay. Let's get him down to the infirmary."

Brigid helped lift Lakesh from the floor, easily managing the small man's slack weight. "I'll be with you in a minute," she said. As DeFore helped Lakesh into a wheelchair, Brigid went to examine the mat-trans. Bry may have gone, but the mat-trans left a record of where he went.

MALLET STOOD on the high, wind-whipped promontory overlooking the Salmon River and peered east. A handful of his men held scattered positions in the brush behind him. None of them moved, knowing that if they could see the people down in the water, they could be seen, as well.

Keeping his back to the scrub pine tree so he couldn't be profiled, the Mag commander trained his field glasses on the oblong shape on the river. The canyon the river fed through was at least 150 feet above the waterline. The striations on the canyon walls showed that the river still occasionally rose that high, but hadn't done so in years.

He focused the magnification, tightening it up. The vessel was a barge, obviously made for the trips up and down the river. The crew moved expertly across the bobbing deck. The strong current shivered through the craft, sometimes lifting the front and back completely clear of the whitecaps, then slamming it back down. Water surged across the flat decks, making footing treacherous, but the crew only moved to man the long poles they used to push against the river bottom and banks to keep the craft's prow forward.

Mallet took the binoculars from his eyes and stored them in their protective case. He passed them back to Iverson as he abandoned his position. "Stand up," he ordered his men. "Spread out along the ridgeline."

Without a word, the Cobaltville Magistrates fell into position, unlimbering the Copperhead assault rifles they carried.

Mallet unslung his own Copperhead and checked the action automatically. The wear and tear of the days traveling across the Outlands was beginning to show in his team. Irritability had set in at being in hostile territory, and tempers occasionally flared. If his command had been any less, he knew they would have started killing one another.

For most of them, the anxiety was caused by being away from Cobaltville. Few of them had traveled past the outer reaches of the ville itself, and fewer still had been past the Utah territories. Back home they had the confidence of familiar surroundings and no supply problems. Fuel was starting to be a major consideration, but Mallet thought he had that figured out. Two days back, they'd crossed paths with a group of Roamers. They'd taken the fuel and tires from the Roamer vehicles that fit their own wags, then Mallet had gone to work on two of the survivors, finding out about a trader who had set up shop farther down the river who kept a supply of gasoline.

They'd been headed there when one of the scouts spotted the barge on the river. They'd found the hidden fort first, but Mallet had reached the decision that pitting his group against the men holding the waystation wasn't a good idea. He had no doubt that his troops would triumph in the end, but the cost in men and supplies would have proved too high.

Taking out the binoculars again, he surveyed the craft. He tried to keep focused on Remar at the tiller, recognizing the man from the few times he'd seen him while negotiating deliveries for Baron Cobalt, but the barge skipped and skated on the turbulent water. Then Mallet caught sight of the two men with Remar, recognizing them almost immediately.

Mallet had known of Grant and Kane back in Cobaltville. Both men had been legends as Magistrates for the baron, then become infamous when they'd deserted the ville. Several stories surrounded the reason why the two men had left, but Mallet wasn't sure any of the stories were true.

There were even stories that had circulated about Kane being dead a time or two. But the man kept turning up.

Hopping and twisting like a snake crossing rad-blasted earth, the barge lunged for the whitewater between the jagged rocks ahead.

"On my mark," Mallet bellowed, knowing they wouldn't be heard over the crashing river below. He put away the binoculars, pulled the Copperhead to his shoulder and pulled on his polycarbonate helmet. "Albright," he said over the helmet link.

"Yes, sir."

"When we rip this barge, I want at least one survivor."

"Yes, sir."

"Iverson," Mallet said, "you're first man up."

The other Mag nodded and settled the long, predark Russian rocket launcher over his shoulder, leaning out over the ridge. A man sat beside him, another finned rocket round already in hand in case the first one wasn't enough.

"Your target?" Mallet asked impatiently.

"I've got it," Iverson said quietly.

Mallet glanced at the barge, still some eighty yards away. "Let them make half the distance," he commanded, "then break the barge up."

"Yes, sir."

Feeling buzzing excitement stirring within him, Mallet stared through the optical image-intensifier scope. The barge was twenty yards from the whitewater, firmly gripped in the violent trough that had hollowed out in the current. The water was shallow there, making the current run even faster. Water spumed ten feet into the air, drenching everything on the other side.

"Iverson," Mallet said confidently, "it's your mark." He watched the man's finger curl on the trigger, whitening from the pressure. "Take the shot."

The whoosh of the rocket leaving the tube washed over the ridgeline. Trailing a plume of smoke, the warhead vectored in on its target.

Chapter 21

DeFore was finishing prepping the back of Lakesh's head when Brigid arrived. DeFore had shaved the hair around the laceration to prevent it from getting into the wound.

"I assure you, DeFore," Lakesh stated in annoyance, "that your ministrations are not necessary. This is merely an inconvenience, a slight swelling that a good night's sleep will surely put behind me." He fidgeted in his chair, obviously not happy about being there.

"You're getting stitches," DeFore informed him.

Lakesh sighed. "I don't wish stitches."

"Don't be difficult."

"I have a headache."

"Which might be a concussion on top of everything else." DeFore unsealed one of the prepacked med trays and sorted through the instruments and medicines available. "I'm also going to keep you under observation for twenty-four hours. So you can either plan on staying here with me, or plan on me being with you."

Brigid stepped into view.

"Yes, dearest Brigid?" Lakesh rasped. "I can tell by your behavior that you have discovered something."

"Bry's destination," she replied.

"And that is?"

DeFore stepped in with a hypodermic in one hand, holding Lakesh's head with the other. "This is going to sting." Smoothly, she started the first of a series of injections of local anesthetic.

Brigid knew the routine from her own times under DeFore's

healing hands. The injections only stung if they didn't outright hurt like hell. "Would you care to guess?"

Lakesh grimaced, his pale blue eyes wide. "No."

"Have you noticed any changes in Bry?" Brigid asked.

"Yes," Lakesh said harshly. "Today he assaulted me. For no reason. And clearly he didn't care how much damage he did." He plucked at the bloodstained smock he wore as if displaying evidence.

"What about before today?"

Lakesh yelped.

"Be still," DeFore ordered. "I'm almost done."

"You're hurting me," Lakesh stated. "I don't remember being in this much pain when I was in surgery."

"That's because you don't remember surgery," DeFore told him. "I could put you out for this, but I thought maybe you'd want to be awake, ready to deal with the Bry problem."

Brigid waited, knowing Lakesh hadn't forgotten her question. She debated, wondering if the man really was distracted by DeFore's efforts or if he was biding his time.

"In answer to your question, dearest Brigid," Lakesh said, "yes and no."

"You weren't in the habit, back in the Cobaltville Historical Division, of letting me get away with an answer like that," Brigid said.

"Yes, I'd noticed some behavioral changes," Lakesh admitted. "But everybody in this complex seems to go through mood swings on a daily basis. Except for darlingest Domi, who remains faithfully the one true constant I have around me."

"Until the last few days," Brigid said, "I would have thought you could have said that about Donald Bry."

"Apparently, we were both wrong about that."

DeFore threaded nylon sutures through a wickedly curved needle. Then she bent to the task of running the needle through Lakesh's numbed flesh.

"Where is Bry?" Lakesh asked.

"In what used to be Washington State before the nuke-caust," Brigid answered. "The same place Kane and Grant are headed."

Lakesh was silent for a moment. "Do you think it's a co-incidence?"

"No."

"Then you believe there is a reason?"

"I'd say there has to be," Brigid told him. "I was thinking perhaps you could tell me why Bry would head there. That area is all Outlands, unsettled and buffeted by intense storm fronts." She'd researched the area over the past few days, wanting to know what Kane was going to be facing.

"I have no idea why he would go there."

"Bry was raised in a ville," Brigid said. "He's not some-one who would enjoy the rigors of a rough life or travel through hard country like that."

"Perhaps he found that role preferable to life under a baron."

"And preferable to life under your guidance?"

"So it would appear," Lakesh admitted glumly. "Though I think Bry had a rather easy life here and before. Compara-tively speaking."

"Would it surprise you to know," Brigid asked, "that a few days ago I saw Bry meeting with a group of coldhearts two days' ride from the redoubt?"

Lakesh's brow furrowed. "Yes. On two counts." He gazed at her steadily while DeFore worked on him. "Number one would be because Bry would not seem the type to risk every-thing in a matter that way. And secondly, that you did not feel it was your place to inform me immediately."

"He knew Bry was out there," DeFore said. "He knew you and Domi were, too."

"Yes, but I didn't know what any of them were doing out there." Lakesh regarded Brigid evenly, obviously irritated by DeFore's input. "Evidently, Bry was not the only person at the redoubt who didn't feel it necessary to let me know they were working off a personal agenda.''

"I followed Bry," Brigid said. "That choice was his, not mine."

"Yet you trailed after him," Lakesh said, "without notifying anyone here at the redoubt. Unless you took darlingest Domi into your confidence."

"No."

"Good, because I'd not willingly suffer anything happening to her." Lakesh paused, his face knotted with nervousness. His eyes narrowed as DeFore added a new stitch, tying it off quickly with the small curved scissors she had.

"What are you going to do about this?" Brigid asked.

Lakesh hesitated. "I don't know. We don't know what the stakes are."

"What did Bry take with him?"

Lakesh didn't answer.

"He didn't leave empty-handed," Brigid said. "I'm certain of that."

"I don't know for sure," Lakesh admitted. "Bry could have copied several of the more sensitive programs I've got in the redoubt's library."

"What kind of programs?" Brigid knew from her own past dealings in Cobaltville's archives that a lot of predark history had been altered, either to conceal the presence of the Archon Directorate or to insure baronial rule.

"I'll have to check."

Brigid nodded. "You need to get it done soon. I'm going to be leaving within the hour, and I'd like to know what I'm heading into."

"What do you mean?"

"I mean Kane and Grant are with Remar," Brigid stated. "Getting a message to them by satellite is out of the question. If Remar learns they have that capability, he could chill them out of suspicion, thinking they were working for Baron Cobalt."

"But why go?" Lakesh tried to wave DeFore away, but she held his head steady.

"Because we don't know what Bry is doing or who he's doing it with."

"He wouldn't hurt Kane and Grant," Lakesh assured her.

"Bry cracked your head open."

"He didn't kill me."

"It could be that he thought he did," Brigid said.

"You can't go off by yourself," Lakesh protested.

Brigid started for the door. "I'm not going to let Kane and Grant walk into a potential ambush without attempting to help them. That's the one thing I know for sure that I can't do."

"Think about what you're doing."

"I have," Brigid told him. She stepped through the door, hoping that the lead Donald Bry had wasn't too much.

DESPITE THE WAY the barge rocked on the troubled waters, Kane split his attention between the whitecapped rapids and the river ahead. His point man's senses flared, drawing his attention up the sides of the canyons.

The trees almost hid the shadows lurking beneath the branches.

Kane peered more closely, making out the tube shape balanced over one man's shoulder. "Grant!" he warned. "Top of the canyon. On the left. Under the trees."

Grant spun, automatically bringing up the mini-Uzi he carried on a strap from his shoulder. The distance ahead and up the canyon wall pressed the outer reaches of the machine pistol's 9 mm Parabellum slugs.

Kane crossed the distance to Remar quickly, forcing the tiller to one side and shoving them into the cotton-mouthed draw of the main rapids.

"What the fuck?" Remar bellowed over the crash of the roaring water.

"Company," Kane yelled. "Up on the ridge." Before he could say anything else, trying to keep his balance on the shifting deck as water streamed over nearly ankle deep, the river erupted to their right only a few yards back. The blast of the warhead surfaced only a moment after the water blew into the air.

The concussion spun new waves through the river and sent a wall of water that poured over the barge's stern, drenching everyone on board. The craft slithered, fighting Remar's and Kane's hands on the tiller, the angry grasp of the river and the blast concussion.

One of Remar's men fell overboard, tumbling into the water. The current's roar almost completely drowned out his frightened cries. He surfaced once, already pulled yards distant from the heavier barge, twisting and turning in a mad scramble of arms and legs. Then he was gone.

Blasterfire crashed in a lethal, stuttering cacophony along the river canyon walls. Bullets made brief dimples in the whitecapped water that popped back up with spitting curls. More bullets hammered against the barge's metal skin, denting or ripping through.

"You got it?" Kane asked Remar.

"I fucking got it," Remar answered between his teeth. He fought the tiller and the crash of the white rapids, corded muscle standing out on his thin arms.

The barge crew had already grabbed the railing and shifted to engage their enemy. Two of the attackers went down under the withering blasterfire, their bodies jerking with the impacts.

Kane made his way forward, lurching across the heaving deck. The river streamed across the deck's metal surface, turning it treacherously slick. Caught in the rapids, the barge lifted and dropped, twisted left and right without warning and acted like a bird caught in a snare.

Another eruption of water sprang from the river in front of the barge. The craft heaved up over the sudden roil of water, shuddering from the impact as the boom filled the canyon. For a moment the barge hung weightless as the current swept the turbulence away. Then it slapped back against the river, throwing men from their feet.

Kane slammed painfully into the railing near the deck-mounted .50-cal machine gun. He grabbed the weapon under the tarp and hauled himself to his feet.

Less than five feet away, a man trying to hold on to the drenched deck lost his grip and slid under the railing, screaming in fear. One of the other men made a wild grab for him, snaring him by the shoulder of his jacket and halting his fall. Together, they managed to get the man back onto the barge.

As it plunged through the rapids, despite its weight and size, Kane felt certain the barge was going to capsize. He held on to the machine gun, watching as the craft drew closer to the snipers atop the canyon walls. Unable to free the machine gun from the canvas tarp easily, he slipped the knife from his boot and hacked at the cords holding it in place. The nylon strands parted easily.

Kane threw the tarp aside as the barge lifted and fell again. Occasional shots still peppered the craft's metal hide, leaving holes and pockmarks in their wake. He reached into the ammo box screwed into the deck, yanked a belt up and slammed it into the breech.

Now that the figures no longer needed the surprise offered by staying under the trees, they stepped out along the ridge but still took cover where they could. The black Mag armor made them look like shadows. The rounded surfaces of the polycarbonate protected them from most of the small-arms fire offered in return from the barge.

Hunkering behind the machine gun, Kane squeezed the trigger, raking the canyon wall as the barge fought the river, throwing out dust geysers in an uneven row. Other rounds chopped branches and leaves from the trees. And two of the Mags went down, slapped back by the heavy bullets.

Kane cursed the river, knowing he couldn't lock on to his targets with the big .50-cal weapon the way he wanted to. Still, his accuracy was enough to break the Magistrate line, causing some of them to draw back. Even with armor, the .50-caliber round was respected.

The man with the rocket launcher held his ground calmly as his partner shoved another shell into place.

The river carried the barge past the ambush site, drawing them away from the Mags at a speed the men couldn't hope to match. But it wasn't out of range for the rocket launcher. One direct hit, Kane knew, and the blast would turn the barge into deadly shrapnel that would leave any potential survivors to the rough mercy of the river.

Kane concentrated the machine-gun fire on the rocket launcher team. Even though he didn't hit the men, the massive rounds dug earthen clods from underneath the edge of the canyon wall where they stood. In the next instant the section of ground crumbled from underfoot.

The man working the reloads stood closer to the edge that crumbled. He dropped over the side, arms and legs flailing as he plummeted fifty or sixty feet to the river. The rapids embraced the Mag at once, sucking him under.

Twisted by the river current, the barge lifted again and slammed back down, then rose once more, lifting until it almost stood on the stern. Unable to continue firing the machine gun, Kane dropped instead and locked his arms around the weapon's support, willing it to stay in place.

Another of Remar's crew slid from the drenched deck and plunged into the vicious river. The survivors screamed curses and prayers as they held on. Out of control, the barge skipped across the rapids, lurching violently from side to side.

Hammered against the barge's metal deck, Kane held on and hoped the craft didn't flip over and bury them beneath the water. He spotted Grant and saw that the big man had wrapped both arms around a railing support.

Just as Kane was certain his arms were about to be pulled from their sockets, the current let up. The barge dropped back to the river surface and fishtailed awkwardly but didn't go airborne anymore.

Snarling curses, his voice hoarse with fear and anger, Remar heaved himself up and grabbed the tiller. During the bumpy ride, the barge had swapped ends a couple times and they were now going backward down the river.

Kane watched Remar struggle with the tiller, unable to gain control of it, then shoved himself to his feet. He crossed the deck carefully and grabbed the tiller, as well.

"Hold the fucker steady," Remar bellowed. "Keep it straight and shallow as you can. If it digs in, we could flip. River's still running too damn fast."

Kane silently agreed, feeling the river current pull and grab at the tiller. The barge twisted and veered, following the pull. Grant and the rest of the crew stayed low, not trusting their legs.

A few of the more violent surges sent Kane crashing against the railing, bruising his side. Then the river grew bigger and broader, and finally calmer. Under Remar's direction, he helped guide the barge to the riverbank. They cut the engines back and held the stern steady while the prow floated around to face forward again. In a handful of minutes, they were under way again.

Kane joined Grant as they checked over the lines securing the wag to the barge. Both of them were completely drenched, still leaving puddles everywhere they went.

Grant brushed water from his face as they secured the lines again, taking out the slack that had been pulled loose. "I don't want to go through that again."

Kane nodded. He shaded his eyes and peered at the canyon walls. "Those Mags aren't going to give up."

"I know. Depending on how long this river is, they'll be along in a few days." Grant tightened the restraining strap, lugging the nuts down with a wrench.

"Remar," Kane said.

The man looked up, surrendering the tiller to one of the crew. He sat and took off one boot, then poured the water from it. "What?"

"Is there any way we can lose those men following us at the end of the river?"

Remar shook his head. "To get to us, they'll have to get a boat somewhere along the way. But they can be had. Lots of folk in the area in small villes got boats. Once they have a boat, they'll find us. Mebbe take a little while, but they seem like they're motivated enough."

"Does Falzone have enough men to hold these people back?" Kane asked.

Remar emptied his other boot. "Yeah, but having them poking around is gonna be like setting off a flare to the others who're looking for the Lost Valley of Wiy Tukay. The Tong keep boats in the area, too."

Kane leaned against the wag, feeling the afternoon sun baking into the metal. The wind plucked at his clothing, giving him a chill, but he knew it would also dry it out before too long.

No matter how he looked at it, Kane knew they were headed into the center of the crosshairs.

Chapter 22

"I do wish you would reconsider," Lakesh stated calmly.

Brigid didn't hesitate on her way to the mat-trans unit. She wore denim pants and boots, a dark green brushed-denim shirt and a black leather jacket scarred from harsh use but still serviceable. A mini-Uzi was slung under her arm. She carried a backpack by the straps in one hand.

"I'm going, Lakesh." Brigid keyed the door open and stepped inside the chamber.

Lakesh, his head bandaged from DeFore's ministrations, looked at her woefully. A couple years ago, Brigid knew, she'd have been feeling guilty at ignoring his wishes. Now she only felt discomfort from her own lingering injuries. The thought of Kane and Grant out there without the knowledge that Bry was a loose cannon took even that away.

"Not going alone."

Brigid turned and stared behind her. Domi entered the doorway across the room dressed in denim pants and hiking boots. The shirtsleeves had been crudely hacked from the garment she wore. She carried a backpack and a jacket in one hand, a baseball cap and a gun belt with the holstered .357 blaster she favored in the other.

"Darlingest Domi?" Lakesh asked. "What do you think you're doing?"

"Going with Brigid," Domi insisted as she stepped into the gateway to join Brigid.

"That may not be such a good idea," Brigid admitted.

"You're going," Domi replied.

"But that doesn't mean you have to."

Domi smiled and shrugged casually. "Grant will like to see me." She hung the gun belt over her shoulder, then pulled on the baseball cap. "Stop arguing."

"I really must protest," Lakesh said. "Losing all of you on some unnecessary jaunt isn't—"

"Isn't what?" Brigid demanded. "Necessary?"

Lakesh was at a loss for words, obviously surprised by the calm anger Brigid displayed.

Brigid stepped inside the mat-trans unit and checked the keypad. Everything still looked operational. "If you want," she said without looking at Lakesh, "we can talk about this when I get back."

"Of course." Lakesh spoke in a dry, lifeless whisper. "I can see you've made up your mind. But later might be too late, mightn't it? I suppose that did cross your mind."

"Yes. But don't worry. I'll take your I-told-you-so to the grave with me."

Lakesh's face soured. "That's not what I meant."

Domi strode into the mat-trans chamber and dropped her backpack on the floor. Reluctantly, she hunkered down against the armaglass wall. "Hate these fuckers," she snarled.

The backpack flap was open enough for Brigid to see all the ammo the albino had packed. "Did you put any food in there?"

"Fuck that," Domi snorted. "Live off land. Plenty of game. Run out of bullets before we run out of animals to eat. No worries about animals. They coldhearts Bry went to see, they chill, no questions." She smiled. "Rather shoot them before they shoot me."

Much as she felt she should be able to, Brigid couldn't bring herself to argue with that.

"Brigid."

Looking up, Brigid spotted DeFore beside a comp station behind Lakesh.

"You watch your back out there," DeFore said. "Whatever you thought about Bry before, all bets are off."

"I know. I will." Brigid finished the activation sequence, then sat against the armaglass wall on the other side of Domi.

The mat-trans unit whined as the energy that powered it brought it up to peak. Fog lifted from the hexagonal floor plates, rising to obscure the interior of the gateway. On the other side of the armaglass, Lakesh's face blurred and lost color.

Despite the fact that she'd made jumps before, Brigid's heart hammered inside her chest. She locked eyes with Domi, watching fear etch into the albino's hard features. Brigid's mind stayed busy, wondering where Bry had gone, telling herself that the man wouldn't have jumped anywhere dangerous, telling herself that it wasn't too late to help Kane and Grant if they needed it.

Then she jumped—and she knew nothing at all.

BRIGID WOKE with a splitting headache and the sour taste of bile in her mouth. She cracked her eyes open against the bright light flooding the mat-trans unit. Nothing moved on the other side of the bottle-green armaglass.

Slowly, she sat up, agonizing over every movement. It had been a bad jump; she was sure of that. She couldn't remember the nightmares that had haunted her, but she still felt them crawling around in the back of her head.

Domi lay sprawled over to the left, the side of her face plastered in her own sickness. Her small breasts rose and fell slowly, indicating that she still lived.

After a dozen even breaths, drawn in through her nose and exhaled through her mouth, Brigid braced her feet against the floor and slid up the armaglass wall. Sharp pangs of nausea racked her stomach, but she breathed through them and they went away.

Domi's head jerked as she regained consciousness. The albino reflexively pulled at the .357, almost freeing it from the holster before Brigid put a hand on hers and stopped the movement. Domi fought her weakly, her eyes struggling to focus.

"It's me, Domi. It's Brigid."

Domi relaxed. "Okay." She closed her eyes, let out a breath and tried opening them again. They focused on Brigid. "Bry?"

"I didn't see him in the room outside the mat-trans unit. But that doesn't mean this place is empty."

"Know where?"

"We're going to have to look. Wait here just a moment." Brigid opened the mat-trans unit's door, the mini-Uzi naked in her fist as she led the way into the outer room.

The redoubt was small, painted all white and set up for efficiency. The comp consoles lined one wall below blank vid screens. Low-key lighting just held back the shadows that threatened the room.

A brief inspection of the storage cabinets showed that all the ammo and weapons had been removed, along with the med supplies. However, she did find a pile of clean towels in the adjoining shower facilities. She wet a towel in the miniature sink beside the lone shower cubicle and returned to Domi.

The albino was sitting up, massaging her jaw.

Brigid offered the wet towel, but Domi's attempt to get it missed by several inches. "Let me," Brigid said. Quickly but tenderly, she washed the albino's pale face. "I can't do anything about your hair, but there's a shower in the next room."

"Kind of stupe to worry about being clean if not check out rest of redoubt," Domi accused.

"No one else is here," Brigid said, putting the wet towel in Domi's hand.

"You sure?"

"Yes." Brigid got up before Domi could argue any further. She knew part of the attitude came from the albino's own embarrassment at being so traumatized by the jump.

Working with the same unhurried but thorough skill that had made her a good archivist, Brigid went through the room. She searched for logs and manuals that she knew should be there, as well as any further journals that might have been left by anyone who'd visited the redoubt. Nothing existed, but she knew things appeared too well taken care of for it to have remained hidden from everyone.

The missing manuals and logs indicated that someone had taken them for study. However, the fact that no guards were posted led her to think that the redoubt was known to the barons, as well. If someone had discovered the redoubt, they obviously hadn't felt they could hold it against a Mag force.

Domi emerged from the mat-trans chamber a few minutes later. "Mebbe we ended up in the wrong place." She stripped off, dropping her clothing onto the stone floor, but kept the .357 in her fist. "Mebbe Bry fixed controls so we go somewhere else. He not stupe about things like that."

Brigid was thinking the same thing when she noticed a piece of white cloth hanging from the room's other door. It barely stuck out from the jamb, hardly showing against the white surface. She crossed the room and pressed the code that in most of the redoubts released the door. She hesitated with her hand on the knob and looked back at Domi.

"Go," the albino said tensely. Still naked, she held the .357 in both hands in front of her.

Brigid pushed the door open and swept the corridor on the other side with the mini-Uzi.

Only the empty corridor filled her view.

But the white cloth remnant dropped to the floor. Brigid picked it up, noting the small blood speck on it. "Feels like the same material Bry's jacket is made of." She blew out her breath. "Soon as you're ready, we can go see where we are."

Domi eared the hammer down on the .357. She walked back to the shower with an exaggerated swing to her hips that Brigid felt certain was done to antagonize. Brigid wasn't prudish, but Domi considered her to be.

Calmly, Brigid reached into her pack and took out a map of the nearby area. Donald Bry had a small lead, but she was certain that the little man was in no shape to travel quickly through harsh terrain. All she needed to find was a piece of ground high enough to let her see what direction he'd gone in.

And hope that no one saw her and Domi first.

KANE SPOTTED the two powerboats sitting low in the water with difficulty. The dark colors of the hulls made them almost invisible against the steel-gray-and-purple horizon. Long fingers of darkness eroded the lingering day and stabbed deeply into the western sky where the sun had dipped over the rim long moments ago. Now that the sun had disappeared, the heat went with it. A wind cold enough to bring goose bumps whipped over Kane.

The barge chugged steadily along toward the two powerboats.

"Got them?" Grant growled restlessly, wrapping his arms around himself to stay warm.

"Yeah." Kane took up the minibinoculars hanging from his neck and focused them on the powerboats. The crafts' size was deceptive against the river. Kane studied them and spotted at least six armed men on each. The men looked small against the boats, letting him know a lot more could be easily hidden belowdecks. A .50-caliber machine gun was mounted on the prow of one while the other held twin 20 mm cannon.

Neither of the powerboats had running lights.

"Easy," Remar said, joining them. "Those ships are ours."

"The checkpoint you were talking about earlier?" Kane asked.

"Yeah."

"I'm surprised that you're letting us see this place," Kane said, "with all the secrecy Falzone has in place."

"Oh," the old man said, chuckling, "you ain't even begun to be surprised yet."

A gentle bump rocked the barge. Kane fisted his shotgun, thinking they were under attack from another shark.

"Jumpy?" Remar cackled and slapped his thigh.

Grant treated the old man to a cold, mirthless grin. "Mebbe, and mebbe we were wondering how good skinny old men could float.''

''You're taking this way too personal,'' Remar assured him. ''Relax. You boys are in the hands of professionals.''

Kane remained on guard, scanning the dark water around the barge. He had no clue at all where he and Grant were. Night made everything seem much worse.

The barge rocked again as it bumped up against something large underwater.

''Feels like we're going to rip the bottom out of the barge,'' Kane said.

''No.'' Remar took a fat-barreled pistol from his side and pointed it skyward. When he pulled the trigger, a flare fired from the pistol, arcing high overhead and bursting into a crimson star.

The flare burned brightly as it floated slowly down in the easterly breeze.

''That's not exactly conducive to keeping a low profile,'' Grant observed.

''Yes and no,'' Remar said. ''If there's anybody out there in boats who we can't see who's keeping an eye on this little meeting, they're going to be using some sort of light-amplification sensors. Night-vision capabilities.''

''The flare robs them of that,'' Kane said. Any kind of light-amplifying device or infrared goggles would react to the flare in a negative way.

Remar nodded as the two powerboats less than a hundred yards in front of them suddenly fired flare guns, as well. The other two flares joined the first and drifted down toward the water.

The barge shivered again as the underwater object struck it once more. This time Kane clearly heard the muted metallic gong noise from the impact that carried through the water. He glanced to port and watched a cylinder a little wider across than the fifty-five-gallon drum of water the barge carried rise above the river's surface. Although the body of water they were on was so huge, Remar had told him the correct name for it still had been a river.

While the three flares were still floating down toward the water, the cylinder held steady beside the barge, then the top flipped open.

"Hurry," Remar urged, waving Kane and Grant toward the cylinder.

Two barge crewman ran out a short, narrow gangplank that thudded home beside the cylinder, only a few inches underwater. A man's silhouette rose above the surface of the cylinder and he stepped onto the gangplank. "Are these the men you were talking about, Remar?"

"Yeah," Remar answered.

The man in the cylinder wore his dark hair cut short and combed forward, giving him a skullcap effect. His eyes were set back in his head, leaving heavy ridges for brows. Standing just less than six feet tall, he was thin, but there was no sign of weakness about him. He wore a short beard, carefully trimmed, and moonlight glinted off gold-hoop earrings in both ears. A Glock 24 .40-caliber semiauto pistol rode in shoulder leather under his left arm. He was dressed in a black turtleneck under a navy woolen sweater with leather-patched elbows and denim pants tucked into calf-high work boots. He looked pale in the darkness, as if he were anemic or didn't get much sun.

His dark eyes apprised Kane and Grant in a heartbeat, and that quickly his decision was made. He strode forward and offered his hand. "I'm Tyler Falzone." His voice remained low and carefully modulated.

Kane introduced himself and Grant, taking Falzone's hand and finding the man's grip surprisingly strong and sure.

"I trust you've had a safe journey," Falzone said.

"If you don't count a run-in with a Mag force," Remar said, "why hell, we've had us a picnic."

Genuine sympathy showed in Falzone's dark, expressive eyes. "You have my apologies for that. My troubles with Baron Cobalt seem to have spilled over on you."

"Barons' problems are everywhere these days," Kane replied. He took an instant liking to Falzone's straightforward way, but wondered how such a mild-mannered individual could lead hard-edged men like Remar and the barge crew.

"We're probably under observation here," Falzone said, glancing at the sky where the flares continued to float down. "And the flares won't hold off the people with night-vision capabilities for long. We'd better go."

"Where?" Kane asked.

Falzone gestured to the cylinder thrusting up from the water. "Down there."

Kane approached the cylinder and peered down into it. Soft green lights from instruments glowed several feet below, giving a hint at the shape and dimensions of the remarkable vehicle resting underwater. "An underwater boat?"

"A sport submersible," Falzone corrected. "After I started salvaging the sunken Northwest Territories, I found out about submersibles that Wei Qiang and the Tong sometimes used down in the Western Isles. I also heard about the sub pirates that plunder the coastlines. It took me eight months of planning and searching, but I caught one."

"How?"

"I put a team down in the Western Isles in a trader boat, made sure people knew I had tech and goods to barter or sell, and set myself up as a target. When the sub pirates came for my boat, I had steel-mesh nets in the water like I'd been fishing. They didn't know I had sonar on board the boat." Falzone gestured toward the conning tower leading into the sub.

Gingerly, Kane stepped over the side and went down the ladder. The conning tower was tight, but he stepped down into the sub in short order.

The sub felt claustrophobic to Kane. The control center was at one end, providing seats for a pilot and copilot, with a navigator's desk to the left of that. The copilot's and navigator's seats were occupied. The navigator looked young, sullen and restless. The copilot was obviously a woman from her build. She kept her attention on the instruments in front of her. Moonlight silvered the water on the other side of the nose windows, creating wispy layers that shifted and moved constantly.

The other end of the sub was filled with diving equipment Kane recognized from mil-spec gear manuals he'd leafed through at the Cerberus redoubt but couldn't identify. Chains held tanks he figured contained oxygen, water or fuel. A round hatch was forward of them on the floor, a wheel-shaped lock on top of it. The air smelled closed-in and left a metallic taste in his mouth. Two bench seats occupied either side of the sub, providing seating for no more than six or eight men.

Grant joined Kane a moment later, having to stoop slightly because he was too tall to stand. He didn't look happy, either.

"When the sub pirates closed in on me," Falzone continued as he slid down the ladder in a practiced maneuver, "I fled. They gave chase, never realizing I was setting them up. Running with the wind, the steel net spread out behind us, it was easy to wrap the net around the sub. The steel strands held, something I wasn't sure they'd do, and fouled the sub's propellers and diving planes. I waited until they ran out of air and surfaced, then I convinced them it would be better for them to surrender the ship. They did, and I let them live. It worked out for all of us."

Remar dogged the conning tower hatch and climbed down into the sub. He took a seat on one of the benches and started rolling a smoke.

"Remar," the woman spoke from the copilot's seat as she checked the instruments.

"Okay, Teresa," Remar grumbled. "Wasn't going to light it. Just wanted the taste in my mouth." He placed the unlit cigarette in his mouth and chewed it casually.

"Have a seat," Falzone invited, dropping into the pilot's chair. "This is my wife, Teresa. Calvin is our navigator."

The young guy at the navigator's station tossed a quick salute without looking up.

"You might want to use the seat belts, as well, to strap in," Falzone said. "The waters through here are somewhat turbulent."

Reluctantly, listening to the whine of the propellers increase and feeling the vibration of the engines suddenly take hold, Kane sat. Grant sat across from him beside Remar, splitting up the fields of fire if it came down to that. However, shooting holes in the sub underwater didn't sound like a good idea.

"What about my wag?" Kane asked.

"The crew will deliver it in a couple days," Remar responded. "Once they make sure nobody from the Heimdall Foundation is following them, they'll turn up. They're taking a different route to where we're going. Anybody tries following them, they're saving them a seat on the last train headed west."

The sub shivered again and the propeller fans growled, then the undersea craft knifed through the water faster than Kane would have thought possible.

Chapter 23

Brigid stepped into the humid night outside the redoubt. A narrow trail ran along a mountain ridge. Six feet in front of her, the land fell away. She couldn't see how far down it went, but the moonlight glistened on treetops several feet below the top of the ridge. An owl hooted, and the sound echoed below, sounding forlorn.

Pausing at the edge of the dropoff, hunkered down against a boulder so she wouldn't be easily skylined, Brigid took her minibinoculars from her pack and flicked them over to infrared. The landscape changed from patchy shadows to different hues of green.

"Nothing there," Domi said.

Brigid remained silent and finished her recon. The infrared capability was sensitive enough to pick up the mountain lion staking out a stream below. Brigid stood and put the minibinoculars away.

"Nothing there," Domi said again, irritation ringing in her voice. "If anything there, owl not be there."

"Unless the owl isn't an owl," Brigid pointed out. She wasn't willing to trust much. She'd believed in Donald Bry and that had almost gotten her killed. "Let's go."

Domi automatically took the lead, and Brigid didn't argue. The trail wound down, zigzagging back and forth across the face of the tall hill. Vegetation stayed thick, but even though t helped to keep them hidden, Brigid knew it also made the going harder. At the bottom of the trail, they found another path that ran alongside the stream.

Brigid held the mini-Uzi in her fist as they passed the area where she'd seen the mountain lion. If the big cat hadn't fed, she felt certain that it wouldn't hesitate about attacking them if it had the chance.

The sound of massive wings slapping the air drew Brigid's attention in time to see the great owl glide from a tree overhead. The bird moved as silently as a shadow and disappeared from sight.

Domi stooped ahead in a little clearing where the moonlight shone down on the trail. She brushed at the ground with her fingers carefully. "Bry's boots."

"How do you know they're his?" Brigid asked.

She stabbed a finger into the boot-print depression in the soft ground. "See mark?" The mark looked like a quarter moon on the boot sole where the big toe would be.

"Yes," Brigid said.

"Back in Cerberus redoubt," Domi explained, "saw mark of Bry's boot in blood left by Lakesh." She placed the ball of her thumb near the quarter-moon divot for measurement. "Same mark there, same mark here."

"I didn't notice that Bry had stepped in Lakesh's blood back at Cerberus."

"Enough of it was on the floor that it was hard not to step in." Domi slid effortlessly to her feet again. "Track fresh. We not too far from Bry. Can tell because the ground still soft and moist from him passing. He waited in redoubt."

"Why wait?"

"For the men who come get him. Their tracks there, too." Domi pointed at the ground again.

"How many men?" Brigid followed Domi, glancing back at the imprints in the soft loam.

"Two, mebbe three. Hard to tell in this light. They didn't stay on path. They were being careful, walking ahead and behind Bry. Sometimes he stepped on their prints, sometimes they stepped on his."

Brigid filed the information away. She wasn't looking to come up on Bry and his associates in the middle of the night

A little farther on, Domi strode out to the stream's edge and touched the scarred bank. Her fingers sank into the slick mud, but even Brigid could spot the groove where something had been dragged across.

"They got in a boat here," the albino said. "Small boat with a strong wooden keel. Can tell wooden because grain shows in places. Keel cut into ground." She touched the ground experimentally. "Ground's still wet, so not long since they passed this way." The moonlight made the stream's depths uncertain.

A loud *blatt* of a small engine spluttered and popped for a moment, then died away.

"Upstream?" Brigid asked, uncertain with the way the noise echoed among all the trees.

"Yeah. Not too far."

"Is there any way to tell which way the boat went?" Brigid asked. It made sense for the boat to go downstream. Unless where it was headed didn't lie in that direction.

Domi spit into the water. "Boat floats. You see any tracks on water?"

The engine spluttered and popped enthusiastically for a moment, then died with a wet, grinding noise.

"Upstream, then," Brigid decided.

Domi nodded and took the lead, vanishing into the leaden shadows made by the heavy foliage and the dark clouds scudding across the face of the quarter moon.

THE DRUMBEATS ECHOED hollowly over the flat expanse of water below the cliff where Mallet lay ready with his team. He cradled his Copperhead in his arms, resting his body weight on his elbows. Since the ambush on Kane and Grant had failed earlier, they'd been on the move constantly. All of them were fatigued, relying on energy reserves that would have sapped most men. He left the faceplate open on his helmet to aid in cooling.

Voices joined the drums, calling out for the mercy of Wiy Tukay.

"Stupe fuckers," Iverson growled as he looked at Mallet. "They don't even know what they're praying to."

"Doesn't matter," Mallet said. "They have boats and we need boats. Looks like we've run out of river."

The darkening sky west of their current position was full of heavy clouds hanging low over the horizon. Lightning sizzled through the vaporous masses, and the heavy ozone smell in the air promised rain.

After they'd raided the fuel depot hours ago, Mallet had questioned the old man who had operated it. The old man had talked about the Wiy Tukay worshipers and their location here. He'd also mentioned that the Wiy Tukay worshipers had boats and were constantly warring with Tyler Falzone's people. Mallet had headed this way at once. They'd left the Sandcats two miles back, hidden in a small box canyon just off the river that led them here.

The drumming reached a crescendo, then began anew. The mouth of the cavern where the Wiy Tukay worshipers had their base cast an irregular patch of yellow light out onto the waves sweeping in. The crash and boom of the waves mixed with the drumming.

"Set the lines," Mallet ordered.

Quickly, two crews set the rappelling lines, tying them around pitons they drove into the ground. The sound of the hammers driving the pitons didn't carry over the crash of the waves and the drumming.

When the lines were set, Mallet divided his team and wrapped the first rappelling line around his stomach and butt in a makeshift harness. He held the lines in his gloved left hand, the Copperhead's stock resting against his chest. He glanced to the left, saw Iverson was ready, closed his face shield and stepped back over the cliff face. He fell.

The Wiy Tukay worshipers had chosen their base well. With the cave facing the water, the only means of approach most

attackers would have was the water. However, the Wiy Tukay
clan hadn't thought about a rappelling attack.

Mallet let the line burn through his gloved hand, touching
the wall once more lightly with his feet and shoving himself
back out again. His slight lead over Iverson was going to work
out well.

Forty feet farther down, he arced out, let go the rappelling
lines to drop the remaining distance quickly and got his first
glimpse of the cave's interior.

Nearly fifty men, women and children occupied the cave.
One huge bonfire in the center of the cave threw dancing shadows across three walls. Groups of five to ten sat around
smaller fires, roasting meat on sticks. They wore ragged clothing that held patched-over patches. Only a few of them had
blasters, most of them single-action pistols, .22 rifles and the
occasional shotgun. Eight powerboats anchored near the
mouth of the cave bobbed restlessly on the water.

In the next heartbeat, lightning sizzled across the sky and
thunder bellowed. At the same time Mallet slid the final distance to the cavern, a man posted as guard near the mouth of
the cave looked up. He lifted the single-action rifle he carried,
fitting it to his shoulder and squinting over the sights at Mallet.

Mercilessly, the Cobaltville Magistrate aimed on the fly and
stroked the Copperhead's trigger. The line of bullets chopped
into the man's chest and tracked up to his face, exploding his
head. Even as the dead man stretched out on the hard stone
floor, Mallet touched down.

The Mag leader swept the people inside the room with his
harsh gaze, seeing them draw back in fear. Even if they didn't
know what the black polycarbonate suits represented, they
knew enough to fear him.

Iverson came to a rest beside him, his own Copperhead up
and ready.

A Wiy Tukay worshiper with a shotgun stood and fired.
The detonation filled the cave as the drums fell silent.

Mallet rocked back as the double-aught buckshot slammed

him backward, but his finger caressed the Copperhead's trigger. Even as the Magistrate's balance came steady again, the Wiy Tukay worshiper stutter-stepped backward and collapsed across one of the smaller cook fires. The sweet stink of burning flesh filled the cave.

More of the Magistrates rappelled into the cave and quickly took up positions. They stood like shadows at the cave's mouth while lightning sliced through the sky behind them and blasted the cave with flashes of harsh bright light.

Incredibly, the Wiy Tukay worshipers laid down their weapons and bowed, placing their palms on the ground in supplication.

RIDING IN THE SUB reminded Kane of flying in a Deathbird, except where the attack Bird always felt heavy slicing through the air, the sub felt buoyant, as if it were on the edge of taking off.

Kane stared hard at the blackness on the other side of the cockpit windows. "I can't see anything out there."

"We're running on sonar," Falzone replied. "Not only does it let me know if other ships are around, but it provides a pretty good map of the river bottom here."

He adjusted a joystick and shifted the small sub to avoid an object forty feet to port. They continued to descend into the black water.

Kane watched through the window as they passed the object, but he never got a look at what it was.

"It was a building," Falzone said. "Overturned and broken. We're cruising above what used to be Leavenworth, Washington." He made a course correction and the minisub headed south, southwest. "In the past, gold drew men here and the fertile lands made them stay. Of course, you can't see any of that now. Then, for a time when the Great Northern Railway Company ran through here—you are familiar with trains?"

"Yes," Kane replied.

"Good. Some people aren't." Falzone made more steering

adjustments. "While the railroad ran through here, Leavenworth was a logging town. That lasted only a short time before the railroad relocated. After that, they became a tourist town. The Cascade Mountain range, which we'll be passing in moments, was part of the attraction."

"How do you know so much about this predark stuff?"

"I read," Falzone answered. "And there are a lot of comp progs my teams and I have found. I'm very restless, hardly sleep more than three or four hours a night."

"Reading's not a characteristic you'd normally find in a guy running sec for a trader," Kane observed.

"Remar's been talking, I see."

"Only enough to get me interested."

"I wasn't always a sec boss." Without a word, Falzone removed his hand from the joystick. As if it had been rehearsed, Teresa's hand quickly took his place and the minisub continued on without interruption. "What about you? You seem to know a lot about any number of things."

Kane gave the man a neutral glance. "I've worked sec for someone since the day I was born."

Falzone lifted an eyebrow. "That surprises me."

Kane let the comment pass without response.

"As I'm sure you must have been surprised by Remar's bit of polish, though he does disguise it well."

"Looks truly deceive," Kane said, and drew a quiet, brimstone-reeking curse from Remar.

"They do indeed," Falzone admitted, regarding Kane speculatively. "Meaning no disrespect to others in this godforsaken world, but there are some men whose main goal in life is to conquer new worlds and to explore questions of nature and self. I freely own up to the fact that I see myself as one of those men."

"Those men," Kane said softly, "are generally the ones whose bodies other villes hang out as warnings to other people who get to feeling questioning."

Falzone laughed good-naturedly. "Perhaps. But I believe

we were put on this planet to do more than survive, Kane. I think we were intended to bend nature and physical laws to our wills. What do you think of that?''

"I'm thinking like that's what caused skydark," Kane replied.

"Knowledge is a very powerful thing, Kane, and in the hands of the wrong men, it is a very wicked tool."

"Baron Cobalt seems like the wrong kind of man."

"If he is a man," Falzone said. "At any rate, whatever Baron Cobalt turns out to be, he is the wrong kind of man. Which is why I've been judicious in what I've been trading with him at all. If I didn't need the blasters he's so willing to trade, he could go fuck himself."

"But you need the blasters," Grant stated.

As the sonar pinged another warning, Teresa made a course correction, picking up another ping almost immediately.

"I do need the blasters," Falzone admitted. "Thankfully, Baron Cobalt believes I don't know that most of the progs I'm trading him are more or less worthless." He frowned. "Or at least he did believe that until one of the shipments I traded him turned out to be laced with a comp virus. Now it appears he has no patience with me."

"And if the Mag force he sent catches up with you?" Grant challenged.

"I'm reasonably certain that they won't," Falzone said. "We're firmly entrenched in our salvage operation."

"You mentioned the Heimdall Foundation," Kane probed.

"Have you heard of them?" Falzone asked, turning back to Kane.

"If I have, I've forgotten," Kane answered.

"They've been around since shortly after skydark," Falzone said. "They believe that the past world was toppled into chaos by alien invaders. They've been interested in gathering evidence to support their theories, and recover lost science, since their inception."

"What's their interest in you?" Kane asked.

"The Lost Valley of Wiy Tukay, of course." Falzone smiled. "During its time, Seattle became a repository and birthplace of thousands of progs used by comps around the world. For a long time, the Heimdall Foundation believed that all the knowledge possibly contained in this area was lost to them forever. I've proved them wrong. Now they want to know what I know. And it appears they'll stop at nothing to get it."

Abruptly, a series of rapid-fire bangs thudded against the minisub's hull. Grant and Kane both jumped, startled by the sudden sounds.

"Relax, it's only debris stirred up by the current," Falzone said. "It happens all the time."

"It sounds like it's almost coming through," Grant said.

"It's not—it just sounds like it. The hull is fiberglass."

Kane swore. "It's not even metal?"

"It's better than metal. Fiberglass is only a layman's term to describe composite compounds of fiber-reinforced plastic resins. This hull is made up of fiberglass featuring multiple layers of woven and biaxial roving."

The harsh popping repeated, but there were still no leaks.

"The seams are all stepped to a separate thickness at each layer," Falzone went on, "kind of like tongue-in-groove carpentry. Or, perhaps, an example more to your familiarity, like the slide on your pistol. They have very tight fits. The finish is sculpted and painted, and each individual minisub put out by this particular manufacturer was done by hand. Contact areas along the lower hull are covered with replaceable, heavy, dense polyethylene plates. We're well protected in here."

"And if you ran into a building?"

The sonar pinged again.

"At this depth and at this speed, we'd crack open like an egg."

THE STORM CONTINUED to rage outside the cave of the Wiy Tukay worshipers. Acid rain pelted the ledge hanging over the river, creating hissing pools of toxic waste that would have burned flesh down to bone.

Mallet raised his free hand to hold his shock troops in place as he stared at the worshipers on their hands and knees before him. His eyes swept the cave as he sought understanding. He glanced at Iverson, but his second's face was masked in the featureless executioner black. Iverson slowly shook his head back and forth.

Then the Wiy Tukay worshipers began chanting. "Men in Black. Men in Black. Men in Black."

Slowly, fearfully, a large, muscular man near the bonfire heating the cave stood. He showed his open hands as the others around him held their positions and stopped chanting.

Mallet stepped toward the other man. He spoke to Iverson and the rest of his troops over the helmet comm. "Hold here." He kept the Copperhead centered between the Wiy Tukay worshiper's eyes as he advanced. Then he spoke through the mask in the harsh voice he'd been trained to use in Cobaltville. "Move and I'll chill you."

"Yes, Man in Black," the man answered immediately. His face held a mixture of fear and awe.

Mallet stopped just out of arm's reach of the man, conscious of every eye on him. More than half of the worshipers were men. Another quarter their number were women. Children made up the rest, ranging in ages from babies to teens.

"Who are you?" Mallet demanded.

"I am Kroger, Man in Black."

Realizing that the Wiy Tukay worshiper wasn't simply referring to the way he was dressed, Mallet asked, "Do you know who I am?"

"You are one of the Men in Black, one of those foretold to arrive with the coming of the angry god, Wiy Tukay, whose fearful hand smote down the world. Can I get a hallelujah, brothers and sisters?"

"Hallelujah!" the other worshipers responded, remaining

on their hands and knees. "The wicked and the unprepared have been stricken down in your name."

The voices died away, leaving the hammering thunder of the storm outside the cave.

"Do you know what you're supposed to do?" Mallet demanded.

"Of course, Man in Black. You are the representative of the one true government, amen."

"Amen!" the group of worshipers cried out.

"All you have to do is tell us what to do, Man in Black," Kroger said. "We have lived all our lives, knowing the fear of Wiy Tukay, doing our best to serve the destroyer of greed and complacence, striking down those who would interfere with the great leveling. When others thought they ruled the world through their comps, our ancestors knew that they were only instruments of the beast, branding the world with its unholy number 666." He paused, the firelight and lightning flickering in his feverish gaze.

Mallet stared at the man. In his time as a Cobaltville Magistrate, he'd seen a lot of Roamers and outlanders who possessed strange beliefs. Some of those beliefs could be traced back to prenukecaust times, and a few even further back than that. But he'd never heard about the Wiy Tukay movement.

"I'm searching for a man named Tyler Falzone," Mallet stated.

"We will help you find the desecrator, Man in Black," Kroger declared fiercely. "We have tried to bring the defiler to divine justice ourselves, but we have failed." Slowly, the man stepped forward. He reached for Mallet's Copperhead.

The Magistrate just managed to stop himself from pulling the trigger.

Gently, Kroger placed the Copperhead's muzzle between his own eyes and released it. "I know we have failed you, Man in Black, but please take only my life and spare those of my family." Sweat ran down the man's face, but the feverish glow never left his eyes. "I live only to die serving the great

Wiy Tukay. Let your righteous anger be with me, not them.''
Slowly, he dropped to his knees, his arms resting at his sides.

"Failure is not accepted," the crowd of worshipers intoned.
"Compliance is not accepted. Wiy Tukay will shield us and
hide us in his glory again by sundering the world and making
it whole once more."

Kroger waited, trembling slightly. "I await deletion, Man
in Black."

"No," Mallet said, pulling the Copperhead's muzzle from
the man's flesh. "No deletion."

"Then I am unworthy of your attention. I will attend to my
own deletion." Kroger yanked a knife from a holster strapped
to his thigh. Lightning flashed across the massive blade as the
man attempted to slash his wrist.

Mallet kicked the blade from the man's hand, signaling his
troops not to attack. Beneath the Magistrate's helmet, Mallet
grinned, enjoying the worshiper's willingness to destroy himself. Perhaps at another time he would have let the man do
that and watched him kick through his final death throes as he
bled out. But for now Mallet needed the worshiper alive.

Keeping the Copperhead out of reach by placing his body
between the worshiper and the blaster, Mallet seized Kroger's
long hair and twisted the man's face up to meet is. "No deletion," he ordered hoarsely. "Do you understand?"

Kroger's lips quivered and spittle dripped from one corner.
"In truth, Man in Black, I do not. Failure is not accepted."

"Failure is not accepted," the worshipers repeated, their
voices filling the cave. They sounded angry, doubtful.

Knowing he stood on the brink of losing control of the
crowd and having to kill them all when there was a chance he
could use them, Mallet shouted, "No deletion until I say failure has been final. Do you understand me?"

A hesitant silence followed for a moment, then they all answered. "Yes, Man in Black."

Mallet stared into Kroger's feverish eyes. "Do you understand?"

Tears tracked the man's cheeks. "Yes, Man in Black. Forgive me, but I had doubts that you would ever come. My people and I have been waiting so long." He wiped at his face with a callused hand. "But we knew with the desecrater Tyler Falzone digging up all the old comps that Wiy Tukay the destroyer would arrive. The madness must end. We must be autonomous again. Humans do not live by the will of the machines."

"Humans do not live by the will of the machines," the other worshipers said. "No one shall be just a number. The census-takers, servants of the machines, must die. Let not every name be known."

"I want to find Tyler Falzone," Mallet repeated. "Can you help me?"

"Yes," Kroger hissed. "We can help you. We have almost succeeded in tracking him and his underwater boats down to their hiding place."

"Good," Mallet said coldly, releasing his grip on the man's hair. "Then you'll take me to him."

"Of course, Man in Black. We live only to do the bidding of the great Wiy Tukay."

"Are there other Wiy Tukay worshipers?" the Magistrate asked.

"Yes."

"And can you get them to join us?"

"Of course. Once they learn you are here, Man in Black, I don't think it would be possible to keep them away."

Mallet turned from the man, smiling beneath his mask as he studied the worshipers. This was working out better than he'd expected. He'd hoped merely to get a few boats to continue the chase. Instead, he had the beginnings of an army.

Chapter 24

The stuttering pop of the engine thundered only a few yards ahead, but the thick brush filling the stream banks prevented Brigid from seeing the source of the noise. Closer now, she also heard other engines roaring in the distance, growing dimmer. Domi was stopped ahead, peering through the brush. Brigid joined her, gently pushing a branch aside so she could look through.

A small, odd boat sat in the stream pulling at a line Brigid assumed led to an anchor. The current tugged at the boat, rocking it from side to side. The big man pulling at the engine starter cord cursed as he rocked the boat even more. Two other men urged him on, watching the surrounding forest nervously.

The man in the middle of the boat stood a little more than six feet tall and carried extra weight that had settled in his stomach. He wore a full beard that looked slightly ragged and unkempt, and his dark brown hair brushed at his shoulders. He was dressed in dark green coveralls and boots, a blue New York Yankees windbreaker pulled tight across his shoulders. A pistol jutted from a holster at his hip.

The boat reminded Brigid of old steam-powered paddle wheelers of the nineteenth century she'd seen in books at Cobaltville. Only this one was constructed with a small crew and cargo in mind. The craft was no more than twenty-five feet in length and half that across. The paddle wheel, equipped with metal-ribbed wooden blades, stuck out a foot and a half on either side of the boat.

"Get that fucking engine started, Wimmer," one of the men

snarled hoarsely. "Those damn Tong will be down on us in no time."

"I'm trying, damn it." Wimmer wrapped the starter cord back around the flywheel on the big engine mounted at the back of the craft. "Probably can't hear us over the noise of those damn fan boats they're driving." He braced a foot against the engine and pulled on the starter cord again.

The motor turned over a handful of times, chugging and popping, and the paddle wheel turned half a rotation, blades slapping at the water. Then it stopped and the men started cursing again.

Wimmer hooked the starter cord again and started winding it around the flywheel.

"Did you check the gas?" one of the men asked.

"Hell, yes," Wimmer declared disgustedly. "You think I'm some kinda stupe?"

"Yeah." The man snickered. "Just wasn't sure which kind." Both the other men were dressed in coveralls and looked as ragged as Wimmer.

"Fuck you, Zandt," Wimmer yelled. "If I didn't have to get this engine started right now, I'd kick your ass." He pulled on the cord, listened to the engine sputter and die, and cursed again.

"Quiet," the third man said. "I hear something."

Brigid strained to hear, watching the men listening intently in the paddle wheeler. She knew the hull on the craft didn't match the marks Domi had found, which meant there had been at least two boats.

In the distance she could still hear the buzzing noise of other engines. Only now, at least one of them was coming back downstream. She couldn't help but wonder where Donald Bry had gotten to.

"Damn Tong are coming back," Zandt stated. "They must have heard us. We've to get out of here."

"Don't fucking panic," Wimmer ordered, striding forward. He took up the rope leading into the water and pulled, bringing the paddle wheeler forward. He knelt, then unhooked the small anchor from a log in the stream. "Grab up them poles. We'll float downstream. We get past the redoubt, mebbe they'll give up on us."

The other two men picked up the long wooden poles lying on the paddle wheeler's deck and went to the starboard and port sides of the boat. They had to push the poles into the stream at least eight feet before they touched the bottom. Angling the poles, the men put all their weight into the effort of getting the paddle wheeler moving, practically climbing up on them to shove the boat forward.

Wimmer joined them, grabbing another long pole and setting himself up beside the man on the starboard side.

From the swiftly increasing sound of the approaching engines, Brigid knew the men weren't going to get clear of the area in time even with the current favoring them. She tapped Domi on the shoulder and withdrew behind the bushes.

"They're gonna catch us, Wimmer," Zandt cried out.

"Goddamn it, I know it. Keep poling," Wimmer urged.

The two new boats were smaller than the paddle wheeler. They were basically triangular in shape, a blunt-nosed prow followed by a rear-directed fan at least five feet across. The flat-bottomed boats skimmed and skipped across the water, hammering the passengers unmercifully. Two-man teams straddled the long seat that ran from prow to fan. The man in front controlled the craft with handlebars and rudder pedals, leaving the man behind to act as gunner.

The pilot of the first fan boat decreased speed and brought his craft around in a tight turn that threw a drenching wave over the paddle wheeler. The gunner twisted and fired immediately, and Brigid recognized the distinctive sound of an AK-47. Tracers flared violent purple every third round, ricocheting sparks from the paddle wheeler deck and smacking into one of the men, knocking him into the water.

Wimmer abandoned the paddle wheeler and raised his pistol in both hands as he took cover beside the tree, then fired deliberately, spacing his shots. Sparks jumped from the fan boat's prow. He had to duck out of sight as the second fan boat's gunner targeted the trees.

The second fan boat slowed dramatically as the engine throbbed in reverse. The gunner stood, bringing his AK-47 to shoulder and unleashing 3-round bursts.

Zandt broke from too little cover aboard the paddle wheeler and dived for the nearest bank. The Tong fan boat gunner targeted him in midleap, and blasterfire nearly cut Zandt in two.

Brigid weighed the options she'd been considering for the past couple moments. She had no clue who Donald Bry had met once he'd stepped from the redoubt, and no real sense of where he'd gone. The Tong being in the area was a good indication that something had gone on, but again she was left not knowing what that was.

The only wild card in the mix was the paddle wheeler crew. If they'd happened to be in the area by happenstance, she'd be back to square one. If they knew something, she couldn't afford to lose them.

She didn't even want to think about dying in the attempt. In the split second she made her decision, she was already in motion, startling Domi by moving unexpectedly.

The albino's ruby eyes stared at her.

Brigid lifted the mini-Uzi, targeted the bottom of the closest fan boat's fuel tank on the port side of the vessel, breathed out and squeezed the trigger. The bullets ripped through the fuel tank, sloshing the contents over the fan boat. She let the machine pistol track up and to the right, striking sparks from the wire cage around the fan boat.

The pilot yelled to his companion and reached for a pistol holstered at his side, twisting his head back to look at Brigid. In the next moment the sparks ignited the spilled fuel.

Evidently, the fuel tank had a bigger internal reservoir than Brigid had expected, possibly extending even under the bench seat for long-range patrols. The explosion ripped through the fan boat, twisting it and throwing it high into the air. An orange-and-yellow ball of flames expanded briefly as the watercraft blew into pieces. The blast punched razor-sharp shards through the gunner standing nearby, knocking him sprawling. The biggest section of the wrecked fan boat came back down and got hung up in the trees wreathed in flames.

Wimmer stuck his head up for an instant, then Domi fired at him, driving him back to cover.

"No!" Brigid ordered. "We need Wimmer alive." She twisted and fired a short burst that tore into the water only inches from the fan boat.

"Wimmer!" Brigid yelled. "Wimmer!"

The blasterfire died away, and the voices of the two Tong members speaking in Chinese sounded.

"Wimmer!" Brigid called again.

"What do you want?" the man asked suspiciously.

"If we get a chance, I want to talk to you."

"Hell, you nearly chilled me."

"It was a mistake. She shot before she realized it was you." Brigid doubted Wimmer would believe it, but she had to try.

The fan boat's engine idled more strongly for a moment as the pilot pulled back against the current until he reached Brigid's position again. Another flurry of bullets ripped into the ground in front of her.

"I don't know you," Wimmer said in the sudden silence that followed. "If I don't know you, I don't trust you."

"I just want to talk," Brigid said.

The Tong members on the fan boat spoke to each other rapidly, too far away for Brigid to overhear.

"About what?" Wimmer demanded.

"The redoubt downstream for one."

"Been there. Ain't interested."

Brigid shifted, peering through the brush at the Tong fan boat. Fear prickled the skin across the back of her neck. "How long do you think it will be before the Tong send reinforcements?" And for that matter, they didn't know that ground troops hadn't been let off farther upstream and were now closing in.

"I'm listening," Wimmer said.

"We could go back to the redoubt," Brigid suggested.

"Might as well crawl into a grave. Get in there, ain't no place to go."

Brigid felt a little better. If the man didn't know the access codes for the mat-trans unit, it was almost certain he was local to the area, not someone who had jumped in like them or Bry. "Do you know a man named Donald Bry?"

"Never heard of him."

The gunner left the fan boat, disappearing at once into the inky shadows.

"Domi," Brigid whispered, turning back to face the other woman. Only Domi wasn't there. Panic pounded at Brigid's temples. She wanted to move because she was certain the Tong warrior had spotted her position. Staying there was like being a sitting duck. But if she moved, Domi might not find her again if more Tong did arrive, and there was every chance the albino girl would kill her by mistake.

"You still there?" Wimmer asked.

"Yes," Brigid replied.

"We got us one loose in the bushes now."

"I know." Brigid strained to hear footsteps in the forest, but it was impossible over the rapid humming of the fan boat's engine.

"Give me some cover from the guy in the fan boat," Wimmer said, "and mebbe I can tilt the odds a little more in our favor."

"When?" Brigid asked, pushing up on her knees.

"We ain't getting any younger," Wimmer declared. He broke cover, drawing fire from the fan-boat pilot at once. The blazing fire from the wreckage hanging in the tree showed the terrain much too clearly.

Brigid squeezed the trigger, causing the fan-boat pilot to accelerate his craft and turn the fan back toward her. Debris and leaves whipped over her, stinging her eyes and blurring her vision. She lost sight of Wimmer instantly. The mini-Uzi's rounds struck sparks from the wire cage over the fan, ringing stridently.

Farther downstream, Wimmer rushed from the forest and a couple feet into the stream before leaping into a low, flat dive. The fan-boat pilot emptied the pistol's magazine in a rush of snapping pops. Water spumed up from the near misses.

Leaning out again, Brigid targeted the fan boat's fuel tank, hoping to have the same response as she did the first time. The mini-Uzi cycled dry before she was able to track onto the fuel tank. She ejected the spent magazine, palmed another one from her pack and tried to fit it into her weapon.

Wimmer's head broke the surface less than five feet from the paddle wheeler. He swam hard for the boat, although Brigid didn't see why. The paddle wheeler didn't even offer cover. His hand caught the boat's edge and he hauled himself up, throwing his upper body over the side.

The magazine jammed, not fitting properly, just as Brigid caught a moving shadow in her peripheral vision coming up quick on her left. She turned and saw the Tong gunman step from the darkness, his cruel face lighted by the fan-boat wreckage hanging in the trees.

The Tong warrior peered at her over the AK-47's muzzle and grinned as his finger tightened on the trigger.

Chapter 25

Brigid Baptiste had never known that time could move so slowly. She was surprised at the cool detachment that filled her, that allowed her to pull at the magazine jammed in the mini-Uzi and free it even as her breath froze in her lungs.

Anam-chara, she thought, and her mind filled with images of Kane in battle and at rest, bloodied and sleeping. She saw him dressed in Magistrate black, a walking nightmare wreathed in death. And she saw him dressed in another suit of armor, this one hundreds of years old with a banner of a gold harp on a field of blue tied around his left arm.

Somewhere in that instant, Brigid believed that her thoughts brushed his, and she knew wherever he was, his thoughts were of her.

Then Domi stepped from behind the Tong warrior. The albino's right arm knocked the assault rifle up so that it fired into the trees while her left hand drew a slim knife blade across his exposed throat. Bloody bubbles blew from his sliced trachea.

The Tong warrior knew death had claimed him, but he turned on his attacker. Domi head-butted him in the mouth, knocking out teeth and splitting his lips. Her bone-white hair came away stained with his blood as he dropped. The albino dived for cover as the fan-boat pilot opened fire, pinning them down.

Brigid moved quickly, her breath coming back into her lungs in a harsh, dry gasp. For the moment, she abandoned the mini-Uzi, shoving it aside in favor of the dead Tong warrior's AK-47. She checked the action, blew the dust from it and knew from her readings rather than her experience that the weapon was almost indestructible. She turned her gaze back to Wimmer aboard the paddle wheeler.

Near the middle of the boat's deck, Wimmer stomped down his foot. Two half doors swung open, releasing a 7.62 mm machine gun that popped up nearly two feet on its swivel mount.

The fan-boat pilot turned his craft again, bringing his field of fire toward the paddle wheeler. He released the handlebar controls for an instant and fired.

Wimmer swung the machine gun around and squeezed the trigger. The full-throated roar filled the forest, and brass glinted in the moonlight and the light from the flaming wreckage. The heavy rounds chewed into the stream and across the fan-boat's prow.

At least one of the Tong gunner's rounds hit Wimmer and knocked him to one side.

Brigid couldn't tell if it had struck the man in the face or chest. Either would be bad. Coolly, she extended her hand under the assault rifle's barrel, lined up the sights on the Tong warrior as he powered up again, then squeezed the trigger deliberately. She aimed for the center of the man's mass, not certain if she should lead him at the distance. If he'd moved only a short distance either way, the trees that had protected Brigid and Domi from his bullets would have interfered with the shot.

The bullet struck the Tong warrior in the chest and drove him from the fan boat. Out of control, the vessel ran up onto the opposite bank and flipped over. The motor ran for a few seconds longer, then coughed, sputtered and died.

Brigid started to get up but Domi caught her arm.

"Wait," the albino whispered. "Listen."

Reluctantly, Brigid did, but her eyes cut to Wimmer aboard the paddle wheeler. The man forced himself up with effort, slowly bobbing up and down on the water where it had become ensnared in a clutch of exposed roots sticking out from the bank.

"Okay," Domi said. "Don't hear no more boats."

Brigid picked up the mini-Uzi and slung it. She paused only long enough to strip the bandolier of extra magazines off the Tong warrior whose throat Domi had cut. If the mini-Uzi was still serviceable, the AK-47 could be used to trade for supplies.

Wimmer weakly managed a sitting position, but brought up his pistol.

Brigid didn't know if Wimmer knew anything about Bry, but she was certain that the paddle boat was the only quick means of escape that they had. She showed none of the hesitation she felt as she raised the assault rifle to her shoulder. "You can talk, or I can shoot."

Wimmer nodded and lowered the pistol. "I guess we'll be talking, then. I think I'm losing too much blood to make it out of here on my own."

"Keep him covered," Brigid told Domi.

"Sure."

Brigid waded into the stream and swam across to the paddle wheeler. The water was cold, turning her to ice in seconds. When she pulled up onto the paddle wheeler, the wind made the chill sensation even worse, prickling her skin and causing her teeth to chatter.

"Come on out," she called to Domi.

The albino plunged into the water without hesitation and clambered aboard the paddle wheeler.

Domi checked on the engine while Brigid retrieved a med kit from the hole in the deck. A quick examination of the spring-loaded device let her drop the machine gun back into concealment. She opened the med kit at about the same time Domi pulled on the starter cord.

The engine coughed and wheezed, then caught. "Easy," the albino said.

Wimmer scowled at her as she took the pilot's seat. "Beginner's luck. But you're going to need me to get us out of here.''

Brigid examined the man's wound with a flashlight. The bullet had entered high on Wimmer's chest and exited even higher on his back, even missing the scapula. She put her hand over the wound but didn't feel any suction. "There's no blood. The bullet missed the lung. That's good news.''

"Still hurts like hell.''

Brigid ignored the complaint as she stuffed the wound with gauze to staunch the bleeding. The capillaries had already started shutting down some of the flow.

"Which way?'' Domi asked as she powered the boat into the middle of the stream.

"Downstream,'' Brigid answered.

"Mebbe Bry not go that way.''

"Is Bry a friend of yours?'' Wimmer asked. He shivered from the pain he experienced as Brigid tended his wound.

"He was,'' Brigid answered. "He's why we came out here.''

"You're from Cobaltville?''

"No.''

Wimmer flicked his gaze back toward Domi in the pilot's chair. "She mentioned Cobaltville.''

"We've been through there,'' Brigid replied. "But it's not where we're from.'' The feeling of truth in the statement surprised her. She didn't know exactly when she'd started thinking of the Cerberus redoubt as home, but she did.

"Where are you from?''

Brigid shook her head, rocking from side to side as Domi sped downstream. "No.''

"You're damn tight-fisted with information,'' Wimmer objected. With the shock hitting his system, his voice didn't sound nearly as gruff as he'd wanted.

"Do you know Bry?'' Brigid asked.

"And if I want to be tightfisted with information?''

Brigid looked at him and spoke calmly. "Right now, I need your boat. I don't need you."

"Do you think you're that cold?"

Brigid was silent for a moment. "I guess it's what you think that matters, right? If you're right and I'm not, you won't know until you test me. If you're wrong and I am that hard, you're going to be snake bait." She glanced at his arm. "Snakes have keen olfactory senses. With the blood trail you'll leave, I'm betting they'd find you in less than five seconds."

Wimmer stared at her. "Olfactory senses."

"They smell things," Brigid said.

"Thought they tasted them, what with the way they flick their tongues out."

"Their tongues gather scent particles," Brigid explained. "Then they stick them into a Jacobson organ in the roof of their mouth."

"You know a lot about snakes, huh?"

"Yes." An image of the snake striking her a few days ago filled Brigid's mind for an instant.

"You talk like some other people I know. Want to show you something." Wimmer rolled up his left sleeve to reveal a tattoo on the inside of his elbow. "Know what this is?"

The tattoo showed a large blue dot with lighter blue rings around it. Two twisted lines of orange ran through it.

Brigid would have remembered the tattoo even without her eidetic memory. At Cobaltville, there had been only whispers of the organization known as the Heimdall Foundation, and most of those were being eradicated in the revisionist history being done. "That's the Heimdall Foundation."

"You're familiar with it?" Wimmer seemed surprised.

"I've heard of it," Brigid said, "but I've never met anyone associated with it." The wind cut into her, biting with jagged icicle fangs.

Wimmer rolled his sleeve back down. "Your friend Bry. Want to give me a description?"

Brigid did, reeling off the information.

"Tatum didn't have Bry's name right," Wimmer said when she was finished, "but he had the description down."

"The Heimdall Foundation is looking for Bry?" Brigid asked.

"Or a guy who fits that size." Wimmer nodded.

"Then you didn't just happen to be out here?"

"No. We were sent to get that Bry guy. Only the Tong got him first."

"The Tong?" Despite what had taken place back at the redoubt, Brigid couldn't imagine Bry meeting up with Wei Qiang's troops.

"Yeah," Wimmer said. "The Heimdall Foundation has been working a deal with your friend—"

"Not so much friend." In the pilot seat, Domi scowled.

"What kind of deal?" Brigid asked.

"Bry has been giving them some kind of files," Wimmer said. "Files that have something to do with aliens coming to our world and destroying it. Biggest bunch of nukeshit I've ever heard of."

Brigid considered that, not believing that Lakesh would give up any of the documents about the Archons. But the Heimdall Foundation's core efforts were devoted to discovering the truth about the aliens. "What was Bry getting out of it?"

Wimmer hesitated, then shrugged. "I don't know."

"You're lying," Brigid said flatly.

Wimmer met her gaze steadily for a moment, then gave in with another shrug. "They were going to get Bry into Tyler Falzone's operation in the Lost Valley of Wiy Tukay."

"How?"

"They've been talking to some of Falzone's people. Not all of them are loyal."

"HERE WE ARE," Falzone said.

Kane stood behind the pilot and copilot as the minisub gently headed toward the surface. The forward lights burned through the shallower depths, which looked blue now that they were nearer the surface. A craggy rock face filled the view screen and small, colorful fish flitted away. Several schools of young fish turned together, looking as if the currents had taken them all at once. Debris from buildings, including steel girders and wags, twisted into the rock.

"Where?" Kane asked.

"Home." Falzone cut the engines entirely, and the minisub floated up as smooth as oil. A sea turtle almost a yard across bumped against the Plexiglas nose window, pulling itself into its shell as it bounced away and disappeared. "You notice all the marine life around this island?"

"Yeah," Kane replied. He felt better now that they were going up. It had taken almost five hours to make the journey, and he never had quite gotten used to being under the sea.

"We feed them," Falzone said, "then we feed on them. It's an ecological cycle that's good for all of us. They could venture out to one of the other islands—and there are hundreds here in this part of the Northwest Territories—but fish this size are prey for everything out there. Every island I've set up has self-sufficiency in mind."

"Every island?" Grant asked.

Falzone nodded. "There's more than one major port for our operation. How many there are is going to be my business. I set it up like this for a couple reasons. It's hard to find an island that can support a population of any size, and for another, I don't like the idea of putting all my eggs in one basket."

"Told you he was a smart guy," Remar said, winking at Kane.

"The major ports are self-contained," Falzone went on as the minisub continued to drift up. "But we rotate ops bases on a lot of others."

"A moving target is hard to hit," Kane observed.

Falzone nodded. "Exactly."

The minisub surfaced, bobbing slightly out of the water before settling back in. Lights swept across the prow, blasting in through the windows strong enough to make Kane blink. After Falzone switched off the sub's lights, Kane was able to make out the figures standing on a C-shaped dock in front of a sheer rock wall.

"So what are you bringing us to?" Kane asked.

"My home," Falzone answered as he flipped switches. The minisub stopped vibrating as the engines died. "I wanted you to see what we're doing here, not just a tin hut in the middle of barren rock." He glanced at Kane and Grant. "Looking at the two of you, I know you're well fed and healthy. Whoever you're working for, you're being well taken care of. And if you're as good as Remar says you are, I want to show you that I can take care of you, too."

Teresa led the way up the short ladder to the conning tower. Falzone motioned for Kane to go next. Teresa was more sure-footed on the ladder, going up it rapidly and releasing the hatch locks, while Kane rocked wider with the minisub's motions as the waves lapped at it. Teresa stepped out and Kane spotted the stars in the night sky above, thinking that maybe he'd been taking them for granted a little too long.

He clambered over the conning tower and dropped onto the minisub's body. The vessel rolled on top of the waves now instead of being inches below. He guessed that Falzone felt pretty secure in his location.

"Careful," Teresa called out. "It's going to be slippery even with the friction pads." She stood on the small dock only inches out of the water.

Kane looked at the ladder attached to the dock. The ladder disappeared below the waterline.

"We're at high tide now," Teresa explained, noticing his interest. "When we're at low tide, the climb's about ten feet."

Kane grabbed one of the dock supports and pulled himself over. "Big difference in water levels. How deep is it here?"

"About a hundred feet," Falzone answered, "almost straight down. Someone hitting the water without a boat isn't going to make it easily. It's a long way between islands." He opened up a rear compartment and spoke to one of the half-dozen men standing on the docks, quietly giving orders for the fuel tanks and oxygen tanks to be filled.

Four of the men instantly started shifting the tanks to a handcart while two of them maintained patrol. Kane noted that the two men maintained military vigilance.

"Yes," Falzone said, noticing Kane's interest, "the people here are very good at what they do. They have a vested interest in what they're protecting. We're family, Kane, and that's worth dying for."

"And worth chilling for," Grant observed.

"Make no mistakes about that," Falzone said. He swept a hand toward a cave in the rock wall ahead. "This way, if you please."

Kane followed Teresa into the cave. Equipment filled the small space and diving supplies hung on rusty iron racks. Metal scaffolding, evidently scavenged then welded, made a circular stairway that followed the cave wall up over a hundred feet. A lantern shone in the hallway above.

"Our staging area," Falzone said. "Oxygen bottles and batteries are charged here."

"What batteries?" Kane asked.

"The minisubs run on rechargeable batteries," Falzone said, "not fuel. Before skydark they were manufactured down in Texas. After I had the one from the Tong, I went looking for more down there, then I brought them up here."

"How many do you have?"

Falzone shook his head. "Not yet. Let's go up. You haven't seen everything yet."

"You were a trader's sec boss," Grant said, shaking his head.

"Mebbe." Falzone smiled. "Humble beginnings, but I've never lacked for ambition."

Kane followed Teresa up the metal scaffolding, aware of how the woman's hips bunched and moved in her pants. He remembered Remar's story of how Falzone had taken the woman away from Carson, the trader he'd started with. Falzone hadn't been strong enough to stand against Carson and his men, but he'd been nervy enough to steal her away.

The scaffolding steps clanged under Kane's boots and echoed hollowly throughout the cave. Then one of the men started a generator and the thumping washed away all other noise.

"What do the generators run on?" Kane asked.

"Grain alcohol," Falzone answered. "Same as the lanterns you see here. We raise the grain ourselves."

"We raise a lot of things ourselves," Teresa added, looking back at Falzone with pride as she reached the lighted hallway.

Kane followed her through the short cavern passageway that wound through the rock wall. The rock was worn smooth, proof of the heavy traffic the passageway entertained.

He counted his steps, hitting forty-three before he saw the trail of smoky alcohol lanterns suddenly end. Wind caressed his face, and he realized the dark opening ahead led outside. Another two steps forward and he made out the stars above, barely skylining the rock wall on the other side of the huge bowl-shaped depression. Falzone's hidden retreat lay spread out below them, the details partially masked by the darkness.

Chapter 26

Rhythmic creaking drew Kane's attention to the hoist elevator at the right of the sheer drop-off ahead. The elevator was secured to a boom arm mounted on the rock wall and was stripped down to a double platform and a center support pole. A thick rope ran through the top and bottom platforms, looping through so a double strand showed. Rope loops on the underside of the top platform made handholds for passengers.

Teresa stepped onto the swaying elevator and Kane trailed her. The uncertain footing left him a little apprehensive. He grabbed a handhold, joined by Grant a moment later. The pulley rope helped stabilize the elevator, but not much. The short, sharp swings the elevator made were still enough to throw a man or cargo over the side.

Kane surveyed the land contained by the high rock wall. He couldn't tell how far across the island was. The ground was more than fifty feet below. The moonlight highlighted the clapboard structures below. There were seventeen of them that Kane could see in the inky shadows, all of them looking like communal dwellings two and three stories tall. There were no trees, no brush, and the area looked as if it had been cleared out. A lot of rock and barren soil showed, as well.

"I know it doesn't look like much," Falzone said, pulling on a pair of gloves and taking up two lit lanterns from one of the guards. Teresa and Remar took a lantern each. Falzone reached for the rope and clicked the pulley release free. The elevator started down with a jerk, but gained speed as he expertly paid the line out. "But that's a community out there."

A gentle lowing sound echoed out in the quiet contained within the bowl.

Kane recognized the noise with difficulty. "That's a cow?"

Falzone grinned. "Yeah. We've got six of them—bull, four cows and a calf. Not enough to eat yet, but I'm hoping for that, too. The cows were hard to come by, but I wanted them. I worked out some trading with the Tong."

"I thought the Tong wanted your head," Grant said.

"Yeah, but they were willing to part with a few cows to get some of the comp progs I dug up from old Seattle. It's only lately that they've turned really aggressive. But that's probably more because of his son."

"He's still trying to cut his father out of the family business," Kane said.

"You know the Qiangs, elder and younger?" Falzone kept the rope moving through the pulleys, but his eyes regarded Kane sharply.

"I met Wei Qiang down in the Western Isles a while back," Kane replied. The encounter had been bloody and something that would be talked about. If Falzone had been doing business with the Tong, he might have heard about it.

"I'd heard about a man named Kane who'd faced Qiang down. You're the same guy?"

"Yeah," Kane said, remembering the incident. "But I wouldn't say I faced him down. It could have went either way."

"But you insulted him and walked away. Not many people do that."

"He's a hard man."

Falzone gently lowered the elevator to the ground and tied off the rope. "We've got chickens, which we have started eating on special occasions, and I'm in the process of nego-tiating for some sheep."

"How big is this island?" Kane asked. A guardhouse was built into the bottom of the rock wall to the left, taking advantage of the natural cover available in the irregularities in the stone.

Falzone waved at the three guards who'd taken up position outside the guardhouse. They stepped back immediately. "It measures almost five miles by four miles across." He waved ahead. "This island, like a lot of others here, was formed by volcanic eruption. The earthshaker bombs tore away the coastline and separated the tectonic plates long enough to trigger volcanoes, then the water rushing in as the coast dropped cooled it rapidly."

"This was a volcano?" Grant asked.

"Yes, but there's little chance of eruption again because the magma activity and earthquake epicenters have moved away from here. This island was created by a stratovolcano, which is why it has this distinctive conical shape." Falzone led the way along a well-worn path.

Kane stayed wary, studying the surroundings and feeling a little bit like the fly that had wandered into the spider's parlor.

"The part of the volcano we're standing in now is called the caldera," Falzone went on. "It's formed when the center of the volcano collapses back into the magma chamber after it has finished venting and starts cooling."

"How did you get to know so much about volcanoes?" Grant asked.

"Volcanoes are part of the sea," Falzone replied. "They formed a number of the island chains around the world. When I came here looking, I knew I'd find an island like this. In fact, I've located a few of them."

The trail wound around a gently rolling hill, past a structure where a half-dozen war wags were housed. Hard-eyed guards stood post there, as well.

"What about water?" Kane asked.

"Water does get to be a problem at times during the hot months," Falzone said, "but between the distillation we do and the rainwater we're able to capture in a cistern, we make do. The only problem is the toxic rains that come through this area. We have to drain the cistern after those and start over.''

"You're able to distill enough water for the people living here and for the livestock?"

Falzone nodded. "And for the farming we do. Plus, there are some islands I've found with caves that go deep beneath the ocean floor here. Some of them are filled with water that's been purified through the cave formation process, leaching all the impurities out through the limestone. We ship water back to the island during those times.''

"We could survive getting cut off from the outside world," Teresa said. "If that's what you're thinking.''

"Until the first toxic rain poisoned the cistern," Kane pointed out.

"There are stockpiles here," the woman said, meeting Kane's gaze forcefully. "We could survive here longer than any ships at sea could sit out there and surround us.''

"Point taken," Kane said.

Falzone led them between a row of buildings that had been put together from salvaged lumber and concrete cinder block. The buildings were boxes, harshly squared off and desperate looking, but they were serviceable.

"Building materials are scare through this area," Falzone said, "as you might imagine. But we've managed to find enough to construct these so far. We still have some people living in tents around these buildings, but we're gradually hoping to house them all.''

"Other people are starting to hear about us," Teresa said. "They don't know where the island is, but they know our ships and they know the minisubs we use. They've heard stories about us that say we're living in some kind of paradise.'' She looked at the buildings with pride. "It's not exactly true, but you can have a family here.''

Kane studied the buildings, noticing people awake and alert in some of the windows. He felt their hot gazes on his back and knew they all regarded him suspiciously. "Not everyone gets in, I gather."

"At the moment," Falzone said, "we're having to be selective. A tradesman, a carpenter, a farmer, a sailor, a tinker who has taught himself mechanical skills or been trained by another, those are the people we're looking for."

"Or for someone who can fight better than the next guy," Grant rumbled.

Falzone looked at him, then shifted his gaze to Kane. "Yes. At first, having someone like that wasn't as important. Now, with the attention we're getting, it is."

"Taking a new person on isn't an easy thing," Teresa said. "You can't take them without their families, and sometimes you get a lot of dependent mouths to feed for one man who can help us build the islands. If we can, we take single people first, and we try to grow slowly."

"Life is hard up here," Falzone said. "If it wasn't for our salvage operations, we wouldn't have the jack to have come this far." He looked at the buildings and shook his head. "I never intended to come this far or grow this big. You get this big, someone's going to notice you."

"DID YOU GET a chance to look at the comp progs I brought you?" Kane inquired at breakfast the following morning.

Falzone nodded. "They all seemed satisfactory. Whoever you have doing these files does really good work."

Breakfast consisted of biscuits and gravy, hash browns, cold oysters on the half shell and wild blackberries. Falzone sat at one of the small round tables outside of the kitchen. Nearly two dozen other tables fanned out around them. All of the tables and chairs were scuffed and scarred, showing obvious signs of wear and tear.

Kane inspected one of the biscuits. "Figured you were living off self-heats. Homemade bread is a surprise."

"In the beginning," Falzone replied, "we did live off self-heats. As soon as we found this place, I searched until I found Olson, too.''

"The cook," Remar said, pouring coffee into their cups. He spoke with his mouth full.

"One thing I learned from Carson," Falzone said, "was that you can't put a big group of men together without being able to feed them. Olson came from Minnesota, spent some time in Ragnarville and had to leave in a hurry when her husband got crossways with the baron."

Kane dug in, wasting no time. "She's a good cook."

Falzone nodded. "She built the brick ovens back in the kitchen as the building was constructed around her. There were a number of restaurants and warehouses in this area, so finding stainless-steel furniture, racks and shelving, as well as baking and cooking equipment, isn't impossible.''

"Stainless-steel pots and things," Remar said, "are good to barter with. Lot of folks out there are wanting them but can't get them. We can."

"There are a few other communities here that make their own fuel," Falzone said. "I trade stainless-steel pipes that they need for their operation for their overflow when I need it. And sometimes I buy it from coldhearts who've successfully raided a fuel supply caravan from Snakefishville or Cobaltville."

Kane raked an oyster from its shell and swallowed it. "That's risky business if they follow you here."

"They don't," Falzone stated quietly. "No one gets to this island who isn't someone I trust."

"It makes me wonder," Kane said, "why you brought us here."

"Because you needed to see what you were buying into, Kane. There was no way to explain this."

Silently, Kane agreed. Sheltered by the volcano crater the way they were, it seemed easy to forget there was an outside world. The wind blew in from the ocean, carrying the brine smell. Despite the hard rock and volcanic sand underfoot, green fields were in evidence on the western end of the crater. Young trees stood out above them.

A little girl's excited voice suddenly interrupted them. "Daddy, Daddy! Look what I have!"

Kane turned and saw a little girl he'd spotted earlier feeding the chickens. She wore a bright yellow dress that she kept folded up and hiking boots. Her legs flashed tan as she ran. Yellow ribbons held up her dark hair. A light dusting of freckles covered her nose. Her smile was big and totally uninhibited, showing the gap where her two front teeth were missing.

Some of the hardness evaporated from Falzone as he turned toward the little girl. He caught her up, lifting her from the ground.

The little girl laughed with glee.

"I'm sorry," Teresa said, smiling broadly, "but once she heard you were back, I couldn't stop her."

"That's okay," Falzone said. He sat the girl on his knee. "And what do you have, Ariel?"

The little girl proudly unfolded her dress to show the contents. "Chicks!"

Three baby chickens sat in the folds of her dress. They looked like little balls of yellow down. Their heads rose up and down as they peeped and looked around fearfully.

"They're Chuckie's chicks," Ariel enthused.

"Chuckie," Teresa said, "was supposed to be a boy chicken. Ariel was really surprised when Chuckie started laying eggs."

Kane nodded, feeling the bond between the parents and their daughter. It was primal, strong and clean like nothing he'd ever seen before.

Falzone talked to his daughter and wife a little longer while Grant and Kane finished their breakfast. Then Ariel had to take the chicks back to their mother. Falzone watched mother and daughter walk off in silence for a moment.

"The other reason I brought you here, Kane," Falzone said, turning back to face him, "is because I'm certain you don't know where you are. There are hundreds of islands out here. You'd search a long time before you found this place. The Tong has searched for it, as have the Heimdall Foundation and the Wiy Tukay worshipers. They've had a better chance of finding us than you have.'' He paused. ''And if I thought for a moment that you knew where we were, or that you posed some kind of threat to my wife or my daughter, I'd chill you in that moment. I hope there aren't any hard feelings.''

''No,'' Kane said evenly, looking at the woman and little girl. ''I wouldn't blame you for trying.'' But he couldn't help thinking about the subcutaneous transponder Lakesh had injected him with. Someone outside Falzone's trusted circle knew the location of the island, and had known it since early that morning when they'd arrived.

DeFore CARRIED a cup of coffee through the empty halls. At that time of morning, most of the Cerberus personnel were already about their assigned tasks. She smothered a yawn after a late night spent with Lakesh in the central control complex. When she'd left, he had still been there.

It didn't surprise her to find him there now.

Lakesh sat in front of one of the comp banks, his fingers laced together before him while his elbows rested on his chair arms. He stared intently at the screen before him, not even aware of her entering the room.

Curious, DeFore moved with quiet deliberation, not tiptoeing but taking care not to make any noise. She stopped a few feet behind Lakesh and inspected the screen. She knew at once from the readout printed in the upper right corner that it was from the satellite visual feed.

The picture was grainy and occasionally faded completely to black, but DeFore could make out the island featured on the screen. Coordinates in the upper right corner gave the location. A ribbon of information pulsed across the bottom of the screen that identified the subject as Kane, following with stats on his heart rate, brain-wave patterns, respiration and blood count.

Lakesh leaned forward and manipulated the mouse, bringing up a pull-down menu. He tapped the buttons, closing in on the island. Two small fishing boats operated in the nearby water. Then the view pulled in even tighter, concentrating on a group of buildings inside the volcano crater that formed the island. The picture shimmered as the magnification intensified.

Kane and Grant got up from the table and followed two other men. DeFore didn't know either of them.

"Have you found Bry?" DeFore asked. "Or are you too busy spying on Kane?"

Calmly, Lakesh tapped the mouse and the comp screen blanked. He turned his chair around and fixed her with a steely gaze. "A slight clearing of the throat would have politely announced your presence. I'm not unwilling to overlook this breach of etiquette."

"Do you feel spied upon?" DeFore asked with a slight edge to her voice.

"No."

"Switching the monitor off like that was pure guilt."

"That would be your opinion."

DeFore stuck her hands in her pockets. "A very professional one, I might add. And I've spent a lot of time with the subject in question."

Lakesh returned her gaze belligerently. "There are things here beyond your realm of understanding."

"Perhaps if you explain them to me," DeFore suggested icily, "and go really slow…"

"Sarcasm doesn't become you."

"Well, I'm going to stay with it until I find something better."

"What are you doing here?"

"I came to check on you."

Lakesh nodded and gently touched his bandaged head. "I

assure you that your intention is appreciated but hardly necessary. Everything is fine.''

"Somehow," DeFore said, taking a penflash from her jacket pocket and shining it into Lakesh's eyes and ears, "I don't think everything is.''

"I'm perfectly fine.''

"There's something inherently wrong with that statement,'' DeFore returned smoothly, "but you're healthy enough. There's no sign of a concussion. Or any other life-threatening situation. Maybe that's a bad thing.''

Lakesh pushed back in his chair. "Are you quite finished? I have work to get back to.''

DeFore looked at him. "What are you really doing, Lakesh?''

"What I have to do in order to insure the survival of this redoubt.''

DeFore stared at the man's back and held the rest of her questions. She let out a slow breath to try to calm herself. "It might help if you talked to the other people involved.''

"No one," Lakesh said, "understands our situation as I do. No one chooses to view it in quite the same manner.''

"Or chooses to view it the way you do?" DeFore shook her head. "It might help if you laid all the cards on the table for them. You picked Kane and Brigid, Lakesh. And by picking them, you picked Grant and Domi. And me.''

Lakesh said nothing.

"And you picked Donald Bry, too. And until yesterday, I wouldn't have imagined he would have ever lifted a hand to you. So why? What agenda is he following? Yours or his?''

"This discussion is ended, DeFore. Please return to your duties. If you find yourself without responsibility, I'm sure I can find you something to do.''

DeFore bit back a scathing retort with effort, then turned and left the room. Whatever was happening out in the Northwest Territories, she was certain Lakesh had a heavy hand in it. What was going to be interesting was how Kane dealt with it when he found out.

KANE SURVEYED the fields at the western end of the crater. Verdant green growth jutted from black loam that looked totally alien against the gray-white ashy sand and rock that filled the crater. Rows of staked tomatoes, hills of potatoes, corn, squash, onions, beans and carrots grew in front of acres of wheat.

"We hauled the dirt in. There was no other way to make this happen," Falzone said.

"That's a lot of work," Kane commented, realizing the enormity of the task.

"Years," Falzone agreed. "We trucked the dirt in from dig sites, freighted it here on boats, then trucked it back here to set up the fields. The ash is a natural fertilizer." He paused, looking over the people out gathering the latest crops. "I had a lot of opposition. Some people believed it was too big, too ambitious."

Ariel ran screaming through the corn rows, making the stalks jump as she swatted them with her hands. She kept looking over her shoulder, squealing at her mother to chase her.

"But it was worth it," Falzone said, smiling as he watched his daughter. "For the last two years, we've been able to put back some in underground storage areas and sell off some surplus."

"All the comforts of home," Grant said.

Kane looked at his friend and knew that Grant was also impressed in spite of his laconic retort.

Falzone watched his wife chase his daughter, then scoop up the little girl and toss her into the air. Ariel screamed in delight, not afraid even for a moment. Teresa caught the little girl, laughing out loud with her.

"It *is* home," Falzone said softly.

For a moment Kane's mind played with what it might be

like to have the kind of life Falzone had built for himself. The sound of the mother and daughter laughing was like nothing else he'd ever heard. He knew the sound of it would haunt him.

Chapter 27

Brigid Baptiste sat in the paddle wheeler's pilot's seat and steered downstream, running slightly ahead of the current. The controls were simple: a joystick to accelerate or reverse the turning wheel, and foot pedals for the boat's rudders.

The morning sun burned into the thick forest above and around her, making the green vivid against the blue sky above. Rabbits and squirrels scampered through the brush and trees, and birds flitted through the air. However, a hunting cat's scream occasionally paralyzed the other wildlife and sent them scurrying for cover.

When the sound of another engine blatted over the paddle wheel's throb, coming from somewhere ahead, Brigid shaded her eyes and cut back on the paddle wheeler's power.

"Not a boat." Domi sat up on the paddle wheeler's deck with her .357 in hand. "Wag engine."

The engine roar sounded different to Brigid, too, but she wasn't as sure of the source as the albino was. She laid her mini-Uzi across her legs.

"Wait," Wimmer called out. "It's them. The people I was supposed to meet." He pointed into the brush to the left.

Two wags sat in the thick brush almost hidden by the shadows. Armed men stood around them. A thin man with a neatly clipped Vandyke and chestnut hair down to his shoulders stepped forward. He wore a leather jacket that hung down to his midthighs. Shotgun shells filled loops across his chest, and the butt of a pistol-grip shotgun showed over his right shoulder. A long hunting knife hung from his right hip in a hand-made leather sheath studded with dyed seashells. Gold earrings gleamed in both ears.

"Wimmer," the man called.

"It's okay, Olney." Wimmer forced himself to his feet and coughed, swaying drunkenly with the fever and the bobbing boat. "We ran into the Tong. They got that guy I went after at the redoubt."

He turned back to Brigid. "Pull over there. I know these guys."

"I don't," Brigid replied, making no move to turn in where the men were.

"Shit, lady," Wimmer complained. "You say you come all this way to find this Bry guy. Hell, I'm telling you they're the best chance you have. You didn't wanna meet nobody, you shoulda turned and went back where you come from."

Reluctantly, Brigid knew it was true. She glanced at Domi.

"In or out," the albino said in a low voice. "No other way. You pick. I got your back either way."

"Miss," Olney called. Other men ran behind him now. "Miss, I promise you that you can trust me. My intentions are honorable."

Miss? Brigid looked at the man again.

Olney ran with his hands spread out at his sides. "I assure you, I offer no threat. Your name is Brigid, right?"

His use of her name almost drove Brigid away. "How do you know my name?"

"Our contact," Olney said, breathing heavily as he trotted along.

"Who's your contact?" Brigid demanded.

"All we know is the name Delphi."

Brigid recognized Delphi as a city in Greece known for its oracles. People went there in ancient times for answers to their problems and portents of the future. "That's no one's name," Brigid declared.

"I know," Olney said. "Greek myth. Apollo the sun god's ville." He stumbled over a tree root and fell, but got up again immediately. "Please. That's all I know. I desperately want to talk to you. If you know about the aliens, I need to know."

Brigid hesitated.

"If you're going to leave," Wimmer said, "at least put in close enough to the bank that I got a chance against those fucking snakes."

"Brigid," Olney called, coming to a stumbling stop. His chest heaved with effort.

Angry with herself for being so indecisive, Brigid swung the boat over to the bank. She stared at Olney, who waited on her.

"Handsome," Domi commented, smiling as she looked at the man. "Handsome men tell best lies."

Brigid ignored the comment.

"Uh, can I put the anchor out?" Wimmer asked, not daring to move because Brigid had him covered with the mini-Uzi.

Brigid got up and kicked out the anchor. The paddle wheeler floated for a moment then came to a stop. She shut off the engine, watching as the two wags advanced cautiously through the forest. She walked through the shallows of the stream and up onto the bank.

Olney came forward slowly, a smile on his face. "I'm Mac Olney." He offered his hand.

Brigid ignored the hand, lifting the mini-Uzi between them meaningfully.

Olney dropped his hand.

"You're with the Heimdall Foundation?" Brigid asked.

"Yes." Olney pushed back his jacket sleeve to reveal the orange-and-blue tattoo. "You're familiar with us?"

"A little."

Olney smiled and nodded. "Then you're interested in the aliens also?"

"I don't know what you're talking about," Brigid replied. "I'm here for Bry."

Olney looked confused.

"The man you were supposed to meet," Brigid explained.

"Is he a friend of yours?"

"I don't know." Brigid looked into the man's eyes, so glacial-gray they were almost colorless. "Is he a friend of yours?"

"Delphi said he had information for us."

"In return for your help in getting him into Tyler Falzone's salvaging operation?" Brigid guessed.

"The plan was to try to get the man you know as Bry into Tyler Falzone's salvage operation so he could get a better look at the things Falzone is bringing up."

"What things?"

"The comp progs. The men we've arranged to deal with on the island don't have comp experience."

"Why didn't you send one of your own people?" Brigid asked.

"Falzone checks for the tattoos," Olney answered. "All of our people are identifiable to one another. It has to be that way."

"To keep people out, or to keep those people in?"

Olney's easy smile lost a little of its luster then. "You ask very pointed questions."

"It only seems that way when people don't want to answer them."

"Touché." Olney looked over his shoulder at the arriving wags and the men scattered throughout the forest. "I would love to explore a further meeting of minds with you. You seem quite intelligent. Perhaps we could compare notes and come up with a possibility as to who Delphi really is."

Brigid returned his gaze completely, aware of the men surrounding them. "I'll go as your guest, but if I ever get the impression you're going to act in a manner that's other than gentlemanly, trust me when I say that I'll chill you if the opportunity presents itself."

Olney put a hand over his heart. "Upon my honor. I shall never offer ill will or malice toward you."

"Okay." Brigid glanced at Domi, to let the albino know she

was accepting for both of them, or to offer her the chance to turn away.

Domi gazed at her silently for a moment, causing Brigid to doubt her own decision. Going out on a limb like this wasn't something she'd normally do, but Lakesh's and Bry's secrets had left her without many resources.

Though there was a lot of things she faulted Kane for, she knew she could trust him with her life. And she was prepared to defend his—if she could. If it wasn't already too late.

Domi nodded, but bared her teeth in a cold smile.

"Excellent," Olney replied. "When we get to the ship, I've got a really good local port I'd like to introduce you to." He smiled, his expression forthright and confident.

Brigid looked at him, feeling slightly uncomfortable with the man's frankness. She heard Domi's voice in the back of her mind again. *Handsome men tell best lies.*

"YOU'VE HANDLED a wag before, right?"

Kane looked at Falzone, who pointed at the copilot's seat in the minisub that Teresa just vacated. "Yeah."

"This won't be much different." Falzone grinned at Kane's hesitation. "Hell, at least out here you don't have to worry about running over something. At least, as long as you don't hit bottom."

Kane looked through the Plexiglas nose. The minisub ran only thirty-five feet below the water, but it was a long swim if something went wrong, and another seventy feet to the bottom of the ocean here if things went even worse.

At the shallow depth, the light turned the water blue and kissed the fish with rainbow colors. A pale pink squid jetted by, tentacles trailing briefly across the windows. Two sea turtles, each at least three feet across, swam above them, looking black with the sun blazing down from above them.

Kane dropped into the seat. If he could fly a Deathbird, surely the slow-moving minisub would prove no real challenge.

Falzone pointed out gauges, familiarizing Kane with what each one was and what it represented. "Most of your control comes off the joystick. It's a fly-by-wire system. The onboard comp reads the joystick position and changes speeds according to the position. The thrusters change with each other. There's no chance of overcontrol that's going to hurt the ship."

Kane moved the joystick experimentally, feeling the changes shudder through the minisub.

"Just remember which way is up," Grant called out, "and I'll be happy."

Remar cackled.

Kane ignored them, intrigued by the slow-motion roll the minisub seemed to operate on. Still, the horizon shifted dramatically.

Falzone tapped the directional arrows by the joystick. "These arrows get darker as you apply more torque, so you don't have to worry about reading your direction all the time. The terrain can fool you, as well. What would be level on dry land isn't necessarily so down here. With this much water, you can get lost."

"How do I handle sharp descents?" Kane asked.

"This minisub has an automatic buoyancy control. Without it, you'd be adjusting buoyancy all the time. You have to set the buoyancy each dive, depending on the cargo and passengers you're carrying. When we pick up the salvaged items we're going to get today, the buoyancy will have to be recalibrated. It's not hard, but it has to be done."

Kane pressed the throttle button and increased the speed, listening to the fans spin harder. He didn't really feel the increase in speed inside the minisub. "What about surfacing?"

"The ascent is managed through the dive planes, generally," Falzone said. "If you lose those and your power systems are still operational, you can add ballast to the air tanks from the extra tanks in the back and slowly surface. If you can't do that, the minisub carries ballast, ten-pound weights that can be dropped through the diver-entry hole in the back of the sub.''

"In all the years we've been operational here," Teresa said, "we've never lost a sub."

"We have lost a few boats to the Wiy Tukay worshipers, though," Falzone said.

Kane enjoyed the feel of the controls. "Torpedo controls?" he asked.

"Launch controls are here," Falzone confirmed, indicating the safety-covered switches overhead. "They're Mk 48 heat seekers, fire-and-forget, but you've got to get them in close to your target."

"Who are the Wiy Tukay worshipers?" Kane asked.

"You've heard of Wiy Tukay, the computer glitch regarding the year 2000 the original comp programmers forgot about when they built the first systems?"

Somewhere in the back of his mind, Kane remembered. Lakesh or Brigid had to have mentioned it. "Y2K. Supposed to have ended the world because of air wags falling from the sky, lots of files getting erased."

"There was a small mass hysteria on New Year's Eve in the year 2000. People expected power supplies to go out and there to be panic in the streets because of the Y2K computer glitch. There were a few problems, but nothing drastic. However, when skydark came on January 20, 2001, a bunch of conspiracy believers in the Seattle area felt certain that it was still Y2K. A lot of people mistakenly thought the end of the last millenium was in 2000, but it was actually in 2001. They behave that there actually was a god called Wiy Tukay and he lies buried out here."

"Why would they think Wiy Tukay lived here?" Kane asked.

"This is where all the major comp industries were," Falzone said. "Originally, they had a place called Silicon Valley in old California where software was made. Several of the big companies relocated to the Seattle area in the late 1990s. They believe Wiy Tukay, if disturbed, will once again end the world. Some say Wiy Tukay is actually a comp prog.''

"What do you believe?" Kane had seen a lot of strange things the Totality Concept had brought to life. He didn't know if he was prepared to write off the possibility of a living comp prog.

"What I believe," Falzone said, "is that this area is loaded with scrip for the taking in the form of salvaged goods.''

"Everything but blasters," Kane said.

"So far. Mebbe they're down there somewhere, but we haven't found them yet.''

"STUPE FUCKERS," Iverson growled as he spit over the side of the sailboat.

Mallet joined his second at the stern railing. He'd just come up from the captain's quarters, which he'd taken for himself, and went through the contents. There hadn't been anything worthwhile, mostly the skeletons of small animals bearing scorch marks from the fires that had presumably killed them. He'd thrown those out, upsetting some of the worshipers, and his fact-finding op had turned out to be primarily a major cleaning.

Below, the Wiy Tukay worshipers seined fish with a small net from the ocean. Mallet didn't recognize any of them, but most of the fish were as long as his arm. As soon as the worshipers had the fish on the deck, several of them beat it to death with clubs or knife hilts. Then, spattered in fish blood, they cheered loudly and offered the sacrifice to Wiy Tukay.

Kroger, the worshiper leader, hooked their latest sacrifice through the gills with his fingers and held it up. "Man in Black," he yelled. "See how we chill in the name of Wiy Tukay, the destroyer of greed and complacence?''

"You serve Wiy Tukay well," Mallet roared back, then added under his breath, "you nukeshit stupe fuckers.''

"If they ever turned on us," Iverson said, "you know it

would be hard to get out of here without getting chilled ourselves."

"They won't turn on us. We're the Men in Black, representatives of the one true government. Mebbe the only hope they have of not being destroyed by an angry god." He looked out to sea as they sailed westward.

Joining their ship were six others, all three-masted cargo ships that had seen better days but remained serviceable. He wasn't sure if they'd been built before skydark or since. There were some shipbuilders in the Northwest Territories who'd had the craft passed down to them by ancestors dating back before skydark. Counting the worshipers and the Magistrates he had left to him, there were several hundred men on the ships sailing for Tyler Falzone's island hideaway.

From what Kroger had said, the Wiy Tukay worshipers had all but found Falzone's island. However, they'd never been able to band together to make an attempt on it. Once the word had gone out that the Men in Black had arrived to take them all back to the one true government, the Wiy Tukay worshipers had flocked in.

"Is the radio working?" Mallet asked.

"Meyer told me it would be up in twenty minutes," Iverson said.

"Let me know as soon as it is," Mallet said. "We're going to want reinforcements once we hit the island. Even if we take it today, it's going to take Baron Cobalt a few days to arrange the staging necessary to get Deathbirds and troops here."

Below, the Wiy Tukay worshipers dragged the net back on deck. This time, though, they'd netted a shark almost six feet long.

The big fish flailed angrily, snapping at the worshipers who were too tightly packed to move back quickly. The shark caught a young man's leg, and swallowed it up to midshin before he could get away. Blood spurted, covering the worshiper's leg and the shark's mouth. The young man screamed in agony.

Mallet lifted his right arm and popped his Sin Eater free. As soon as the firing stud touched his finger, he emptied the magazine into the shark's head, blowing its brains out in a pink-and-gray mess across the deck.

The worshipers drew back hurriedly, trying to free their fallen member.

Iverson grunted in disgust. "These fuckers are totally stupe. Hope the reinforcements get here in a hurry before I start shooting these bastards myself."

Mallet put the Sin Eater away with a flick of his wrist, then went belowdecks. The sails popped and cracked overhead, punctuating the worshipers' screams and curses and sounding like blaster shots. The Mag commander took up a double-bitted ax from the ship's supplies and walked over to the worshiper who still had his leg in the dead shark's mouth.

"Man in Black! Man in Black!" the worshipers chanted.

A quick survey of the wounded man's leg told Mallet it was too far gone to be saved. He lifted the ax and swung, cutting through the lacerations and broken bone the shark had left. Mallet loved the feel of the flesh and bone shearing away.

The stricken worshiper tried to get away but succeeded in only pulling away from his own leg, leaving the limb in the grinning shark's mouth. The wounded man screamed and seized his own stump, blood spurting everywhere.

Mallet moved quickly, reversing the ax and butt-stroking the man across the face. The helmet mask covered the savage smile that twisted his lips. The smile became even more warped when the worshipers started cheering him for chopping the man's leg off.

"The Man in Black has saved Frankie!"

"Get a tourniquet on his leg before he bleeds out," Mallet commanded. While they hurried to do his bidding, he turned and buried the ax blade in the ruin left of the shark's head. The meaty smack felt good to him. Waiting until they reached Falzone's island to do any more killing was going to be hard.

Chapter 28

"Did you sleep well?"

Brigid Baptiste stopped in midyawn and glanced over her shoulder to see Mac Olney standing on the cargo ship's deck. She felt a little embarrassed at the man's direct gaze, even more embarrassed that she hadn't heard him approach. "I slept longer than I intended to." The sun was high overhead, letting her know she'd slept almost into the middle of the next day.

"Probably needed it after being up all night with Wimmer on that river," Olney observed.

Brigid nodded, knowing it was true. She still hadn't healed completely from her previous wounds, and being up all night hadn't helped. She and Domi had been assigned quarters after they'd reached the Heimdall Foundation ship late the previous evening after traveling to the edge of the Cific Ocean.

Brigid had gone because there was nothing she could do about Donald Bry's capture by the Tong, and she knew that Kane was out there somewhere on the sea. Olney, or at least some of the Heimdall Foundation members, knew where Tyler Falzone's island was. She hoped to find Kane there, maybe figure out what to do about Bry.

And with Lakesh, she silently added, because she was certain Lakesh was the mysterious Delphi whom Olney had mentioned.

"What about something to eat?" Olney asked. "*Starseeker* has a galley aboard."

Brigid's stomach rumbled expectantly, but she concentrated on her safety first. "Domi?"

Olney pointed aft. "Fishing."

Following the indicated direction, Brigid glanced aft and spotted Domi on near the stern railing. She had a pole in her hand and was staring intently into the water. A handful of men gathered around her, calling encouragement and laughing.

"Has she caught anything?" Brigid asked.

"A few tuna," Olney said. "Helps stock the larder, and she seems genuinely amused. So how about breakfast?"

"Yes, please."

Olney led the way and Brigid followed. He wore the same leather vest that he had the day before, as well as the shotgun in the shoulder scabbard, but his clothes were fresh. Brigid felt embarrassed by her own clothing because she'd slept in them.

The galley was small but held a stainless-steel kitchen and three tiny booths equipped with tables. Olney waved to one of them. "Sit."

Brigid did after a little hesitation. The galley was small enough that it was hard to keep from feeling that her privacy was being invaded by Olney's proximity.

"How do you like your eggs?" Olney asked, reaching into a small refrigerator, then taking down a small frying pan from overhead.

"I can do that." Brigid started to get up from the booth.

"No," Olney said, smiling. "You're our guest. I insist."

Brigid remained standing, uncertain what to say next. His behavior was something she wasn't prepared for.

"Please," Olney added, waiting.

Brigid sat, turning her gaze from him, but there was little else to look at in the galley. The ship rolled gently as it sailed.

"You didn't answer." Olney placed a cup of coffee on the table in front of her.

"What?" she asked, feeling flustered.

"How you like your eggs." Olney nodded at the coffee cup. "You might want to hang on to that cup. We're sailing smoothly right now, but there's no guarantee that's going to keep up. The currents around here are hard to predict at times.''

"Scrambled." Brigid took possession of the cup, her fingers gliding smoothly against his callused ones for a moment. The touch was electric. She dropped her gaze from his. Thankfully, he returned to the grill. She was beginning to have serious doubts about her decision not to return to Cerberus redoubt.

"So where are we headed?" she asked.

Eggshells cracked, then hissing started. The smell of butter and eggs joined the aroma of coffee.

"To join up with another foundation ship," Olney answered. "Toast? It's panfried, but we have jelly."

"Okay." The smell of frying meat joined the other smells, drawing Brigid's attention.

"Bacon," Olney explained, pushing pieces of meat around in another pan. "We eat a lot of fish, but we trade with some of the local villes that hunt wild pigs in this area. Meat's a little gamy, but it's a change from a constant diet of fish."

Brigid returned her attention to her coffee, trying to organize her thoughts and figure out a plan of action. However, she couldn't ignore the fact that Olney was making breakfast. "Why are we joining up with the other foundation ship?" she asked.

"Because I need to get permission to get you into the foundation," Olney replied.

"Why?"

"Because they're as sec paranoid as you are."

"No, I mean why would I want to go there?"

"You don't?"

"I didn't say that." Brigid felt a little irritated, but she knew most of it was because she was out of control of what was going on around her. She tried to remember when the last time was that she'd been in control of her circumstances, and realized that she couldn't. Nor could she remember what it had felt like.

"Good, because I'd like to take you there. I think you'd like it."

"Why?"

"Why what?"

Brigid almost asked him why he wanted to take him there, but she didn't. "Why do you think I'd like it?"

"Because you seem like a person with more learning than most. There are some educated people at the Heimdall Foundation."

"You're educated," Brigid said.

Olney laughed gently. "I like to think so. But I haven't specialized like a lot of the people at the foundation have. I've got more or less a superficial education. Just enough to be dangerous. Not always a pleasant thought to the people who run the foundation."

"You've got more than a superficial education."

"Get to know me better," Olney entreated as he placed two heaped plates on the table. He sat across from her, and his knees touched hers briefly. "Then let me know what you think."

Brigid hesitated, then picked up her fork and picked at the food on her plate. "All right," she said, and her answer surprised even her.

MALLET STARED angrily at the broken radio scattered across the small communications room aboard the Wiy Tukay worshipers' ship. Despite the promises he'd made, Meyer hadn't been able to repair the radio, and none of the Wiy Tukay worshipers had working radios. They weren't believed necessary.

The Magistrate stood nervously on the other side of the room. He was young and scared, and at the moment, having trouble swallowing.

"Why?" Mallet asked again, struggling not to trigger his Sin Eater and blast the man's brains through the back of his head.

"Don't have the parts I need, sir," Meyer replied. He knew better than to say he was sorry. Men who admitted weakness to Mallet died, and everyone serving under him for any length of time knew that.

"Then we'll need to get more parts," Mallet said in a tight voice. He turned to Iverson as he headed back out onto the deck. "You said a ship was spotted earlier?"

"Yes, sir," Iverson responded. "About ten minutes ago. It stayed away from us and we returned the favor."

"Did you identify it?" Mallet strode up the stern castle.

"No, sir."

"Did you ask any of these fuckers onboard?"

"No, sir."

"Then what the hell are you doing standing here? Get it done. If these Wiy Tukay fuckers have got radio, I'm betting that some of the other locals do, too. If we find out theirs is working, we'll take it."

"Yes, sir."

Mallet stood in the stern and listened to Iverson's boots drum on the deck. He shouted out questions at once to the worshipers assigned to help act as lookouts. The Mag commander glared across the sun-kissed waves and thought about Kane and Grant. They couldn't be far away. Maybe they weren't any farther than Tyler Falzone's operation.

The possibility made Mallet eager.

Iverson thumped back up the companionway leading to the stern castle. "Kroger identified the ship. It belongs to something called the Heimdall Foundation."

Mallet turned over the name in his head. "Does that mean anything to you?"

"No, sir."

Mallet nodded. "What did Kroger say about them?"

"That they're madmen," Iverson answered. "Supposed to be searching for aliens that caused skydark."

"Outlanders, you mean?"

"No, sir. Men from another planet."

Mallet shook his head and growled. "Most stupe thing I ever heard of."

"Yes, sir," Iverson replied. "However, Kroger did confirm that the Heimdall Foundation ship does have a radio."

Mallet nodded. "Fair enough. Tells those bastards to get this tub turned around." He gazed out at the sea, straining to spot the other ship somewhere in the distance. "Let's see if we can catch that damn ship."

KANE RESTED on the circular metal tower. Most of the structure's windows were cracked and broken out now, but the interior was still big enough to provide Falzone's men a semipermanent command center and fort.

The tower had been constructed in two layers. The top layer was nearly a hundred feet across, and the second layer was nearer 150 feet across. All the metal below the platform was flaking and rusting, slowly being digested by the sea.

Kane and Grant sat along the outer rim of the tower nearly two hundred feet above the sea surface. Cool wind blew in from the south, prickling their skin, and the sun was deep into the western horizon, promising a beautiful sunset due to all the pollutants in the air. The tower rocked back and forth a few inches with the surge of the sea.

Remar sat bare legged a few feet away, a fishing pole in his hands and a .30-30 lying close to hand. Smoke wreathed his head as he watched the red-and-white float gently riding the ocean swells that slapped at the tower's spindly, barnacle-encrusted legs.

The minisub floated at the end of a tether below, riding the waves in the shadow of a cargo ship that worked above salvage sites.

Kane held a bowl of chowder filled with pieces of meat and ate hungrily.

"Do you know anything about this building?" Falzone asked. He sat with Teresa, a thin blanket pulled about them to knock off some of the wind.

"No," Kane replied.

"It was called the Space Needle," Falzone said. "Before skydark, people from different villes used to gather for big marketing trades. Usually, it was for business, bringing new interest in later trades. The Space Needle was built for the 1962 Seattle World's Fair. It has a concrete foundation 120 feet across and thirty feet deep. At one time, the Space Needle stood about six hundred feet tall. All the quakes in the area restructured the landscape below us. Some of the nearby buildings are buried under nearly two hundred feet of rock and silt, but some of them were pushed to the top. They were some of the first looted."

"Doesn't look like this part has ever been under water," Grant said.

"I don't think so." Falzone scooped up another bite of chowder, eating slowly. He kept his gaze trained on the horizon. "Got plenty of dents and bullet holes in it, though. Even before we took it over to use as an observation post and communications relay, other people used it for target practice."

Kane tore off a chunk of bread and dipped it into the bowl of honey at his side. Everything was warm, fresh from the kitchen that had been cobbled together inside the tower. The stoves burned wood, which had to be hauled in from dry land or cured after being salvaged from below. Gray smoke from the chimney colored the sky.

"You haven't said what you think about what we're doing out here, Kane," Falzone said.

Kane chewed the bread for a moment, then swallowed and reached for the coffee cup at his side. The gentle sway of the tower remained unnerving, but it lulled him, too.

"You're building a future," Kane replied. He glanced at the men scattered around the tower and still manning the cargo ship below. None of them were in the water. Falzone had explained that mutie sharks and other giant sea creatures inhabited the area. "Not many are doing that these days."

"And?" Falzone pressed.

"It's an admirable thing," Kane added.

"What about you, Grant?" Falzone asked.

"Not many could do what you've done," Grant said. "Especially having to work this hard at it."

Falzone grinned, but his humor was thin, worn from all the long hours of the salvage. "Both of you are deliberately avoiding the question I'm asking, and you know it."

Kane hesitated a moment. "About whether or not we'd fit in?"

Falzone nodded. "We can always use good men. We lost one today to a mutie fish. Replacing him won't be easy."

"I don't know," Kane replied. He felt a little uncomfortable with the answer. If Falzone decided that they knew too much about his operation to set free, Kane had no doubt that the man would order them killed. But at the same time he felt certain that Falzone would recognize a bald-faced lie.

"Why?"

"For one," Kane said, "this terrain is not what I'm used to. There's too much water here for my taste. I wasn't trained to fight on water, and that's what you're going to be doing sooner or later. Whether you want to or not."

"Because our communities are growing," Falzone said.

"And because you can't turn invisible," Kane agreed. "Wei Qiang knows you're here, and so does Baron Cobalt. Both of them want what you're digging up."

"I know."

"You can't defend yourself against either of them," Kane said.

"If I can get the blasters we need from Cobaltville," Falzone said, "I think we can."

"No," Kane stated, "you're too small. Either one of those forces will roll over you and crush you when they track you down and decide chilling you is worth their time."

Teresa's face hardened. "Those are harsh words, Kane."

Kane nodded, looking at the woman. "And they're made only more harsh because they're true. Falzone knows it."

Teresa looked at her man.

Falzone let out a deep breath. "Kane's telling it like it is. It's the same thing Remar's been talking about."

"If you stayed smaller," Kane said, "you'd have a better chance. If you found a way to be more autonomous."

"I know. But then there's question of how small is too small, and how small is small enough."

"It's also a question of where you decide to light down," Grant growled. "You came out here seeking a fortune, sell the gear and comp progs you could salvage here. You just couldn't know those same comp progs could draw the attention of Baron Cobaltville and Wei Qiang so much."

"No. That was only supposed to be small trade. Enough to tide us over."

Seagulls heeled over in the sky in the distance, then dived down to pick up debris being dumped over the cargo ship's side. The scavenging birds battled one another for delectable scraps.

"So what do Wei Qiang and Baron Cobalt want?" Grant asked.

Falzone shook his head. "I don't know. But whatever it is, they both want it really badly."

"You've got to have some idea," Kane said.

After a moment, Falzone said, "Mebbe I do. You know about the redoubts?"

Kane nodded.

"Some people have a mythology about the makers of the redoubts," Falzone said. "There are people who say they were made by secret government organizations for the purpose of fighting the wars they were constantly involved in. Some say they were bases used to do scientific experiments that they didn't want the rest of the world to know about. Others say that the world was ruled by a handful of people who jumped from country to country by some kind of device found in most of the redoubts—puppet masters that controlled all the wars that kept them rich and getting richer. Then there's the Heimdall Foundation, believing that skydark was the result of opposition to aliens from another planet.''

Kane remained silent, waiting as the sky continued to darken around them, turning purple-black, the color of a bruised plum.

''Whatever is hidden beneath these waters and on these islands,'' Falzone said, ''is important to someone. But everything I've been able to learn from Wei Qiang's people and Baron Cobalt's is that they're interested in learning more about the redoubts and who made them.''

Maybe the Tong war leader wanted to know more about the people who'd constructed the redoubts, Kane reasoned, but the barons were more interested in making sure that knowledge didn't leak out into the wrong hands. Maybe Lakesh was in the same category.

''The Tong and the barons both have large armies,'' Kane pointed out, ''and when it comes to interest in this, you're caught in the middle. With the way you're operating now, you're in a no-man's-land.''

Falzone nodded and grinned weakly. ''Mebbe you're right. Mebbe a man would have to be stupe to throw in with me. But I can't just pack these people off the islands where I've set them up. There are too many of them, and I don't have enough ships. And where the hell would I take them?''

''I don't know,'' Kane admitted.

''I made them promises when I recruited them and brought them out here,'' Falzone said. ''I stick to the word I give a man, Kane. It's important to me.'' He paused, searching the skyline or unable to maintain eye contact. ''We've already started our first generation of island born. My little girl is one of them.''

Teresa turned to him and held him tightly. Tears glittered on her face.

Kane felt the breeze turning colder as he realized Falzone was definitely aware of the harsh choices facing him.

"What would you suggest I do?" Falzone asked after a little while.

"There's an old saying," Kane said quietly. "I don't know where it comes from, but they talk about it a lot in the Outlands. The enemy of my enemy is my friend."

"Giving me a choice of aligning myself with the Tong or with Baron Cobalt?"

"Yeah."

"Which would you rather make a deal with?" Falzone's glare was a hard challenge.

"Neither."

"You don't have a deal with either of those groups, do you?" Falzone asked.

"No."

"And you expect me to pick one?"

"You're in a position that you're going to have to," Kane stated.

Anger showed dark and ugly on Falzone's face.

Kane knew he hadn't backed the man into the corner, but he was also aware that Falzone could decide to focus all his frustration on him at the moment. It wouldn't solve anything, but men had gotten dead for a lot less. Kane kept his hand loose and ready, the Sin Eater holstered along his wrist, hidden by his shirtsleeve. As much as he liked Falzone, Kane wasn't prepared to die in the other man's place. Grant moved slightly, as did Remar, and Kane knew if things turned hostile, there would be a lot of dead men.

Then the moment passed and Falzone managed to pull his anger back inside. "You're right, of course," Falzone said in a dead voice. "I've already been considering that. But there are no guarantees that either of those groups will let us remain independent."

"You're not independent now," Kane said. "You're just now realizing that. But if you make the right deal, you can be. To a degree."

"But to what degree?"

"Mebbe enough for you to live with," Kane said. "Mebbe only enough to live long enough to see your daughter grow up. A man only has a certain amount of control over his life. Once he realizes that, he's free and trapped at the same time."

"But which to choose?" Falzone asked. "Cobaltville is so far away, and the Tong culture is so different than what we know."

"Sometimes," Grant growled, "enemies have a tendency to sort themselves out. Right now, you don't have to make an immediate decision."

Falzone pointed out to sea.

Kane turned to look, spotting the ship against the western horizon, backlit by the setting sun. The sails belled, filled with wind.

"The Tong," Falzone said. "They know we have this post here. They patrol the area from time to time, just to let us know they're there."

It was also a grim reminder, Kane knew, that the decision facing Falzone was closer than anyone wanted to admit.

Chapter 29

"Got it!"

Domi's whoop of sheer, savage joy brought a smile to Brigid's lips as she stood in *Starseeker*'s stern section. The albino girl worked the reel on the huge rod. She pulled the big tuna in, cranking the reel to take up the slack.

Twilight turned the Cific Ocean a gray-green flecked with silvery reflections, but every now and then Brigid spotted pools of phosphorescence. Mac Olney had explained that the green-and-yellow glow was from schools of fish, night feeders that were often as vicious and hungry as South American piranha. White curlers rolled toward the distant shore far from sight. The cool night air brought white wisps of fog with it.

"She's having fun," Olney said, nodding toward Domi. "But I don't understand how she's been able to do this for hours."

The crew around Domi shouted out excitedly as the big yellowfin tuna broke the water surface. The fish was more than three feet long, and Olney had guessed that it weighed roughly a hundred pounds. The biggest tuna that Olney had seen hauled aboard was just over two hundred pounds, though he'd heard stories of tuna big enough to pull a man from a small boat and swallow him whole.

"Domi lives for the hunt," Brigid said.

"She must," Olney agreed.

The albino sat in a fishing chair bolted to the deck, her pale white legs out before her, bare feet braced against the railing as she strained with all her might.

The yellowfin tuna cleared the water again for just a moment, the long second dorsal fins trailing almost back to the anal fins, which fit the description Brigid had read about the fish. Brigid watched the fight between Domi and the fish with interest.

Domi swore viciously, her curses descriptive enough to give momentary pause even to the sailors around her, then they roared with laughter again and cheered her on.

"And there's no mistaking her enthusiasm," Olney stated dryly.

Brigid smiled even bigger. "No. I've never met anyone like her."

"Probably wouldn't be able to stand it if you did," Olney commented.

Brigid felt him looking at her again and tried to ignore it. His attention was nearly constant, but wasn't entirely unwelcome. They'd spent the afternoon talking, and she had been surprised at his knowledge about the sea and many other topics, as well.

Olney was gregarious, willing to talk and discuss and draw conclusions, and he loved books. He'd even showed her a collection of novels and textbooks he'd traded for during his last trip through the coastal lands. Some of them were bound for the Heimdall Foundation libraries, but some were going into his personal library. Wherever the foundation was, Mac Olney had also built a home.

The images his talk conjured up sparked Brigid's imagination. From his description, she'd pictured a small house with a fence and small garden beds for flowers and vegetables. Fruit trees stood in the backyard, though Olney had admitted only the cherry trees consistently bore fruit.

It sounded different than anything Brigid Baptiste had ever seen, and part of her wanted to see it. Olney had overtly extended the invitation.

Domi fought the tuna to the surface again after it dived deep. The big fish twirled and jumped, arching its body, then it slammed back down against the ocean. The albino cursed again, setting off a new round of cheerful encouragement.

Olney laughed out loud. "Reminds me of Hemingway's *The Old Man and the Sea*. Only with cursing."

"That," Brigid said, "was a good book."

"Oh, then you've read it?"

"Yes."

"Like it?"

"I understood it," Brigid replied.

Olney leaned a hip against the railing, only inches from Brigid, so close that she could feel the heat of him against the chill of the night. Her flesh was covered in goose bumps, and she honestly didn't know if it was the cool air or Olney's close proximity that caused it.

"You're very well read," Olney observed.

"I worked in a library," Brigid said.

"But not now?"

She had deliberately avoided any questions concerning where she was from or what she had done there. "I still do some."

"But you enjoy that kind of work?"

"Yes."

Domi cursed some more and yanked on the pole again, quickly taking up more slack and bringing the tuna within fifty yards of *Starseeker*'s stern. The sails popped slightly overhead, punctuating the cheering.

"The Heimdall Foundation has extensive libraries," Olney said. "However, it's hard to find the proper personnel to staff the libraries. They're always looking for good people."

Brigid let the statement pass.

The crew cheered again as Domi won another couple of yards against the big fish. Brigid guessed that only the albino's feral constitution and iron will kept her in the seat.

After the latest round of cheering died away, Olney said, "You know, with the moonlight in your hair like that, it looks like it's aflame, a burning halo surrounding your face."

Brigid didn't say anything.

"You're a beautiful woman, Brigid Baptiste," Olney stated.

"Look—" Brigid began to say.

"Mac," Olney said. "Call me Mac."

Brigid avoided that. "Don't make me feel uncomfortable." She eyed him directly.

After a moment, Olney nodded. "Okay, so you're not married, but maybe there's someone in your life after all."

"No. Definitely not that, either." But Brigid couldn't help thinking of Kane and wondering where he was.

"Then maybe I should go slower."

"Maybe you should—" Brigid stopped as foul curses from Domi and all the sailors drew her attention. She followed their gazes down to the water.

A green phosphorescent pool streaked underwater toward the tuna, overtaking it quickly. At the urging of the men around her, Domi yanked harder on the fishing pole. The yellowfin tuna cleared the water again, but this time several of the phosphorescent fish clung to it. The predatory fish looked less than six inches long, but they fastened on to the tuna like leeches. Blood masked the tuna's bright colors. Then it vanished below the water again.

Domi continued pulling on the fishing pole. The tuna struggled harder than it had for the past dozen minutes or longer. The big fish swam to both sides and tried to dive deeper. Then it abruptly gave up fighting altogether. Domi quickly reeled the tuna in.

Brigid peered over the ship's side and saw the glowing pool surrounding the tuna's body as it surfaced. The piranha-like fish still clung to the tuna's corpse, but most of the meat had already been stripped from the skeleton.

Domi continued shouting out curses and reeling up the corpse remnant. Most of the small fish dropped away, phosphorescent teardrops returning to the sea. Only a dozen or so of the small fish remained when the tuna was hauled over the railing and thumped against the deck. The sailors quickly stomped the fish into glowing green smears against the deck.

"Mebbe they'll save some of it," Olney said. "A few breakfast steaks, mebbe enough for a few stews." He was grinning as Domi continued her verbal assault on the phosphorescent pool slowly gathering its individual parts and swimming away.

"Mac!"

Brigid glanced over at the urgency in the man's voice.

"What is it?" Olney demanded, taking long strides toward the stern companionway.

The man standing there was in his late forties, gray-haired and lean. He wore a handblaster in a shoulder rig and a concerned look. "*Sounder*. She's being stalked by another ship."

"Who?" Olney asked, following the other man down the stairs.

Brigid trailed after them, wondering if she might be better off taking a break from Olney while she had the chance to sort through her own feelings. But she couldn't. Falzone's people weren't friendly with the foundation people, and it was possible that Kane and Grant might be on that pursuing ship.

"Don't know," the other man answered. "Dawson can't identify her as Tong or one of Falzone's."

Brigid remained behind them as they sprinted across the deck, drawing the attention of the crew. Less than a minute later, they were in the small nav-comm station.

The radio transmission kept breaking up. Olney had explained that fallout residue in the area from skydark and the volcanic activity caused communications problems.

"...don't know...these fuckers are...tacked on to my ass and ain't letting go," a man's strained voice announced. "*Starseeker*...copy?"

Olney picked up the headset and leaned down to speak into the mike. "We're here, Dawson. Do you copy?" He turned to the comm operator. "Can you get a fix on his signal?"

"I'm trying now," the comm officer replied.

The radio crackled. "...copy, *Starseeker?* We...son of a bitch...firing...don't know who the hell...hit us..."

Brigid listened intently, hearing the cannonade of heavy-caliber weapons mixed in with small-arms fire.

"Dawson!" Olney called. "Damn it, Dawson, stay with me!" He glanced up at the comm officer. "Find that damn ship—*now!*"

"YOU KNOW," Mallet said as he stood on the prow of the Wiy Tukay ship holding a Copperhead assault rifle, "for stupe fuckers, Kroger and his group sail really well."

At his side, Iverson nodded.

The fleeing ship raced only a few yards ahead of them. The worshiper sailors had come up behind the ship and stolen the wind, allowing their prey only a few brief seconds of wind that barely filled their sails as they crested waves ahead of them. Their running lights created small pools against the dark water.

"Are those cannon ready?" Mallet demanded. They'd stripped the cannon from the Sandcats when they had left them and taken the Wiy Tukay ship. Mounting them aboard the worshipers' vessel had taken little time and improved their firepower dramatically.

"Yes, sir."

"Then hit them again," Mallet commanded. "And tell those bastards if they hit that comm station, I'll have their heads."

"Yes, sir." Iverson shouted the order.

Immediately, the 20 mm cannon belched fire against the night. They'd fired from the bottom of a trough, shooting up at the fleeing ship. Only two of the 20 mm rounds hit the ship, but one of them took out the main mast, shattering it three or four feet above the deck. At least four sailors were blown into the dark water, all of them in pieces. The fleeing ship slowed dramatically with the loss of sails that were now draped amidships.

Mallet waited impatiently as the vessel he commanded overtook the other ship. Sailors gathered along the other ship's rail tried to make a stand as they closed the final few yards, but they couldn't hold any kind of line against fully armored Magistrates.

Autofire from the Copperheads blasted the crew from the railing and broke the resistance immediately. The Wiy Tukay worshipers threw grappling lines with ease, snaring the other ship. Despite the skill the worshipers used, the two ships slammed together hard, almost knocking Mallet from his feet.

"Rake the decks with the .50-cal blasters," Mallet yelled over the gunfire, "then we take the ship."

Iverson relayed the order. The .50-cal gunners hammered the deck with the bullets, tearing away chunks of wood, beating down the pockets of resistance that remained. Then the Wiy Tukay supporters pulled the grappling lines tight while the helmsman steered their ship into their prey.

Mallet led the rush over the railing, landing heavily as he misjudged the drop and the ship slipped down the side of a wave. He had to put a hand out to steady himself, then staggered again as one of the foundation sailors fired at his chest.

The Mag armor stopped the round and most of the blunt trauma, then Mallet returned fire. The Copperhead spit a zigzag line of bullets that stitched the man from hip to shoulder, knocking him down.

"Follow the Man in Black!" Kroger screamed as he landed beside Mallet. "Follow the Man in Black!" The Wiy Tukay worshipers exploded over the side of the ship, and there was no mercy in them. They killed most of the ship's crew outright, but some of them were still alive when the worshipers threw them into the sea.

Behind the faceplate of the helmet, Mallet grinned. The worshipers possessed hearts that were even colder than most Magistrates' hearts. Once Baron Cobalt took over the Northwest Territories, Mallet determined to put in for a transfer.

The Mag commander ran across the ship's deck and toward

the comm office. He slung the Copperhead and popped the Sin Eater free of his wrist.

The door was locked.

Mallet fired a half-dozen rounds through the lock, turning it to scrap metal in a heartbeat. He lifted a boot and drove it into the door, ripping it open. Two men scrambled inside the room, firing at him immediately, scoring the black armor again and again. Calmly, Mallet pointed the Sin Eater in their direction and shot them both through the head, dropping them.

A brief glance showed him that the radio was intact and working, still broadcasting. "Dawson, this is *Starseeker!* Damn it, come in!"

Mallet switched off the radio and turned back to the doorway. A Magistrate stood there, ready to back him up.

"Cover this room," Mallet ordered. "Nobody in or out unless you personally hear from me."

"Yes, sir." The Magistrate stepped into position in front of the door as Mallet brushed by.

Outside, Mallet gazed in satisfaction at the carnage scattered across the deck. Two separate fires burned at the stern. A few worshipers were down and the way their lax bodies shifted across the deck, the Mag commander knew they wouldn't be getting back up.

Unlimbering the Copperhead again and inserting a fresh magazine, Mallet stepped out onto the deck. The last few sailors threw down their weapons and held up their hands, dropping to their knees. Kroger held the worshipers in check, glancing at Mallet expectantly.

"Chill them," Mallet ordered, then opened fire.

The sailors tried to scramble to safety, to recover their weapons or to charge Mallet and the worshipers. But they couldn't get their feet under them on the blood-slick deck. They died in seconds.

Mallet turned from the scene, eagerly searching for more victims as the Wiy Tukay worshipers screamed in exultation. He opened the comm channel. "Iverson."

"Yes, sir."

"Get Meyer up to the comm room and strip that radio out." Mallet strode across the deck, walking easier with the rolling gait of the sea. It was still unfamiliar, but he'd grown more accustomed to it. "Then plant those plas ex charges. They made contact with someone, and I don't know how far out they are. I want to eliminate the possibility of survivors."

BRIGID STOOD in *Starseeker*'s prow with Olney and Domi. The horizon had gone fully black now as night had settled over the sea.

Olney consulted the digital compass he held. Tense frustration showed in every line of his body. Dawson was obviously a friend.

"We should be almost on top of them according to the last reading we took," Olney said. "But you can't tell with these damn things sometimes. They're not linked to global positioning satellites."

"You have an operational satellite?" Brigid asked. That hadn't shown up in any of the data she'd read on the Heimdall Foundation.

Olney shook his head. "Every now and again, we can hack into satellites used by the barons. It's a very dangerous thing, and not something that's done unless as a last resort. Our techs believe there are other satellites possibly still operational in space, but we haven't managed to link with any of them. We've come close a couple times. That's one of the reasons we have crews out to follow the satellites that fall to earth."

"There!" someone shouted.

Brigid stared hard into the night again, then barely made out the dark silhouette of a ship on the horizon as it crested a wave. Running lights still showed on the ship's rigging and railing.

"Is it Dawson's ship?" she asked.

Olney nodded tensely. "Yeah."

"Perhaps they escaped."

"I don't know." Olney stared into the night. "Her main mast has been shattered. That's why most of the sails are down."

"There's another ship!" someone shouted.

Brigid scanned the horizon and spotted the other ship, all its sails intact and tacking into the wind as they were. The ship rolled over a wave, then sparks flared along the stern.

"Cannon!" Olney yelled, grabbing Brigid by the shoulder and pulling her down behind the railing.

Chapter 30

Back pressed against *Starseeker*'s wooden railing, Brigid felt the concussion of the cannon rounds and heard the detonations before she heard the scream of them passing through the air. Water splashed over *Starseeker*'s bows in droplets rather than waves, letting her know that the cannon rounds had landed a fair distance away, but the sounds of the detonations made it seem that the explosions were nearly on top of them.

"Missed us!" someone shouted.

"Thought we'd caught the last train headed west for sure that time!" another man shouted.

Olney stood, partially drenched from the spray.

Brigid pushed up beside him, listening to the scream of secondary rounds that had already hit the water, as well.

"We're out of their range," Olney declared.

The other ship fired only a few more times, but made no effort to change course, vanishing slowly over the crest of the next wave. Even as it did, the stricken foundation ship blew up, ruptured and twisted by at least four separate explosions. The glare of the explosions highlighted the faces of *Starseeker*'s crew.

Olney cursed softly, almost devoid of feeling. Then he gave orders to close in on the ship before it disappeared completely beneath the water.

Having to tack against the wind slowed *Starseeker* by precious minutes. By the time the ship reached the other vessel, the wreckage had burned nearly to the waterline, the fires seemingly dancing on top of the sea, reflected in hundreds of facets created by the irregular ocean surface.

Brigid studied the dying ship dispassionately, trying to keep her distance from the corpses she spotted on the ship's remains, as well as in the dark water. Even as she watched, small, green glowing pools swam toward the torn bodies and started feeding on them.

"Over here!" someone yelled weakly. "Over here!"

Olney ran around the railing and grabbed a line. He tied it to the railing, then dived into the water toward the man barely keeping his head up. Once Olney had the sailor, crewmen pulled them back aboard *Starseeker*.

They laid the wounded man on the deck, working at him and Olney quickly to strip away at least a dozen of the piranha-type scavengers. Blood flowed onto the deck from both men, but Olney ignored it.

Gazing at the rescued man, Brigid felt certain that he wouldn't live to see the dawn. A massive wooden splinter from ship's planking nearly two feet long protruded from his left side.

"Who did this?" Olney demanded gently.

The man's eyes rolled in their orbits, and he strained to focus. "Mags," he gasped. "Magistrates helping the Wiy Tukay people." He shuddered suddenly and lay still, but his chest still rose and fell almost imperceptibly.

"Magistrates," someone said over the slap of waves against the ship.

"What the hell are they doing out here?"

"Never been here before."

Olney covered the wounded man with a blanket, then gave orders to get him below and get him some medical treatment. He joined Brigid at the railing.

"Only one thing comes immediately to mind that would interest Magistrates," Olney stated quietly. "And that's Tyler Falzone's ville of islands."

Brigid silently agreed. "Falzone needs to know they're coming."

Olney glanced out at the darkness. The wrecked ship was

slowly dropping under the sea. "If we get too close to the Magistrates, they could end up chilling us, too."

"Leaving Falzone and his people to die wouldn't help the foundation's interest," Brigid pointed out.

"I know."

"How far away is Falzone's island?"

"Two, three days depending on the sea and the wind. But that's asking everyone on this ship to put their lives at risk while we pursue them. We don't have enough manpower to stand against Magistrates."

Brigid was silent for a moment. "No, but there are two men who should be with Falzone by now. Kane and Grant. They're friends. If they know about the coming attack, it could make all the difference."

Olney looked at her. "How sure are you about that?"

"Your other choice is to lose the chance at forging a relationship with Falzone."

"Which would you do?" Olney asked.

"I believe in Kane and Grant," Brigid said. "When it comes to something like this, they're the best at what they do."

"Funny." Olney grinned. "You speak highly of them, but you don't sound like you're fully approving."

"I'm not," Brigid replied honestly.

TWO NIGHTS LATER, Mallet lay in the bottom of the johnboat, stretched out prone, a sniper rifle in his hands. He watched his target through the light-amplifying scope, not bothering to adjust for the rise and fall of the waves that continually lifted and dropped the small craft.

They were almost three hundred yards out, invisible against the black ocean because the johnboat had such a low profile. The mast lay in the bottom of the boat, the sail neatly furled around it.

The boat crested a wave, then started the gentle fall into the next trough. The tide slowly carried the boat toward the island

Kroger had identified as belonging to Tyler Falzone. They'd spent the past three hours watching the island's security, determining the best points of egress. It had all come down to the cave near the docks. Security hadn't changed until twenty minutes ago, so Mallet felt good about assuming another shift change was at least two and a half hours away.

"Iverson," Mallet said quietly over the helmet comm.

"Yes, sir."

"On my mark, take down your targets." Mallet tightened his finger on the sniper rifle. They'd identified seven guards watching over the dock area and the cave. Mallet, Iverson and two other men in johnboats surrounded the island's dock. All of them were accomplished snipers.

"Yes, sir."

Mallet waited, knowing he had to pick off at least two of the security guards. He put the sniper rifle's crosshairs over the man smoking a cigarette in the cave mouth, the magnification bringing the man's face into view.

"Go," Mallet whispered softly, then squeezed the trigger.

On the island, the first guard toppled to the ground, dead instantly when the bullet cored through his brain. The silenced rifle made only a coughing noise, and even if that carried across the water, Mallet knew it would never be heard by any of the men at the docks.

Mallet moved to the right, aware of another man falling from the dock into the water. Mallet brought the crosshairs over his second target as the johnboat started to ride up the next wave.

The man moved quickly, racing for the cave mouth. Mallet fired twice with deliberation, watching as at least one of the bullets took the man in the chest a half second later. When the guard sprawled on the stone floor, Mallet put another round through the back of his head.

Moving slightly, Mallet raked the small shoreline before the cave and saw that all the targets had been taken down. He keyed the comm. "Okay, let's move in." He sat up and motioned to the Wiy Tukay worshipers manning the boat.

The worshipers used oars, pulling fiercely to get the boat in close to the island.

Mallet stepped out onto the docks, waiting less than a handful of minutes for the crews from the other four boats to join him. He led the recce, making sure no one was left alive inside the cave.

"Iverson, disconnect that bomb," Mallet ordered, referring to the self-destruct system set up inside the cave. Then he headed up the metal stairway, his boots banging.

A man stepped from the shadows above, spotted Mallet and the other invaders and turned to run. Still using the sniper rifle, firing at nearly point-blank range, the Mag commander blew the man's heart through the front of his chest. At the top of the stairway, Mallet stepped over the corpse and kept going, following the passageway to the hand-powered elevator.

He gazed out over the ville. Only a few fires and lanterns burned. A handful of men moved around the dwellings, not knowing that death was among them.

Mallet grinned in anticipation. He'd already contacted Baron Cobalt. Reserves from Cobaltville would meet him at a prearranged location along the mainland in three days.

But for now, ransacking the ville was totally his operation. He gathered his troops and began the descent.

DEFORE ENTERED the command center with the intent of checking on her final patient before retiring for the night. Lakesh had been strangely silent the past few days, and she wasn't at all certain what the cause was.

As he had been every day, Lakesh was seated in front of the monitor, his fingers steepled before him. What little sleep he'd had had been spent in the chair.

For the first time, DeFore realized how important Donald Bry was to Lakesh's daily routines. With Bry manning the monitors, at least Lakesh occasionally got out of the central command center and slept in his own bed.

DeFore cleared her throat as she crossed the floor. Despite the physical transformation that took years off his appearance on their last mission in China, sheer exhaustion showed in Lakesh's movements as his head turned toward her. His eyes were bloodshot and red-rimmed below his unkempt hair.

"Thank you for that, me dear DeFore," Lakesh said almost listlessly. "A modicum of civility and courtesy extended at this moment is definitely appreciated."

"Glad to know that," DeFore said. "I came to take your vitals."

"You could have done that through the infirmary comps."

"Then I thought perhaps I'd work on my bedside manner."

"Ah, a return to sarcasm and snideness."

"You seem more comfortable with me there."

A wan smile touched Lakesh's face. "In truth, perhaps I am." He returned his attention to the monitor.

DeFore took his wrist and began timing his pulse. Her eyes strayed to the monitor. Wherever the scene was being transmitted from over the sat-link, it was dark. But shadows moved in the night, punctuated by the sudden blaze of muzzle-flashes. In the time it took to count Lakesh's advanced heart rate, a number of people had died and several small structures had been set afire.

Lakesh made no move to hide the events from her.

Then, in the light of one of the fired buildings, DeFore saw two men in Magistrate black pursuing other victims with cold-blooded efficiency.

"Do you know what you're witnessing, my dear DeFore?" Lakesh asked.

"No," DeFore answered. "Your heart rate's up. You need to get more rest if you're going to heal properly."

"There's no rest for the wicked," Lakesh said. "What

you're witnessing is the death of a small, nearly complete paradise. And I had a hand in it.''

"The paradise?" DeFore asked, surprised.

"No. In the destruction of that paradise."

DeFore wanted to say that she didn't find that too surprising, since it wasn't a paradise that Lakesh didn't control. But somehow she just didn't have the heart. So she said nothing at all.

The destruction continued across the monitor as the sat-link cycled through programmed views, some closer than others. The Magistrates, DeFore saw, obviously led another group in the destruction of the first. The second group didn't offer much resistance, being overpowered almost completely and seemingly made up mostly of adolescent children and women.

"Those people are there," Lakesh said, "as surely as if I'd put them there myself."

"I'm sure you had your reasons," DeFore said, not too unkindly.

"Indeed, my dear DeFore, I did. And they most definitely were not to meet these ends."

"Are Kane and Grant there? Or Brigid and Domi?"

"No," Lakesh answered tiredly. "But they will be."

"And then what will happen?" DeFore asked.

Lakesh sat quietly for a moment, then finally shook his head. "I honestly don't know, but they are going to be in the gravest danger and there's not much I can do to help them."

"TALK TO ME, bitch!" Mallet backhanded the frightened woman in front of him, splitting her lip and knocking her from her feet. The staccato roar of blasterfire was slowing around him. The Magistrates and the Wiy Tukay worshipers were taking no hostages; the only people who lived were those quick enough to leave the ville.

The woman sobbed and remained on the ground, illuminated by the burning buildings only a few feet away.

Mallet felt the heat from the burning buildings, warm

against the cool air that filled the island. He reached for the woman and dragged her to her knees. Purple bruising already stained her cheek. "Tell me where Falzone is," he commanded.

"He isn't here," the woman answered, trying to cover her face. She was the fourth person to tell Mallet that, and he believed her.

Anger surged through the Magistrate commander, and he stopped himself just short of killing the woman. The terrified look on her face showed him that she knew that. "Where is he?"

"Salvaging," the woman replied, keeping her arms wrapped over her head.

"Where?"

"Don't know. Don't know."

"How do you get in touch with him?" Mallet slapped the woman's hands from her head, then kicked her in the face.

The woman fell to the ground, hacking and coughing and spitting out broken teeth. "Radio. That's all I know. I swear."

"What frequency on the comm?" Mallet stayed alert, watching as his men formed a protective ring around him.

"Don't know." Snot and blood mixed, running from the woman's nose, down over her mouth and off her chin. Once, she'd been pretty, but she never would be again. Mallet took a certain vicious pleasure in that.

"Who would know?" Mallet demanded.

"Carlson. Don't know where he is. Mebbe in the cave—"

That was no help because everyone in the cave outpost was dead. Mallet stepped back and twisted his wrist, freeing the Sin Eater.

The woman covered her head again, as if her arms would turn bullets. "Wait! Don't chill me! Falzone's little girl is still here if she isn't dead!"

Mallet breathed in deeply. Over the years he'd learned that some people put great store by their children. It was a special weakness that made victims more vulnerable. He kept a smile from his face with effort. "Show me," he ordered. He yanked the woman to her feet.

The woman cringed from his painful grip, then pointed at a house farther up the side of the wall.

Mallet pushed the woman toward the house, waving his men into positions around them. The worshipers crowed in fierce delight as they ran down the final would-be defilers of their god.

The house proved to be a narrow two-story that hadn't been touched yet. Mallet followed the woman inside. "What is the girl's name?" the Mag commander asked.

"Ariel," the woman replied, having trouble speaking through her broken and swollen mouth. "I watch her sometimes when Falzone and his woman are gone."

"What woman?"

"The little girl's mother."

"The mother is with Falzone?" Mallet grinned. Things were definitely improving.

"Yeah. They stay together all the time."

Mallet followed the woman through the small neat rooms, listening to her call out for the little girl. Blasterfire had nearly died completely away except for the occasional burst, but the screams of victims carried on. The Wiy Tukay worshipers had demonstrated a bloodthirsty and sadistic streak that Mallet truly appreciated.

Then the sound of a strangled cry caught Mallet's attention. He turned his gaze toward the narrow stairway leading up to the second floor. A thin, frightened shadow clung to the stair railing.

Mallet took a small flash from his belt, switched it on and played it over the tiny girl hiding in the corner of the landing. She shielded her eyes with a thin arm, her other arm around a doll made from rags.

"Ariel," Mallet called in a stern voice.

"Go away!" the little girl shrieked. "Go away! I want my mommy! I want my daddy!"

Grinning wolfishly, Mallet switched off the flash and strode over to the girl. She watched him, her eyes terrified and yellow from the reflection of the fires burning outside. At the last second, she screamed again and tried to run away. Effortlessly, Mallet caught the girl by the ankle and dragged her from the stairs. She whipped and spun and shrieked, clawing at him like a cat and beating at him with the doll.

"Don't!" the woman yelled, running toward Mallet.

The Magistrate knew the reaction stemmed from the woman's own guilt in the matter. He'd seen it a few times, more often from women when small children were involved. Mercilessly, he lifted the Sin Eater and shot the woman through the face four times, knocking her body back and dissolving her features into crimson ruin.

The little girl screamed again.

Mallet dropped the girl beside the dead woman, releasing her ankle and quickly moving his hand to her throat. He squeezed tight enough to shut her up. "Stop screaming," he ordered. "Stop screaming or I'll chill you right here."

But the little girl couldn't stop screaming. Her fear of him had pushed her past all reason. She hugged the doll to her fiercely and tried to scream again.

Mallet strangled the little girl, clamping his big hand around her throat until he saw her eyes roll up into her head. The doll slid lifelessly from her arms.

Chapter 31

"They won't get any closer," Falzone said. "They're just spying on us, trying to see where we've come from, mebbe figure out what we got."

Kane stood at the cargo ship's railing with Grant, Falzone and Remar. Kane trained his field glasses on the Chinese ship and scanned the deck.

The ship was definitely Tong design, a style he'd become familiar with while tracking Ambika in the Western Isles. Constructed of arches and angles, and carrying three squared-off sails that folded into neat sections, the ship looked ancient. With the cherry-red lacquer finish broken up by thin black lines, it appeared to be covered in gleaming blood. A great, roaring dragon figurehead sprouted along the prow, reaching out into the wind with its painted claws.

The Tong ship carried a full complement of cannon that had been cast in Wei Qiang's foundries in the Western Isles. The weapons were based on eighteenth-century designs and used old-fashioned black powder, as well, but Kane knew from personal experience how deadly they were. With proper handling and targeting, the cannon could reduce another ship to matchsticks in minutes. A few modern cannons and .50-cal deck gun backed the cannon.

"Do they know who you are?" Kane asked. Early morning painted golds and pinks on the waters to the east.

Falzone nodded. "I'm known to them. Qiang makes sure his officers have pix of me. We've found them on a couple ships we've fought."

Kane studied the sea around the Tong ship.

"Looking for another ship?" Falzone asked.

"Yeah," Kane said.

"You won't find it. This far up into the Seattle area, I made it a point to torpedo Qiang's ships any time there's more than one in a group."

"With the minisubs?" Grant asked. Teresa prowled underwater in the minisub now. Falzone had chosen to let himself be seen.

Falzone nodded. "We come up on them in the night when their sec is at its weakest, then blow them out of the water. How many ships did we take down before Qiang got it through his head, Remar?"

"Twenty. Twenty-five," Remar answered, rolling another cigarette.

"Ships are expensive properties, Kane," Falzone said. "A man owning them isn't going to want to spend them foolishly. They're too hard to replace, and you don't want to be without them for long if you're depending on them for defense."

"Why didn't Qiang send Tong minisubs after you?" Kane asked.

"Shit," Remar said, "they tried that. But that didn't work out for them, either."

"I know these waters," Falzone stated. "I know the safe areas and the dangerous ones. When I fight, whether on the water or under it, I fight on a battlefield I choose, and I fight to win."

"There's been times," Remar added, "that the battlefields he's arranged have been infested with damn chewers or hollowguts, guaranteeing anybody thrown overboard one fuckin' hard death." The old man grinned and scratched at his scarred knob of an ear. "Kinda added to the stories those bastards tell about him."

Kane nodded. The chewers were the phosphorescent piranha that swam through this part of the Cific Ocean in schools, and the hollowguts were mutie jellyfish that measured over thirty feet across and had tentacles capable of paralyzing and killing prey as big as they were. All of those species included humans as part of their diet.

"Then why allow even one ship to watch you?" Grant asked.

"I can't destroy them all," Falzone answered, "and there have been times that the Tong have lent a hand when one of my salvage ships was under attack by the Wiy Tukay worshipers. In the meantime the Tong have a nasty habit of attacking and chilling anyone in these waters that don't fly one of my flags. Thins out the pirates."

"Kinda like having your own pet sharks." Remar cackled.

"And usually," Falzone said, "the Tong are the first that I trade with. If they get to watch me, I've got a direct source for trading, as well as a loose sec arrangement."

"Then why not enter into a stronger relationship with them?" Kane asked.

"Because," Falzone said, "they don't have weps to spare the way that I need them. That's why I've been trading with Baron Cobalt. I want those blasters. Hell, I *need* them if I'm going to keep operating the way I have."

Kane thought about the Cerberus redoubt. The only way to truly remain autonomous in the Outlands was to be unknown and hidden, and to have everything that was necessary to that lifestyle. Falzone didn't have that luxury. And caring about his people the way he did only made him a bigger target.

"So if you decided to trade with Baron Cobalt exclusively—" Kane said.

"Wei Qiang would have my head if he could," Falzone finished. "I won't agree to a deal with Baron Cobalt because I don't trust him, and because any kind of allegiance he's going to offer would only be lip service. If a war here with the Tong got too costly, the baron would pull up stakes." He paused, watching the Chinese ship. "That's why I'm not trying to work a deal with the Tong, Kane. If Baron Cobalt decided to overinvest in this area and nuke me out of business, the Tong might pull up, too. Neither of them wants to do that until they get the maps I have of this area.''

Kane nodded. ''Mebbe. But Baron Cobalt has other worries going on right now, too. An arrangement with the Tong might make him reconsider this whole area as just too expensive.''

''Perhaps. But I won't know that until I make that arrangement. And I'm not going to get there any time soon.''

Kane watched the Tong ship, sedately matching the pace the salvage ship was setting. ''So what do you do now?''

''With them watching?''

''Yeah.''

''Clean the ship,'' Falzone answered. ''Hold off salvaging. Wait for them to get bored and move on. It usually doesn't take more than a day or so.''

''Falzone!'' a crewman called from the comm station in the prow. The man's face was tight, anxious.

Falzone excused himself and walked away.

Grant leaned a hip against the railing, arms crossed over his chest as he stared at the Chinese ship. ''This man is in the eye of a storm that could break at any time.''

Kane silently agreed.

''Yet,'' Grant went on, ''instead of being worried about it, Falzone seems to be happier than a pig in slop.'' He paused, then grinned sourly. ''I ever mention to you how much he reminds me of you?''

''No. But there's a lot about Falzone that I admire and respect.''

''He can't remain on his own out here,'' Grant said softly. ''Not with the way everything here is shaping up.''

''I think he's beginning to realize that.'' Kane used his field glasses again, scanning the Tong ship and being scanned in return.

''Trouble,'' Grant breathed at his side.

Kane turned slowly and watched Falzone come back down from the comm station in the prow. All humor and life seemed to have deserted the man, but he kept his face implacable.

Falzone joined them at the railing again, but his attention was solely riveted on the Tong ship. "Do you know a woman named Brigid Baptiste?"

The question turned Kane cold inside, opening up a dozen different possibilities in just those few words. "Yeah."

"She's going to want to talk to you," Falzone said. "I told her she'd have to wait a while because I wanted to talk to you first."

Kane nodded, remaining noncommittal.

"Baptiste came in with a Heimdall Foundation ship," Falzone said. "Do you know anything about that?"

"No," Kane replied. "I didn't even know she was out here."

Falzone stared at Kane's eyes. "I believe you. What is she to you?"

"A friend."

"What is she doing with the foundation people?"

"I won't know the answer to that until I ask her."

Falzone was quiet for a moment, then when he spoke again his voice was husky and harsh. "Ships carrying Wiy Tukay worshipers and Magistrates attacked my island last night."

Kane waited, remembering the fields and the homes, the little girl with the sun in her hair who had been so excited about baby chickens. He made himself go cold and emotionless inside because it was the only way he could deal with the information he was certain Falzone was going to tell him.

"A Magistrate named Mallet led the group," Falzone said. "He left a couple people alive just to tell me that. He also said he wanted the maps I've made and found that show where all the comp businesses were before skydark. He took my little girl, Kane. He took her and he left word that if I didn't deliver those maps within the next three days, he was going to chill her, then come back for me. So I guess I need to know where you fit into this thing."

Kane was suddenly aware of how Remar and the rest of the

crew were positioned around Grant and him. One wrong move and he knew there would be a lot of falling bodies.

"I'm going to help you," Kane stated.

"I've got a lot of men ready to back me up on this play," Falzone said. "Why should I need you?"

"Because this is a one-percenter play," Grant growled, "and you know it. When it comes to the time the shit hits the fan, Kane and I have stood through the worst of it."

Falzone just stared at them.

"You're too close to it," Kane said. "They have your daughter."

"And don't you fucking forget it," Falzone whispered coldly.

"Your people are used to you leading," Kane went on. "You can't back away from this thing, and you can't control it, either. You need someone on the outside of it to handle it. That's the only way you're going to get her back alive."

Falzone breathed raggedly, barely managing control.

Kane waited, keeping his hand ready to go for the blaster at his hip.

"Tyler," Remar said softly, "these boys are right. They're right about the dangers here, and they're right about the way you got your nose all opened up over this. And you know it, too."

Falzone shook his head slightly, never breaking eye contact with Kane.

Remar stepped up beside Falzone easily. "The Mags, mebbe they'll settle for getting the maps, but they're gonna figure that's only one set of 'em. They'll think you might give another set of maps to the Tong just so they can devil 'em while they're searching for whatever the hell it is Baron Cobalt figures is so goddamn important. So they'll chill you, and if they chill you, ain't no use keepin' Ariel alive no more."

Falzone spun on the man, and for a moment Kane thought he was actually going to hit him. Remar didn't flinch. "Fuck you, Remar," Falzone said heatedly. "Don't you ever say that about my daughter again. She isn't going to die. I won't allow that."

"Get mad all you want," Remar said, "but you know that's what this Mallet fucker is wantin' you to do. You get mad, and he'll take your head off at your shoulders with no more thinkin' than if he'd been swattin' a fly."

Falzone's left eye twitched.

"I've seen these two men in action a few times," Remar said. "We ain't got nobody, 'cept mebbe me back when I was in my prime, that can even hold a candle to them. You want to get Ariel back safe and sound and in one piece, you're gonna need a small team to get to her and get her outta whatever hell she's in. Kane and Grant, whatever else they are, I'm thinkin' they're the beginnin' of that."

Restrained emotion made Falzone shake slightly.

"You listenin' to me?" Remar asked.

"Yeah." Falzone let out a harsh ragged breath that sounded more like a pained gasp. "I hear you."

"Where are the Magistrates and Wiy Tukay worshipers?" Kane asked.

"They sailed east," Falzone said. "That's all anyone knows. Damn ocean is huge to go looking for them. Probably headed for the mainland."

"Then I have something else for you," Kane added. "I can locate that ship for you." At least, Lakesh could with the satellite views into the area. "The people I work with have access to a working satellite with a spying camera."

"There's only one reason the Magistrate ships are running," Falzone said.

"To lead us into a trap," Grant said.

Falzone nodded. "Survivors from another ship Mallet attacked told the foundation crew that Mallet was after their comm gear."

"Mallet has called someone else as backup," Kane said.

Turning his eyes from Kane, Falzone stared across the water

at the Chinese ship earnestly. "Then we need to raise an army, as well. Are you ready to talk to the Tong?"

"Yeah," Kane replied.

"Then let's do that first," Falzone said. "Because telling my wife that her baby has been taken is going to be even worse."

KANE CLIMBED the ladder leading up to the Tong ship's deck, following Falzone.

The Chinese captain, dressed in a black-and-white robe and wearing a sword on his hip, met them at the railing. The man appeared to be in his late forties, medium built, with a goatee showing only a few gray hairs. He stood in a relaxed stance, his hands crossed behind him, but Kane got the impression the man was a coiled spring waiting to snap if the meeting went wrong.

"I am Lik-Tsun Rong," the captain said. "Commanding officer of *Blessed Butterfly*. Welcome aboard my ship. My master, Wei Qiang, extends his wishes for your comfort and safety."

Kane and Remar flanked Falzone, leaving Grant and the three other men of their party covering their backs. They kept a path open to the railing and the longboat below. No effort was made to take their weapons from them.

"I'm Tyler Falzone," Falzone said.

"I'm well aware of who you are, Mr. Falzone," Rong stated. "I'm also well aware that you've never stepped foot on one of my master's ships, so I will admit to some curiosity about your choice to do so now."

"I've come to make a deal with Qiang," Falzone stated evenly. "If he can cover his end of it."

Rong nodded, but his eyes never left the group before him. "As a captain in my master's navy, I am empowered to act as Wei Qiang's agent."

"I want to speak to Qiang," Falzone insisted.

Rong considered that for a moment. "Radio contact from

here is possible, but I dare not interrupt my master unless it is a matter of some import.''

"Fine,'' Falzone said. He turned and headed back for the railing. ''Then we're done here.''

Kane kept the shotgun in his fist, ready to bring it up. The crew glanced toward the captain, who remained absolutely motionless, his eyes fixed on Falzone's back. Remar just grinned and shifted the cigar Kane had given him to the other side of his mouth.

"Mr. Falzone,'' Rong called out neutrally, ''perhaps an arrangement could be made.''

Coolly, Falzone stood by the railing and turned back. ''I won't settle for anything less than speaking to Qiang.''

"Of course. Please accept my apologies.'' Rong held up a hand. ''My personal quarters are this way. I will arrange an audience with my master. Please make yourselves comfortable.'' A young boy dressed in the maritime black uniform like the rest of the crew stepped forward and waved for them to accompany him.

Falzone led the way. Kane, Remar and Grant fell into step behind him. The cool breeze of the morning blew over the ship, rattling the rigging and twisting the folds of the rectangular sails. And Kane knew the whole way that unseen snipers had them in their sights.

IT TOOK more than twenty minutes to set up the radio connection to Wei Qiang, and when it came through, there were still fitful scratchy noises and instances of dead air.

Kane remained by the doorway with Grant standing tandem. Neither of them spoke. Falzone knew what he had to do. They just had to cover his back while he did it.

The captain's quarters were small but neat and carefully arranged. A few books occupied a shelf over the hand-carved desk in front of the bed. An intricately designed Oriental rug covered the hardwood floor. Red lacquered paneling covered the walls, each with mythical scenes burned into them depicting dragons and warriors and ghosts.

Kane didn't know what all the pictures were about, but assumed they were from stories Rong had read, or maybe from some aspect of his culture. He knew Brigid would probably recognize them, and thinking of her brought other troubling thoughts. He had no idea what she was doing in the Northwest Territories or how she'd tied up with the Heimdall Foundation.

Despite the tension involved in the situation, Falzone conducted himself well—even when he told Qiang about his daughter. Falzone sat on the small chair by the porthole, talking calmly but looking through the porthole out to sea.

Rong's cabin boy poured green tea for all of them, then left.

Qiang's voice sounded like cool leather. "Once I agree to this bargain with you, Mr. Falzone, I shall hold you accountable as long as you live. You do understand that?"

Kane listened to the calm certainty in the old man's voice. When he'd first met Qiang, Kane had been impressed. The old man was ruthless, but he backed it with complete fearlessness.

"Yes," Falzone answered. "But you need to understand me, too. If you don't help me save my daughter, if she is lost, we don't have a deal."

"That is not acceptable," Qiang said sharply. "Getting my troops into that area is going to be a hardship for me. Financially, I am risking much, and I am stripping away my own defenses to provide even this small chance for your daughter."

"I don't give a fuck," Falzone said. "My daughter is at risk, and if you can't live with that, neither can I."

"Surely," Qiang said evenly, "you can see that you can't deal with Baron Cobalt after this."

"If you can't help me," Falzone said, "then I'm asking help from the wrong man, and that's an ace on the line. Cobaltville still has the blasters I need to stand against the Wiy Tukay worshipers. If I can't depend on you for this, I don't need you."

Captain Rong breathed in shallowly, but said nothing.

"I can stand against you, Qiang," Falzone said, "that's why you haven't taken a harder stance against me. I can duck and hide in these islands and chill anybody you send after me for a long time. And you still won't know where the Lost Valley goods are. I'm entering into this deal because there's a chance to save my daughter, not because I've suddenly become enamored of you."

Captain Rong cleared his throat delicately.

Falzone spun on the man. "If you got something caught in your throat, get outside and take care of it."

"Captain Rong believes you should not be so indelicate with me," Qiang said amid the hiss and pop of the radio.

"This is a fucking indelicate situation," Falzone said. "I'm going to lay my cards on the table so you can get a good look at them."

"Agreed," Qiang stated. "A most honorable way of doing business."

"From the way I hear it, honor isn't exactly your strong suit," Falzone said, "but you're greedy enough to buy into this. And it'll be a chance to strike back at Baron Cobalt."

"Agreed," Qiang said. "Since we are both being up front about our motivations."

"How soon can you have support teams in the area?" Falzone asked.

"That answer," Qiang replied, "will surprise you. Men under my command in those territories recently came into possession of a man named Donald Bry."

The announcement surprised Kane.

"I knew from their questioning of him that someone was about to make a move against you. So I have been preparing for a while. I have been told I can have ships and airplanes there within thirty hours."

"Rescuing the girl," Kane said, "is going to be left up to us."

Falzone glanced up at Kane.

Only the crackle of white noise echoed inside the captain's quarters for a moment.

"I know your voice," Qiang said.

"We've met," Kane replied. "Down in Autarkic a while back. I came in with Christensen on *Sloop John B.*"

"Kane," Qiang stated. "I remember you. You slew Ambika."

"Mebbe." The woman warrior's body had never been recovered. "But I want you to know we're going to ramrod the rescue operation."

"I have men capable of—" Qiang began.

"No," Falzone said. "Kane works this end of the salvage."

A moment passed. "As you wish, but once the battle is joined with the Cobaltville forces, should it come to that, my men will act as they see fit."

"That's fine," Falzone said. "And once my daughter is out of there alive, we have a deal."

"Kane," Qiang said in a cold voice, "you should know that my bargain with Mr. Falzone rests squarely on your shoulders. If you should fail him, you will also fail me. And in this endeavor, Mr. Falzone's wrath—even though his daughter is involved—will in no way match mine."

"Sure," Kane said, "but if your people fuck this up by jumping the gun on us, trust me when I say that I'll hold you accountable."

Qiang made no response.

"And I want Donald Bry," Kane went on.

"Why?"

"Because he has information I need."

"Was he working for you when he came into these territories?" Qiang asked.

"No."

"Then what is he to you?"

"Information. I want to know who all the players are."

"Very well. Captain Rong?"

"Yes, Lord Qiang?" the captain responded.

"See to it that your prisoner is transferred into Mr. Falzone's custody."

"At once, Lord Qiang."

"Mr. Falzone," Qiang said, "I wish you good fortune on the rescue of your daughter. I have found it to be most...*unpleasant* to lose family."

"Thank you," Falzone replied.

Qiang ended the radio communication.

TWO OF CAPTAIN RONG'S crewmen brought Donald Bry up onto the deck. The little man showed hard wear and a scruffiness Kane had never seen in him. Bry didn't look too relieved to see Kane waiting on him. The crewmen took Bry's cuffs off and left him with Kane.

"We're going to need to talk," Kane stated.

Bry nodded but didn't say anything.

"You may contact my ship," Captain Rong told Falzone, "if you need anything. And all the coordinating efforts will be done through me."

"That's fine," Falzone said.

"I have three daughters myself, Mr. Falzone," Captain Rong said. "My son serves as my cabin boy so that we can spend time together and I can further his training. I teach him the things a warrior and a sailor needs to learn. Family is very important to me. I would not see you lose your daughter." He offered his hand.

Falzone took the Tong captain's hand and shook it. He didn't speak.

Kane waited until Falzone was clear of the deck, then motioned Bry over the side. Kane dropped into the longboat beside Grant.

Captain Rong leaned on the railing, looking back at them. The dragon on the prow clawed the waves that broke across it.

"You got an idea of how we're supposed to pull this off?" Grant whispered.

"Yeah," Kane said. "At least, I've got the beginnings of an idea."

Chapter 32

"That's Kane?" Mac Olney asked.

Brigid watched Kane step out of the minisub onto the docks fronting the cave mouth leading into Tyler Falzone's island. "Yes," she replied.

"He's not as big as I thought he would be from the way you described him," Olney stated.

Brigid let the statement pass without comment. She'd never described Kane physically. Cool winds blew in from the ocean and the crash of waves underscored her conversation with Olney. The coarse, sour smell of burned buildings and death lingered over the island.

Falzone's guards watched over Brigid and Olney, but they weren't overbearing. When the foundation ship had arrived at the island, they'd immediately surrendered, trusting Falzone's mercy and Kane's presence at Brigid's insistence. They'd been there for the past twenty-eight hours, sequestered to a holding area while awaiting Falzone's arrival from the salvage site where he'd been. During that time, Brigid had also been aware that the Magistrates who'd attacked the island were increasing their lead.

During that time, she'd also spoken with Kane over the radio, explaining how she'd come to be with the Heimdall Foundation people and learning that Kane now had possession of Donald Bry from the Chinese.

A sudden excited squeal rang out below. Domi broke from her guards and ran to Grant, who caught her up in his arms and laughed out loud.

"You don't seem as excited to see your friends as Domi does," Olney observed.

"I'm glad they're here," Brigid said, "but I'm more reserved than Domi is."

Olney nodded but didn't say anything.

Brigid waited, watching as Kane moved toward her. He was totally focused, his blue-gray eyes looking stormy. He stepped up into the cave with her. "We need to talk, Baptiste." He glanced at Olney and dismissed the foundation man. "You can bring your new friend if you want."

Brigid barely curbed a heated response.

"Not overly friendly, is he?" Olney asked.

"No," Brigid responded. "Not even on a good day." She watched Kane's broad back as he ascended the metal staircase inside the lookout cave. She wondered how much of his shortness was due to the pressures he was under now, and how much was due to the fact that Olney was with her.

"Mebbe Falzone needs to rethink who he's going to send after his little girl," Olney said.

Brigid turned to the foundation man. "No. If there's any person I'd trust to get that little girl out of this situation, it's Kane. Don't make any mistakes about that." She left him standing there, not really understanding why she'd defended Kane so brusquely.

KANE SAT inside the wag he and Grant had brought from the Cerberus redoubt. He held the radio handset that connected him to Lakesh, watching the faces around him.

Donald Bry sat farthest away, his gaze resting uncomfortably on the burned-out shells of the homes around them. Since he'd been returned to them, Bry had only answered Kane's questions, offering no defense for his actions and only as much explanation as he could get away with.

Domi sat beside Grant, her attention riveted on the big man. Falzone conferred with his men only a short distance away, but Teresa was nowhere to be found. Discovering that her daughter was in enemy hands had been a lot for her to handle, and Kane supposed it was only natural that the woman placed part of the blame on Falzone.

And Brigid sat close to the foundation man, Mac Olney. Or maybe, Kane irritably conceded, the foundation man sat close to her. They'd been talking quietly among themselves, which bothered Kane on a level he wasn't ready to admit to even to himself.

"Lakesh," Kane called over the radio.

"I'm here, friend Kane. I've been expecting you to call." Despite the fact that his machinations had been found out, Lakesh didn't sound overly defensive. The old man sounded tired. He really hadn't been happy to find out Kane had helped engineer the deal between Falzone and Wei Qiang.

"You were the one who boobied the files Falzone traded to Baron Cobalt," Kane accused.

"Yes," Lakesh admitted. "After we found out about the salvage operation in the Northwest Territories, I couldn't allow it to go unchecked. I had Bry set himself up with some of the comp prog suppliers that networked with Falzone's traders, and began trading files back to Falzone that I knew he would be able to trade to Baron Cobalt. I built the viruses that affected Cobaltville's comps."

"Intending to set the Magistrates loose on Remar and other people Falzone had been using to trade through."

"Yes. The fact that you and Grant were caught in the cross fire at the gaudy came as a surprise to me. I had no way of knowing. My intention was to slow Falzone's trading with Baron Cobalt and get Bry inside Falzone's salvaging to get a better understanding of what it is Baron Cobalt searches for so desperately there," Lakesh went on. "Bry would have been able to keep an eye on developments there for us."

"You don't know what Baron Cobalt is searching for?" Kane asked.

"No, I don't. I'd hoped Bry would have been able to uncover that."

Kane didn't know whether to believe the man about that or not. Lakesh had a history of playing things close to the vest, and was always guileless until he'd been found out.

"Why did you fake Bry's attack on you?" Brigid demanded.

"All of you," Lakesh said, "involved yourselves in this. With Kane and Grant in the area, it seemed more possible that the Heimdall Foundation's ability to get him inside Falzone's camp would work. However, if you happened to see Bry there, you needed to be convinced that he had become a traitor to our cause and treat him accordingly."

"To *your* cause, you mean," Grant growled.

Lakesh ignored the comment. "Of course, I'd no way of knowing the Tong would capture Bry. And friend Bry, if you are there, I am glad that no harm has come to you."

Bry only shook his head.

"You knew the Magistrates were following us," Kane said.

"Yes, though I didn't know any of them would go to these lengths."

"This would have ran more simply if you'd have let us know what was going on," Kane said.

"Would they indeed, friend Kane?" Lakesh sounded more sarcastic then, but his words lacked their usual sting. "Baron Cobalt has even taken precautions to make sure the other barons haven't learned of his search among the ruins of Seattle and the second Silicon Valley that existed preskydark. If I had not precipitated these events in the manner that I chose, had I not added the catalyst of the comp progs with viruses in them that elicited Baron Cobalt's decision to treat Tyler Falzone as an enemy rather than a trader, we would have learned nothing."

"You've still learned nothing if you don't know what Cobalt's after," Kane said. "You succeeded in getting over half the ville here chilled, and now there's a little girl's life on the line because of it."

"Events could have just as easily worked out the way I had engineered them," Lakesh said.

Kane curbed his anger and focused on the present situation. Lakesh had his way of looking at things and there would be no persuading him that he'd acted in any way wrongly. "I want Mallet's ship, Lakesh. Get it found and get back to me."

There was a momentary pause. "What will you do when I find his ship, friend Kane?"

"I'm going to rescue that little girl," Kane replied.

"And what happens after that? Will you stay there, or will you return?"

Kane paused, suddenly aware that he had no ready answer. "Find the ship." He broke the radio connection and glanced at Brigid, who was talking quietly with Mac Olney again. Maybe they all had new roads open to them.

"I SEE THE SHIP," Brigid stated calmly, staring through her field glasses on *Starseeker*'s prow deck. Nearly a mile away, Mallet's ship crested a wave, riding high, then slipping down the other side until only the tall masts showed. The other ships were spread around it.

For the past two days, Falzone had gathered ships from different islands, putting the word out that Cobaltville Magistrates had invaded his home and taken his daughter. At first the response from the other islands was muted. None of the people there wanted to involve themselves too much. But they'd come at last. Fourteen ships sailed in the ragtag convoy navigated by Lakesh from the Cerberus redoubt.

From the reports the few survivors at Falzone's island had given, there were no more than a half-dozen Wiy Tukay ships. But Brigid knew they were sailing into battle. She could tell from the way Mallet's course had changed that he was receiving directions from someone else, and that someone else had to be heading up the assault force coming from Cobaltville.

Lakesh had confirmed the arrival of the Magistrate troops,

as well, tracking them from Cobaltville. With that information, Lakesh had triangulated a course that would bring Falzone's people and Qiang's navy to the meeting place, shaving nearly a day off the Tong's travel time.

Kane's plan called for engaging Mallet's ship before it reached the rendezvous point. The first thing Mallet would do would be to remove the young girl from the ship.

And if the girl was turned over to the ground troops, there was little chance they would be able to rescue her.

"Why didn't Kane ask you to be one of his party?" Mac Olney stood beside her, his eyes locked on to the uneven horizon where the Wiy Tukay ships sailed.

"Because he knows that I'm nowhere near the warrior he and Grant and Domi are," Brigid answered.

"And you're comfortable with that distinction?"

Brigid glanced at the foundation man, trying to figure out how she felt about him. "Yes. It's a fair assessment."

"Ah, but Brigid Baptiste," Olney said with a slight smile, "you strike me as every inch the warrior maid."

"Flattery isn't something that I approve of."

"Perhaps not, but it does sound nice, doesn't it? And coming in with Wimmer after the fight with the Chinese Tong members was no easy thing."

"Kane also left me here to coordinate the ships," Brigid said.

"I'm glad you feel that way." Olney loosened the shotgun in the shoulder scabbard. "I thought perhaps he was a bit jealous of my relationship with you."

"We," Brigid said clearly, "don't have a relationship." The thought, though, wasn't totally off-putting. Kane had been wrapped up in planning the various stages of the rescue operation and outfitting the ships, much of it done on the way. Olney's humor during that time had been very much appreciated.

"The lack of a relationship could be quickly remedied," Olney said. "Unless you find me just totally unappealing."

Brigid foundered for a moment, not quite sure how to respond.

Then Falzone joined them, his face anxious. He'd come aboard *Starseeker* so his own ships wouldn't be seen. *Starseeker* still flew the Heimdall Foundation flag, and Kane's plan was that Mallet would believe the foundation ship was out for revenge.

"They're only five miles out from the coastline according to the latest reading your friend Lakesh has," Falzone said, peering out at the other ship. He'd been manning the comm station, coordinating the other ships, as well as the Tong. It was still questionable whether the Tong would arrive in time.

"Does Kane know?" Brigid asked.

"Yes. He's making his move now." Falzone breathed out harshly. "I should be with him."

"Your place is here," Brigid said. "Your people will follow you better if they see you. Kane explained that." Kane had also privately told Brigid that Falzone's presence during the rescue mission could complicate things due to the man's emotional involvement. She'd agreed.

"I know." Falzone watched the Wiy Tukay ships like a hawk. "But I can't help feeling I should be there."

"You can do more here," Brigid said. "How long until Mallet reaches the coast at his present speed?"

"Fifteen, twenty minutes. The Cobaltville troops are already in place."

"What about the Tong?"

"Lakesh says they're still a question, but Captain Rong tells me he already has planes in the air. As soon as Kane is in place, they'll begin their approach."

"Falzone," a man yelled from the comm station.

Brigid, Olney and Falzone all looked back.

"Kane says it's time."

Falzone cursed softly, then raised his voice. "Ready the cannon."

"Cannon ready," the gun crews roared back.

Brigid watched as the Wiy Tukay ship crested another tall roller, then sank on the other side. *Starseeker* ran slightly south of the enemy ship, able to bring the port broadside cannon into play. From the books she'd read on naval war battles of the eighteenth and nineteenth centuries, she knew that the time to strike was at hand. She turned to Falzone.

"God help me," Falzone whispered hoarsely, looking at her, "I can't give the order." Unshed tears glimmered in his eyes.

Locking eyes with the man, Brigid raised her own voice. "Gun crews ready."

"Ready."

Brigid watched from the corner of her eye as Mallet's ship rose from the next trough. "Fire!"

Immediately, *Starseeker* shuddered as all the port-side cannon thundered. Clouds of roiling black smoke from the coarse black powder rolled across the deck, staining the gun crews.

The cannonballs sped across the gray-green sea and intentionally fell short of the mark. The misses were close enough that Brigid felt certain Mallet wouldn't think they hadn't been aimed at the ship.

Then the Wiy Tukay ships opened fire. Most of the cannonballs didn't touch *Starseeker,* but three or four bounced from her reinforced sides, and one ripped through the top rigging.

"Swab those cannon out!" Falzone roared, no longer frozen by his own fear. "I want those fuckers to think we're raining death down on them!"

The gun crews prepared the cannon, running wet cloths down inside the barrels, then loading up to go again.

Brigid watched the Wiy Tukay ships, knowing they had to continue to miss Mallet's ship while staying alive themselves and avoid the return fire that was sure to come. All of their lives were measured in minutes. When Mallet and his crew got close enough to the coastline, she had no doubts that the newly arrived Cobaltville troops would quickly join in.

"HOLD US STEADY," Kane ordered, peering through the Plexiglas nose of the minisub. He peered up at the shadow of Mallet's ship less than thirty feet above them.

"I am," Teresa replied fiercely. She handled the controls easily, adding thrust as she maneuvered the minisub up. Next to Falzone, she was the best minisub handler among the salvagers.

Even though Kane hadn't wanted to bring the woman along because of her personal involvement, Teresa was completely professional. The minisub glided under the ship and rose slowly, matching speeds.

Clad in a wet suit and wearing air tanks, Kane wished he could have brought the polycarbonate Mag suit from its hiding place in the wag back on Falzone's island. But that would have led to more questions than he cared to answer, and possible confusion aboard the Wiy Tukay ship, as well.

The distance between the minisub and the ship dropped to twenty-five feet, then twenty, then fifteen. Teresa held the distance at about ten feet. The water was shallow enough that they could be seen from above if anyone looked carefully enough.

"You've got eighteen minutes before we reach the shore," Teresa called out, concentrating on the ship above. She turned and faced Kane. "You bring my daughter back to me."

Wordlessly, Kane turned back to Grant, Domi, Remar and the three salvage men Falzone had assigned to him. All of them were outfitted with spearguns and H&K MP-5 machine pistols in waterproof sheaths. The three salvage men had hand drills and saws tied at their belts.

Kane removed the hatch at the rear of the minisub, adjusted his mask and took the tether Grant handed him, then fell back into the water. Kane slid through the water, quickly falling behind the minisub. Before he could draw his first breath, he hit the end of the tether and thought for a moment his arms were going to be pulled from their sockets. The ship sailed above him, cutting through the sea.

A moment later Remar followed him out onto the line, moving carefully.

Using his swim fins, Kane arched his body and glided up toward the ship, coming within ten feet of the hull. He fisted the speargun looped around his wrist, made sure the line remained tied to the spear and fired into the middle of the ship.

The spear crossed the distance in a silvery flash, and the *thunk* of razored barbs biting into the wood reached Kane's ears, altered by the water. He yanked on the rope attached to the spear and found it secure. Letting go of the tether to the minisub, knowing if the spear slipped that he wouldn't be able to swim and keep up with the ship, he quickly pulled himself toward the target ship.

Remar came next, firing his own line into the ship's hull. Domi, then Grant and the other three men did the same, clinging to the underside of the ship like parasites. Teresa kept the minisub close.

The three salvage men started to work instantly, tying themselves up close to the ship, then plunging their hand drills into the softwood.

Kane recharged his speargun. At the rate their hearts were beating and the exertion they were making to stay attached to the ship, he knew the single air tanks wouldn't last long. And even if they made it to the shoreline, the Cobaltville troops stood waiting.

They were definitely working a one-percenter.

Once the salvage team had pilot holes drilled, they abandoned the drills and pulled out the narrow-bladed jigsaws and started cutting out a circular area roughly three-feet wide, each working at a different point to meet the others.

Kane knew the Wiy Tukay ship was already taking on water, but Mallet and the crew already had their distraction. Cannonballs from the foundation ship Falzone currently skippered fell between thirty and fifty yards short of Mallet's vessel. The massive balls entered the water in a whirl of confusion, trailing streamers of bubbles, then slowed until they finally dropped sedately toward the ocean floor.

One of the salvage men cut himself badly. Blood slipped through the water in greasy sheets, but he didn't quit working. In little over a minute, they'd cut through the ship's bottom and the water pressure forced the wooden section in.

Cannonballs continued to fall into the sea, proof that Falzone and his crew were keeping up their part of the distraction. Kane doubted anyone aboard Mallet's ship noticed they were suddenly taking on water. He caught the edge of the hole and pulled himself through, stepping into the darkness of the cargo hold. Despite the ship's length, water already swirled around his ankles. He stripped out of the air tank and fins, dropping them where he stood.

Kane took a small flash from his weight belt and waited as Grant, Domi, Remar and one of the salvagers crawled into the belly of the ship. Kane played the light around the cargo hold, briefly noting the small collection of crates, spare parts, and stores of food and sailcloth. According to the surveillance Lakesh had done, the little girl, Ariel, was being kept in the captain's quarters.

Thundering explosions sounded from overhead as the cannon fired again. The ship settled more deeply into the water for a moment as the recoils pushed it down. Water sprang up from the hole in the hull like an artesian well, almost as high as Kane was tall.

"Shark!" the salvager climbing through the hole squalled loudly enough to fill the cargo hold.

"Quiet, damn it!" Grant growled, reaching down to clap a hand over the other man's mouth and grab him under one arm. The man kicked and fought in Grant's grip, struggling to get inside the ship.

Then a sudden fountain of blood bubbled up with the water filling the ship. When Grant yanked, he only pulled up the man's upper body. A piece of broken spine and entrails were all that remained of the salvager's lower body.

The man opened his mouth to scream, but only blood spewed out. His eyes glazed over and his arms went still.

"Son of a bitch!" Grant whispered hoarsely. He threw away the torso he held. Domi stood at Grant's side, her blaster in her hands, a look of amused disgust on her bone-white face.

"Fuckin' sharks," Remar grunted. "Got to where they follow some ships near the coastline at times. Slaver ships in this area sometimes throw bodies overboard when slaves catch sickness and die. Sharks don't catch no sickness, and they damn sure ain't gonna turn away a free meal."

A footfall through the water ahead of Kane warned him of the approaching crewman. Kane turned quickly, bringing up the speargun and firing from the point.

The barbed spear leaped from the speargun and crossed twenty feet, catching the Wiy Tukay crewman in the throat and pinning him to the wooden crate behind him. The man dropped his weapon, reflexively reaching for the spear in his throat. He kicked, sloshing in the water, as Kane calmly reloaded the speargun.

"What about the other man?" Kane asked.

Grant stuck his head down through the holed hull for only an instant to look for the other salvager. "Gone."

"Let's go." Kane took the lead, his point man's senses flaring. By the time he passed the crate, the man pinned to it was already dead, suspended only by the spear through his throat.

Kane knew without looking at his chron that they were all running out of time.

"THERE'S THE COAST!" Falzone yelled amid the din of explosions coming from *Starseeker*'s cannon.

Brigid peered in the direction Falzone pointed, spotting the erratic line of Cobaltville Sandcats and Deathbirds along the broken terrain of the shoreline. Magistrates in black polycarbonate armor stood in between the war wags, their weapons at the ready.

"When we get within their range," Olney said, "we're all chilled."

Two of the Deathbirds lifted from the shore, arcing back over the land briefly, then breaking straight out toward *Starseeker*. "We're going to be within their range anyway," Brigid said. "Get the deck guns ready."

Falzone called out the order and crews ran to man the .50-cal deck guns.

"Their heat seekers aren't going to do them any good," Brigid said, "but they still have the nose cannon and rockets."

In seconds, the Deathbirds swooped over *Starseeker,* their blades whipping through the air. Bullets from the chain guns chewed across the deck and punched holes in the sailcloth. Two men fell from the gun crews, their bodies turned into a series of bloody, ruptured craters by the big rounds. Rigging parted and drooped, allowing the sails to luff and snap free. The deck guns never touched either of the two Deathbirds.

Immediately, the Wiy Tukay ships fanned out, intent on turning back and taking advantage of the air cover. The two lead ships spread out, opening overlapping fields of fire.

Glancing at the sky, Brigid watched as the pair of Deathbirds came back around for another pass. This time the pilots skimmed even lower, the rotors beating waves across the ocean surface as they swept in to attack.

Chapter 33

The ladder leading out of the cargo hold led to the stern section amidships, leaving Kane the whole deck to cross between the cannon crews. He glanced back at Grant, unable to speak over the roar of the cannons firing.

Grant spoke, and even though Kane couldn't hear him, he could read his friend's lips: "Fucking one-percenter."

Kane nodded, knowing the biggest danger they were going to face was the armored Magistrates among the Wiy Tukay worshipers. Kane waited while the starboard gun crews rolled their cannon back to recharge. Then, while their attention was centered primarily on their weapons, he pushed free of the cargo hold and sprinted.

His mind flew, assessing all the variables that suddenly took shape before him, slowing time. He lived on his razor-edged quickness and decisive ability. Some of the port-side gun crews spotted him and went for their weapons.

Kane brought up the machine pistol he'd accepted from Falzone's stores, firing short bursts as he ran across the reeling deck. Two men went down, then three and four, knocked back over the cannon they were assigned to. Target number five was a worshiper who stepped out in front of Kane. The man's face was vicious, his mouth distended as he yelled. Kane emptied the last of the MP-5's clip into the man's mouth, shattering his head and blowing it back over the Magistrate trying to get position behind the man.

Temporarily blinded by blood and flying brain matter, the Magistrate held his fire.

Kane kept running, putting all his strength into his stride, aware that Grant had fired his blaster dry behind him. Kane went low, staying loose, taking the shock of hitting the Magistrate on his shoulder. It still felt as if he'd gone head to head with an anvil, but the Mag dropped to the deck.

Off balance but recovering quickly, Kane pushed himself up, drawing the knife from the sheath on his leg. He rapped the Magistrate on his head with the machine pistol as the man struggled to his knees. When the Mag's head went backward from the impact, Kane slashed his throat with the knife. Crimson spilled down the front of the polycarbonate armor.

"Chill them!"

Kane didn't know who shouted the order, but he knew it came from the prow ahead. Letting go of the machine pistol so it hung from the leash around his wrist, he picked up the dying Magistrate's Copperhead. He wheeled, bringing up the assault rifle, the knife still bloody in his other fist.

A Wiy Tukay worshiper stood at the top of the prow over the door to the captain's quarters. He swung the 7.62 mm machine gun mounted on the deck around in Kane's direction.

Domi blasted two other worshipers who fired at them, sending their bodies tumbling away. Grant switched magazines on his machine pistol, his eyes bright with combat heat. He stutter-stepped as a round cored into his thigh, but he remained standing, bellowing in pain and rage. Domi wheeled and cursed, shooting into the center mass of the man that had wounded Grant, putting him down.

The Copperhead came into Kane's arms like a long-lost lover. His finger caressed the trigger, and a 3-round burst took off the top of the Wiy Tukay worshiper's head. The corpse stumbled back from the machine gun even as Kane surged forward again.

Kane focused on the door to the captain's quarters. "Grant!" Bullets whizzed around his head, letting him know most of the crew was aware the ship had been invaded.

"Yeah!" Grant responded.

"You got the door!"

Grant made no response, but ran headlong for the door.

Kane stepped aside, shoving Domi roughly forward after Grant. He jerked Remar into motion, as well. The old man was bleeding from at least two wounds on his arm and shoulder, but was still ready to make a fight of it.

The last salvager didn't make it to Kane, going down in a blaze of gunfire. His body hit the deck at Kane's feet, blood spattering the desk from his mouth as he tried to scream.

Mind spinning, searching for the edge he needed to keep the rest of his group together, Kane spotted the powder barrels in the cannon pits that were used to reload the artillery.

A bullet caught Kane in the left hip, spinning him sideways, but he remained focused on his target. He squeezed the trigger, aiming for the powder keg farthest away from him on the starboard side.

The powder keg exploded a heartbeat later, the superheated bullets setting fire to the coarse grains. If the gunpowder had been refined, Kane knew it would have exploded faster and more powerfully. As it was, he had time to turn and start running before the first barrel detonated.

The explosion hurled the gun crew in all directions and spread flames throughout the sails and rigging. The concussion knocked Kane off balance, but he kept his feet.

Grant reached the door to the captain's quarters, paused momentarily, then drew back and drove a shoulder against the door. The lock gave with a shriek that was heard even above the next powder keg exploding in the gun pits.

Debris filled the air, jagged pieces of railing and deck, chunks and hunks of men's bodies, and cannonballs rolled loose, as well. Hoarse screams of the wounded pierced the air.

Grant shoved inside the captain's quarters with Domi on his heels. Kane drove Remar forward, throwing both of them through the door and falling to the floor as bullets followed them. They slid across the floor.

Kane kicked the door closed, watching as it sagged a little on its hinges, but the wood was thick enough to hold out the bullets for a moment. He glanced around the room, seeing only that it was empty, thinking that they were well and truly fucked, that Mallet had moved the girl somewhere and Lakesh hadn't caught it.

"Here," Grant growled, reaching under the bed.

Ariel came reluctantly at first, then she wrapped her arms around Grant's thick neck. "Remar!" she screamed, seeing the old man. "Want my mommy!"

"I know, child," Remar said, breathing raggedly, blood streaming from his wounds. "Gonna get you there in just a little bit. You just sit tight."

Kane stood and peered through the crack between the door and door frame. Fires had spread across the ship's deck from the gun crew pits. They'd lost at least four or five of them, including the crews, but the smoke from the burned gunpowder and the fires made that end of the ship cloudy.

"We got girl," Domi stated tersely. "Now what?"

"I don't know," Kane said. "This is the part I was going to figure out when we got here."

"We here," Domi pointed out.

"Damn," Kane said, "and here I was thinking I needed to check the map again."

"Not funny," Domi said, glaring around the captain's quarters. "Feel like rat. All trapped. Nowhere to go."

Without warning, .50-cal bullets chewed through the door, ripping free long splinters and digging into the wall on the opposite side of the room. Grant dropped to the floor with Ariel, who put her hands over her ears.

"Mallet!" Kane yelled. "You're going to get the girl chilled!"

A man in Mag black strode from the swirling smoke at the ship's stern. He turned and popped his Sin Eater free, taking instant aim on the man firing the .50-cal machine gun. He fired at once, ripping the man's face to shreds.

"Hold your fire!" Mallet roared. "Next man that fires without my order, I'll chill myself!"

Blasterfire ceased immediately.

"Get those damn fires put out!" Mallet ordered, pointing to the starboard side of the ship.

Kane cautiously surveyed the deck that he could see. Chaos ruled aboard the ship. Although the exploding powder kegs hadn't caused extensive structural damage, they had blown the hell out of the ship.

And although Mallet still wasn't aware of it, his ship was still sinking. Kane could already feel the ship rolling heavier with all the extra water it had taken on.

"Give up the girl, Kane," Mallet called out.

"Let us go free if we do?" Kane asked.

"Hell, no," Mallet replied.

"Don't see why I should do it, then."

"That way she gets to live. You obviously want her to live if you went to all this trouble to come find her."

"I've always been more concerned about my own neck," Kane replied. "That's what they teach you as a Magistrate. You know that. A dead Magistrate is just worm food, but a live one is a weapon of the baron, just waiting to be used again." He scanned the room, thinking quickly, trying to find some way out of their predicament.

The little girl clung fearfully to Grant, shaking. She kept repeating, "Want Mommy! Want Mommy!"

"I'll give you a quick, clean death," Mallet yelled. "I'll promise you that."

Kane remembered the tortured bodies of the dead men he and Grant had found in the pass when they'd linked up with Remar to begin the journey to the Northwest Territories. He knew that Mallet wasn't one to let death be easy when it didn't have to be.

"Kane!" Mallet yelled.

"I'm thinking," Kane yelled back. He heard Deathbird chain guns and cannon in the distance and knew that Brigid and Falzone were obviously under attack, as well.

Time was running out for all of them.

FORCING HERSELF to wait, blowing her breath out to keep from hyperventilating, Brigid watched the lead Deathbird scream by overhead, trying not to think about the dead and wounded men the chain guns left in their wake. Then she stepped out and brought up her machine pistol, aiming for the rear rotor, the weakest part of the aircraft. Her finger tightened on the trigger, firing through the whole clip.

The bullets struck the rotor, doing enough damage to destroy it. The pilot fought for control but just couldn't get the Deathbird back. The aircraft plunged to the sea, the whirling blades breaking into shrapnel as they struck the water. The pieces chopped into the cockpit, starting an explosion that ripped through the craft. The Deathbird sank in seconds.

A brief flurry of cheering ripped raggedly from the throats of the crew, but it was quickly drowned out when they noticed two more Deathbirds streaking for them from the coast.

"They see the other ships now," Falzone said. "They know it's more than just us."

As she reloaded, Brigid glanced back to the west and saw Falzone's other ships sailing toward them.

"Going to be too little way the hell too late." Falzone's voice had gone raw and dead ever since the explosions aboard Mallet's ship. He'd lost hope.

"It's never too late," Brigid said, surprised at her own stubbornness. "Kane will never give up."

"For all you know," Falzone said quietly, "Kane's already dead."

"No," Brigid said with conviction. "He's alive. If he were dead, I'd know it. And if he's alive, I'm willing to bet your daughter is alive, too."

Starseeker's deck guns came to life, and Brigid glanced up to see Mac Olney manning the one mounted in the stern. The withering barrage of fire turned the approaching Deathbird aside for the moment, drawing another cheer from the crew.

But there was no mistaking the other two wasp shapes that hurtled slightly above the ocean surface at them.

"Look!" one of the crew yelled. "Planes!"

Brigid turned and glanced into the sky, shading her eyes against the harsh sun. It took her a moment to find them even with them being crimson against the cerulean sky. There were a dozen planes, grouped in threes, flying point and two wingmen.

"Wei Qiang's people made it," Falzone whispered in disbelief.

Brigid smiled.

"Falzone," the comm officer yelled, "the Tong are wanting to know when they can start attacking the ships."

"Not until I know Kane and my daughter are clear of them," Falzone yelled back. "Tell them to take out the beach units."

Even farther behind the approaching salvage ships was a large navy of red-lacquered warships flying imperial dragon flags.

Brigid glanced back at Mallet's ship. It was still swaddled in black smoke that obscured view of much of the deck. But somewhere on that ship, she knew Kane still lived and fought.

"KANE!" Mallet roared.

Kane ignored the man for the moment, gazing at the floor of the captain's quarters. The cargo hold lay below. He glanced up at Grant. "Rip that bed out of the wall and turn it over."

Over the long years they'd been together, Grant knew better than to question. He passed Ariel to Remar, who talked to her like a grandpa at a Sunday dinner, keeping himself and the little girl calm.

"Turn the bed on its side," Kane instructed. "We're going to need it for protection."

"Those .50-cal rounds will chew right through the bed," Grant said, ripping the structure from the wall.

"Kane!" Mallet yelled.

"We won't be here then," Kane said. He took the small

block of plas-ex he had at his belt. Explosives were always good to have, he'd learned, and he hadn't hesitated about taking them when he'd found them in Falzone's armory. He pinched off a chunk of the gray-white claylike material, then flattened it against the floor. He glanced at Domi and Remar. "Get behind the bed." He added a remote-control detonator to the plas-ex, then joined the others.

"Answer me, Kane!" Mallet yelled.

"Pull the mattress tight," Kane instructed. He turned to Remar. "Cover her ears."

Remar did as he was told, hunkering his own good ear deep into his shoulder.

Kane touched the remote-control detonator, setting off the charge. Trapped in the room as it was, the explosion was hellishly loud. The concussive force rocked them all back against the wall. Kane's head hit so hard he had black spots in his vision and felt as if he were waking up from a deep sleep. The little girl screamed, her mouth wide and her eyes closed.

Grant kicked the mattress away. When it fell to the floor, the mattress was shredded on one side from the force of the blast, and smoldering pockets clung to the material.

The blast had opened the floor, though, leaving a hole nearly five feet across and cracks that split the deck boards. Jagged, splintered ends surrounded the hole.

Kane shone his flash into the hold, finding the water-covered floor just over twenty feet below. He glanced at Grant. "You first. Then Domi. She protects you while I lower the little girl to you."

Grant nodded, then levered himself over the side of the hole, dropping and rolling when he hit. He was on his feet instantly, reaching up for Domi. Once Domi was safely on her feet, he reached up for the little girl.

Kane eased the little girl down as far as he could, then dropped her the rest of the way. She screamed all the way into Grant's arms.

"Move!" Kane yelled. "Get her to the sub."

Domi had her blaster up and firing, proof that at least part of the crew had been sent belowdecks to either check on the leak or possibly to shoot up into the floor under the captain's quarters.

An onslaught of .50-cal rounds suddenly burst through the door, tearing away a third of it.

Kane and Remar hugged the floor.

"Shit!" Remar cursed. "We're gettin' down to the bone on this one, Kane."

Kane grabbed the old man's hand. "Go. I'll catch up."

"I could stay," Remar offered.

The .50-cal rumbled again, spitting more bullets into the room.

"Stay and do what?" Kane asked. "Catch the last train west?" He shook his head. "I'm not staying here for that."

Remar nodded doubtfully. "See you on the other side of it, then."

"You will," Kane said. He held the old man's hand as far down into the hold as he could, then let go.

Grant was wading through waist-deep water, heading for the hole that had been cut through the hull.

"Hold up!" Kane yelled. "I'm throwing my blaster out!"

Mallet gave the order to cease-fire.

Kane worked quickly, smashing the last of the plas-ex along the Copperhead's buttstock so it wouldn't be very noticeable. Then he added a remote detonator.

"Kane," Mallet yelled.

Standing, gazing through the huge hole left by the .50-cal rounds, Kane studied the deck. Men were shifting, and the way they watched let him know some of them were already crawling on top of the captain's quarters. But beyond them, he spotted the red air wags and tall ships of the Tong. Wei Qiang had delivered after all.

"Looks like you may not win this one," Kane said. "If you're interested, I'll accept a surrender."

"Fuck you, Kane," Mallet roared. "You're a dead man."

Kane opened the door wide enough to kick the Copperhead through, praying the plas-ex and detonator stayed on the weapon and was operable. The assault rifle skidded to a stop amidships, thirty feet from Mallet.

"Now come out," Mallet commanded.

Kane spun away from the doorway and dropped, catching himself briefly on the edges of the hole in the floor. Splinters tore at his hands and fingers, then he dropped the rest of the way into the hold. He collapsed, letting his legs go limp under him because he didn't want to take a chance on breaking an ankle.

He came up on his knees, sputtering, the cold water already up to his chin. He got his bearings, noticing the men running down the companionway alongside the hold. Grant, Domi, Remar and the little girl were gone. If their luck held, Teresa would have the minisub within easy reach because none of them would be able to find the abandoned scuba gear in the water.

The only thing that concerned Kane were the sharks. If Teresa wasn't waiting, it was a sure bet the sharks were.

Kane raised the machine pistol from the water and aimed at the men running down the companionway. Squeezing the trigger, he sent three of them spinning, dropping into the water that now filled the hold and was still rising.

Kane dodged to the side as muzzle-flashes flared from the cargo hold entrance in the deck. He heard Mallet screaming orders. Then Kane was underwater, shoving a hand up only long enough to trigger the detonator.

The deck above him went to pieces, creating a hole nearly twenty feet across. It opened up near the stern, well away from where he'd dropped the Copperhead. The assault rifle had either slid or someone had picked it up and moved it.

As the deck above crashed into the cargo hold, propelled by the plas-ex knocking everything down, light also filled part of the ship's interior. Water ran between the boxes, crates, extra sailcloth and equipment. Bodies floated on the water, torn and bloodied, most of them not even whole, some of them with broken sections of planks driven through them.

And through the hole in the deck, Kane saw a few Death-birds being hunted by three and four times as many of Wei Qiang's red-lacquered air wags. The Tong craft were little more than flying coffins, holding no armor at all, crafted of light wood and canvas, and powered by small engines. Still, they came equipped with machine guns and hand-thrown bombs. Even all of the Cobaltville Magistrates with Sandcats and Deathbirds couldn't stand against that kind of consistent, suicidal pressure Wei Qiang commanded from his troops.

The ship lurched suddenly as the cargo hold full of water caused it to shift.

Kane threw himself into the water. It was deep enough to swim easily in the cargo hold now. He knew if he didn't get out of the dying ship quickly enough that he would go down with it, pulled to the bottom by the undertow.

It took him two tries to find the opening that had been cut in the bottom of the ship. He blew out his breath, filling his lungs with fresh air. There was every possibility that Teresa would have left once she had her daughter onboard. Kane hoped that she hadn't.

A crate floated toward him, a body bobbing next to it.

Kane shoved the crate away, getting ready to dive through the opening in the hull. Then Mallet rose up from the water looking like a wild man. Kane grabbed the Mag's wrist, then stepped inside the man's defense and headbutted him. Balling his right fist, Kane drove a short jab into Mallet's neck beneath the helmet, hoping to catch the man full in the throat and break his trachea.

Mallet dodged, turning his head and taking the blow along his jaw. He backhanded Kane in the face, nearly knocking him down and freeing the Sin Eater. Kane maintained his hold on the Mag weapon, knowing he was dead if he lost it. Blood trickled across his lips from his nose. His vision blurred for a moment from the pain.

"Gonna die, Kane," Mallet promised, drawing back his fist and driving it toward Kane's face.

Unwilling to release his hold on Mallet's Sin Eater, Kane dodged, feeling Mallet's fist skim along the side of his face, tearing at his ear. Kane raised his knee, driving it into Mallet's crotch, but the polycarbonate armor kept the blow from being debilitating.

Mallet swung again and howled with rage. The blow caught Kane on top of the shoulder, briefly numbing his arm. Kane drew his knife and stabbed at Mallet's throat, expecting the man to dodge back from the blade.

Instead, Mallet turned to face the knife, catching the point on the helmet's face shield. The blade was sharp enough that it embedded in the shield, sending fracture lines skating across the material. Kane drew the knife back and plunged it into the man's face again and again, splintering the shield, knocking jagged pieces free. Suddenly one bloodshot eye was open to Kane's attack.

Before Kane could ram the blade home, the ship lurched again, sinking quickly in the stern. The floor tilted treacherously. Off balance, unable to get secure footing due to buoyancy from the water flooding the cargo hold and the slippery wood, Kane fell, pulling the Sin Eater into line.

Mallet fired immediately.

One of the bullets hit Kane on his lower left side, just under his ribs. White-hot pain seared through his mind, but he knew he was lucky because the wound was through-and-through the flesh and didn't bounce off the ribs where it could have fractured bones or been deflected internally.

Kane dived instantly, listening to the bullets splat against the water and watching some of them leave streamers in the water only inches away. With the sunlight pouring down through the huge hole ruptured in the ship's deck, the hole in the hull was easier to find.

Staying underwater, Kane swam for the hole. He felt the water pushing at him as he neared the breach, continuing to stream into the cargo ship. He fought it, managing to swim strongly enough to catch the edges of the hole. Just as he started to pull himself through, something seized his ankle.

Clinging to the hole, fighting the pull of the waters rushing in and the grip on his ankle, Kane glanced back and saw Mallet rip his own knife free. Kane lashed out with his free foot, stomping into Mallet's helmet hard enough to break the man's grip.

Kane pulled himself through the hole, his lungs already aching for oxygen. He stared down through the water, spotting the minisub thirty feet below, spotting Grant, Domi, Remar and Teresa through the Plexiglas nose.

Grant was shouting and pointing to Kane's left.

Turning in the indicated direction, Kane spotted the large mutie shark cruising effortlessly through the water over forty yards away. The creature came around serenely, its black eye focusing on Kane. The cruel mouth gaped open to reveal huge teeth.

Then it felt like a burning brand lay along Kane's jaw. Murky red blood stained the water near Kane's face, letting him know he'd been cut. He flared out instinctively, moving away from the broad blade that flashed in the water. He turned over and found Mallet coming straight for him, knife poised to strike again.

Kane blocked his attacker's knife wrist, peering through the shattered remnants of the face shield. Only cold, naked fury showed in Mallet's gaze. Throwing punches underwater was almost impossible, but the knives were pure death. Kane thrust at Mallet's face, but the Mag commander turned his head and blocked the blow with his helmet.

From the corner of his eye, feeling as though his lungs were going to explode, Kane saw the shark swimming toward them. Mallet hadn't seemed to notice the creature at all, intent on killing Kane.

Mallet lunged, jabbing his knife at Kane's face.

Blood continued to flow from the wound on Kane's jaw,

streaming into the water and clouding his vision. He pulled himself inside Mallet's reach, barely avoiding the knife. Then he threw his left arm out, locking it around and behind Mallet's right arm, trapping it and preventing him from using the knife again.

Mallet struggled to get free, lifting his legs and driving his boots against Kane's thighs, fighting to be free.

Dizzy from exertion and the lack of oxygen, Kane held on stubbornly. The cargo ship pulled at him as it sank lower in the water, headed for the bottom far below now. He and Mallet remained just beyond the tug of the undertow claiming the ship.

The shark swam faster now, coming straight at them.

Kane focused on the savage creature, kicking out, wishing he had the swim fins still, willing himself to survive. Drawn by Kane's intent gaze, Mallet stopped struggling long enough to glance back over his shoulder.

By that time the shark was already on them.

Horror filled Mallet's face as he realized what was happening. He screamed, air bubbles exploding from his mouth and through the shattered faceplate. Then the shark took him, locking on to his midsection because he was between the creature and Kane.

The shark ripped Mallet from Kane's grip, stripping him like a toy from a child.

Caught by the slipstream of the mutie shark's passage, Kane twisted and flailed, then slammed up against the creature's body. He recovered quickly, watching as the shark bit down, cracking the polycarbonate armor easily. Bits and pieces of Mallet floated down and away as the shark closed its mouth. A blood fog foamed from the shark's mouth. Mallet's legs kicked until one of them fell off and began the long, slow descent to the ocean floor. Before it could go far, however, another shark swooped in and snatched it up, then came at Kane.

Galvanized into action, Kane swam for the rear of the minisub, kicking strongly, not knowing if he had enough speed and strength and air to make it. He felt the shark closing in on him, sensing the great creature's full attention. Then he saw Grant drop into the water from the rear of the minisub, leveling a speargun.

When Grant fired, the spear missed Kane by inches, darting by his face. Keeping focused on the minisub, knowing he'd be aware of the moment the shark got him instead, Kane surprised himself when he reached Grant.

Glancing over his shoulder, Kane spotted the shark behind him, swimming away from the minisub now, a spear protruding from its head. Lungs near bursting, vision filled with black spots, Kane swam up under the minisub and pulled himself through the hatch.

Kane didn't have the strength to haul himself up at first. Remar grabbed him by the back of the wet suit and pulled him aboard. Sucking air gratefully, Kane fell to the minisub's deck and lay there, his hands over his head to open his lungs better.

Teresa sat in the pilot's seat with Ariel held protectively in her lap. The little girl held tightly to her mother.

Grant came in through the hatch, then reached down to help Kane to his feet.

"You're cut up some," Remar remarked.

"I've been worse," Kane said.

Domi rummaged through a first-aid kit.

"Get us topside," Kane told Teresa. "It looked like Qiang and his forces had everything well in hand, but I want to be on hand to help out."

As Teresa brought the minisub around, Kane watched the darkening sea drink down the broken cargo ship, streaming debris and corpses in its wake.

Epilogue

Kane surveyed the rocky coastline as he carried the 7.62 mm machine gun he'd salvaged toward the nearest longboat Falzone had assigned to ferry recovered items to the waiting cargo ships. His face still hurt where Mallet had cut him.

The battle between the Cobaltville Magistrates, Falzone's people and the Tong had raged for nearly two hours after the Tong had arrived. For the first thirty minutes the engagement had been vicious and bloody, with both sides throwing everything they had into it. Then both sides had pulled back to a degree, jockeying for position. In the end, the Tong's disposable aircraft had proved the turning point.

Some of the Sandcats destroyed along the beach still burned. A few corpses of Deathbirds and their crews lay shattered across the rocky beachfront, but there were even more of the canvas-and-red-lacquer air wags Qiang had called on to be sacrificed in the battle. Terns and gulls were already working over the corpses, and crabs crawled over the bodies lying at the water's edge. The sea had taken everyone that had gone into it.

Falzone and the Tong members maintained an uneasy alliance, and Kane knew if the Tong warlord hadn't needed or wanted the information so badly from Falzone, they'd probably all be dead now. At least, they wouldn't be scavenging parts from the abandoned Sandcats and Deathbirds, or stripping weapons and extra ammo from the dead that had been left behind.

Kane placed the machine gun into the longboat.

"You look like you could use a rest."

Turning, Kane saw Brigid Baptiste approaching with her arms full of med supplies raided from the Sandcats. Smoke and soot stained her face, and the honey-gold hair was disheveled.

"I'll be fine," Kane growled.

"You always are." Brigid placed the med supplies in the longboat. "I've got some self-heats from the ship's stores up on the hill." She pointed to a copse of trees on a ridge forty feet up the hillside. "It's not a banquet, but it'll be hot."

Kane's first reaction was to turn her down. During the salvaging operation, she'd been hanging around Mac Olney, the Heimdall Foundation man, or maybe he'd been hanging around her. "What about Olney?"

Brigid looked up at him. "What about him?"

Kane stopped himself short of saying something they'd both regret. "All right."

"All right?" Brigid lifted an eyebrow.

"The self-heats," Kane said. "Something was said about a rest."

Brigid nodded and led the way, following a game trail up the side of the hill to the ridge.

As Kane sat on the ground, he was suddenly aware of how dirty and blood covered he was. He wished he'd thought to clean up. Sitting on the ridge, he could peer out over the battlefield, another in a long list of ones he'd seen. None of them were forgettable.

The slapping crush of the waves rolling in over the rocks sounded peaceful. The voices of the men working below, speaking English and Chinese, reached his ears, punctuated by the cries of the seabirds. Despite the death and destruction lying at the bottom of the ridge, the sky and sea met in a gauzy haze of blues and gray-green in the distance. The salt air came in thick and heavy, mixed with burned-rubber and death smells.

It wasn't a picnic spot and had only a view of hell.

Brigid passed out the self-heats, then surprised him with a

bottle of wine. "One of the Sandcats," she explained. "I claimed it as part of a personal salvage."

A memory touched Kane then and turned him cold. In one of those other lives that he could barely remember sharing with Brigid—if it all wasn't something drawn strictly from his imagination—she'd said goodbye to him forever over a bottle of wine. He couldn't remember where they'd been or why the decision had been made.

She poured the wine into two plastic cups.

Kane breathed the aroma in, finding it sharp and sour and pungent. He sipped, and it tasted bitter but good at the same time.

"What are you going to do now?" Brigid asked.

"Stay here a couple days and work with Falzone, help him get back on his feet. Then Grant, Domi and I are going to head back to the Cerberus redoubt."

"Why? Falzone would welcome you with open arms."

Kane shook his head. "This is their place, Baptiste. It isn't mine. I know that whether Falzone wants to admit it or not."

"He could use you."

"Yeah. Probably. But I've got my own path to find."

"And where will that take you?"

"I don't know, Baptiste. I only know that this isn't it."

"Lakesh wants to talk to you soon."

A wolfish smile touched Kane's lips. "Let him stew for a while. It won't hurt him."

"He lied to you about this, you know," Brigid said. "He lied to all of us."

"That's his way," Kane said. "For better or worse, that's Lakesh's way of dealing with things."

"So you're going to stay with him?"

"For now," Kane replied. "But he knows he's really stretched things thin between all of us this time."

"This could be a good place to settle down," Brigid declared.

"I'm not ready for that." Kane glanced at her, feeling his

stomach tighten as he asked the question he was afraid of. "What about you, Baptiste? Are you going to stay here? Olney doesn't seem like he'd mind."

"Olney's a good man, I think."

Kane nodded, not trusting his throat for a moment. "I think so, too."

"And if I chose to stay?" Brigid asked, locking eyes with his.

"That would be your choice, Baptiste. Personally, I can think of worse places to be." Kane meant it, but he hated saying it.

Brigid sipped her wine and looked out at the battlefield. "I can't."

Her reply surprised him. "You could if you wanted to."

She shook her head, no longer looking at him, wrapping her arms around her legs. "I'm afraid."

"Of what?"

"Wanting something I'm not ready for."

"What do you think you're not ready for?"

"Someone like Olney. Someone who would want me to build my life around his."

"Would that be such a bad thing?" Kane asked softly. He nodded toward Falzone and Teresa, who had staked out a small section of the beach away from the dead. They sat talking quietly, watching Ariel occasionally building a sandcastle and running barefoot through the white-foamed waves. "They seem to make it work."

"It's not that easy, Kane, and you know it."

"If you worked at it hard enough, mebbe it could become easy."

Brigid laughed, but tears splashed on her sunburned cheeks. "Work hard to make something easy? Only you would look at it like that."

"Everything easy," Kane said, "was hard once. Otherwise it wouldn't be worth doing."

"I'm going back to the Cerberus redoubt, too," Brigid said.

Kane's stomach muscles unclenched slightly, and he breathed more easily. "Okay," he said softly. Then, before he could stop himself, he added, "I'm glad, Brigid."

"Don't be," she said, "because if the time should come and things feel right, I'll go, Kane. Never mistake that."

"I know," Kane said. And if she did, he knew that he would miss her. Quietly, he dug into the self-heat, not even really aware of what it was, just enjoying the company. For however long it lasted.

Take
2 explosive books
plus a
mystery bonus
FREE